THE RING KEEPER

Also by AJ Park

Seven Rivers Series
Forgotten Rebellion
River in the Sand

Guardians of the Horsemen Series
Silver Song
War's Ending
The Exiled Horseman
Sea and Iron

Stand Alone Novels
The Ring Keeper
Poisoned Splinter

THE RING KEEPER

AJ PARK

StarTree Press

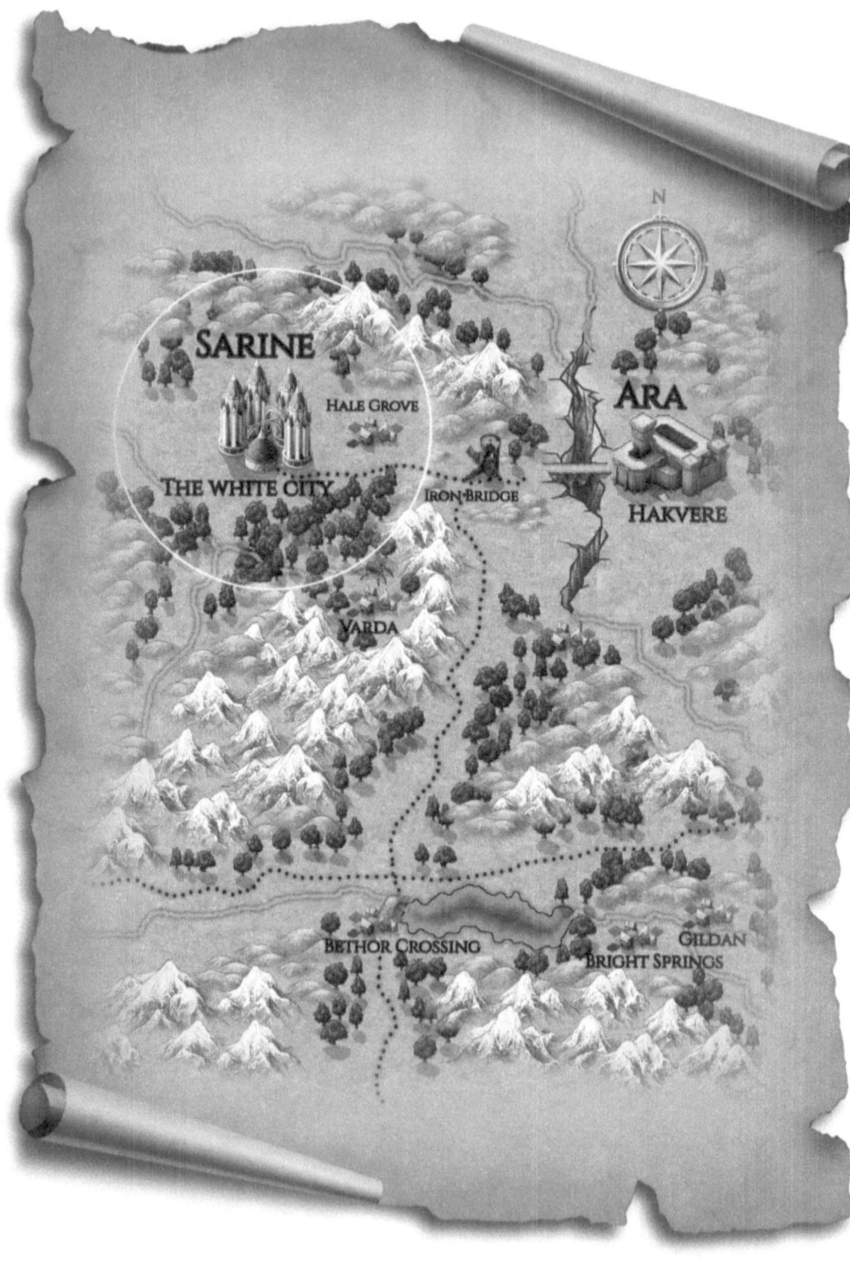

N
SARINE
HALE GROVE
THE WHITE CITY
IRON BRIDGE
ARA
HAKVERE
VARDA
BETHOR CROSSING
GILDAN
BRIGHT SPRINGS

PROLOGUE

Year of Warding 37, Sarine-Ara Border

CALLONEN

H IS WORSENING ILLNESS MADE travel difficult. Emperor Callonen wished for the strength to ride his horse as he always had instead of sitting in a carriage. At least his guards offered him the small kindness of not mentioning the change. No one dared speak of his deteriorating physical condition. They all hoped he would get better. He needed a solution. If he didn't fine one, Callonen's death would leave every person in his empire vulnerable.

The carriage rolled toward the edge of the Warding, surrounded by a protective army. Sarine couldn't afford to allow any harm to come to their emperor. Without him, and the enchanted defense of the Warding he wielded, the demons would destroy their people.

"Emperor, I think we should have ignored his message," General Gray said from his seat opposite, his expression sober behind his dark beard. "What could he possibly have to say that will aid us? It's too dangerous for you to be so near the border."

Callonen's stomach clenched. The message from his traitorous brother had been unexpected in the extreme. Years ago, the last time they had spoken face to face, Haldreth had driven a dagger into Callonen's heart. Only a miracle had saved him that day.

No, not a miracle. A young woman had saved him. She had loved him and sacrificed everything to save his life. The memory of Allia awoke a sharp familiar pain in his chest. He recalled the sound of her voice, the way her golden hair had caught the sun, the touch of her hands. She had seen his true self more clearly than anyone else. In all these years without her, he had not felt whole. For a moment, he concentrated on breathing, focusing on controlling his emotions enough to speak again. "No. He will not aid us."

"Then why should we hear what he has to say?" Gray protested. "He plans to destroy us. This whole meeting is probably a trap."

"We won't leave the Warding," Callonen assured him. "For now, we still have the power to keep the demons out of our land. Maybe can learn something useful from what he says."

The edge of the Warding, invisible to the human eye, was defined by lines of armed men on both sides. Outside, the heavily armed troops of Ara in blue uniforms congregated. Inside the protection of the Warding, Callonen's men stood guard in orderly rows.

As the carriage stopped, Callonen drew in a deep breath. A strong urge to escape flooded through him. He would order them all to turn around instead of going through with this. How could he face his brother again after what Haldreth had done? He'd been a peaceful man all his life, but now Callonen felt the urge to attack, to make his brother pay for the pain he'd caused. Haldreth deserved to die for the crimes he'd committed.

General Gray moved to the door and got out, turning back, subtly providing support. As Callonen stood upright, exhaustion dragged at his limbs, pain twisted through his muscles and joints. No matter how his body felt, he had to face his brother. For a moment, he feared he couldn't walk without aid. Gray remained close beside him, ready if that should be the case.

Callonen moved forward, one step and then another. His loyal soldiers in dark green uniforms lined his path on either side. They were good men, every one of them. He would do what he had to do to protect them and the rest of his people.

With halting steps, Callonen walked toward the front, attempting to conceal his weakness as much as he could. A familiar figure approached the border from the other side. Haldreth's appearance hadn't changed much. Dark hair and beard, their father's brown eyes. He looked older, but he remained a mirror image of Callonen, his identical twin.

Callonen was the one who had changed. The illness had attacked his body, aging him prematurely. The changes were obvious now, as he faced his brother across the empty space between the soldiers, and he saw the triumph on Haldreth's face.

"Callonen!" Haldreth called jovially. "It's good to see you, brother!"

Ignoring his pain and weakness, all of Callonen's muscles clenched, tightening with a visceral need to attack. His jaw clenched back the words that threatened to come out in a flood of despair and pain. *You took Allia from me. I loved her with all my heart, and she was everything to me! I intended to cherish her for the rest of my life.* Despite knowing that Haldreth would hear the desperation in his voice, he couldn't prevent the question that escaped his lips. "Where is she?"

A long, awkward moment of silence fell. The soldiers on both sides stood perfectly still while Callonen faced his brother.

At first, Haldreth's face betrayed no emotion other than vague confusion. "Who?"

Callonen glared at him, attempting to control the trembling in his hands.

Haldreth's eyes widened in realization. "Oh, you're talking about that servant girl who worked at the palace. The two of you were... friends."

Hot rage flooded through Callonen and he struggled to keep his body still, his expression calm. Haldreth meant to goad him, to force him to lose his remaining shreds of control.

Haldreth laughed coldly. "Let the past go, brother. It was a long time ago. Seventeen years is a long time to hold a grudge. I can't believe you're still asking about her." He tapped his chin as he thought. "What was her name? Hannah? Leah...?"

"Allia." Callonen hadn't spoken her name aloud in years. The pain was too great.

Haldreth smiled, slapping his thigh. "That's right," he rubbed his chin. "I remember now. Allia." He shook his head. "Not the smartest girl. For some reason, she never would cooperate with me, no matter how I tried. She's long gone."

Callonen hadn't thought his heart could hurt more, but the pain in his chest increased at his brother's words. Haldreth had taken Allia, determined to control her for her power. He would have used *any* means to force her to his will.

"I didn't ask you here to talk about her," Haldreth said. "I wanted to know how you were. You don't look well, brother."

"No," Callonen ground out. His brother knew that already.

Haldreth shook his head in mock sympathy. "That's terrible. How long has this been going on? Probably about four months now?"

Fear, like a silver of ice, penetrated Callonen as everything came together at the words. Four months. "It's a spell," he gasped. He looked up at his brother. "You did the same thing to father, didn't you? I should have realized."

Haldreth raised his eyebrows. "Me? How could I affect our dear departed father's health? I haven't been in Sarine for years."

"Before you left, I saw your spell book with an enchantment to cause someone to die of old age within a year. Father wasn't even sixty, and he could have had many good years. How could you—" Callonen felt his knees weaken, and he swayed on his feet. Gray stepped closer, taking his arm to support him.

Haldreth's cold eyes bored into Callonen's. "If you believe that's true, then you know exactly how much time you have left. Just a few short months. We are family. I thought we should speak once more before it was all over. Perhaps you already knew that Allia gave birth to a child."

Yes. Callonen had received that news.

"You haven't found her, have you?" Haldreth asked, his voice deceptively casual.

Callonen's voice shook with rage. "I would never tell you where she is!"

Haldreth smiled. "So, you don't know either. No matter. I sent my demons to hunt her. It's only a matter of time before they find her."

Unable to leave the Warding himself, Callonen had sent many of his best people to search for the child over the years. They still searched. There seemed little hope they would find the girl before Haldreth's dark servants did.

"Dear brother," Haldreth said, shaking his head, "why are you still trying to fight me? Sarine *will* be mine. You have nothing left. Give up now. You don't have long anyway, and there's no cure for your illness."

Giving up seemed logical. If so many other lives hadn't depended on him, Callonen would have done it long ago. But Haldreth had lied about one thing. There *was* a cure for his condition, Allia's enchanted ring. There would be hope if they could find the ring.

Hope.

Haldreth nodded to his soldiers. Yelling, they drew their weapons and surged forward to attack.

PART ONE

FLIGHT

CHAPTER ONE

YEAR OF WARDING 38, BRIGHT SPRINGS, KETHEL

ANA

TRAVELERS RARELY USED THE rutted dirt track running past the only inn in Bright Springs. But all morning, carts and wagons rolled along. Ana saw them through the windows as she cleaned the tables and swept the floors. The harvest had just begun. It was too soon for anyone to be taking their crops to market, and it made no sense for so many to be traveling.

By midday, a noisy crowd of villagers and travelers packed the inn. No one wanted a room for the night, but they all wanted a meal. In the kitchen, Tari prepared food as fast as she could. Ana ran back and forth with orders, coins and heavy trays laden with food. Fergen would be pleased. This might be the most profitable day the innkeeper had ever had.

Fergen entered the common room, his gray hair and stocky frame familiar among the crowd of strangers. He led another group to the last empty table. "Why are so many people on the road today?"

Ana hurried over to take their order.

"I'm not staying in Gildan," a big bearded man in the worn clothes of a farmer was telling the innkeeper. "Harvest or no harvest. My grandfather lived in the old kingdom more than sixty-five years ago. He was there when it fell. If the same thing is happening here, we want no part of it."

"The same thing?" Fergen asked. "What are you talking about?"

"The village of Gildan was attacked," the man growled. "And the day after, anyone who had gotten even a scratch was burning with fever. They were poisoned. I'm not the only one who remembers what happened in the dark times. It was the Shekkar."

The room froze. One of the villagers dropped a mug, and it broke on the floor. A terrified silence replaced the voices.

"Are you telling me the Shekkar attacked Gildan?" Fergen finally asked into the ringing silence.

"They came in the middle of the night. We didn't see them, but I know it was them!" The man faced Fergen.

"How do you know? The Shekkar haven't been seen for nearly forty years. Not since the old emperor destroyed them with his enchanted sword. Who could have brought them back?"

The bearded man shook his head. "I don't know who, but someone did. In the north, there have been rumors of them for years, but they've never come anywhere near here, until now. I'm not waiting around for them to come after my family." He waved a big hand at his wife and children, clustered around the table. He nodded toward the road, where wagons were still rolling along. "I'm not the only one who thinks so. We've worked all year for this harvest, and it makes me sick to leave before we can bring it in. But I'd rather abandon it than be dead."

His words echoed around the room. The unnatural stillness dissipated slowly as the crowd resumed eating and talking. Their voices were hushed now. Ana gathered the pieces of the broken pottery into her apron, collected a few coins, and left the farmer and his family with a pitcher and mugs while she went to the kitchen for their food.

It took hours for Ana and Fergen to finish serving the midday meal. The inn's kitchen was empty of food save for a few scraps and an enormous stack of dirty dishes. Ana found Tari surveying the pile, a look of dismay on her kind face.

"What a day," the cook exclaimed. "We'd better clean these quick. There will be more customers here tonight. Can you work on them while I start some meat roasting?"

Ana tied back her hair and was busy at the washbasin when Fergen came in, running a hand through his gray hair. "Did you ever see such a crowd?"

"Not in Bright Springs," Tari answered. "Did you find out where they're going?"

Fergen glanced at Ana and gave the cook a warning look.

Ana turned from washing dishes to face him. "You don't have to hide it from me. I heard what they said." She was sixteen, no longer a child who would wail and cry in fright. "What are the Shekkar?"

At the word, Tari dropped the dish she was drying onto the floor, where it landed with a loud clatter.

Fergen took a deep breath, his lips tight, and his face unsmiling. "They're demons."

When the dishes were finally finished and Fergen gave her permission to take a break, Ana left the kitchen and walked up the hill into the quiet woods. She craved the silence of the trees after the noise and bustle of the inn.

A little way up the hill, she came to her favorite oak tree. Over the years, she'd climbed it so many times that she had worn the bark on its limbs smooth from finding the same handholds over and over again. The late afternoon sun filtered down through the leaves and made a pattern of light and shade on her skin as she sat in the wide fork between the branches, hidden from sight. This had been her secret place as a child, and it was still a haven of peace and solitude for her.

Beyond the edge of the woods, she saw houses and bits of the fields where farmers brought in their harvest. Nothing could be heard but the tranquil murmur of oak leaves in the breeze.

She wanted to stay until the sun set, but Fergen expected her back in time to help with the dinner rush. It had been the same every night for the nine years she'd lived at the inn, though today had been far busier than usual. Fergen, the kind old innkeeper, had taken her in, a child alone in the world, after her grandmother died.

In the stillness, Ana heard the distinct sound of footsteps beneath the tree. Was it one of the boys from the village? She looked down through the branches.

Two strangers walked between the trees, pausing every few steps to bend low and look at the ground. Ana knew everyone in Bright Springs, and she'd never seen these men before. Were they part of the crowd of travelers today? If that was true, what were they doing in the woods?

Silently, she watched them. They wore packs on their backs, confirming her guess that they were traveling. The one with dark hair knelt on the ground, looking at something. The other had light hair that hung in unruly waves. "Are you sure?"

The kneeling man looked up from the ground. He frowned behind a short dark beard, and his brows were pulled together in worry. "The tracks are clear. No human made these. You can see the marks of their claws in the soil. They're here."

He stood, and Ana's eyes widened as she stared at the long blade at his side. She realized the other man wore a similar weapon strapped across his back, the hilt sticking out above his pack. No one in Bright Springs wore a sword. She'd never seen weapons that big before.

"When?" The man with light hair rubbed the back of his neck.

"They look fresh. I'd say, last night."

"It's this town, then. It has to be. They passed through Gildan on their way here. Everyone in this place is in danger. If they were here last night, they'll be back as soon as it gets dark. She must be here, and we have to find the girl before they do." He turned and took a step away.

The dark-haired man shook his head. "Not the town. Here. The tracks are everywhere around this tree." He pointed to several places surrounding the oak. He paused, looking down toward the inn, the way Ana had come. Bending down, he examined the ground. "These tracks don't match the others. Someone walked here."

Peering down between the branches, Ana watched him. He examined her tracks along the path she'd taken from the inn into the woods. No one had ever bothered to follow her before. She wasn't important enough, unless it had something to do with her secret. Ana possessed a strange ring. It was silver, set with a sparkling green gem. Peculiar symbols marked the inside of the band. On her deathbed, her grandmother had warned Ana never to tell anyone about it. All these years, she'd worn the ring on a leather cord around her neck, hidden beneath her clothes. It was a constant reminder of the secret, but until now, she hadn't given much thought to her grandmother's warning. She pressed her hand against the stone, feeling a strange tingle in her skin like the ring had a life of its own.

The men followed her tracks a little way down the hill. Ana breathed a sigh of relief as they went away. Then they turned and came back to the base of her oak. "See the tracks there. They come right to the tree."

Ana pressed herself against the bark, out of sight. These men were following her, and from their conversation, they weren't the only ones. Her stomach tightened. All the talk in the inn that day ran through her mind. Now strange tracks had led these men to this very spot. No one but Ana ever came here.

One of the men climbed the tree. Ana heard his boots against the bark and the soft sound of his breath as he pulled himself up. Soon, he appeared between the branches, and they stared at each other. Her eyes darted to his shoulder, wondering if he still carried his sword, but he'd taken it off with his pack before he climbed the tree. He wore a dagger at his belt, but his hands were nowhere near the hilt.

Up close, he looked barely older than the village boys who worked in the fields. His expression seemed friendly. He had a straight nose and a strong jaw covered by a short beard.

"Who are you? And why are you following me?" she demanded.

She didn't know these men. Maybe they were dangerous.

Seating himself on a branch, the young man raised his empty hands palm out in a nonthreatening gesture. "I'm sorry I startled you. Please, don't be afraid." His voice sounded kind. "I'm trying to find someone. She's in danger, and we came to help."

Ana stared back at him. That wasn't what she'd been expecting him to say. What was he talking about? It almost sounded as if he knew about the secret. Grandmother had been very clear that Ana should tell no one because it was dangerous. Something terrible had pursued Ana years ago when she was a baby. Could it be the same thing that had left tracks all around her tree?

"Do you wear a ring? Silver, set with a green stone?"

Ana's eyes widened. How could he know about it? Was he a friend or an enemy?

She stared back into his eyes and held up her hands. "No. This village is too poor for anyone to wear jewelry."

He returned her gaze. "I know it's a secret. But if you or someone you know has the ring, you're in great danger." He looked at her with serious gray eyes. "My name is Zarek." Pointing to his friend on the ground, he continued, "That's Dane down there. May I ask your name?"

She'd been warned never to share her real name, so she gave him the shorter version she'd used all her life. "Ana."

Zarek met her eyes, his expression earnest. "I promise we would never hurt you, Ana. We came to help. There are dangerous things in this world, and we've sworn an oath to find the girl with the ring, protect her and take her to safety. Do you believe me? We only want to help."

She stared into his eyes and nodded toward the ground. "Tell me what made those tracks."

He cleared his throat and rubbed the back of his neck before he finally spoke. "Shekkar. Demons."

Ana drew in a sharp breath, her eyes wide. Even before the rumors she'd heard today, the village boys used to tell stories about Shekkar just to frighten her. Everyone knew demons would rip you apart if they caught you. They had destroyed an entire kingdom, their poison killing thousands. Now, it wasn't just an old story. "And you think they're following me?"

He stared at her for a moment before he nodded.

Cold dread twisted her stomach. If the Shekkar were hunting her, they would kill her. She had no way to run fast enough or far enough to escape them. Tears welled in her eyes, and she blinked them back. Ana was too old to cry like a baby. She didn't want Zarek to notice.

"They're coming soon. We need to go!"

He was right. His words startled her into motion, and she followed him as he climbed down.

"Hurry," Dane called up from the ground. "It will be dark soon. We have to get everyone indoors. The whole town is in danger!"

"We have to tell Fergen." Ana pointed down the hill toward the inn.

"Is that where you live?" Dane asked.

"Yes."

Dane looked at Zarek. "The Shekkar will follow her trail there. But the rest of the people should barricade themselves in their houses. I'll meet you at the inn. Get her inside. Tell them to bar the doors."

Zarek removed his sword from its place on his pack and belted it around his waist.

Ana led him to the back door, and she ran into the kitchen. "Tari, where's Fergen?" she asked the gray-haired cook.

"What's going on? Who is that?" Tari eyed Zarek in confusion.

Fergen appeared in the kitchen door. "Hurry, Ana! Almost every table is already full." His eyes tightened in suspicion as he looked at Zarek. "Who are you?"

"My name is Zarek. I serve the Emperor of Sarine. I came to warn you that the inn is going to be attacked."

The blood drained from Fergen's face, and he took a step backward. "When? Who? Not the—"

"Shekkar. Demons of dark magic," Zarek said. "My friend has gone to warn the rest of the village. The demons will be here soon. We need to bar the doors and windows. Get everyone out of here. Tell them to stay hidden indoors. Go now!"

Fergen ran back to the common room, and he only had to utter one strangled word, "Shekkar." His customers scattered at his warning.

Ana helped Fergen pull the heavy shutters closed, and he dropped the latches into place. They barred the front door.

"The demons are coming. You should go too," Zarek said, putting his hand on Fergen's shoulder, gesturing toward the kitchen door.

Fergen glanced down at Ana. "What about Ana? If she's not safe here—"

Zarek met Ana's eyes, then looked back at the innkeeper. "They're following her."

Ana's stomach clenched.

Fergen stood beside her and put his arm protectively around her shoulders. "If she's in danger, I'm not leaving her."

Ana turned to hug him tightly. He had always treated her with kindness, even though she was only an orphan.

"There's no way you can fight them." Zarek shook his head. "They'll only kill you if you stay. Take the cook and run. Get somewhere secure. Find a place to hide!"

Fergen didn't want to go, but Ana couldn't let him get hurt because of her. She threw her arms around him. "You've done so much for me. You always took good care of me. Please don't let them kill you! I couldn't bear it."

He held her close. "Every day I've had you in my life, I've been grateful. I love you Ana, please be safe!" He kissed the top of her head and released her. "I'm sorry. I'm so sorry." He took Tari by the arm, and they disappeared into the gathering darkness.

Ana helped Zarek check the doors and windows again. Then he pushed chairs and tables against the front door.

Outside, night covered the village. Dane ran in through the back door. He slammed it behind him and slid the heavy bar across it. "I told them to get indoors and stay there." He was breathing hard. "They didn't all listen." As if to punctuate his words, a scream rang out from somewhere in the darkness.

Ana stood trembling. Fergen was gone, along with everyone else she knew. No one was left except these two strangers.

Outside, something clawed at the door, and Ana didn't dare to breathe. It scratched at the walls, hunting for a way inside. A hard blow struck the door. It held. From the other side came a shriek of frustration. Ana cringed away from the sound.

Zarek gripped the hilt of his dagger and took a deep breath. His jaw clenched. Dane came into the dining room, drew his sword, and stood watching the door, tense and ready, the weapon in his hand. From outside in the dark, they heard terrified voices and running feet. Someone was out there. They called out, and Ana wanted to help them. A man screamed first, then a woman.

Zarek drew his sword and held the weapon ready, his eyes on the door.

Outside, it grew silent. Whoever had been out there, they made no other sound. Ana took a deep breath, then another. The quiet didn't last. More blows came at the front door, and more shrieking. The door creaked and groaned and shook on its hinges. Would it keep them out? Or would the thing outside find more of her friends and neighbors and kill them? Would it find Fergen and Tari?

She couldn't stand that. "They're looking for me! If I go out there, will they take me and leave the others alone?"

"You can't do that, Ana," Zarek said firmly. "They can't get the ring. If they do, many more people will die."

"People are dying now! Can't you just take the ring and go?"

He shook his head. "It's too late for that. They're already following you."

"They're breaking in. You're going to have to take Ana and run," Dane said. "Get ready to slip out the back door."

Zarek took Ana's hand and headed for the kitchen.

The attack against the door redoubled. Ana heard blows from all around the building now. From the front of the inn, they heard the sounds of breaking wood and shattering glass. Abruptly, the assault on the back door ceased.

Zarek met her eyes. The muscles of his jaw clenched. "Get ready to run."

"It's time." Dane's voice sounded hard as he looked at Zarek. "You're faster than I am. Take her and go. I'll hold them off and then follow you."

Ana's breath came fast and shallow, and her heart pounded in her throat. Zarek raised his sword.

"Go. Now!" Dane ordered, standing in the kitchen doorway, his blade in his hand. Several black shapes burst through the front door, shrieking. Dane held his sword ready.

Zarek pulled Ana through the back door. She screamed as a black shape towered above them, blocking their path. Shoving her back, he attacked the black thing.

The demon screeched and tried to claw at them, but Zarek's sword deflected the blow. Ana heard its razor-sharp claws scrape against the metal. While his sword held the creature back, he drew his dagger. The blade glowed faintly green in the darkness. He struck at the demon, driving the blade home until it fell, unmoving.

"Run!" Zarek ordered, tucking the dagger back into its sheath.

They dashed away from the village, following the edge of a stream, stumbling over the uneven ground in the moonlight. Ana ran as fast as she could, but it didn't feel fast enough. Zarek pulled her along, urging her to greater speed.

The night was quiet around them, except for their rapid breathing and the sound of their feet pounding against the ground. Ana looked back over her shoulder and saw Dane behind them, running hard. Beyond him, black shapes followed. But Zarek was heading the wrong way.

"Don't go—" she gasped, pointing ahead of them. "There's—cliff—"

Zarek didn't listen. For a few moments, they widened the gap between them and their pursuers. But the demons would soon cut off their escape. The small stream beside the town drained into a larger river that had carved a deep cleft in the land, and Zarek was coming to the brink of the cliff. He stopped and looked over the edge. Ana glimpsed a black chasm with a silver ribbon of water at the bottom.

Dane caught up with them. "That way!" He pointed along the edge of the canyon. They followed the cliff downstream.

The Shekkar cut across the distance, heading straight for them, gaining fast. Ana could hear the demons clearly now, and their horrible voices sounded triumphant. They were about to claim their prize. She stopped on the brink of the cliff, frozen, the yawning space open below her. Zarek had placed himself between Ana and the Shekkar, his sword in one hand and his dagger in the other. But there were too many enemies to fight, and they charged toward him, black claws outstretched.

The foremost of the creatures struck at him. He blocked the blow with his sword, but poisonous claws seized the weapon, twisting it out of his grip. A flash of moonlight lit the sword blade as it spun away, landing behind the demon.

Zarek sheathed his knife and darted straight toward Ana. As his shoulder slammed into her, his arm seized her waist, and his momentum propelled them out into the black abyss. Ana screamed as they fell.

Chapter Two

Year of Warding 38, Kethel's Countryside

ANA

COLD AIR RUSHED BY Ana as she fell, the black rock of the canyon flashing past. They struck the water, and from that height, it felt like a solid wall. Her face and arms exploded in pain. Their momentum sent them deep under the surface. The impact tore her away from Zarek and knocked the breath from her lungs.

She flailed, frantically trying to find her way back to the surface of the dark water. There was nothing to hold on to, and the current tossed her in all directions. Something seized her leg, pulling her. Confused and disoriented, she felt like she was being dragged deeper into the water.

Ana felt them break the surface, and dimly, she realized Zarek had brought her back from the depths. He towed her toward the bank, hauled her out of the water onto the gravel shore and struck her back. A little water ran from her mouth. Additional blows brought up more, and she coughed violently. She sucked air into her lungs and felt the stones of the bank beneath her as she lay, coughing and gasping.

Dane slogged through the shallows toward them. "Is she hurt?" He knelt down beside them.

"We hit hard. She has water in her lungs." Zarek ran his hand through his hair. "I didn't mean to hurt her. I wouldn't have jumped—I didn't know what else to do!"

"You did what you had to do." Dane bent over Ana. "Carry her and watch her. We'll check on her again when it gets light. Come on, we need to go."

Ana's lungs burned, and she still wasn't sure which way was up. Zarek slid one arm under her shoulders and the other beneath her knees and picked her up. He must be very strong because he easily got to his feet holding her. No one had held her like this since she was a small child. She wanted to tell him to put her down, except she couldn't gather the breath to speak and she wasn't sure she could walk.

The dark canyon walls towered above them, the moonlight gleaming on smooth rock. Ana hid her face in the front of Zarek's shirt. Her ribs throbbed where his shoulder had struck her, her skin felt raw where she'd hit the water, and her soaking wet clothes felt chill in the night air. Unsuccessfully, she tried to hold back the tears that escaped from the corners of her eyes. Now she was crying like a baby and being carried like one.

They kept going. Ana had several more bouts of violent coughing, but when they passed, she breathed more easily.

Zarek set her down to walk, but exhaustion slowed her steps. She struggled along until, eventually, the rose pink of dawn lit the east. Dane stopped in a sheltered place beside some rocks and took off his pack and sword. Ana collapsed to the ground. Zarek dropped his own gear and sat near her. It felt good to be still, and she rested her back against the stone.

"How badly are you hurt?" Zarek asked. Putting one finger under her chin, he gently turned her face to the morning light to examine where she'd struck the water. His brows lowered, and his mouth turned down in a frown. "I'm sorry." He released her chin and shook his head.

But Ana knew he'd done the best he could. If he hadn't jumped with her, the demons would have caught them. "I..." She swallowed and tried again. "You didn't let them catch us." She spoke with difficulty, and her throat felt raw from coughing up river water.

Zarek stared back at her, his eyes widening in surprise at her answer.

"Where are we?" She scanned their surroundings. This was already farther from home than she'd ever been before.

"We're at the bottom of the canyon below the village. This river flows down into Lake Bethor."

Everyone she had known, the only home she remembered, had been left behind last night. She looked at Zarek. Another fit of coughing passed before she could speak again. "Did they kill everyone in the village?"

He rubbed the back of his neck. "I don't think so. Most of them are safe."

"What about Fergen and Tari? What if the demons killed them?"

"They didn't," Dane said from where he sat on a rock nearby.

"How can you be sure?"

He took a deep breath and met her eyes. "Because the demons are following us."

Ana felt a sharp twist of fear in her belly, and she shivered. This was it. They were all going to die. As soon as night fell, the Shekkar would hunt them. And this time there would be no shelter, no cliff to help them escape.

A muscle in Zarek's jaw tightened.

Ana's chest constricted until she couldn't breathe. Her voice sounded strangled. "They're going to kill us. We're going to die."

Dane came over to her and bent to one knee, gripping her shoulders. His brown eyes appeared stern. "We are not going to die. We are going to run, but we can escape them."

Ana looked back at him. "How is that possible? I've heard the stories. If they don't tear us apart, they're going to poison us, and there's no cure."

"There is one cure," Zarek said. "The ring. You do have it, don't you? It's the reason they're following you."

Ana hadn't trusted them with her secret before, but what choice did she have now? They had both saved her life last night, at great risk to themselves. If they wanted to harm her, why would they do that?

She clutched the ring where it hung under her shirt. Pulling it out, she drew the cord over her head and made a fist around the ring. "This is why they're following me? Then let's get rid of it!" She stood up, faced the churning white water of the river, and drew her arm back to throw.

They launched into motion so quickly, she barely saw them moving before they both gripped her wrist.

"Don't!" Dane pleaded. "You can't. If we lose that ring, the empire of Sarine will fall and no place in the world will be safe from the demons. Many more people will die. Besides, it's too late. The Shekkar are already hunting us."

That was too much pressure. Ana didn't want the lives of thousands of people to be in her hands. She scrunched her eyes closed, but that didn't stop the tears from running down her cheeks. Closing her hand tightly around the ring, she sank to the ground, and they released her arm.

How could she possibly escape the Shekkar? Ana shook her head. "It's only a matter of time before they kill me."

"We won't let that happen," Dane promised.

Beside him, Zarek nodded in agreement. He rose and took a deep breath, as if to shake off the worry, and grabbed his sodden pack. From inside, he retrieved his flint and started gathering sticks. Still clutching the ring, Ana got up and stretched her stiff, sore muscles. She hung the cord back around her neck and began gathering wood. Dane helped too, and in a little while, they had a good fire going. Ana sat with her knees pulled up to her chest, as close to the flames as she could.

They spread wet clothes and blankets from their packs to dry on the bushes. Zarek peeled off his wet jacket and shirt and hung them up. He lay back on the sandy riverbank with his eyes closed.

Ana blinked and looked back at Dane. "You promised you would protect me. What if they kill you?"

Dane rubbed his face and met her gaze. "If something happens to one of us, you could use the ring."

"What do you mean... use it?" Ana stared at them in confusion.

"You don't know what it does?" Zarek sat up, his eyebrows raised in surprise.

Ana shook her head. It was a ring. Was it supposed to... do something?

"That ring can heal any injury," Zarek said.

Ana stared back at him in shock. "What? How?" Then her eyes widened. "Do you mean that back there, I could have saved the lives of those who were injured?"

Dane shook his head. "No. The demons would have caught us too. We would have to escape them before you'd have a chance to use it. And you can only heal one person at a time. The ring uses your strength and will to heal, but the process is painful. It would be several days before you could do it again."

"But if one of you were injured, then I could heal you?"

"Yes."

"What if I can't do it?"

"We're hoping that you can," Dane said. "We serve the Emperor of Sarine, and he wields a magical power called the Warding that keeps the demons out of Sarine. All we have to do is get over the border before they catch us. The emperor is ill, and we're hoping you can heal him. If he dies, the Warding will disappear, and the demons will destroy Sarine."

"And you think I can heal him? Why don't we give the ring to someone else?"

Zarek got up from where he'd been resting and sat beside Ana. "Once you put it on your finger, it will not come off again. The ring belongs to you."

He was right. Ana didn't want to give it away. The ring was the only possession her mother had left her. Maybe she wouldn't have actually been able to throw it in the river, even to save her own life. Pulling the cord from beneath her collar, she stared at the ring. Strange symbols were engraved on the inside of the band, and the green gem sparkled in the sunlight. What would it be like to heal someone? Painful, they had warned her. But she wasn't willing to give up this final link to her family.

She removed the leather cord and slid it onto her finger. It fit exactly.

Zarek was worried about her. They were all in danger, and he felt sorry for the shock and pain she had been through in the last several hours. He wanted to keep her safe.

Ana's eyes widened, and she gasped. Zarek was still there, standing beside her. He hadn't moved or spoken, but now that she wore the ring, she could sense what he was feeling.

He was determined to protect her and get her safely to Sarine. And Zarek would never harm her. She felt his loyalty, as if she knew what was in his heart. She stared at him in wonder. "You really do want to help me."

Zarek grinned. "I told you I did."

She took a step nearer to Dane and found she could sense him, too. His feelings shared the same desire to protect her, and the same loyalty to Sarine.

Last night, Ana hadn't had much choice but to trust them, and she wondered if it had been foolish. If she believed this new sense, then she had been right to count on these men.

"Maybe we can make it." With this new knowledge, she felt more hopeful. "If they catch up, can we fight them? I don't know how." She looked at Dane's sword. "But you both do."

Dane sighed. "I wish I could. Ordinary weapons don't hurt them. That dagger is the only thing we possess that can." He pointed to Zarek's weapon.

Zarek sat up and patted the hilt. "The dagger is enchanted with the power to kill demons, just like Emperor Caldoreth's sword, Blackbane. I didn't know for sure it would work until last night, but I killed one of them."

"That's more than anyone else has done since the sword was stolen," Dane said. He felt hope and relief when he said it, and Ana relaxed a little.

"The wizard Zarekathus helped Caldoreth found the empire of Sarine. His son Callonen is emperor now," Zarek said.

"Za—re—kath—us?" Ana stumbled over the name.

"Just remember, Zarek-athus," Dane said, grinning. He nodded at Zarek. "His mother named him after the wizard. I think she hoped he would grow up to be a brilliant scholar."

Zarek smacked his friend.

Dane only laughed. "You're better with a blade than a pen and ink." He glanced at Ana. "Zarek might be young, but he's the most skilled soldier in Sarine."

Ana gazed at Zarek with wide eyes. He shifted uncomfortably under her attention.

Turning back to Dane, she asked, "You mean he can beat you?"

Dane grinned. "He can beat anyone. Here." He tossed her a damp shirt. "Put this on and hang up your clothes. I'll stay with you, and Zarek can find us something to eat."

Ana took the shirt and went behind the rocks to change. It felt strange to put on clothing that didn't belong to her. Dane's spare shirt was much too large, which was a blessing after she peeled off her soaked pants. The hem came nearly to her knees, and she had to roll the sleeves up to expose her hands. She felt embarrassed to walk around partially dressed in front of two men who had been strangers only a few hours ago. But it was much better than wearing wet clothes.

Dane had pulled off his shirt and jacket while she was gone and now hung them up.

She touched the fabric of her borrowed shirt. He could have had at least one dry piece of clothing if he hadn't shared with her. "Thank you," she said. She hung up her tunic, pants and jacket and huddled close to the flames.

He turned at the sound of her voice and smiled. "You're welcome."

It didn't take Zarek long to come back with a rabbit. He sat down by the fire and began skinning and cleaning it. His hands moved skillfully. When he finished, he placed the rabbit on a spit over the fire to roast and went to scrub his hands at the edge of the river.

"How far is it to the Warding?" Ana asked, looking up at him as he returned to the fire.

He rubbed his wet hands against his pants. "It will take several weeks to get there," he admitted.

"Don't worry. We'll make it," Dane promised.

"Why do the demons want the ring?" she asked.

"They serve the king of Ara. He wants to destroy Sarine. And right now, Emperor Callonen is very sick," Dane said. "But we know he's still alive because the demons are chasing us. If he dies, they won't bother with us. They will simply go to Sarine and destroy it. We were searching for the ring to save his life."

Ana felt her stomach twist. "And if I can't heal him... it would be like... back there? The demons would kill everyone? How do you know it will work? Have you seen it heal before?"

"When I was little, back in Sarine, a young woman named Allia saved my life with the ring," Zarek said.

The blood drained from her face at the sound of the familiar name. Before she died, Grandmother had told Ana her mother's name was Allia.

"You know that name?" Zarek asked, observing her reaction. "Then you are Cirana? After all this time, we finally found you?"

She nodded. "Allia was my mother. But Grandmother told me never to tell, that if people knew, it would be dangerous. I guess she was right."

Zarek nodded.

"But, Allia—you know her? Where is she?"

"I knew her," he corrected quickly. "I'm very sorry, but she died many years ago."

Ana's momentary hope crumbled. All her life, she'd wondered about her mother. Had Allia loved her? Why hadn't they stayed together? It made sense that she was dead. If Allia had been alive and had loved her, she wouldn't have left Ana alone.

Ana nodded sadly. "I understand. But will you tell me about her? My grandmother said she named me Cirana. I've never told anyone my real name before. Everyone always just called me Ana. You said you knew her. What did she look like? Tell me everything you remember about her."

"I remember her." Dane shook his head sorrowfully. "It was the first year I joined the Emperor's Guard. Half the soldiers in the palace were secretly in love with her. She had the most beautiful smile, and she was always kind to everyone."

"It was almost seventeen years ago," Zarek said. He turned the meat roasting over the fire. "I was only six when she left the city. My parents were so grateful to her for saving my life. I remember she had long golden hair, lighter than yours. Her eyes were different. I don't remember exactly, maybe green? My father and his friend Harrow went to look for Allia. Harrow was badly hurt on the way back, but he made it to the Warding and said he'd hidden Allia's child and the ring. He must have meant you. We guessed she'd passed the ring on to you before she died."

"So we can ask Harrow about it!"

Zarek shook his head. "The Shekkar had attacked him. He didn't survive their poison."

"Your father and his friend rescued me." Ana looked at him. Her mind tried to avoid the terrible truth. "But your father... He came back, didn't he?"

Staring back at her, Zarek shook his head.

The truth settled over Ana. It was her fault he had lost his father. Tears stung her eyes. "You must hate me." She felt her hands clenching into fists. "I'm the reason he's dead. You loved your father, and he's dead because of me."

Zarek took her hand. At his kind touch, she allowed her fingers to relax into his. It felt good, and she appreciated the comfort he offered as it flowed through her. "That's not true, Ana. Stop and breathe. With the ring, you can tell what I'm feeling. You know I don't feel that way. I don't hate you. My father thought that protecting you and your mother was worth risking his life for. I will do the same. I promise I won't let anything hurt you."

For six nights, they followed the canyon downward. The white river roared beside Ana, reminding her not to slip. Zarek frequently offered his hand to help her down from the boulders. The cliffs on either side of the river had gradually lowered, but they had spent the long nights climbing through the rocks. Ana pushed hard to keep up with them.

Tonight, the stars turned slowly in the clear sky above them. When Ana turned to look at Zarek, and she saw him staring behind them. Was something back there?

"Dane! Demons!" Zarek yelled above the sound of the water. Dane looked back. "Behind us?"

Zarek pointed back the way they had come.

CHAPTER THREE

YEAR OF WARDING 38, KETHEL'S COUNTRYSIDE

ANA

WITH TERROR CHURNING INSIDE her, Ana moved as fast as she could down through the jagged boulders. The river grew calmer and slower as they descended. Soon, she heard the demons too.

"Hurry," Dane yelled. "The rocks drop off on this side. We need to get across the river." They waded out into the icy water.

The Shekkar were close now, snarling and growling words in their indecipherable language. As the frigid water rose to her waist, Ana couldn't take her eyes off them. They seemed darker than the night surrounding them. The first of them had reached the edge of the river.

Zarek paused beside her and stared back at them in disbelief. He had told her that the demons refused to enter water, but she hadn't quite believed it. But it was true. They wouldn't even put their feet in it. Why didn't they walk into the water?

Ana stood between Zarek and Dane. They had their weapons out and stood ready, waiting for an attack. They watched the demons, who snarled and gnashed their teeth, but never entered the water. It felt like a year passed, and Ana's feet were numb with cold. Nothing changed. Ana heard more demons coming. They were on both sides of the river now.

"We have to move," Dane yelled above the roar of the water.

"Hold on to me." Zarek grabbed Ana's arm. They plunged into the bitter cold water, and the current took them. Ana couldn't see the demons any more. But they wouldn't give up so easily. Maybe Zarek and Dane could get a little ahead of them this way. Zarek pushed off the rocks with his boots and swam in the deeper places. The water felt icy.

Ana clung to him, shivering violently. They'd been in the river for so long. All she wanted to do was sleep. The sound of the water faded, and it didn't seem so cold. But everything was dark, and her eyelids were heavy.

Voices interrupted her rest. "Ana! Ana, please wake up."

Someone shook her and rubbed her numb arms and legs. It did not feel good.

"Stop," she protested.

"Ana!"

She recognized Dane's urgent voice. "Wake up."

"Too tired..." she mumbled.

"Please, Ana?"

That was Zarek. He felt worried. They were both worried. Why? What was so wrong with sleeping? She dragged her eyelids open and saw them both bending over her with the starry sky behind them. Shivers racked her numb body.

"Take off your wet clothes and wrap up in this." Dane held out a blanket. "There's no one else here. We'll turn our backs."

Zarek helped her sit up. She gazed with longing at the dry blanket. They turned around as she undressed and wrapped herself up in it. "Are we safe?" she asked, her voice still shaken by her shivering.

Rousing slightly, she realized they were in a boat. How had they gotten here from the river?

"We're safe for now," Dane said. "Rest."

Ana curled into a ball and pulled the blanket tight around herself. Dane tossed another cover over her. "Thank you," she murmured. "Please don't make me jump in the river again?"

"Not tonight," Dane promised.

Ana woke to the delicious feeling of warm sunlight on her face. She lay still wrapped in the blanket, and huddled against Zarek's back. They were in a wooden fishing boat with a single sail. Dane stood a few feet away, tying off a rope attached to the canvas. When she lifted her head, she saw water surrounding them in all directions. Was this the lake Zarek had been talking about days ago?

It felt so good to be warm. Zarek still slept, his only motion the steady rhythm of his breathing until he shifted in his sleep, rolling onto his back.

He wore a silver charm on a chain around his neck. It stood out against his bare skin. She'd never seen anything like it. The intricate pendant had been formed into the shape of a tiny sword and hammer crossed.

The sun was high before Ana had any interest in getting up. Zarek woke up and turned to look at her. "Feeling better?"

She nodded. "You?"

"Better." He nodded.

"What is that?" She pointed to the charm.

He smiled. "It belonged to my mother. My father had one just like it."

She returned his smile. It felt good to feel safe for a moment. But Zarek was hungry, and Ana could sense it. And at the reminder, her own empty stomach complained. Her clothes were nearly dry, and beneath the blanket, she pulled them on. Dane had found some rods and lines, and he sat at the back of the boat, watching a line trailing into the water.

"Do you like fishing?" he asked her.

"Yes." Ana sat beside him in the sunshine and threw another line into the lake. They'd been fishing for hours when Ana squeaked and reeled in her line. She pulled a struggling silver fish into the boat.

Dane laughed. "You're amazing," he exclaimed.

She smiled at his praise and held up the fish. "I don't like to clean them," she said. "It makes my hands smell like fish."

"Don't worry!" Dane assured her. "Zarek loves to cut fish."

"So does Dane," Zarek protested. But he didn't complain much. Taking the fish from her, he used his knife to cut long filets off the bones.

"There's no way to build a fire." Ana glanced around the little boat.

Dane did the same. "Not unless you want to burn a hole in the hull."

Ana's stomach growled. She watched as Zarek put a raw piece in his mouth and chewed. She'd never eaten fish without cooking it before. But she was hungry and followed his lead.

"Where are we going?" Ana asked when she woke up in the morning and peered over the side of the boat.

"There's a town called Bethor Crossing at the end of the lake," Dane said. "From there, the road leads north toward Sarine. We'll leave the boat outside town and not take it to the docks."

Her eyes widened. "You stole it?"

"Borrowed," Zarek corrected, with a grin. "Borrowed without permission. The man should thank us. If we hadn't thrown him in the lake, the Shekkar would have gotten him. We saved his life."

"Will he be able to find his boat?"

"I hope so."

"Will the Shekkar be waiting for us when we land?" Ana felt a twinge of worry.

"No," Dane told her. "It's a big lake. And now we have confirmed they won't go into the water. If we stay near lakes and streams at night, we will slow them down. Then we can try to get ahead of them during the daylight. I think we've lost them for the moment. But we'll move quickly when we get there, just in case."

Another night passed on the dark water, and it had been eight days since the demons attacked Bright Springs. Just before dawn, Dane landed the boat in a quiet place a little distance from the docks. The lights from the houses and shops were near and bright. They gathered their belongings and walked toward the town.

"We can buy supplies here and get something to eat, and then we'll be on our way," Dane said.

"Good idea," Zarek agreed.

Ana had never been so hungry. She stared greedily at the gardens behind the houses as they passed, her mouth watering at the sight of the vegetables. Some of the yards even had chickens. Images of the roast chicken Tari made back at the inn stuck in her mind as she walked.

The town of Bethor Crossing had grown up around the meeting of roads along the western border of Kethel. One road ran east, deeper into the kingdom of Kethel, and one west toward the land of Paraman. The northern road led to Sarine and Ara.

Despite the early hour, the streets were busy with people coming and going and merchants setting out their wares. Everyone seemed to be in a hurry. Horses, carts and wagons filled the roads. Many of the buildings were tall, rising two and three stories, and a maze of streets wound between them.

Ana looked around at everything with wide eyes. Bright Springs would fit into one tiny corner of this town. She stuck close to Dane and Zarek.

The three of them walked along the street to an inn with a sign advertising hot meals. They went inside and sat at a table.

A waitress came up to them. "What'll it be?"

"Breakfast," Zarek said.

"You have money?" she asked, eyeing their well-worn clothes.

"Of course we do," Zarek said, irritated. He dug coins out of his pocket and put them down on the table.

"All right, all right—" the waitress wiped her hands on her apron. "I didn't mean anything."

"It's fine," Zarek said.

"I'll just get you some breakfast." She hurried away, looking uncomfortable.

"Rude," Zarek complained. "Just because we look like homeless wanderers." He winked at Ana, and she returned his gaze uncertainly. "Maybe we are a little dirty, but she has no idea who we are!" He smiled and hushed his voice confidentially. "I'm pretty sure you're a princess, traveling in disguise."

Ana couldn't help but smile. She'd worked at the inn for years, and no one had ever mistaken her for a princess. "Then you could both be brave knights in shining armor."

Zarek made a face. "Do you have any idea how much that stuff weighs?"

Dane grinned. "We would be honored to be your knights, Princess."

The waitress returned with bowls of steaming porridge and cream, thick slices of bacon, and a fresh loaf of bread. It was all Ana could do not to moan with longing. As soon as the woman turned away, Ana stuck a hot, crispy piece of bacon into her mouth, entranced by the rich savory taste. They'd already come so far, and they'd been so cold and hungry.

"Your fish was great, but this is so good," Zarek said with his mouth full. Dane nodded and kept chewing. Ana smiled.

They ate everything so quickly that the waitress brought them each another bowl, and they finished those too. When they were finally done, they left the inn.

"We need to get moving," Dane said as they made their way through the busy streets. "There's a man with a farm just outside town. He'll sell me a couple of horses. It'll use the last of the coin I got from our outpost two months ago, but I should have enough. We're going home now. Buy supplies and meet me there."

Zarek nodded, and Dane disappeared into the crowd. Ana walked beside Zarek as they turned a few corners and entered a shop. The place appeared to have everything, with tall piles of goods stacked on shelves reaching to the ceiling and overflowing. They picked out dried meat, fruit, nuts and dry biscuits that would stay good forever. Zarek chose a warm cloak that would fit Ana. He paid the shopkeeper some coins and put everything into his pack, and they went back out into the street.

A few minutes of walking brought them to the crossroads in the center of town, one road leading off in each direction. Zarek took the road heading north. It was thronged with people. Ana followed him as he made a path through the crowd.

They came to the end of a large stone bridge spanning the wide river. People on foot made way as carts and wagons passed them. From the middle of the bridge, Ana looked upriver to the lake they had sailed across. When they reached the road on the far side, the crowds thinned a little. The buildings became farther apart until finally there weren't any more.

Outside of town lay an encampment made up of neat rows of tents. Some of them displayed a gray-and-white flag. Men were coming and going between them, dressed in gray uniforms. "They serve the king of Kethel, gathering here to protect the bridge from the Arans," Zarek said. He and Ana continued past the camp.

Three of the gray-uniformed men stood on the road, hands on their sword hilts, blocking their path. One of them was a huge man. The others flanked him. These men looked like they didn't want to let them pass. What did they want? Zarek didn't alter his pace or turn aside. When they didn't move, he stopped, facing them, Ana at his side. Her middle tightened in fear as Zarek faced the three soldiers. His stance remained casual, his expression relaxed. "Good morning, gentlemen." He didn't look afraid at all.

"Good morning," the big one said, grinning. That smile made Ana feel smaller.

"You're doing a fine job protecting the border," Zarek said.

"War is brewing," the man said, no longer smiling. "Ara's army is growing. We need more men to protect our border."

"Well, I wish you the best with your search," Zarek replied. "If I see anyone who'd like to join you, I'll send them this way. There's nothing else I can do for you now."

"Is that so?" The big man looked Zarek up and down.

"My errand is urgent," Zarek said. "I cannot delay."

"Urgent, is it?" They snickered and spread out to block the road. "What's so urgent?" the big man asked. "You'd like soldiering, boy. Plenty of food, and the wages are fair. Come on—join us."

"Your offer is kind, but I have other business." Zarek met the man's eyes steadily and squared his shoulders.

"You're pretty cocky for a farm boy. Come with us."

"Get out of my way," Zarek ordered.

All three of them laughed. Ana's chest constricted. They were in trouble. Zarek took the pack from his back and handed it to Ana, giving her a quick, confident nod, as if he wanted to assure her that everything was going to be fine.

He turned back to face the three men. "I said, get out of my way."

The leader was still smiling. Deliberately, he drew his sword, pointing it at Zarek's chest. "With an attitude like that, you could be a captain someday. Come with us, boy. We'll make a soldier out of you."

"I'm already a soldier." Zarek darted to one side, away from the sword, and expertly kicked the man's knee. He toppled with a yell.

What happened next was so fast Ana's eyes could barely follow. The other two men tried to grab Zarek, but he moved much too quickly. By the time Ana had taken a breath, they both lay on the ground.

The leader got back to his feet. With an enraged roar, he charged with his fists flailing. Zarek sidestepped his attack and drove his fist into the man's side as he passed. A few more blows sent him back to the ground with his friends.

Zarek turned back to Ana, who stared at him in shock. He took the pack, slung it over his shoulder, and offered her his hand. "Come on." They hurried away.

A little farther along the road, they saw Dane coming back to meet them, mounted on a sturdy black horse and leading a brown one. He held his arm out to Ana. "Come on, Princess. You can ride with me for a while." He pulled her up behind him. "What took you so long?" he asked Zarek.

"After we crossed the bridge, we stopped to chat with the soldiers." Zarek swung into the saddle.

"The man I bought the horses from said they're signing on any man between fifteen and sixty. They're getting worried about Ara."

Dane glanced back at the army camp, and they rode quickly away.

"Did they try to stop Zarek?" Dane asked Ana over his shoulder.

"There were three of them with swords! I was so scared. But he beat all of them. How can he fight so well?"

"I told you he was the best soldier in Sarine. He's had years of training and practice."

"Has he been doing this since he was a little boy?"

Dane sighed. "Yes. He's my friend, and I wish he could have been a child a little longer. His father was Talon, a captain of the Emperor's Guard and the emperor's most trusted friend. When Zarek got the news that Talon wasn't coming back, he started training. I've never seen anyone work so hard."

For a few days, they continued to see gray-uniformed soldiers. Dane shook his head. "If Kethel has its army out here, the Arans do too. We need to be careful." They stayed under the cover of woods as often as possible and took turns keeping watch as they rested.

On horseback, they made good time for several days and nights of travel. It had been two weeks since they left Bethor Crossing. They still followed the road toward Sarine, even though they didn't ride on the road itself. Instead, they rode through woods and fields, which made their progress slower, but Dane thought it was better to stay out of sight.

One afternoon, they halted in a small group of trees for a meal and to rest the horses. They could hear the sounds of running water nearby. After they ate, Zarek said, "I'm going to wash and get some water. I'll be back in a moment."

Dane nodded, leaning back against a tree trunk while Ana curled up to rest.

CHAPTER FOUR

YEAR OF WARDING 38, KETHEL'S COUNTRYSIDE

ZAREK

WHEN ZAREK STARTED BACK toward the others, he froze halfway up the riverbank. Movement caught his eye, and his stomach dropped. It wasn't Ana and Dane.

He saw several armed men in the dark-blue tunics and black armor of Ara's army. A few of them had already taken Dane's horses and were far down the hill.

How had he not seen the men sooner? Zarek sprinted toward them. The sun flashed off the polished metal of weapons, and he heard the ringing as blades met.

In the middle, Dane fought for his life. Zarek pushed himself to run faster.

Dane fell to the ground as the soldiers disappeared into the trees.

Seconds later, Zarek dropped to the ground beside his friend. "Dane!" He pressed his hands to the worst of the wounds, trying to slow the bleeding.

Dane's eyes were wide in shock. "They found the ring. They took Ana!"

"Just hold on! She can use the ring on you!" Zarek placed Dane's hand over the wound. "Keep your hand here. I'll get her back!"

Dane nodded without speaking, his face pale.

Zarek wiped his bloody hands on his pants, picked up Dane's sword, and ran after the soldiers. They were keeping out of sight under the cover of the little groups of trees. That was good. If they'd been out in the open, they would have seen him coming.

He couldn't let them take Ana.

The two men who made up their rearguard barely had time to reach for their weapons as Zarek struck them down. When he crashed into the larger group of them, they all stopped and turned on him. Zarek moved faster than anyone else. That's what Dane always said. Zarek needed it now.

Three of the Arans fell to the ground quickly, and the other four whirled around to face him. One of them seized Ana and began dragging her away, kicking and fighting, while the other three advanced on him, their swords ready.

They came at him from both sides. As he blocked a thrust coming from the left, one of the others snagged Zarek's side with the point of his blade. He gritted his teeth against the pain, but he would not give up so easily. They slashed through his guard twice more. But the wounds weren't deep, and he kept fighting.

From the corner of his eye, he saw the man who had Ana strike her, then throw her over his shoulder and run. Zarek defeated the last of the three men and bolted after Ana's captor.

He had to stop the man before he escaped with her. Everything depended on the ring. Zarek ran, his feet pounding against the ground as he gained on the man.

Despite his burden, the Aran moved as fast as he could. Ana struggled and her body partially blocked his view, so he didn't see Zarek coming until he tackled the man from the side. They tumbled to the ground in a tangle of arms and legs. The Aran had lost his grip on Ana, and she scrambled away from him.

Rolling to his feet, the soldier drew his sword. He aimed a blow at the girl, and Zarek leapt forward to deflect the blade. When he wasn't quite fast enough, the Aran's blade sliced across Ana's back and she cried out in pain. Zarek pushed the weapon away from her, placing himself between them. He traded blows with the Aran, as he saw Ana circle around to get behind the man.

She hit the soldier with a sturdy tree branch, and he lurched forward, completely off balance.

Taking advantage of the distraction, Zarek landed a slash to the man's side. It wasn't deep enough to stop him, but the man jumped back away from them both. He stared at Zarek for a moment and then turned and fled down the hill toward the rest of the Aran troops.

Zarek ran after him, but he stopped after only a few strides. He couldn't leave Ana here alone, and they had to help Dane.

When he turned back to her, Ana stared at Zarek, frozen in shock. "Dane!" she gasped. "They hurt Dane. He tried to keep them from taking me, and I saw them strike him. You said the ring could heal him!"

Ana and Zarek ran back the way they had come.

Dane lay where Zarek had left him. His hand no longer covered the wound. It had fallen to one side. A small trail of blood ran from his mouth.

Ana knelt beside him and put her hand on his forehead. "Heal him!" she cried. "I don't know how to make it work. How do I make it work?"

Dane's eyes stared at nothing. He lay utterly still. Zarek looked at the wound. Dane's heart no longer pumped blood from the gash. "You said I could heal him!" Ana yelled. "Why isn't it working? Why?"

"It's not working because he's dead. It's too late. Too late..." Zarek dropped to the ground, letting the sword fall from his hand, holding onto his friend.

"He can't be dead. You said the ring could heal any injury! We have to help him!" She shook Zarek's arm.

He threw off her hands. "I've seen the ring heal before, but there's nothing I know of that can bring back the dead."

Zarek touched his friend's face and closed his empty eyes. The weight of it settled on him. Dane was dead. Zarek was the last one left to complete their quest. The fate of his nation rested on him now. All those people. His chest constricted, and he couldn't breathe. What was he going to do?

Ana bent over Dane, sobbing. "He tried to save me. It's my fault!" Dane had been Zarek's friend for many years, and his only companion since they left Sarine nearly a year ago. He was the one who had guided and led them. How could Zarek do this alone?

The grief stabbed at him as painfully as the sword blades had. How could he go on without Dane?

The soldiers who had attacked them weren't alone. Dane had hoped to continue as they had been going, crossing the river at Iron Bridge and following the road into Sarine. If Aran troops were between them and the bridge, they didn't have a chance that way. "What do I do, Dane?" He realized he'd asked the question out loud. Dane couldn't answer him. And Zarek couldn't talk like that in front of Ana. She relied on him to protect her.

He had to keep going.

As if waking up, he glanced around and saw the sun lowering into the west. They needed to move. More soldiers could arrive anytime. He took a deep breath and wiped his hand across his eyes.

He picked up Dane's pack. There was something about looking through Dane's meager belongings that he'd carried so far. Zarek felt tears on his face as he transferred the food into his own pack, as well as Dane's cloak and blanket.

Casting aside the now-empty pack, Zarek took his friend's sword belt and put it on. He picked up the weapon from the ground. "I'll keep your sword." Zarek looked down at his friend. "I'll try to carry it as well as you did."

Shouldering his pack, Zarek glanced around in the gathering darkness. The horses were gone, and the Aran army blocked the way north. He couldn't go east toward Ara, and he couldn't go back. To the west rose the mountains, the lofty peaks already capped with snow. Sarine and the safety of the Warding lay on the other side, if only they could reach them. They had to go through the mountains. And if Zarek chose the wrong path, they would die.

Zarek looked down toward the road. As the evening darkened, he saw watch fires that could only belong to the Aran army. Some of the small points of light were moving. Torches.

They were advancing this way. It made sense they would come looking for their companions. Zarek gripped the fallen man's shoulder. "You were the best friend I ever had. Goodbye, Dane."

"We have to go, Ana," he said. "They're coming."

She clung to Dane's hand. "We can't just leave him!"

"We have to." He pulled her away.

She struggled against his hold at first, but she knew they had no other choice.

CHAPTER FIVE

YEAR OF WARDING 38, MOUNTAINS OF SARINE

ANA

EVERY TIME ANA CLOSED her eyes, she thought of Dane. If not for her, he'd still be alive. The guilt sat like acid in her belly. She and Zarek walked in silence for days and nights, not knowing what to say. He felt it too. They halted at dawn and rested against a ridge of rocks. Zarek sat beside her, silent, staring at the ground.

Tentatively, she reached out and touched his arm. "I tried to fight them," she said. "But I don't know how."

"I do," Zarek said bitterly. "That's all I've done my whole life, learn to fight. Dane was my best friend. If I hadn't left, we could have held them back together..."

"It wasn't your fault," Ana protested. "They were looking for me. If not for me, they wouldn't have killed him."

"You can't blame this on yourself!"

"I miss him," Ana said. "There aren't very many people in the world who care about me."

"Dane wasn't the only one. I care about you too. You can't think this was your fault. You didn't cause any of it."

She looked up into his gray eyes. "Neither did you."

By sunset, they were walking uphill again. Ana longed for a soft, warm bed with a feather pillow and thick blankets. She remembered her little room at the back of the inn. It seemed a distant memory of comfort now that they spent the dark hours of every night stumbling through ravines and hillsides choked with brush. It continued to get colder and sometimes rained, but they wrapped their cloaks around themselves and kept walking. The valley looked far below them now.

Ana grew too tired to think or wonder much about anything. She had to keep going. Keep climbing. Follow Zarek. He was tireless, his long legs always ready to walk or run.

Dane should have been there beside them. Ana shut her eyes tightly against the image of him lying unmoving on the ground.

It had been a week since they left the lowlands. They climbed steadily up the slopes of a mountain, following the course of the river. Sometimes they passed through thick forest. At this higher altitude, the leaves were already golden against the dark green of the pines.

Often, they had to force their way through the underbrush. Ana had long scratches on her legs from finding thorn bushes in the dark.

But the Shekkar hadn't found them yet, and they hadn't seen any more Aran soldiers.

As Ana and Zarek climbed higher, the air grew thinner and colder, and the forest shrank to short scrubby trees, sculpted by the wind. Ana looked back and saw the land spread out below them in a patch-work of farmlands. She could see the river and the distant lake. Beyond them were the hills where the town of Bright Springs lay. It had been her home for as long as she could remember.

How quickly her life had changed. Ana had left behind everything she'd ever known, except her secrets.

That night, heavy clouds moved in and rain fell intermittently. Ana shivered from the chill and stumbled in exhaustion. A patch of clear sky passed them, and in the faint moonlight, they crossed a sharp stony ridge. Ana could see in all directions from the top. The white glow touched the peaks and forest, and the jagged mountains spread all around them. The lowlands were dark except for a few distant points of light.

Zarek pointed northwest toward a glimmer, barely visible in the distance. "I think that's the city." Ana squinted, but it appeared to be a long way away.

They began their descent cautiously. She looked down into a deep valley in front of them, and on the far side of it, another steep ridge, even higher than the one they were on. How were they going to get up that?

An icy wind blew in their faces, carrying the first few drops of rain with it. Ana followed Zarek down through the rocks. The storm came in with a flash of lightning and thunder rolled between the peaks. A thick curtain of rain reached them, soaking them in moments. Ana's foot slipped on a stone, slick with rain, throwing her off balance. She toppled, clawing at the rocks on the edge of a precipice, trying to regain her grip, but she couldn't find anything solid to hold on to. She fell.

In the moment of impact, she knew she was hurt, and she wondered if she was dead. A blinding pain came from her head and one arm. The world spun around her, and she couldn't see properly. She stayed still, gasping and trying to breathe, trying to push the pain back enough to have room in her mind for thought.

Slowly, the world righted itself. In the flashes of lightning, she could see a little. After pushing herself up with her good arm, she held the injured one against her chest and used her good hand to shield her eyes from the rain. Ana had landed on a narrow ledge, with sheer rocks above and a black abyss below. She bit back a startled cry when she saw how close to the edge she had come, and she realized she couldn't see the bottom in the dark. If she'd fallen off that...

"Zarek!" Ana yelled. The wind carried the sound of her voice away. There was no response. She looked back up at the way she had fallen. Could she climb up? There were handholds and footholds.

It would be just like the oak tree back home.

She got to her feet. Everything spun around her again, and she nearly threw up. She leaned against the rock wall, breathing slowly and steadily, waiting for the dizziness to pass. Her wrist throbbed unmercifully, and she couldn't make her hand work.

Whatever she did, she would have to do it with one hand. Stepping to the first foothold, she gripped a handhold. She brought her other foot up. That was it. Her injured arm refused to work.

She moved to the next foothold she could reach and tried to stand quickly and grab a higher handhold with her good hand. When her fingers couldn't latch on in time, she fell back. Defeated, she sat down on the ledge and huddled against the rocks, her injured arm cradled close to her body.

CHAPTER SIX

YEAR OF WARDING 38, MOUNTAINS OF SARINE

ANA

ANA DID NOT KNOW how long she sat there shivering. It felt like years. What would happen if Zarek didn't find her? If she waited here, either she would freeze to death or the Shekkar would find her. Or she could try to climb, but she'd most likely fall.

Which one would be better?

The ends of a rope appeared over the edge of the cliff. A few moments later, boots and then the rest of Zarek came into view as he lowered himself onto the ledge. She felt tears of relief running from her eyes.

"Ana!" He knelt beside her and dropped his pack. He took out a piece of cloth and held it against her head.

Zarek was here. He had come to help her. She reached out with her good arm and clung to him. "You found me!"

"I will always come to find you," he promised. She felt his words in her heart. For such a long time, she had been alone, but she believed Zarek when he said he would always be there.

"Are you hurt anywhere else?"

"My arm," she said through gritted teeth.

He drew back to look. "Can I see it?"

She held the injured limb tight against her chest. "No, don't touch it! Can't the ring heal it?"

"I'm afraid it doesn't work that way. I won't touch your arm for now," he said. "We need to get off this cliff and find shelter."

That sounded wonderful. But how? Zarek looked off the edge. The rain continued, but the sky had brightened slightly. Somewhere beyond the storm, dawn had come.

Zarek pointed down through the dark rocks and trees. "I see a way. Can you hold on to my back?"

She obeyed awkwardly, with only one arm. Ana wrapped her good arm over his shoulder and around his chest, and her legs around his waist. She closed her eyes tightly as he swung out onto the rope. But after a moment, she peeked again. They hadn't fallen. They hung from the rope, and he lowered them both slowly, his feet against the cliff face.

In a few moments, they had reached a wider ledge with a few trees. She let out a breath in relief. Zarek had been right. He could get them down safely.

Ana sat against the rocks while Zarek retrieved the rope. He looked down again, planning their next step. This time, he used one of the sturdy, stunted trees on the ledge to anchor the rope.

"Ready?" he asked.

Ana clung to him as they climbed down another cliff. They made it down a few more sections until they could put the rope away and scramble down between the rocks. By then, it had grown lighter. Eventually, they reached the valley floor and started along it.

Zarek found a sheltered spot under some boulders at the bottom of the cliff face. It was dry in there, and Ana sat down gratefully. It felt wonderful to be off the cliff, and day had come, bringing temporary safety from the demons. The rain couldn't reach her beneath the rocks. She wrapped herself into a ball, still shivering. A sharp pain radiated from her arm, but at least she didn't have to decide which way to die.

Rubbing his chilled hands together, Zarek started gathering sticks and soon had a fire going. Ana huddled close to the warmth.

He took blankets from the pack and wrapped her in them. When she touched her head with her good hand, she felt a large, swollen lump on one side. It still bled a little. Zarek gave her a piece of cloth, and she held it gingerly against the place.

"Now, let me see your arm," he said firmly.

"No—it hurts. Don't touch it."

"Please, Ana. I just want to look at it."

The light had brightened enough now that they could both see that her forearm had swollen badly and turned purple.

"Oh, no," Zarek said. "I'm sure it's broken." Running a hand through his wavy hair, he took a few deep breaths and stood up to pace back and forth, muttering.

"If we could find a village, they might have a healer. But there's no one, not till we get to the edge of Sarine, and we still have a long way to go. We need to do something now." He stopped pacing and turned to Ana. "If we stop or turn back, we won't make it. They will catch us. We have to go on. And that means we have to do what we can for that arm, now."

She looked up at him. "What do you think we should do?" Zarek took a deep breath. "We have to get the bone back in place. Then we can make a splint to hold it still. We don't really have any other choice."

With his knife, he shaped some pieces of wood to fit her arm. Then he laid out more cloth to use for bandages, cutting them into strips and setting them on a rock. "Come sit here." Zarek pointed to another rock near the one where he had set his supplies.

She obeyed him. "What are you going to do?"

He bent to one knee and met her gaze. His gray eyes looked very serious. "We have to fix this so we can go on," he said. "I wish you could just use the ring to heal yourself. If I had any other way to help, any other choice, I would use it—but there isn't. We have to go on. Do you understand what I'm telling you?"

She understood. They would die if they stopped. She knew it and nodded.

"I have to move the bone back into place," he said. "It's going to hurt. A lot."

Tears welled in her eyes and ran down her cheeks. The pain was already severe. "Please don't make it hurt more," she pleaded. "It already hurts."

"I know," he said. "But we have to do it so it can heal."

"What if it doesn't heal?"

"I promise it will in time. But we have to get the bone in place first. Ready?" he asked. There were beads of sweat on his forehead.

"No," she protested.

He took a firm grip on her arm and pulled hard to force the bone back into place. She screamed. It hurt worse than anything she'd ever felt before. She would have jerked her arm away from him, but he held it securely. For a few moments, she saw nothing but light. As her vision returned, she saw Zarek wrapping her forearm against the splints. He wound the strips of cloth around the splints, cinching them firmly in place. When he finished, he helped her lie down by the fire and covered her in all the blankets.

"I'm sorry," he said, his expression miserable. She couldn't seem to answer.

Ana woke from a fitful sleep made up of a mixture of utter exhaustion and the sharp ache of her forearm. She felt dizzy and nauseated. When Zarek saw her awake, he bent over her. "How are you feeling?" he asked. His brows drew together in worry.

With her good arm, she pushed herself into a sitting position. She still felt dizzy, but after a few moments, the world stopped spinning and settled into its normal place. Her mouth felt dry, and she gratefully accepted the water Zarek held out to her.

When she'd finished drinking, he offered her berries and fish. "I'm not hungry," she said.

"Please, eat." He put a comforting hand on her shoulder. "You have to keep your strength up. We can't stay here."

She looked up at the sky. The sun nearly touched the horizon. It would be dark soon, and they needed to move. So she ate the fish and berries, and they went on.

It didn't take long to cross the narrow valley floor. They passed fields of shale and boulders and thickets of small, dense trees. They stepped on rocks to cross a shallow stream. Soon, they climbed again. Upward, always upward.

For the first few nights after Ana's fall, her arm ached constantly as they walked, and her head throbbed. Some of the way Zarek carried her, and she was far too tired and sore to be embarrassed about it. They had to keep moving. If they stopped, they would die. There was no debate, and it wouldn't do any good to complain. They kept going. The temperature dropped, and though the weather had been dry since the night of her fall, they suffered from the chill. When they stopped to rest, Ana lay huddled into a ball on the cold stone, too weary to go on any more. Her teeth chattered and shivers racked her body. "C-Can we build a f-fire? P-Please?"

"There's not enough wood," Zarek said, sitting down beside her. "I'm sorry."

Her fingers and toes felt numb, and she thought she would never be warm again. If she fell asleep against this icy stone, maybe she wouldn't wake up again. "A-Are we g-going to d-die?"

Zarek looked down at her sternly. "We will not die. I promise."

"But it's so c-cold."

"Do you want to sit by me? It'll be warmer," he offered.

Ana moved closer and huddled against him. He put his arm around her and wrapped his cloak around them both. It felt good. He was so warm, and she felt safe beside him.

"In a few more days, we'll be out of the mountains," Zarek said. "By then, we'll be almost to the Warding. Your arm is healing. Soon, you won't even notice it anymore. And when we get back to the city, you can have anything you want."

"A-Anything?"

"Yes."

"D-Do you think they would give me a blanket and a pillow?"

He laughed. "I'm sure they will, and a feather bed to go with them. Try to rest. Things will be better soon."

"Then you don't think we're going to die?"

"No," he said. "I'm sorry I let you fall, and I promise I will do everything I can to keep you safe."

He really meant it. She could feel it. It was more than just the sound of his voice. She could sense that he truly believed they would make it.

"Why would you do so much for me?" she asked.

His arm tightened around her. "You're a good person. And you don't deserve to die just because of the ring. You're brave and kind, and you deserve to live and be happy. Now get some rest."

He sang a song to her, and as she listened to his voice, her fears faded. His song was about a blacksmith. "Fire and water... hammer and tongs..."

He pulled out the charm he wore around his neck. "My grandfather was a blacksmith, and he taught my father to work with a hammer. Later, my father trained as a soldier and learned to use a sword. This charm tells the story of my family."

She drifted off, comforted by his voice.

❧

When Ana woke again, she was still huddled close against Zarek. The light of day faded fast as they got up and gathered their things. He offered his hand to pull her back to her feet. Stiff and exhausted, she accepted the help. Night surrounded them and they went on, still climbing. Ana decided she would give anything just to walk downhill for a while.

Tall, forbidding peaks loomed ahead of them in the starlight. The sky seemed very near, and Ana thought she could reach out and touch the clouds as they passed. The more she walked, the more her arm throbbed.

Zarek led them up a steep slope through the rocks. It was hard to keep up with him, and he seemed to be in a hurry.

The night grew colder as they climbed, sapping energy and will. It felt like they would be scrambling between the stones forever. It would have been much easier if Ana had both hands to help her balance. Still, she kept going as long as she could, until the end of her strength. She sank down onto a rock.

"Come on," Zarek said, putting his pack on her. "I'll carry you for a while."

"Thank you."

He bent to one knee so Ana could climb onto his back. A bitter wind blew down from the mountaintops, and she shivered and huddled as close to Zarek as she could. His back felt warm against her, but soon the cold crept in from all sides.

On they went, until they left the last few stunted trees behind them, and nothing remained but bare rock and snow. He was strong, able to keep going, even carrying her. The wind picked up, carrying snowflakes with it.

Ana couldn't remember anything but the cold and the snow.

Heavy sleepiness came over her, and she closed her eyes.

She woke with a jolt when Zarek set her down. The wind still howled, and the snow still fell. They huddled against the downwind side of a boulder.

Sleepiness came over her again, and the cold retreated. The snow covered her like a blanket that no longer felt icy and wet. She drifted off.

"Ana!"

Someone shouted her name. But the sleepiness remained too heavy to shake off.

"Ana!"

Now something shook her, roughly. Why couldn't they just leave her alone?

"Stop," she protested. "Sleeping..."

But the shaking grew more insistent, and the voice kept calling her. "Wake up!" it demanded.

She didn't want to wake up. The voice. She knew that voice. It was Zarek, and he sounded angry. Why was he angry? Why couldn't he, just this once, let her rest? "I can't wake up," she said. "Please, please let me sleep."

"Wake up," he repeated.

"No."

"Ana, please!" His voice sounded pleading now.

"I'm getting warm. Please let me sleep."

"You have to get up and walk," he shouted above the wind. His voice sounded far away.

"I can't walk," she groaned.

"Get up and walk or you'll die."

"I don't care." She meant it, too. At that moment, she really didn't care. She had gone on as long as she could.

"You do care," he protested. "Please, Ana. Please."

He pulled at her now, dragging her to her feet. Her limbs felt like lead, and her knees collapsed under her.

"Please don't make me walk anymore," she begged, sinking back to the ground. "I can't do it."

"You have to," he insisted, pulling her once more to her feet.

Ana opened her eyes and saw rocks and snow, and Zarek's face tight with fear. Why was he so worried? She took a step. His arm supported and guided her. Another step. With his help, she found the strength to keep moving.

CHAPTER SEVEN

YEAR OF WARDING 38, MOUNTAINS OF SARINE

ANA

THE PATH STILL ROSE steeply ahead of Zarek and Ana, and after struggling to get up the hill, she realized she had grown a little warmer. The sleepiness retreated, and she felt more alert. But they didn't stop. The rest of the night stretched into an eternity of climbing through the driving snow. The gray light of dawn came slowly. With the new day, the wind died down, but the snow still fell. Zarek led them to a cleft in the rocks. He found a small space inside where no snow had fallen, and they were out of the wind. He helped her inside, and she collapsed on the rock floor. Her injured arm ached dreadfully. Through the pain, cold and weariness, she realized Zarek was rubbing her arms and legs. He stopped after a while and held her close, wrapping them both in his cloak.

Ana felt weak, and her stomach pinched. They'd already eaten everything they had with them. Zarek was hungry too.

"We'll cross the ridge tonight," he promised. "We're almost there."

ZAREK

When Ana and Zarek woke in the afternoon, they left their shelter and started walking again. They climbed until the night grew old.

Finally, Zarek saw the top. It was a sharp wall of rocks with a narrow fissure between them. The passage barely allowed room for a person to slip through.

Zarek heard a sound in the stillness. Shekkar.

No. Not now.

They needed to get through the passage. Zarek looked down the hill. He saw black shapes against the patches of snow. He had hoped the cold would hide their scent more. The demons appeared to avoid the snow, and maybe it slowed them down, but now they were coming fast.

Zarek reached the edge of the fissure and gripped Ana's shoulder. He pointed through the crack. "Go through. Find somewhere to hide on the other side."

"No!" she protested, planting her feet stubbornly. "We're both going through."

He shook his head. "If we do, the demons will catch us. I can hold them back here. Go now. Run!"

He could tell she wanted to argue, but she obeyed, running through the narrow pass and disappearing. He'd done everything he could for Ana.

Run. Hide. Don't let them catch you.

Zarek took a deep breath, wiped his sweaty palms on his pants, and drew his weapons. His dagger cast a faint green glow as he stood in the cleft between the rocks, watching the Shekkar run up the slope. At least they wouldn't be able to surround him, and he could hold them off for a while. How many were there? A dozen?

Shrieking in triumph as they spotted him, the demons rushed forward. When the first one reached Zarek, it struck at him with its claws. His sword blocked the blow, and the demon screamed when his knife bit. He drove the blade in a second time, and the creature toppled over. Heedless of their fallen comrade, the others leapt across the crumpled form to attack. Zarek held them back with his sword as they snarled and snapped at him and tried to reach him in the narrow space.

Their attack forced him deeper into the passageway. Black claws slashed at him, and he blocked them with the sword, only to feel burning pain as a second blow ripped into the flesh of his arm and shoulder. He drove his dagger into the nearest demon, and it collapsed with a final snarl.

Shekkar claws raked across his face. His head burned like fire, and he could no longer see properly. Searing pain took over as poisonous claws tore into his chest, and he heard himself scream. It sounded like it came from a great distance.

Dimly, he heard a demon shriek as if it had discovered something. Ana's trail?

Zarek lay on the ground. Quiet surrounded him, and he was alone. He closed his hand, futilely searching for his weapons. He had to get up, to go after them. They were hunting Ana, and she had no one to help her.

Get up.

But it was too late. His limbs twitched when he tried to move, but that was all. His body throbbed with scorching pain, except where it touched the chilling stone and snow. He felt his warm blood escaping from many wounds. It wouldn't be long now. Was this how Dane had felt? Lying alone and hurt, feeling the life draining out of him, waiting for help that didn't come in time? With one eye, Zarek saw the white stars in the black sky above him. He would have screamed from the pain, but he didn't have the breath or energy. He passed in and out of consciousness.

The periods of oblivion granted a blessed relief from the agony. How many times would he wake back up? The stars faded.

When he woke again, he saw morning sunlight, and the thin clear sky of the mountains. The only sound came from the wind whistling in the passage between the rocks.

ANA

At dawn, Ana left the tree where she had hidden until the demons disappeared with the first light. Then she stumbled back up the hill as fast as her tired legs would go. Reaching the passage, she started through it. Just beyond the opening, she saw Zarek, and her stomach twisted into a knot. She couldn't breathe, feeling the desperate need to help him and hoping she hadn't arrived too late.

"Zarek!" She ran and knelt beside him. When she saw what they had done, her empty belly heaved. Blood covered him. Claws had slashed his face, raking across his forehead and destroying one eye, but she couldn't look away from the long gaping wound in his chest. She sensed the agony of his broken body.

No. That was impossible. He could not still be alive. But he had to be. She sensed his pain. Ana touched his forehead.

A flash of green light came from the ring, and for a moment, she became Zarek. Her flesh and skin shredded, her ribs ripped out of place. She felt searing pain from the wounds. There was no hope of surviving. No hope of recovering. The damage was too severe.

It could not be. The part of them that was Ana bent all her will on taking the pain away. Zarek must live. Zarek must be whole and happy. He must smile and be full of energy and ready to do anything.

He must live.

The pain overwhelmed her, and she screamed until oblivion claimed her.

ZAREK

Zarek heard Ana scream and sat up to find her crumpled beside him. "Ana!" he rolled her onto her back, checking her breathing, looking for any sign of injury.

Her breath was steady, her heart beat regularly. She was alive. The pain must have passed, leaving her face peaceful. She'd done it. She'd healed him. But who would ask someone else to experience that kind of pain? Zarek knew exactly what it had felt like, and he would never have given the agony to someone he cared for. Zarek took a deep breath. When he touched his face, he found it whole and uninjured. His eye? He could see normally with it. Gazing down at himself, he saw his clothes slashed and covered in blood. Through the gaping rent in his shirt, he saw a long scar across his chest.

Suddenly, he couldn't breathe. His mind flashed back to the hours he lay alone. The burning pain had consumed him. He'd been dying, his body destroyed beyond recovery. His life had been over.

Zarek sank to the ground and cried.

Ana had taken his pain on herself, and she had healed him.

The sun was high in the sky. As soon as night fell, the deadly pursuit would resume. Zarek wiped his face with his hands and took a deep breath.

They had to get out of here. He searched the ground for his dagger. The enchanted weapon had destroyed two of the Shekkar before they'd taken him down. His efforts produced the hilt, but the blade had broken. He threw the pieces into his pack, buckled his sword to it, and slung it onto his back. Kneeling, Zarek picked Ana up in his arms and headed down the mountain.

ANA

Ana did not know how long the nothingness lasted. She didn't know if she was alive or dead, and she didn't really care. Either way, the pain had passed, and she was content.

Gradually, sounds and sensations invaded the silence. Once she thought she heard someone calling her name. She felt motion from time to time. Above all else, she felt the cold.

When Ana finally woke, she found herself resting uncomfortably across something hard. The last thing she remembered clearly was Zarek lying on the ground. She had to help him. Opening her eyes, she saw snow, rocks and mountain. They were moving. Someone carried her over his shoulder. Where was Zarek? She couldn't leave him injured. He needed help. "Please, we have to help Zarek," she cried. But she faded out again.

⌒

When Ana woke, the light looked different, and she lay on the ground. Someone sat nearby. "Where's Zarek?" she gasped.

He turned, allowing her to see his face. Zarek. His clothes were torn and stained with blood, his hair matted with it. But he was alive.

A wave of relief washed over her.

He came near and bent over her. "Are you all right, Ana?"

When he leaned close, she saw his face didn't look exactly as it had. Now he had two thin white scars that ran from his forehead, over his eyebrow, and down across his cheekbone to his jaw.

It had all been real. It hadn't been a nightmare. But he was all right now. Somehow, Zarek was all right.

He helped her drink some water, and then her eyes closed again. She drifted in and out of consciousness, only occasionally aware of her surroundings. She felt something warm against her lips. When she smelled meat, she opened her mouth to accept a bite and savored the most wonderful thing she'd ever eaten. She didn't even know how long it had been since her last meal.

"What is it?" she murmured.

"Grouse," Zarek said, offering her another bite.

She opened her eyes and saw him against a background of green forest. He looked well and whole. "When I saw what the demons had done, I thought you were dead," she confessed. "You sent me away, and you knew they would kill you..." Tears welled in her eyes, and she closed them as if that would shut out the picture of his slashed and bleeding body. "How can you be all right?"

"Because of the ring." His gray eyes met hers. "You healed me."

Now she remembered a flash of green light and pain so severe she'd been sure she wouldn't survive it. She'd thought they would both be dead. "It hurt," she admitted.

He nodded slowly. "I know it hurt you. Thank you for doing that for me."

"I couldn't let you die."

"Thanks," he smiled. "Now we have to take care of you. Can I see your arm?"

She intended to hold it out to him, but nothing happened when she tried. "I can't move," she realized, fear twisting through her. "What's wrong with me?"

"I've seen this before, years ago, when Allia used the ring. It's because you used its power," he said. "You'll feel better in a few days." He checked the splint on her arm and prepared to go on.

Zarek carried her, and she slept much of the time. She wasn't sure how long it had been. Gradually, she managed to stay awake longer. She could move her hands and feet and finally walk again.

They had come down a long way from the peaks. It grew warmer, and Zarek found food in the forest. Never as much as they wanted. But enough to keep them going.

࿐

One night, as they descended the slopes, they heard the Shekkar behind them in the trees. Ana's stomach clenched.

No. This couldn't happen again. They had to get away.

Zarek threw Ana over his shoulder and ran. Branches slapped at them and brush snagged them, but he kept going. Ana could hear the demons, but she couldn't see anything from that position. She heard Zarek splash into water, and she saw a dark river. His steps lurched up the far bank, and they ran again.

The night lasted forever, and Ana wasn't even conscious for all of it. She knew Zarek still ran, still carried her. She could hear the demons, sometimes faintly, sometimes near. They couldn't seem to lose them. It remained the same for all the dark hours of the night. She grew ever more uncomfortable, but Zarek was doing all he could, and she had no way to help him.

❧

Ana woke up to the impact of them hitting the ground. Forest surrounded them, and the layers of pine needles absorbed some of the shock. The light of dawn shone down through the trees. Zarek lay on his face.

"Zarek!" She shook him. He didn't respond. "Please wake up. Are you hurt?"

He answered with a muffled groan. She pushed hard and rolled him onto his side. "I'm all right," he mumbled without opening his eyes.

"What's wrong?"

"Can't run anymore..."

He'd been running all night, carrying her.

She brought him water and wiped the sweat from his face with a cloth. "Rest," she said, wrapping a blanket around him. His skin was pale.

Zarek needed rest and food. Ana had to move slowly, but she could walk. She searched the area for something to eat. She picked berries and dug up some edible roots, quickly rinsing them in the river. It wasn't much of a meal.

When she got back to him, he still hadn't moved. She wiped his face with the cloth again and gave him more water. He drank and turned to look up at her. "Ana? What happened? What time is it?"

"Almost midday," she said.

"Midday—" He shook his head and dragged himself into a sitting position. His color was better, but he still appeared exhausted.

"I brought you some berries." She held them out to him.

"Thank you," he said, eating one from her hand.

"Eat them all," she ordered.

He obeyed. Then she gave him the roots, and he ate those too. "Feel better?" she asked.

He smiled slightly. "Yes." He drank more water, then stiffly got to his feet.

"What are we going to do tonight?" she asked. He still seemed too tired to run.

"Let's see if we can lose them before then," he said.

She gathered their things and put them in the pack, the sword still buckled to it. She shouldered them both, and they went on.

Zarek moved slower than usual. But they kept moving, and at least they were going downhill. They followed the river as it cascaded down the mountainside.

Below them, spreading across the hills, ran a heavy dark line of forest. "What is that?" she asked Zarek.

"The Forest of Varda," he said.

"Do we have to go through it?"

"Yes. There is an old road that would be easier to travel, but it's far east of here. After last night, I'm afraid the Shekkar are too close for that."

"Then we go through," she said. "They're only trees, right?"

He looked back at her, and she could feel that he didn't want to go into the forest. There was obviously something he wasn't saying.

She stared at him with eyebrows furrowed. "Well, what is it?"

"What is what?"

"What is the thing you're not telling me?" she demanded.

"I—" he faltered. "It's not a nice place." He took the pack from her, removing the sword and slinging its belt around his waist.

"Why?"

"Does it matter?" he countered. "We have to go that way. We're heading for the narrowest part of the forest."

The decision made, they entered the woods, and they walked as fast as they could all that afternoon. Even though Zarek was tired, Ana still struggled to keep up. As they traveled deeper into the forest, the trees grew thicker and larger, draped with moss and vines. It was gloomy under the dark branches and the air felt stuffy.

"You're right. It's not a nice forest," Ana said, looking at the gnarled trees. "I don't like it."

"Me neither," Zarek agreed.

Darkness came early under the trees, and soon they couldn't see anything. Zarek kindled a small fire and made a crude torch. It was risky to make a light, but they had to see to keep moving. "We have to be able to find our way out."

Black night fell around them, and they could see no end to the woods. There was no light anywhere except the small flickering gleam from the torch.

"We have to hurry," Zarek urged. "Can you run?"

They ran, stumbling over fallen branches and tree roots in the faint torchlight.

"Zarek!" Ana paused, gasping for breath. He stopped and turned back to her.

"Can we rest?" she begged. "Please!"

"No!"

They both heard a snarl from back the way they had come. Shekkar.

CHAPTER EIGHT

YEAR OF WARDING 38, MOUNTAINS OF SARINE

ANA

Z AREK TOOK ANA'S HAND and they ran, struggling through the thick growth. They came to a small stream. "Step in the water," he said. He dropped the torch, and it hissed and went out, leaving them in complete darkness. Zarek grabbed her arm. "Stay close," he whispered.

They felt their way through treacherous footing in the water. The stones were mossy and slippery, and brush and overhanging branches scratched them. Trailing vines tried to entangle them and clung to their hands and faces.

They stumbled a long way in utter blackness. Pausing for a moment, they listened hard over the sound of the water, but could hear no sign of pursuit.

"I'm going to make a light again," he said, slogging to the bank.

He made a tiny fire to start another makeshift torch.

In the flickering light, several dark shapes on the branches overhead skittered back into the shadows.

"What are those?" A shiver of fear went down her spine, and Ana stepped closer to him.

"Squirrels," Zarek said, taking her hand. "Come on. Keep moving."

His hand surrounding hers felt good. She took comfort from his strength.

They went on, the glimmer of light from the torch helping their progress. Now they could see trailing lines hanging everywhere, and they passed the remains of animals, large and small, tightly wrapped in the entangling threads.

Ana stared at them with a growing knot in her stomach. "What lives here?" she demanded.

Zarek opened his mouth to reply.

But before he could speak, she said, "And don't lie to me again!" He shut his mouth without saying anything. Just then, the torchlight illuminated a large, eight-legged shape that lowered itself on a line, right in their path.

"Spiders!" Ana screamed. She'd never seen one so big. It was the size of Fergen's favorite serving platter back at the inn.

Zarek swung the torch at it, knocking the spider far away into the dark.

Ana clutched his arm. "Please get us out of here!"

"Keep going!" Zarek said. "We need to get through the woods."

ZAREK

Zarek wasn't sure when he realized the spiders were following them. It seemed they had multiplied since the last time he'd been here as a boy. Every time he looked back, clusters of eyes glittered in the torchlight.

Dark, many-legged shapes ran along their webs, skittering out of reach of the light. They made almost no sound, but they grew bolder with every passing moment, as if they didn't want their prey to escape.

Ana huddled close to Zarek, shuddering. They went on. The night had to be nearly over by now.

Beside him, Ana screamed. He turned just in time to see a spider scuttle off into the brush.

"It bit me!" She held out her arm. The spider had left two bleeding puncture wounds just above her elbow and the splint she still wore.

"We can't stop," Zarek said, pulling her forward. "We have to get out."

It wouldn't help to tell her the spiders were venomous. And more of them followed all the time. They couldn't stop now. And Zarek still couldn't see the end of the dark trees.

In a few moments, it was going to be too late. He'd chosen to bring them into this forest. Would any of the other routes they might have taken turned out any better? How sad that they would die here after all they'd been through.

Zarek felt the revolting touch of a spider's hairy legs and a hot sting of pain above his shoulder blade. He pushed on, waving the torch desperately. It drove the creatures back only a little, but he thought he saw a light ahead.

"It hurts." Ana moaned, holding her arm.

"We're almost there," Zarek encouraged. "Keep going!" He felt another bite higher on his shoulder.

The light grew stronger. They stumbled through the underbrush toward it. As they crossed another small stream, Ana caught her toe and fell on the rocks. He dropped the torch into the water and pulled her back to her feet. They reached the edge of the trees and stepped out into the morning light.

Zarek looked over his shoulder. In the woods behind them, night remained, the shadows alive, but nothing followed them past the last tree.

Ana's body shook convulsively. "I can't see." She slumped to the ground.

Zarek half carried, half-dragged her along until they were a safe distance from the edge of the forest. He laid her gently on the grass and sank to his knees. He remembered an herb from his childhood. It would cure the spider's poison if only he could find it. Red... something. It was difficult to think. Red... vine, red... berries? Red... It was redleaf. That was the plant.

On his hands and knees, he searched. Everything seemed gray and dim, and the edges of the plants blurred together.

At last, he found it. Crawling back to where she lay, he crushed the leaves between his fingers and rubbed them into the poison bite on her arm. Checking her arms and neck and back, he saw no more bites.

He took more of the plant and reached for his shoulder to apply it. Zarek extended his hand toward the second bite, but the light grew dimmer until he couldn't see at all.

Zarek woke with his face in the dirt. He sat up with a start. It was dark, and he was freezing. The pain and sickness had vanished entirely. He put a hand to the back of his shoulder. The poisoned bites were gone. Ana must have healed him.

She lay unconscious beside him. But they were both alive.

Zarek carried her all that night, not daring to rest even for a moment. The demons couldn't be very far away. When it got light enough to see, he searched for more of the redleaf and found some along the path. He crushed the leaves and rubbed them into the wound on Ana's arm. The bite looked awful, swollen and oozing. He wrapped her arm, hoping that it would help.

The sun had not yet risen when he came to a small farm. All was quiet. Zarek slipped into the barn, where a cow stood quietly chewing her cud. No horse.

He set Ana on a pile of hay and took a bucket from the wall. It had been many years since he'd tried to milk a cow, but he was starving. The cow was gentle and only watched him curiously, swishing her tail. When he had enough milk, he tried to wake Ana, but she lay there, unresponsive. With no way to carry the milk with him, he drank it all.

He found a sack of grain in a corner and put a handful in his mouth to chew. Quickly, he cut a corner off Ana's cloak and tied more of the grain in it. Lifting Ana into his arms, he moved on.

They passed a few more farms, and Zarek walked all that day with only a brief rest. Ana had not stirred, and he worried he was moving too slowly. They were near the Warding. Just a few more miles and they would be safe.

Night fell quickly. He was so hungry his insides felt hollow, but he couldn't stop now.

In the dark hours of the night, as the moon fell toward the west, Zarek heard one of the Shekkar shriek behind him. He saw another farm ahead and ran for the barn. With a horse, they had a better chance of escaping.

Inside, he found a sturdy, shaggy farm horse, not built for speed, but at least it was a horse. Setting Ana down for a moment, Zarek tossed a bridle on it. He picked up the girl and set her astride the animal's back and led it out the door. He leapt up after her. The demons were closer now, and the horse whinnied and snorted in terror. The farmer ran out of his house, shouting at Zarek to stop. When a shriek came from the woods, the man stopped yelling and bolted back toward his door.

The horse ran. It seemed to know that something terrible pursued them.

Zarek kept one arm around Ana's waist to hold her in place as she slumped against him. They had no other choice but to continue on. He guided the horse northwest toward the Warding. For a while, the Shekkar gained on them. They grew so close that he could hear their insane voices clearly.

Ana woke with a gasp. "Zarek, demons!" She clutched at him in terror.

"I think the horse can outrun them."

They galloped on across the meadows and through little patches of woods. They were almost there. Zarek came out from underneath the trees into an open field.

The Warding lay directly ahead. He saw the tents of Sarine's army camped on the inside. Watch fires clustered along both sides of the border. Between him and his friends were encampments of Aran troops stretching along the Warding in both directions as far as he could see.

Behind him, the demons shrieked. Zarek urged the horse toward the Warding, hoping to reach the border before the Aran soldiers could stop him. Already they shouted in alarm and raised their weapons.

Zarek drew his sword. At his urging, the farm horse charged into a group of Aran soldiers gathering to block his path.

A man ran at him, thrusting his blade at Zarek. He blocked the blow and kicked the man hard in the jaw. The man reeled backward, but two more took his place. With one arm, Zarek held on to Ana, and with the other, he fought them off, trying to push through to the border. Over the clash of metal, he heard the Shekkar getting closer. The Aran soldiers only needed to slow them down enough for the demons to catch them.

Zarek shouted the signal cry familiar to all of Sarine's soldiers. They couldn't know who was trying to cross the border. But they could see someone fighting the Arans. Would they help?

Ana screamed as more Arans ran at them from the other side.

Already, enemies surrounded them.

Hearing the sudden pounding of hooves as more horses approached, Zarek saw Sarine's soldiers coming.

He attacked his foes with renewed determination. His friends crashed into the Arans, scattering them. Zarek pushed back the last few men who tried to stop him and raised his blade.

"For Sarine!" he yelled.

His rescuers raised their blades in answer. Together they drove back their enemies and urged their horses toward the Warding, pounding across the border at a gallop. They halted and turned, ready to fight any of the Arans who crossed the line.

The Shekkar ran between their human allies until they reached the invisible barrier. Screaming in frustration, they clawed at the Warding, trying to get in.

For a long moment, the enemies faced each other, their weapons raised. But the Aran soldiers didn't go any further than the border. Slowly they lowered their weapons and moved away.

Zarek put away his sword, staring at the demons, his heart pounding. It was insane to be so close to them and not run. But they couldn't get through the Warding.

He turned away from them and slid off the horse, pulling Ana with him. Zarek had done it. He'd gotten Ana safely inside. They had cheated death.

From where she lay against him, Ana raised her head to stare at the Shekkar with wide brown eyes. After a moment, she put her arms around his neck, buried her face in his shoulder, and cried quietly.

He held her a little closer. "It's all right," Zarek he murmured. "They can't get in. You're safe now."

In the light of the watch fire, he glanced around at the soldiers staring at him. Many of their faces were familiar. These were the men he'd worked and trained with. "Hal?" he asked, picking out the auburn hair belonging to his old friend. "Look at you, promoted to sergeant."

"It's Zarek!" Sergeant Hal's mouth fell open a little, and his eyes widened. "How did you... What are you... I thought you were dead!" He looked Zarek up and down, his gaze pausing on his friend's torn and bloodstained clothes. Hal's eyes came to rest on the girl in Zarek's arms. "Is that... her? Is she all right?"

Zarek nodded. "She will be."

"Come with me," Hal said. "I'll find you someplace to rest."

Hal led Zarek through the camp to a neat row of small white tents. Pushing a tent flap back, he said, "This one is empty."

Zarek crawled into the tent on his knees to set Ana down on the blankets inside. He covered her warmly and went back out to find his friend waiting.

"You don't look like you've been eating well," Hal observed, handing him a bowl of food.

"I'm all right," Zarek insisted, but he took the bowl and began to eat. "How is the emperor?" he asked around a mouthful.

"Not good," Hal admitted, running a hand through his hair. "They're sending more troops out here every day to reinforce the border, but if the Shekkar get in, it won't help us."

"I need to get to the city," Zarek said. "We're almost out of time."

"I'll have a horse ready for you at first light," Sergeant Hal promised. "And I'll send a couple of soldiers with you. If you stop at the Blue Oak Inn, Rosie will give you fresh horses. For now, eat and get some sleep."

Zarek obeyed. When he lay down to rest, he realized he still heard the demons in the distance. It went against his every instinct to relax with them so near. He'd survived by listening to those instincts.

The blankets felt warm and soft, but despite his exhaustion, it took him hours to doze off.

Not long after he finally did, Ana woke him by sitting bolt upright with a gasp on the other side of the tent. "Zarek! I hear demons. We have to run—" She reached over to clutch his arm. "Why are you lying down? Are you hurt?"

"It's all right, Ana," he said, putting his hand over hers. "We're inside the Warding. They can't hurt us anymore."

She burst into tears, and he pulled her into his arms. "It's going to be all right now. Rest."

Gradually, her sobbing stilled and her breathing evened out. He gently eased her head back onto her pillow and covered her.

⁓

At the first light of dawn, Hal brought them bowls of hot porridge. Zarek shook Ana's shoulder. "I'm awake," she muttered without opening her eyes.

"It's time to eat."

That woke her up. She sat up and looked around. "I still feel dizzy." She rubbed her head.

"It's because of the spider's poison. It will feel better in a few days."

"You took her through the forest?" Hal exclaimed, shaking his head in disapproval.

"It was that or the Shekkar," Zarek protested.

Hal's expression was concerned. "I have a jar of redleaf paste. We see people who've been bitten once in a while. I'll get it after you've eaten."

"Is this an army camp?" Ana asked, looking around at the tent and at Hal.

"Yes. This is Sergeant Hal." He pointed to his friend, who knelt in the tent door with two bowls in his hands. "Sergeant, this is Ana."

"I am honored to meet you," Hal said, holding out a bowl.

She stared at it in amazement for a moment before taking it from him and picking up the spoon. She took a bite. "Thank you!" she said with her mouth full.

"You're welcome," Hal said. "I'll bring you some bread too." He glanced at Zarek's pack. "I guess you ran out of supplies?"

"Several days ago," Zarek explained. "With the Aran army guarding the road, we came over the mountains."

As the sun rose higher, Zarek lifted Ana into the saddle and mounted the horse behind her. Hal had provided food and blankets for their journey. Two other soldiers were ready to ride with them. Zarek set a pace that would cover plenty of ground. Ana dozed as they rode, her head resting on his arm.

The day's ride brought them to the Blue Oak Inn. Night had already fallen when Zarek turned off the road in front of the long, low building. He could just make out the figure of a spreading tree on the familiar sign. Curtains hung in the wide windows and flowerbeds lined the path to the door. The whole place had a comforting air.

Zarek slipped off the horse with the sleeping girl in his arms. The other soldiers followed him. He carried her through the door into a wide room, furnished with tables and chairs and a large fireplace. The room was nearly empty, except for a couple of men who sat at a table in the corner.

A plump, gray-haired woman came out of the kitchen when she heard the door. She stared at him for a long moment, then her gaze dropped to the girl he held in his arms. "Is she hurt?"

He shook his head. "No. Just worn out."

She looked back at him as if she couldn't believe what her eyes told her. "Zarek?" she asked finally. "Is it really you? You look awful."

CHAPTER NINE

YEAR OF WARDING 38, HALE GROVE, SARINE

ZAREK

ZAREK STOOD IN THE doorway facing the gray-haired innkeeper. Her usual smile was absent from her face, her expression frozen with shock.

He grinned. "Hello, Rosie."

"What have you been doing?" she demanded, attempting to hug him despite the girl in his arms. "You're thin as a rail, and you look like you haven't slept or washed in weeks," she exclaimed. "I almost didn't recognize you."

"I have been busy," he admitted. "Do you have rooms for us?"

"Of course," Rosie said. "Come with me."

They followed her down the long hall, and she opened a door. "You two can stay in here," she invited the soldiers. They murmured their thanks and went inside.

She held a door open for Zarek. "You can put her here," she said. "Do you want another room for yourself?"

"I can't leave her," Zarek explained. Ana was sound asleep, and he couldn't leave her alone in a strange place. She wouldn't know where they were when she woke. He needed to stay close so she wouldn't be frightened. He put Ana down on one of the beds.

"Who is she?" Rosie asked, looking down at the sleeping girl. "Her name is Ana," he said.

"You haven't had her running out in the wilds, have you?" Rosie demanded.

"I—" Zarek began.

"You have! I can see you have!" she scolded. "Look at her. She's half-starved and bandaged here and there. What have you done to her?" Zarek rubbed his forehead, remembering their adventures. He sighed. "I had no choice. We barely made it. But we'll be in the city in two or three more days if we ride fast, and she'll have plenty of time to rest there."

"I'll get you something to eat." Rosie disappeared and returned with a tray filled with hot soup and bread slathered with butter.

"Thank you, Rosie," Zarek said fervently, savoring a mouthful of warm bread.

"You never liked my cooking this much before," Rosie said.

"Oh, I did," Zarek protested. "And I haven't had fresh bread since—" he paused, unable to remember.

"You need to eat better!"

"I agree," Zarek said, still chewing. Gently, he shook Ana until she stirred a little. "Can you eat?" he asked.

The girl roused enough to eat some bread and soup and was asleep again as soon as she swallowed her last bite.

"She looks so tired," Rosie said.

"She needs a good long rest," Zarek admitted. "I'll make sure she gets it."

"You'd better," Rosie warned, as she tucked the blanket around the sleeping girl. "I'll have horses ready early for the four of you."

❧

In the morning, Ana and Zarek met the two soldiers in the common room for breakfast. Almost as soon as they sat down, Rosie arrived with food. "I can't believe I'm letting you sit at my table looking like that." She pointed at Zarek's ruined clothes and unshaven face. "Maybe I can borrow something for you to wear."

"Don't worry," Zarek protested. "We'll soon be back in the city. And we need to hurry. Have you heard any news about the emperor?"

Rosie sighed and shook her head. "Nothing good. Captain Toren came through yesterday with a large company of men heading for the border. He said the emperor was getting worse every day. There isn't much time."

"We need to go," Zarek said, stuffing the last bite of bread into his mouth and standing up.

The horses stood in the yard, waiting for them. Rosie followed them out the door. She hugged Zarek and kissed Ana on the cheek.

"Thank you so much," Ana said.

"Take care, my dear," Rosie responded. "Make sure Zarek is a good boy. And take this." She handed Ana a sack. "It's food for your journey."

"Thank you for everything, Rosie."

The soldiers were already in their saddles. Zarek stopped at her side. "Are you strong enough to ride alone? I can ride with you if you want me to."

Ana appreciated his concern, but the night's rest had done her good. "I think I can."

He helped her into her saddle and then mounted his own horse.

They rode away, waving farewell.

A short distance from the inn, they crossed the Hale River bridge and continued on toward the White City.

ANA

By their second day of riding, Ana looked at the countryside with interest. They passed beautiful farms, orchards and peaceful villages. The bustle of harvest had passed, leaving the land quiet. Everything flashed past as they galloped along, and the sun shone down warmly. Best of all, she was no longer hungry. She'd almost forgotten what it felt like to sleep all night in a bed, wake up to find warm water to wash, and to eat breakfast at a table with forks and spoons. She felt much stronger.

Zarek had the redleaf cream Hal had given him. Every time they halted, he applied it to the bite on Ana's arm. Day by day, it was healing.

"You've seen those spiders before," Ana said, guiding her horse to ride beside Zarek. "Did they bite you?"

"Yes, when I was six. My mother and I rode through the forest and they attacked us."

She drew in a quick breath, remembering their own time in the forest. "How did you get out?"

"My father and Emperor Callonen found us. I don't remember that part. I was almost dead."

"Is that when Allia saved your life?"

Zarek nodded. "She brought me back with the ring. Her skill and quick thinking saved my mother too, and several more people. She was the only one who knew to use redleaf to stop the poison."

"So Emperor Callonen knew Allia?"

"Yes," Zarek said.

"Did he know her well?"

"They were engaged to be married," Zarek said finally.

Ana's eyes widened in surprise. "My mother was engaged to an emperor? But—"

"Don't ask me to tell you everything," Zarek interrupted. "Emperor Callonen should be the one to share their story."

They stopped for the night at an outpost run by Sarine's army. While the food wasn't as good as Rosie's, they ate well and rested and were on their way early. As they rode on, Ana saw a tall white tower peeping between the hills. "What is that?" she asked in wonder.

Zarek grinned. "That, Lady Cirana, is the White City, the Heart of the Warding, and the home of the emperor."

"What's it like there?" she asked, feeling her stomach quiver. It seemed enormous and would be full of people. Would she be able to find her way around? What would happen to her when they got there?

"It's the best," Zarek assured her.

"And the emperor?"

"He is a powerful man. The Warding gives him an awareness of everyone within it."

"Do you mean he knows what they're doing?" How overwhelming would it be to sense everyone at once? Ana couldn't imagine a person who was able to do that.

"Yes," Zarek said. "Maybe it's a little like the ring. They were both created by your great-grandfather, the wizard Zarekathus. You can sense what people are feeling. The emperor is very perceptive. No one can lie to him."

What would the emperor be like, this man who knew everything about everyone? And could he sense her coming, even now? What would he think of her?

In the middle of the day, when they stopped and ate the food Rosie had packed for them, Ana walked around to stretch her legs. She breathed deeply and smiled as she felt strength returning to her limbs.

The towers of the city shone in the sun as they drew nearer. Finally, in the evening, when the white stone of the walls glowed pink in the fading rays of the sun, they came over the last hill and Ana saw the entire city. She had never seen anything so magnificent. A tall, smooth wall surrounded it and inside stood many buildings and towers. It looked strong, but also beautiful, and the enormous gates stood open.

If Ana had been alone, the armed guards at the gates would have frightened her. But Zarek didn't hesitate at all. He followed their companions, and the guards stood aside without questioning them.

The two soldiers who had ridden to the city with them bade them farewell and headed toward the barracks. Zarek and Ana followed streets paved with flagstones toward the center of the city. "That's where the emperor lives." Zarek pointed to some of the tallest towers. The palace occupied the highest ground in the city, so it seemed even loftier from below.

They made their way up the hill until they came at last to the gate of the white palace. They were ragged and dirty, and Ana felt like a beggar at the door. She was only an orphan who waited on tables at an inn. Surely, she could never belong in a place like this. There were more guards, heavily armed and wearing white-and-gold uniforms. Ana felt her stomach quiver with nervousness. "Halt!" one of them ordered, raising his hand. Zarek pulled his mount to a stop and jumped to the ground. She slid off her horse, staring at the guards in apprehension, and stood beside Zarek. He gave her hand a comforting squeeze. The soldiers must have recognized him, for they saluted.

"Thank you," Zarek said, returning their salute.

The biggest of them slapped him on the back and said, "Welcome home."

"Are we in time? Is the emperor still alive?"

"He's very weak. We have every man armed and ready to fight in case the Warding fails, but all is quiet, so he must still live. They have not yet ordered us to bar the gates."

"We'll go to him now," Zarek said.

The palace halls were wide and white, and they passed few other people. No one questioned them, though Ana thought they must look terribly out of place. Her boots were dirty, her clothes torn and stained, and her hair tangled.

Zarek knew exactly where to go. He led them up curving staircases, around corners, and across wide halls with marble floors. Ana had never been in a building as grand as this one before. At last, they arrived at the emperor's room. Three men wearing huge swords guarded the door. But as before, when they saw Zarek, they let him through without question. Dane had once told Ana that Zarek was the most skilled soldier in Sarine. Clearly, he was very important here. All the guards treated him with obvious respect. They entered the room and saw the emperor lying in a large bed, attended by several people. Zarek went straight to his bedside, knelt and took his hand. "Emperor Callonen, we found the ring!" Zarek beckoned Ana forward.

When she looked down at the emperor, he appeared ancient, his face gray and tired.

When he saw her, he closed his eyes and tears leaked from beneath his lashes. After a moment, he gazed up at her and asked, "Allia?"

"No. She was my mother. I'm Cirana," she said. "But I've always been called Ana."

"I'm sorry," he murmured. "I thought I was—" He took a breath, appearing to gather the strength to speak. "You look so very like her... Cirana. What a beautiful name. My dear, do you know how the ring works? Are you willing to heal me?"

She studied him for a long moment. His eyes were a deep, warm brown. The same color she saw whenever she looked in a mirror. His expression was sad, but his voice was kind, and Ana liked him at once. She could sense he was a good person, and she wanted him to be well.

"I have used the ring before. And I want to help you." She sat on the edge of the bed and reached out to touch him.

ZAREK

Zarek saw Ana stiffen as her fingers touched Emperor Callonen. Her muscles clenched and tears ran down her cheeks. She shook with pain, but she didn't cry out. In a moment, it passed, and Zarek caught her as she collapsed.

The emperor rose to his feet and looked down at Ana. "Is she all right?"

Zarek bent to listen to her breathing. "I think so."

"Allia's child. She looks so much like her mother. I can't believe you found her. And you kept her safe. You saved Sarine!"

The gratitude in Callonen's expression was so profound it embarrassed Zarek. For a moment, he didn't know what to say. "She saved us," he said, looking down at Ana. "She's a brave girl, and she's been through so much. We protected her as well as we could..."

Zarek turned away. Ana had been hurt so often during their journey, despite all his efforts. And Dane had given his life protecting her.

As if he could read Zarek's mind, Emperor Callonen asked, "What happened to Dane?"

Zarek felt his stomach clench. "Aran soldiers attacked Dane when he tried to defend Ana. He was hurt. I hoped Ana could use the ring, but by the time we got back to him, it was too late."

Emperor Callonen gripped Zarek's shoulder. "I'm so sorry. I want you to tell me everything, but first, we must take care of her. And you should rest and eat. I'm so proud of you. You did this impossible thing, and our empire owes you a great debt."

"I'm honored to have served the empire well." Zarek bowed his head.

And he had saved Ana. That was even more important. She was a rare and wonderful person, and he couldn't stand the thought of the demons destroying her.

Zarek carried Ana through the halls with the emperor at his side. Everyone stared in amazement. No one but his closest advisers had seen Callonen for some time. It had been months since he'd been able to leave his room. Now, he appeared well and strong.

They brought Ana to the head of the imperial household, a kind, red-haired woman named Tess.

"My lord," Tess exclaimed when she saw them. "You're well again!" She rushed forward to hug Emperor Callonen.

"Look." He turned to show her the girl in Zarek's arms.

Tess burst into tears.

"You recognize her then?"

"Of course I do," Tess said. "But how can it be? She looks just like Allia—" She fell silent abruptly.

After a moment, she wiped her eyes, bowed to the emperor and said, "Follow me. We will take care of her."

Tess led them to a large bedroom, one of the finest rooms in the palace. Zarek set Ana on the soft bed. "I'll be back later to check on her," he promised. He left Emperor Callonen standing beside Tess, as she looked down at Ana's sleeping face.

Zarek returned to his own rooms. It had been almost a year since he'd been there, but he didn't see a speck of dust anywhere. The room looked just as it always had, elegant and comfortable.

He eyed the bed longingly, but he was far too dirty. He went to the large bathtub and was pleasantly surprised to find it already full of hot water. Tess seemed to read his mind. She ran the palace so well he hardly ever had to ask for anything.

When he had bathed and shaved, he found clean clothes in his wardrobe. These were a little dusty, but he was sure if he had given Tess any warning at all, they would have been washed for him. It felt strange to be wearing something clean, not his old clothes. He'd been gone for so long.

The bed still looked soft and tempting, but he couldn't relax until he checked on Ana. His gaze moved back and forth between a pair of new, polished boots set neatly in the bottom of the wardrobe and his old, comfortable, dirty ones. Unable to decide, he left the room in stocking feet.

It was late by then, and hardly anyone remained in the halls. Zarek went back to the room where he had left Ana. When he knocked softly, Tess let him in. He went to the side of the bed and looked down at the girl. She'd been bathed and dressed in a soft white nightgown. With what must have taken great effort, someone had combed her long, honey-colored hair until it was smooth. The healers had been there to examine her arm and clean and wrap her injuries, and Tess was just finishing putting a soothing salve on her bruises and scratches.

"She's still sleeping," Tess whispered.

"Thank you for taking care of her," Zarek said to Tess. "She's had such a hard time."

Tess nodded. "I can see she has, poor thing."

"She's very brave," he said. "She saved all of us tonight. You've seen the ring work before. You know she'll sleep for days yet."

"Yes," Tess said. "And it is Allia's ring, isn't it? How did she come to have it? I mean, how could she have gotten away after Allia gave it to her? None of the others escaped. Harrow said he'd hidden her. But that's the only thing we knew."

"Ana told me that Harrow gave her to an old woman who cared for her until she died nine years ago. After her death, Ana stayed with the innkeeper in Bright Springs," Zarek said. "She's had the ring as long as she can remember."

"And she knows Allia was her mother? This sweet girl has endured so much. We're not the only ones who lost loved ones."

"I know Allia was your best friend, and you loved Harrow."

"And Talon was your father," Tess said, taking his hand. "So much tragedy..."

Zarek looked down at the sleeping girl. "The others are gone, but now, beyond all hope, we've found her."

Tess brushed a lock of hair from Ana's face, looking down at her silently.

"I can watch over her," Zarek said. "Go to bed, Tess. I'm sure you've had a long day."

"I'm fine," Tess protested. "You just got back."

"I will stay with her," Zarek repeated. Tess nodded and turned to go.

"And Tess, thank you for sending the hot water."

Pausing in the doorway, she smiled. "Do you need anything else?"

"If anyone is still awake in the kitchen, please have them find me something to eat," he said. "And make sure they send breakfast in the morning."

CHAPTER TEN

YEAR OF WARDING 38, WHITE CITY, SARINE

ANA

A NA WOKE SLOWLY FROM a beautiful, peaceful dream about a white palace in the sky, where she rested on a soft feathery cloud. While she kept her eyes closed, the dream would last, and she wouldn't have to get up and start running again.

"Ana?"

She heard Zarek's voice. "Don't wake me up," she murmured without opening her eyes. "I'm dreaming of a beautiful palace. And I'm too tired to run anymore."

He laughed.

"Do we have to go?"

"No. But you can open your eyes."

Cautiously, she opened them and saw the morning sun shining on white walls. Zarek sat in a large, soft chair beside the bed. She gazed around in wonder. "It's real." The room was more luxurious than any she'd ever seen. There were tall windows on one wall, with long, rich draperies. Ornate wardrobes, thick carpets and tables with vases of flowers furnished the room.

Deep comfortable chairs were drawn up before a magnificent fireplace, with a bright fire burning in it.

"Are you sure this isn't a dream?" she whispered. "What happened?"

"We've done it, that's what happened. We made it to the city, and you healed the emperor."

"Everything is all right then? The Shekkar can't come here?"

"No. Thanks to you, the emperor is now well and strong, and his power will continue to protect this land."

Ana smiled and nestled deeper into the feather bed. She stared at her hands.

"What are you looking at?" Zarek asked curiously.

"My fingernails are clean."

He laughed again. "Will you have your breakfast, my lady?"

"Yes, please!" Her empty stomach growled. Zarek brought a silver tray loaded with buttered toast, eggs and fruit and set it on her lap. It smelled delicious.

"Do you need help?" he asked.

She was too weak to lift her arms. Her fingers moved at her command, but no more. "I can't move." She looked up at him apologetically.

"Don't worry," he replied. "You'll feel better in a couple of days, and I don't mind helping you."

She looked up at him. "Are you sure?"

"Very sure." Zarek placed a thick pillow behind her. "All you have to do is open your mouth."

The food tasted wonderful, finer than she had ever eaten, and even better after the last few weeks of hunger.

"Is it better than my cooking?"

"Maybe a little," she said with a grin. "You're pretty good at cooking over a fire."

Zarek laughed. "I'll have to give up the rest of my work to focus on cooking."

"Aren't you hungry?" she asked, swallowing a piece of thickly buttered toast.

"No, I ate already."

She stared at him as she chewed. "You look different," she said thoughtfully. And then she felt her face grow hot with embarrassment when she realized what the change was.

Zarek was clean. He had bathed and shaved. His hair was washed and trimmed. His worn trousers and jacket had been exchanged for a spotless white tunic.

"You look like a king," she said, staring at him. She felt very awkward amid the luxury of her new surroundings. But Zarek stood, bowed to her, and smiled, and she couldn't help but smile back.

There was a knock at the door, and the guard came in. "His Majesty, the Emperor of Sarine is here."

Ana didn't feel ready to meet the emperor. He was here now? Her insides twisted with nervousness. She looked at Zarek.

He seemed calm. "We're ready."

"Why is the emperor here?" she whispered urgently.

"He's come to see you," Zarek said. "I'll give you two some time to talk." He went to the door.

"You're leaving? But... I should get up at least," she protested, trying unsuccessfully again to move.

The guards opened the door, and the emperor himself came in. Ana felt herself shaking with nervousness. She didn't know how to act in front of an emperor.

He did not look like the same man she'd met when they had arrived. Rather than appearing frail and weak, he stood tall and powerful. His clothes were ornate and his bearing commanding. His hair, which had been thin and gray when she had last seen him, was now thick and dark. The lines of pain and worry were gone from his face. Before, she'd thought him elderly. Now she realized he was barely middle-aged.

She felt the need to stand in his presence, or at least to do something.

He seemed to realize this.

"Please rest, Cirana." His voice sounded just as kind as it had before, and as he drew nearer, she sensed it represented his true nature.

She felt more relaxed and lay back against the pillows to look at him.

"May I?" He sat down in the chair by the bed.

What could she say to him?

She watched him silently as he smiled at her from the chair Zarek had vacated. "Are you feeling all right this morning?" he asked.

She nodded, still afraid to speak to him.

"My name is Callonen," the emperor said. "I'm so glad you're here. Do you have everything you need?"

She took in the luxurious room and the silver breakfast tray. "Everything is beautiful... Thank you," she stammered.

"I am so grateful for what you did," the emperor—Callonen—said. "You saved my life. Because of you, all the people within the Warding will remain under my protection. You're safe here. But outside... the Shekkar would find you."

Ana felt her stomach clench. Memories of their flight washed over her. She never wanted to be running from demons again. "Please, can I stay here?"

Callonen looked at her with penetrating brown eyes. "Yes! Of course. I want you to stay," he said. "Your journey was very difficult. You endured great pain, and so did Zarek. We are all relieved to have you here safely. Perhaps you already know that I cared deeply for your mother and feel the pain of her loss every day. With your permission, I offer you a place in my household. I promise to do everything possible to protect and help you."

"Thank you," she exclaimed, relief washing over her. She had been fortunate that Grandmother and Fergen had taken care of her. Now, Callonen offered her a home here. She gazed up at him. "You're sure you don't mind? I can take care of myself, and I'll do whatever I can to help. I know how to cook and clean, and I can work."

"Thank you for your offer, Ana. You have already done a great service to Sarine, one that no one else could have done. If it becomes necessary for me to ask for your help again, I will remember your offer."

She had been worried about what would happen to her when she got here. With the demons roaming outside the Warding, returning to her old life in Bright Springs would be impossible. But to be part of Emperor Callonen's household? That was so much more than she had expected.

Ana could sense he was truly happy to have her here and wanted to help. She took a deep breath, and the butterflies in her stomach eased. Being with him felt comfortable. She took another deep breath, and the tension in her shoulders relaxed.

"I learned a little about your journey. Zarek told me you were very brave," Emperor Callonen said.

Ana felt her cheeks heat and looked away. "That's not true. I'm not brave at all," she confessed.

"He told me otherwise."

Her eyes widened. "How could he say that? I was terrified. He took care of me, and Dane did too. They did so much to help me. I'm very grateful to them."

"Dane was a good man," Callonen said.

"I tried to save him," she said, feeling her eyes brim with tears. "We both did. Zarek fought so many soldiers, but when we got back... Dane was..."

"I'm sorry," Callonen said. "He was my friend too."

❧

All that day, Ana couldn't get out of bed, forcing her to wait before she explored her new surroundings. It had grown very quiet when everyone had left her to rest. She dozed for a while and had plenty of time to think. There were still so many questions she wanted answers to.

Zarek had said the emperor might help her discover more about her parents. She resolved to ask him as soon as she could.

There was a knock at the door, and Ana saw a woman with red hair and a kind face peeking in. "May I come in?" she asked.

"Yes, of course."

The woman smiled and came over to Ana's bedside. "I'm Tess, the head of the household. Your mother was a dear friend of mine. If you need anything, I'll be pleased to see to it."

"Zarek told me about you, that you've already helped me." Ana smiled. "Thank you. Everyone here has been so kind."

"We're all happy to have you here," Tess said, setting a dinner tray on Ana's lap.

༄

The next morning, Ana woke to see sunlight streaming through the tall windows. She felt much stronger, and though stiff and tired, her legs worked just fine. Someone had removed the splint from her arm, and gingerly she stretched and flexed it. The muscles felt weak from disuse, but it was much better. She slid out of bed and set about exploring her room.

She discovered that one section of the windows included a door that led to a balcony. Ana went out and found she could see most of the city, as well as hills, forests and farmlands. The autumn morning was chill, and the air crisp. The stone felt cold under her bare feet. She shivered in her nightdress and went back inside to warm her toes by the fire. It was so good to have warm feet.

She peeked into the wardrobe and found a dress, noticing it was her size. Back in Bright Springs, she'd barely ever worn a dress before, and this one seemed nice enough for a queen.

Tess came while Ana was still admiring the dress. "Do you like it? We can have more made soon, when you're feeling better," she said. "You can choose the fabric if you'd like."

"Really?" Ana's hands brushed the smooth skirt. "I've only worn a dress once before. I'd feel a little funny."

"You'll get used to it," Tess promised with a smile. She took out the garment. Ana put it on and Tess buttoned her up the back.

"Everything is so different here. I'm afraid I'll do something wrong."

"Don't worry," Tess said. "The emperor cares a great deal about you. And if he is on your side, you can do anything you want in this city."

Ana looked up at her. "Why would he care about me? Is it because of my mother?"

"You'll have to ask him that yourself."

"Can I see him? I only want to talk to him for a moment."

"Of course."

Ana followed Tess through the halls until they came to an enormous room. It was full of people, and Emperor Callonen sat on a throne on a raised platform at one end. Many of his subjects waited to speak to him. Tess slipped past them, went to the emperor, and murmured in his ear.

"I'm sorry," he said, raising his hand. "I will continue audiences tomorrow." Amid murmurs of disappointment, the emperor rose and walked out a small door at the back of the room. Tess led Ana through the crowd, following him. The guards opened the door.

"I'll see you in a little while," Tess said, nodding toward the entrance. Ana went inside and closed the door behind her.

Emperor Callonen stood in front of the fireplace.

"I didn't mean to interrupt, Emperor. I can wait if you don't have time," she said hesitantly, looking up at him. He wore a dark coat with elaborate trim and a snowy white linen shirt underneath. On his belt, he wore a dagger with an ornate golden hilt, and a golden crown sat on his head. He had been very busy before she interrupted. Would it bother him?

But he smiled warmly and said, "Not at all. Please sit down, my dear." He held a chair out for her. She sat. The room was a comfortable size after the enormous hall. It contained a table and a few large chairs.

"What can I do for you?" he asked, removing the crown and dropping it unceremoniously onto the table. He sat down opposite her.

"I..." But when she met his warm brown eyes, she felt his genuine concern for her and wondered why he cared so much. "I have questions," she said.

"What can I tell you?"

Ana stared straight into his eyes. "Can you tell me about my parents?"

Pain filled his expression, and she could sense that this question caused him to feel hurt, betrayal, and anger. She was sorry about that, but she had to understand.

He took her hand and said, "I believe Allia was your mother. Your own information supports this as well. We think the woman who raised you received you from a man named Harrow, one of my bravest soldiers. Harrow was attempting to rescue you and Allia."

"Where is my mother now?" Ana whispered. "Is she alive? Zarek said she died. I'm hoping he was wrong."

Emperor Callonen closed his eyes. She could sense his overwhelming sadness.

He said, "I believe she is dead."

"What happened to her?" Ana asked.

He was silent for a while, staring into the fire. When he looked back at her, his face was despairing. "I don't like to speak of it. But I will tell you, even though it was the greatest failure of my life."

Ana waited for him to continue.

"Allia was the most important person to me. Nearly eighteen years ago, she came to the city to work, and I fell in love with her. I loved her with all my heart and soul. I loved her smile, her eyes. You look just like her, except for the color of your eyes. She was so wise, so kind and full of life, and the most beautiful girl I had ever seen. I asked her to marry me, and she agreed to be my queen. She wore the ring with the green stone, just as you wear it now. But my twin brother Haldreth craved the power of the ring. He was determined to destroy me and my empire, so he abducted Allia. I went after her, of course. But I failed to save her."

Emperor Callonen seemed so miserable that Ana felt tears on her own cheeks. She went to him and put her arms around his neck. "I'm sorry you lost her. I believe you did all you could," she whispered. He held her, and it felt so comforting. Did having a father feel like this?

His voice was quiet. "I felt broken without her. I wanted to rescue her more than anything."

"You really loved her." Ana could sense the depth of his feelings. There was so much more to this than he was saying. He felt angry and despairing, but knew there was nothing he could do now to fix the situation. Yet guilt gnawed at him. He didn't allow any of these feelings to show.

Instead, he held her at arm's length and looked directly into her eyes. Despite his warring emotions, his gaze was warm and kind. "Oh yes," he said. "I loved her. I would have given my life to save her. But my father died, and the Warding passed to me. I couldn't leave my people unprotected. I might have gone after Allia anyway, except my friend Talon offered to go in my place."

He remained silent for so long that Ana wondered if he had decided not to tell her any more. "Talon was Zarek's father?" she asked.

Callonen nodded.

"And he went, didn't he?" she asked. It obviously hurt for him to talk about this, but she needed to hear the story.

"He went, taking Harrow with him," Callonen said, "and he never came back. Harrow returned, badly injured, saying that my brother would not find the ring or the baby. We realized he must have meant Allia's child, and we assumed you had the ring, but he died without telling us where you were. We couldn't find you."

"And you think that before he got hurt, he gave me to my grandmother. At least, she always said she was my grandmother. Now I know she wasn't, actually. I never knew anyone was looking for me," Ana said.

"I hope you can forgive me," Callonen said. "If only I could have found you sooner, I would have taken care of you gladly. You could have grown up here in the palace."

"I didn't need a palace," Ana said. "All I wanted was to know where I came from and if I belonged to anyone. Do you know who my father is?"

Ana had been hoping that she'd already asked the most painful questions. But now he stared at her silently.

Was she in trouble? He was the emperor, and maybe she had pushed him too far. She could sense the tension and a mix of other emotions this question caused him to feel, despair, anger, disappointment, inadequacy. Ana stood frozen, wishing she hadn't asked. "You don't have to answer," she said, trying to spare his feelings.

Callonen took a deep breath. "I was here. And you were born in Ara. There is no way I can know for sure. As much as I wish I were your father, Allia and I never went that far in our relationship. So, I know I'm not. And I don't know exactly what happened, so I can't answer your question. But no matter what the answer is, I'm very happy to have you here."

"Thank you for everything you told me," Ana said, hugging him. "I know it hurts to remember."

"It does," he agreed. "But you needed your questions answered, and I will always answer them if I can. I'm sorry it's such a sad tale. Neither you nor your mother deserved what happened to you. I longed to spend the rest of my life with Allia. I would have. Instead, my brother abducted her and took her to Ara."

That night, asleep in her beautiful room, Ana dreamed of being with her mother. At first Ana was happy, but then something pursued them. They ran, but Ana knew with horror that she couldn't run fast enough to escape. She stopped, gasping, looking for danger in all directions. Then she heard Zarek shout, "run!" and Ana ran again. When she looked back, the Shekkar were there, tall, black and horrible. They surrounded Zarek, snapping at him with cruel jaws and slashing at him with razor-sharp claws, and she screamed. Someone shook her, but the dream still held her. Trapped in the vision, watching Zarek's blood flowing onto the ground, she couldn't stop screaming.

Someone shook her again, then pressed a cool cloth to her face.

Ana opened her eyes and saw Tess bending over her.

"It's all right," Tess said soothingly, taking her hand and stroking it.

But it wasn't all right. She had seen the demons attacking Zarek. "Where is Zarek?" Panic twisted through her.

Tess's voice sounded calm. "He's asleep. It's very late. But he is safe. Can you go back to sleep?"

Ana shook her head. "No! I have to go back. I have to help him!"

"Don't worry," Tess assured her. "Zarek is fine."

But the dream had been too real. No matter how often they told her Zarek was safe, she just couldn't believe it.

"Where is he?"

Finally, she saw his face above her. His brows drew together, and his jaw was tight with worry. Her eyes searched his features for any sign of injury.

"I thought they had killed you!" She clung to him, gasping. "There was nothing I could do. Blood everywhere."

He put his arms around her and hugged her. "It's all over now. It's all behind us. We're safe now. Safe."

A silver of relief penetrated her fear. She felt tears on her face. "They killed you," she sobbed, holding onto him.

He drew back to meet her eyes, his voice steady. "Look at me. I'm fine. I'm not hurt. We are safe here."

He held her close again, staying with her as she gradually calmed. He was here, warm and alive. Slowly, the horror of the dream faded. With his arms around her, she drifted back into sleep.

CHAPTER ELEVEN

YEAR OF WARDING 38, WHITE CITY, SARINE

ANA

THERE WERE OTHER NIGHTS when Ana woke screaming. Sometimes in her nightmares she was back at Fergen's inn, while the demons broke down the doors and rushed into a room where all her friends waited, defenseless.

Sometimes in dreams, she saw Dane raising his blade to defend her from a dozen men who wanted to take her away. She struggled against the arms that seized her. Dane swung his sword, fighting them all, but there were too many. His jaw clenched, his eyes wide with shock as their blades penetrated his body. He sank to his knees, clutching his side while blood ran from under his hands. Then he lay on the ground, his eyes staring at nothing, and no matter how she tried, it was too late to save him.

In other nightmares, she ran in the dark, knowing the demons pursued her, inches from reaching her. But when she turned around, nothing was there. Still running, she tripped over something in the dark. It was Zarek's lifeless body.

In the end, they always had to call Zarek. Only he could calm her down enough to sleep again. He was the only one who understood what she saw.

One night, as Ana got into bed, she saw a spider on the wall. She shrieked and ran out into the hall.

"What is it?" asked the guard, half-drawing his sword.

"A spider!"

The guard stared at her in disbelief. Then he laughed and put his weapon away.

She hung her head, ashamed.

Zarek came down the hall just then. "Ana? What's wrong?"

"A spider," she confessed in a small voice. She didn't want him to laugh at her too. But he didn't. He nodded gravely and went in to kill it for her.

In the first few days after his recovery, Emperor Callonen had sent men back to the place where Dane had died, to lay him to rest properly if they could. They also took a message from Ana to Bright Springs. She wanted Fergen and Tari to know how grateful she was for their kindness, and to let them know she was safe. She hoped that with her gone, the Shekkar would not return.

When the messengers returned to the city, Ana was relieved to learn that Fergen and Tari had survived that terrible night, although demons had killed several of their neighbors.

Two weeks after Ana arrived in the city, the emperor held a grand banquet.

"I'm throwing this party for you," Callonen told Ana as they shared breakfast. "But we must keep the ring a secret. I can't tell everyone about it, or even about what you can do. My empire owes you a debt of gratitude, and I'd like to tell my people everything you've done for us. But it's better for you if I don't."

So, officially, the banquet honored the emperor's miraculous recovery. No one but a few of his most trusted advisers had seen him during the last stages of his illness, and he'd told Ana it would be good for him to be among his people again. He promised her music and dancing and wonderful food.

Even though she hadn't yet completely recovered from her ordeal, Ana was brimming with excitement for the coming event. Tess spent hours teaching her how to dance, and on the day of the party, she brought Ana a new dress. Ana gasped when she saw the delicate fabric in a soft shade of blue. "This color will be beautiful on you with those brown eyes," Tess said. "I'll help you dress."

"Thank you so much!" Ana hugged Tess impulsively.

When evening finally arrived, Tess helped Ana into the gown and arranged her hair. Then, when it was time, they walked to the doors of the great hall.

Ana peeked inside. It was brilliantly lit and full of people. She hesitated at the door, not sure what to do and abruptly nervous, for a herald announced each guest as they arrived and she didn't know the proper words to say to him.

"Don't worry. Everything's going to be fine," Tess whispered to her.

Zarek appeared at Ana's side and offered her his arm. He spoke to the herald. Ana took a deep breath, then placed her hand in the crook of his arm. As they walked in, the herald cried, "Captain Zarek of the Emperor's Guard and Lady Cirana." Everyone politely applauded as they entered.

Ana leaned closer to speak to him. "You never told me you were a captain in the Emperor's Guard."

He grinned. "You never asked me."

Zarek wore a dark-gray tunic trimmed with silver and a shining white cloak. He looked very handsome in the fine clothes, and his smile was charming. After their travels together, she already knew he was brave and kind.

"You look nice," she whispered shyly, looking up at him.

"So do you," he replied, smiling. "But I'd rather wear my old boots any day."

His praise made her feel warm inside.

They crossed the room to join the emperor, who stood chatting with a large group of people. Emperor Callonen introduced her to many of the guests, and the ladies smiled and nodded at her, while the men bowed and kissed her hand. It made her feel like a princess instead of an orphan who lived at an inn. She met several of Callonen's advisers and General Gray, as well as two or three diplomats visiting Sarine from other kingdoms.

The group moved to the tables and sat down. Ana had Zarek at her side, and she had so much fun that she barely had time to worry about making mistakes. The dinner was magnificent.

After they had eaten, the music and dancing began.

A young lady with long, dark hair and a beautiful crimson gown approached their table and asked Zarek if she could have a word with him. He stood. "If you would excuse me for a few moments, Lady Cirana?"

Ana nodded and smiled at him. He winked at her as he bowed to the woman and kissed her hand. The lady took his arm, and they disappeared out onto the balcony. Ana watched them go. It shouldn't have surprised her that he attracted attention, or that he had friends here. She swallowed hard. Of course, there would be young ladies who enjoyed his attention. Just because Ana had been alone with him all these weeks didn't mean he would prefer her company now. But she wished it had been her on Zarek's arm. How could she tell him?

She glanced at Callonen, who still sat at the table, and smiled. "Aren't you going to dance?"

His eyebrows raised. "Me? I haven't danced since..." His words trailed off, and she could tell the memory made him sad.

She didn't want him to feel sad. "I've never been to a party like this!" She looked around at the lights and the people in formal clothes and sparkling jewelry. "And I've never danced in front of anyone."

Callonen met her eyes and smiled, his sorrow receding. "We had better fix that." He got to his feet, straightened his shoulders and offered her his hand. "Lady Cirana, will you do me the honor of joining me for a dance?"

Ana smiled up at him and did her best curtsy, spreading the flowing skirts of her gown as she had seen so many other women do this evening. "I would be delighted." She took his hand.

Everyone in the room stared at the emperor. Were they surprised to see him dance? He put his hand to her waist, and she put hers on his shoulder. It felt like he knew how to spin and turn exactly right, and Ana decided that dancing was lovely.

They twirled around the floor for two entire songs until Callonen led her back to the edge of the dancing. "Thank you, my dear." He smiled down at her. "It's been far too long. But now, I think there is someone waiting to take my place."

Ana turned around in surprise and saw a young man standing there. He was elegantly dressed in a green tunic and had dark hair. "Would you like to dance?" he asked, smiling at her nervously.

Ana nodded. "Yes, thank you."

She felt a touch of awkwardness and didn't know what to say to him. But Tess's lessons paid off, and she thought she did all right. The boy didn't move as confidently as Callonen had. Instead, they moved in slow circles, only a little stiffly, and Ana managed not to step on his toes.

A while later, there was another young man, this one sandy-haired. He wore a pleasant smile and the white-and-gold uniform of the Emperor's Guard.

Between dances, Ana still had plenty of time to watch. Zarek stood out in his brilliant white cloak. He danced very well. She already knew he could be graceful when he wanted to be. Ana noticed his boots, new and polished, and she remembered the ones he'd worn on their journey—old and worn, with holes in them from all the miles he'd traveled. Those were the ones he'd rather be wearing.

For so long, she'd seen him in old ragged clothes. Tonight, if she didn't know this well-dressed nobleman was him, she might not have recognized him. The fine clothes didn't seem to matter to him, he still acted the same. As Ana watched, he danced with many ladies, and they were all beautiful. She thought they admired his handsome features.

Zarek bowed to a woman seated alone in a corner. Her dress was elegant, and her hair had the same golden waves as Zarek, with a touch of gray at the temples. She took his offered hand, and they joined the dancing. For several turns, she smiled up at Zarek. They talked together. But, at something he said, her smile disappeared.

Though neither of them missed a step in the dance, anger appeared on her face. Zarek's eyebrows drew together stubbornly. When the music ended, he bowed stiffly to her, and Ana saw her ask him something. His answer did not please her.

The woman turned her back on him and left the room, fury written on her face. After a few moments, Zarek found another partner and rejoined the dancing.

At the end of the next song, he returned to Ana. "Are you enjoying yourself?" he asked.

"Oh, yes," she smiled up at him. "It all seems like a dream."

"Did you save a dance for me?" Zarek asked. He turned his charming smile on her, and she couldn't stop herself from responding. The room suddenly felt warmer.

"I didn't think you would ask," she said. The crowd was full of other young ladies who all seemed eager to spend time with him.

"How could I not?" he replied, his eyebrows raised in surprise. He offered his hand. "I've been waiting all evening for the opportunity."

Feeling a little breathless, she took the offered hand, and they joined the dancing.

"And how do you like Sarine so far, Lady Cirana?"

She smiled up at him. "It's wonderful, Captain Zarek, just as you promised. You were right about everything."

"I apologize that your journey here was a little... demanding."

Her eyebrows shot up in surprise. Demanding? That wasn't the word that came to mind when she remembered their adventures.

She beckoned, and he bent down so she could whisper in his ear. "Thank you for everything you did for me."

His gray eyes met hers. "It was my honor to serve you, my lady."

Gradually, Ana became accustomed to her new life. At times, she still had terrifying nightmares, but they grew less frequent. She was happy.

As autumn faded into a quiet winter, she made new friends. And Zarek was often in the city. Sometimes they went riding, and she loved spending time with him. He knew his way around the emperor's lands and was friends with many of the soldiers. One day, he took Ana with him to the practice field.

"Would you like to shoot?" Zarek asked as they observed several soldiers practicing archery.

"I'll try," she said. "I'm sure you're already skilled at it."

"Of course," he teased. They selected a spot beside two other soldiers. One of them was tall and lanky, the other of medium height with pale blond hair. "Renard, Wes, this is Lady Cirana."

The two soldiers bowed respectfully, and she curtsied in response. "It's very nice to meet you both."

"Would you like to try, my lady?" Renard, the tall soldier, asked. "Have you ever shot before?"

She shook her head.

"Like this." He demonstrated how to draw the bow, aim along the shaft of the arrow, and release. His blue eyes squinted as he focused on his mark. He loosed the shot, and the arrow lodged in the very edge of the target, almost missing it entirely. Zarek and Wes laughed.

"The wind must have thrown off my shot," Renard protested, staring at the target, his brows knit in frustration. The others only laughed harder. He flushed with embarrassment and handed the bow to Ana.

Ana found it hard to draw the bowstring back, but she pulled it as far as she could and aimed. Her first shot missed the target, and her second, but the third struck the edge.

"Well done," Zarek exclaimed.

"You're already just as good as Renard," Wes said.

Ana smiled at their praise.

⸙

On an unseasonably warm day in late winter, Ana wandered into a part of the palace she had never seen before. The building always had another hall or wing to explore. It would take several months to discover it all.

Near the outer wall, she found a garden. When Ana peeked through the door, she saw a woman sitting by herself. Her wavy, golden hair was touched with gray at the temples. Fine lines marked the corners of her eyes and mouth. The garden around her seemed dead, awaiting the approach of spring.

Ana knew she had seen the woman before, but it took her a moment to remember where. The emperor's banquet. She was the one who had danced with Zarek and then left, angry with him.

"Hello," Ana said.

"Hello, Cirana," the woman replied.

Ana's eyes widened. "You know my name?"

"Everyone knows who you are."

Ana flushed a little at her words, feeling like an awkward country girl. "May I ask who you are?"

"My name is Mirithel."

"I saw you at the banquet. You were angry with Zarek. Why?"

Mirithel closed her eyes for a moment and drew in a deep breath.

Fearing she'd said something wrong, Ana's stomach tightened.

"He's my son."

Ana gasped. "You're his mother? Then why would you be upset with him? He's brave and strong. And kind."

"I asked him to promise me he would not put himself in danger, but he is determined to ignore my wishes. Of course, he's brave! Just like his father... I loved my husband more than anything, and he died on a quest for Emperor Callonen. I cannot endure losing my son in the same way."

Guilt and sympathy flooded through Ana. Talon had left Sarine to look for her, putting himself in danger to save her. She could sense Mirithel still grieved for his loss, even after all this time. She loved Zarek and desperately wanted him to be safe.

Ana had caused all this. Nothing she could say would change that. She couldn't face Mirithel any longer and fled without another word.

MIRITHEL

Mirithel shook her head. She shouldn't have been so hard on the girl. It wasn't really her fault, and there was nothing Cirana could have done to prevent Talon and Zarek from risking themselves.

The boy was willful and even more stubborn than his father had been. Years ago, when he'd been a little boy, she'd made a desperate effort to stop him from becoming a soldier. She couldn't bear the thought of him being killed like his father.

She hadn't meant to think of Talon. His absence still hurt. Even after all these years, she heard his voice in her mind and remembered the touch of his hands, the way it felt to have his strong arms around her, the flutter of excitement in her chest when he smiled at her. And he'd been a good father, always so gentle with their son. Mirithel opened her eyes and started when she saw Zarek. She couldn't help it when she'd been lost in memories of Talon. Zarek had grown up to look so much like him, tall and gray-eyed. And the older their son grew, the more he resembled Talon, until it hurt Mirithel to look at him.

Zarek's brows drew together in concern. "Mother? Are you all right?"

She looked up at him and reached out to take his hands. "Zarek, I'm sorry I was angry the night of the banquet."

He sat down beside her. "It's all right. I understand why you felt that way, but I'm home now, safe. Still, I don't want you to be upset if I need to travel again."

"Is there another girl that needs rescuing?" Mirithel could hear the bitterness in her own voice.

"No."

"Do you know what it felt like, waiting here for all those months? I was afraid you wouldn't make it back. Dane didn't. You can't tell me you weren't in just as much danger. And you came back looking like you hadn't eaten in six months."

"I know. I'm sorry, Mother. But I had to go. They would have killed Ana if I hadn't."

"A girl is worth risking your life for?"

"She is."

"She was just here. She seems ordinary," Mirithel protested.

Zarek shook his head. "You know nothing about her. You have no idea what our journey was like! We jumped off a cliff into the river, and she nearly died in the water. She fell off a ledge and broke her arm in the mountains. I had to force her to walk through a snowstorm so she wouldn't die from the cold. And every single night, the demons were chasing us. She's the bravest person I've ever known. And if she hadn't healed the emperor, the Shekkar would have come here and destroyed the city. Do you know what they're like, really?"

"I saw it," Mirithel whispered. "When Harrow came back, and your father... didn't..."

The memory burned in her mind. She would never forget the deep gashes in Harrow's skin or the blood turned black from the demon's poison. Talon would have endured the same pain.

"Well, I have seen it many times now. Felt it even! If Ana hadn't healed me, I wouldn't be here. They have no mercy, not for anyone. Not for you, not for her. They wouldn't spare her because she's young, or alone, or couldn't defend herself. They would have torn her to pieces, and then they would have come after you."

Mirithel hung her head, tears slipping from her eyes. She knew he was right, but she couldn't help clinging to Zarek. He was all she had left. "I'm sorry," she whispered. "I should not be angry with you or with her." Looking up to meet his gaze, she traced the lines of the scars from his forehead across his cheek.

His expression was determined. "I need you to understand why I had to do it."

"Oh, Zarek." She pulled him close. "What would I do without you?"

"I know how you feel," he said, "and I'm sorry Father's gone. But I still have to live my life."

"You could have chosen some less dangerous life."

"But I didn't. I chose this long ago," Zarek said.

She drew back. "Has Callonen asked you to go out again?" she demanded.

"No. This has nothing to do with Callonen. For now, he's ordered me to stay in the city."

A sigh of relief passed her lips. "Please, obey his orders. Stay here. Whatever it is, let someone else go. You don't ever have to leave the Warding again."

"I can't promise you I won't," Zarek said stubbornly. "I want to protect this land, to protect you. Would you really have me stay here? Safe? Wait until I grow old and die and my life has meant nothing? Is that really what you want?"

She couldn't answer him.

CHAPTER TWELVE

YEAR OF WARDING 39, WHITE CITY, SARINE

ANA

WHEN ANA HEARD A knock at her door, she hastily wiped her eyes and nose, hoping to hide that she'd been crying. "Come in," she called from where she sat curled on the couch across from the fireplace.

It was Zarek. Taking one look at her face, he said, "So you met my mother today." He took a seat beside her.

She couldn't hide how she felt from him. "Yes."

"And she wasn't very nice, was she?" Zarek asked.

Ana shook her head. "It's not that. Your father died trying to rescue me. I understand why she doesn't like me. She's just worried about you."

"I know," Zarek said. "But I'll bet she made you think I was only in danger because of you?"

"No," Ana lied, but she couldn't meet his eyes.

"I know how it is," he said, lifting her chin until she was looking into his eyes. "She made you feel that if not for you, I would never have been outside the Warding."

Ana nodded. "I didn't want you to get hurt protecting me. I never want anyone to be hurt because of me again." She wiped tears from her face.

He put his arm around her shoulders. "I understand," Zarek said. "But no one else is like you. You can help other people who are hurting. You kept me safe out there too. We saved each other, and that means we'll be friends forever."

She smiled and leaned into him. "Friends forever!" His arm tightened around her.

"I'm not sure what's going to happen in the future, but there's a chance I might have to go away for a while," he admitted. "We're going to have to do something to save Sarine."

She drew back and glared at him. "You said you'd stay here."

"I know," he said.

"If you leave the Warding, how will you stay safe without me?" she asked. Sudden determination filled her. "I'll come with you. That way, if you get hurt, I can heal you. I'll walk fast and try not to slow you down too much."

"Ana..." he said.

She looked down, knowing what he was going to say. If he needed to leave, he couldn't take her with him.

"Ana."

Looking up, she met his gaze, her eyes full of tears.

"This is important," Zarek said, grasping her shoulders and looking straight into her eyes. "Whether I am here or not, you must never leave the Warding for any reason. Don't even go near it. Do you understand?"

"Yes," she agreed.

"The king of Ara, the one who sent the Shekkar, he wants your ring, and if he could lure you out of the Warding, he would take you."

Ana drew in a quick breath.

"I'm not trying to frighten you," Zarek said. "You're safe here, but you must never leave the Warding. Promise me."

"I promise," she said.

"Even if I have to be away, the emperor will protect you," Zarek said. "He cares about you."

"How long will you be gone?"

"I'm not sure," he said. "Nothing has been decided yet."

"Will it be dangerous?"

"No!" Zarek scoffed.

She didn't think he was being completely honest. "Are you sure?"

"I'll be safe. Don't worry. Even if I have to leave and it takes a while, I'll be back." Zarek kissed her forehead, then stood and left the room. Ana contemplated the doorway he had disappeared through. How could he ask people not to worry about him? He was great at fighting, but his bravery often put him in danger. No wonder his mother was upset.

ZAREK

The morning after his conversation with Ana, Emperor Callonen gathered his advisers and Zarek in his council room. General Gray, a stocky man with dark hair and beard, the leader of Sarine's army, was among them. Everyone sat silently at the long table.

"Thank you for coming," Callonen said. "I am grateful to be seated here with you once more. But our enemy is still out there, and we need to decide what to do."

"We are so grateful that you're still with us. Without you, our empire would already have fallen," General Gray said.

The men around the table voiced their agreement, and everyone applauded and congratulated him until Callonen held up his hand for silence. "I appreciate your support, and I admit it was a very close call," he said. "Thank you all for your loyalty. But we owe a debt of gratitude to Zarek and Cirana, for without them, Sarine might already be gone."

Zarek shook his head. "So many others helped."

Callonen bowed his head sadly. "I feel the weight of all those who have died."

"We have to do something about it," Zarek exclaimed. "The demons are still out there, and they are merciless. We need a way to destroy them. Your father killed the Shekkar who destroyed the old kingdom. We've all heard the story of how he defeated them and Sarine was founded."

Emperor Callonen's face was grave. "He used an ancient enchanted sword to kill them. Blackbane. I was only a child, but I remember. I even held the sword once."

"Didn't he pass the weapon on to you?" General Gray asked.

Callonen shook his head. "Blackbane was stolen. Now, when we desperately need the sword's power, we have no way to fight the Shekkar. Zarek is the only one in recent years to fight them and survive. Many years ago, Zarekathus created three smaller weapons bearing the same enchantment. Two are lost, and I gave mine to Zarek before he left to find Cirana." He turned to Zarek. "Tell them what happened."

"I killed one of the Shekkar in Bright Springs and two more in the mountains using the enchanted knife. But the last time they came, there were too many. The blade was broken."

"How did you survive their attack?" General Gray asked.

Zarek's stomach clenched at the memory of that night. He shook his head. "I didn't. If Ana hadn't used the ring to heal me, I would have died."

"How many demons were there?" General Gray asked. "It only took a few of them to destroy the old kingdom."

Zarek remembered that night vividly—the cold air, the scent of snow, and the black shapes running at him. He would never forget the feeling of knowing he couldn't stop them all, and that as soon as they had finished with him, they would hunt down Ana.

The others were staring at him, so Zarek cleared his throat and spoke. "I think about twenty. Without a weapon to fight them, it doesn't really matter. Even one of them could kill hundreds of us." He turned to Callonen. "Do you know who stole the sword?"

Callonen was silent for a long moment. His dark eyes were hard. "My brother must have taken it before he went to Ara."

"Without the sword, our only recourse is to hide within the Warding. Do we really want to live like caged rabbits?" General Gray asked, shaking his head.

"Even if we try, how long can that last?" Zarek protested. "Either Callonen will die or Haldreth will find a way to break the

Warding." Of course, protecting their nation wouldn't be easy when their only chance of defense lay in the hands of their enemy. It took him a moment to think it over. He glanced around the table and then met Callonen's eyes. "We know what we have to do." All along, he'd been afraid this would be the only solution. "We have to go to Ara."

The group erupted into heated discussion. Zarek saw the despair on Callonen's face.

After a long moment, the emperor raised his hand, silencing everyone. "When my brother left Sarine, he stole many magical artifacts that belonged to the wizard, including the one he may have used to awaken the Shekkar. His power is precious to him, and he will have these things well guarded. We've had scouts watching Ara constantly for years. He's still at Hakvere, and the place is impenetrable. It would be impossible to sneak in."

"But those weapons are our only chance to defeat him!" Zarek protested.

General Gray met his gaze. "You're talking about infiltrating the fortress, locating the weapons, and escaping with them. Then, you'd need to reach the Warding. There are too many demons for one man to battle all at once. Even with the sword, you'd need a way to fight them one by one." Gray shook his head. "If I thought your plan had any chance of success, I'd go myself. But I don't."

"I know a way into Ara," a captain said. "They're recruiting men from the lands around."

It was the best idea they'd heard yet. "I'll join the Aran army," Zarek said.

"No!" Callonen protested.

General Gray seemed to consider it. "That might succeed. But being a recruit in his army is a very long way from being close enough to Haldreth to even get into the fortress of Hakvere, let alone anywhere near the armory."

Zarek nodded. "It would be difficult, and it would take years. But we have to try."

"It might work," another captain said. "I would go. We could send more than one man."

"And if you're caught?" General Gray protested. "Ara is not a pleasant place for its enemies. They would torture you until you revealed the others."

"That's why I would go alone," Zarek said.

Callonen stood abruptly. "No one is going to Ara," he said flatly. Everyone stared at him in silence. He turned around without saying another word and left the room.

Zarek went about his work without speaking of Ara again. When he saw Callonen, the emperor's expression remained strained, and he pinned Zarek with that penetrating stare, as if he could see into Zarek's soul. He probably could. No one cared to defy the emperor. He would know if they did.

A week after the meeting, Zarek rode out of the city at dawn with orders to ride with the company heading for Sergeant Hal's camp near the Warding. They would provide the camp with supplies and messages and stay to assist Hal for several days. As they traveled, Zarek had plenty of time to think about the insurmountable problem they faced.

The Shekkar gave their master a deadly advantage. With them on his side, no one could defeat the king of Ara. He would keep attacking until he owned the entire world. And who could stop him?

Zarek understood why Callonen had forbidden him to go after the sword. He knew enough of the festering pain in the emperor's heart. Talon had been Callonen's best friend. The emperor felt like he'd killed Talon himself, and Mirithel had never forgiven him. He'd never forgiven himself.

Callonen could never send anyone to find the sword, and Zarek knew in his heart it was a mistake. Maybe the kind of fatal mistake that destroyed nations. Without a weapon against the dark magic, Sarine would fall. After all, Callonen could not live forever. Sooner or later, darkness would come. Unless someone stopped it.

At noon on the fourth day of their ride, the company reached the camp at the edge of the Warding. Sergeant Hal greeted them. They gathered in the command tent to hear Hal's reports and give him the messages from General Gray.

Long after everyone slept, Zarek lay awake, staring at the tent canvas above him. Silence shrouded the camp. Unable to rest, he slipped from his bed. It was time to act.

He lit a lantern and covered it so only a sliver of light escaped. At this hour, the command tent was empty and silent. He allowed a little more light out and looked around. It didn't take him long to find what he needed—parchment, quill and ink. Taking a seat at the desk, he began to write.

CALLONEN

In the middle of the night, Callonen sat bolt upright, his blanket falling away. He slid out of bed and stumbled to the door. The startled guard outside jumped as the emperor threw the door open.

"Where's Gray?" Callonen demanded.

"A-Asleep, my emperor."

"Find him! Please! I need him!"

A few moments later, General Gray entered the room, wearing a robe tossed hastily over his nightclothes. Despite his attire, his eyes were alert. "What's wrong, Emperor?"

Callonen invited Gray into his room and shut the door behind them. "Zarek is at the edge of the Warding, and he's decided to disobey my commands."

"Treason?" Gray asked.

Callonen shook his head. "No. He's more loyal to me than anyone. He's so loyal that he's convinced the only way to save Sarine is to go to Ara."

Gray's eyes widened in surprise. "You ordered him not to. I'll send a detachment of men to follow him at once. Is he at the east border?"

"Yes, Sergeant Hal's camp," Callonen said. "Tell them to hurry. Please! He can't do this."

"They'll be riding within ten minutes," Gray promised, hurrying out the door.

Callonen collapsed into a chair, shaking his head. It was already too late. He should have known what Zarek would do. He should have locked the boy in the dungeon instead of letting him go anywhere near the Warding.

Maybe Zarek would still change his mind. Unable to rest, Callonen rose and paced back and forth. His thoughts focused on Zarek, long miles away, at the edge of Callonen's power.

He would go to Ara, Zarek decided. He was leaving now, tonight, and he would join the Aran army. Pulling off his dark-green uniform, he folded it carefully, almost reverently, laying his armor and weapons neatly on top of it. He set two letters with the other things. Nothing remained to identify him as a servant of the emperor. He was sorry to disobey, but he loved his family and his nation, and he couldn't bear to see them destroyed. Somehow, he would find the sword.

Zarek vanished into the night.

Callonen sank to his knees. "No!" he yelled at the wall.

The guards came running in. "What can we do, Emperor?" But there was nothing anyone could do now.

Four days later, Callonen sat at the table in the council chamber with General Gray and several of the captains. They had been deep in conversation when a soldier knocked.

"Message for you, Emperor." The man placed two letters and the rest of Zarek's things in front of Callonen. He stared at them and took in a slow breath. He wanted to shout, and he felt the urge to smash something.

At least he hadn't been taken completely by surprise. He already knew what Zarek had done. But seeing the evidence in front of him made it worse. His anger drained away, sick sorrow taking its place. He picked up the letter Zarek had addressed to his mother. "Please take this to Lady Mirithel."

The guard at the door took the letter and left.

For several long moments, they sat in uncomfortable silence before Callonen opened the letter addressed to him. Zarek's explanation was exactly what he had expected. Callonen already knew what the words would say. But that wouldn't shift the blame from Callonen if anything should happen to the boy. There were many dangers along the path that Zarek had chosen, and Callonen couldn't stop his mind from reviewing each of them, one by one.

Callonen held the letter up. "Zarek's explanation for his actions. It's exactly as we discussed. He's gone to Ara, against my orders."

The door banged open, and Mirithel marched in, her eyes blazing. The Warding gave Callonen a much deeper sense of what was happening in her mind. She felt crazed, filled with despair and rage. She wanted him to suffer, as he had caused her to suffer. It was just, after all. He deserved her anger.

Callonen got to his feet facing her, not trying to resist, even though he knew exactly what she was about to do. She raised her fist and punched him in the jaw with all her strength. He stumbled backward, and the room exploded into chaos. The soldiers leapt to their feet, and a couple of them drew their swords. General Gray seized Mirithel by the arms, holding her immobile.

His face throbbing, the emperor regained his footing and turned back to face her.

"You did this!" she screamed. "How could you? After what you did to Talon? Zarek was all I had left!"

"I commanded him not to go," Callonen said.

"That's not true!" she insisted. "You need him. You sent him to Ara!"

"I ordered that no one should go!" Callonen protested.

"It's true," General Gray affirmed.

But Zarek hadn't listened. And Callonen had been foolish enough to think he would obey his emperor's command. The boy was stubborn and would do what he believed to be right. He would try to help Callonen and Sarine, even if he'd been ordered not to.

"I sent men to stop him," Callonen said. "They are still following him. I ordered them to bring him back, by force, if necessary."

Mirithel stared at him.

"I didn't send him!" Callonen insisted, suddenly desperate for her to believe him. "I wouldn't—"

She wrenched her arm away from Gray and stormed out the door, the note from her son still clenched in her fist.

ANA

Zarek had gone. The news had moved quickly through the palace. Ana heard all sorts of rumors. Some claimed that he was a traitor and had renounced his oath to the emperor. She never believed that, but she wanted to know what had happened.

Ana found Callonen standing at the edge of the parapet, looking out over the city as the sun sank behind the distant mountains. She stood beside him.

He turned to look down at her. "I knew you would have to ask, eventually."

And she could sense that he wasn't happy about it. "You don't have to tell me."

"No? I'm sure there are many people ready to tell you what they think happened."

"That's why I came to ask you," Ana said. "I've heard several tales that Zarek is a traitor, that he betrayed you, and I can't believe that."

Callonen took a deep breath. "Zarek has already seen his share of danger. So, when he presented a plan to go to Ara and search for a weapon to kill the demons, I could not agree to it."

A sudden chill settled in her belly. "He went to Ara?" No matter what Zarek claimed, his errand would be dangerous. Maybe even hopeless.

Callonen shook his head. "I should have locked him up before he could go."

"But he's quick." Everyone knew that. Ana had seen it. "He went out against your orders, and that's why people are saying he's a traitor?"

Callonen nodded, his mouth a tight line.

"But you will forgive him when he comes back, won't you? You wouldn't punish him?"

"I would welcome him home. Even so, he might find himself cleaning the stables for the rest of his life instead of leading my guard."

CHAPTER THIRTEEN

YEAR OF WARDING 39, WHITE CITY, SARINE

ANA

AT FIRST, ANA WAITED every day for news, but none came. Zarek did not return, even as winter wore away and spring came to the White City. Several more of the emperor's men were still abroad. Fear clutched at Ana every time she heard the Shekkar had killed someone, and she waited in desperation to find out if it was Zarek.

Once they brought back a man who had been attacked by a demon. When Ana entered the room, she closed her eyes tightly against the sight of his body, torn beyond recognition. She could feel it wasn't Zarek, but she could still sense the man's pain, and she had to heal him. After the agony and the unconsciousness passed and she woke again, he came to offer his gratitude and his wife wept at Ana's bedside.

After meeting them, Ana didn't mind that it had hurt so much. She was glad of the ring and that the woman didn't have to go home as a widow.

❧

The seasons came and went until, by the Sarine calendar, it was the fortieth year of the Warding. Ana was nearly eighteen, and she never stopped asking for news of Zarek even though he'd been gone almost a year.

In Callonen's care, Ana had everything she could want—in fact, far more than she ever thought to want. There were always fresh flowers in her room and beautiful clothes; every luxury she could imagine. He always made time for her if she wanted to talk.

Callonen treated her as if she were really his child, and she gave him the affection she would have given a father, doing anything she could to help him. They often shared meals, and he would stop or postpone his work for her. Even when important people visited the emperor, he made them wait in order to give his attention to Ana.

Tess was there to mother her, and she became a wonderful friend, always there if Ana needed her. And as she grew older, there were things she didn't want to discuss with Callonen.

❧

One night, Ana and Callonen stood on the west tower watching the sunset, as they often did. "You've done very well in your studies," he said.

"Thank you." His praise made her feel appreciated. As always, he was much too generous. "I've enjoyed learning about the customs of the nations around us."

"Good." He sounded pleased. "I hoped you might assist me. The king and queen of Paraman will make a state visit here next week. They don't like me much, and I thought perhaps you could help me smooth things over. We want very much to keep them as friends since we need all the allies we can get. The king of Kethel is so afraid of Ara that he won't even talk to me."

"You want me to help you entertain a king and queen?" she asked, surprised.

"Yes. You've studied the protocols. I could really use your help." He turned and smiled. "That is, if you don't mind."

She hugged him. Callonen should know she would do anything he asked. "Of course I will. But tell me, why don't they like you?"

He cleared his throat and looked away. "I, uh..."

She put her hand on his shoulder. "You're embarrassed. This had better be a good story." She looked at him expectantly, waiting for him to go on.

"Many years ago, my father signed a treaty with Paraman. Things were going well, the two nations on friendly terms. The king of Paraman had a beautiful daughter, and he hoped she would marry advantageously for his kingdom. He and my father spoke, and she came here to visit."

"They were hoping you would marry her, and she was horrible?" Ana guessed.

Callonen smiled. "She wasn't horrible. She was very nice, and I have to admit, every bit as beautiful as rumor had reported."

"Did she fall madly in love with you?"

He shrugged. "I hope not. I don't think we knew each other that well, and I never meant to hurt her."

"But you didn't like her?"

"It wasn't even that. I just couldn't look at her in that way. I couldn't think of anyone but Allia. No matter how badly everyone wanted me to marry someone else, I couldn't do it. My father was furious when I sent the princess back to Paraman. And her parents have avoided me since then. They are still our allies and have remained in contact, but it's been many years since they have agreed to visit." Ana knew Callonen was still in love with Allia. She could sense the loss and pain he felt, and she wished she had some way to heal him.

When the king and queen of Paraman visited, and they were civil and respectful. Ana could tell they loved their people and were kindly rulers, and she enjoyed getting to know them. The leaders of both nations had many of the same concerns. Neither of them were friends of Ara. And Ara was expanding in all directions, their armies rapidly growing as people flocked to join them in exchange for safety from the demons.

"We can't just stand by and let them take over," Callonen said, over the council room table.

The king of Paraman was a tall man with iron gray hair and beard. He didn't look happy.

"Are you asking me to send out my troops against the Shekkar?" he exclaimed. "You know as well as I do that no one has any defense against them!"

"Only the Warding, Your Majesty," Ana said. "No other land can keep them out."

The king paused to take a deep breath. "I suppose that is true."

"And I will always offer sanctuary inside the Warding for anyone who wishes to enter," Callonen said. "If Ara destroys the rest of Kethel, they may turn toward Paraman, despite the distance between."

"I fear Ara is determined to swallow every other nation," the king said, shaking his head. "I would rather side with you than with them, but I don't have the power to stop them."

Ana's mind flashed back to Zarek and his quest to find a way to defeat the demons. Had he failed, even been killed far away from home? Could he still be searching?

By the time they finished negotiating, Paraman agreed to maintain their alliance with Sarine, though they would not send troops against the demons. At the farewell banquet, Ana danced with the king of Paraman.

He smiled at her. "Lady Cirana. You've made our stay here very pleasant. And your help with our discussions was very welcome."

Ana returned his smile. "I'm glad. We count you among our friends."

The king nodded. "Our nations have a long history of friendship, and the misunderstanding with my daughter was long ago. It stung at the time, but she met someone else and has been happily married for many years. Despite the bad feelings over it, I know Emperor Callonen is a good man, and he's lucky to have you to help him."

When Ana joined Callonen for the next dance, he seemed delighted. "You're amazing, Ana," he exclaimed. "They adore you, and thanks to you, they've decided to overlook my shortcomings."

Ana laughed. "I think you give me too much credit."

In the months that followed, Ana became deeply involved in running the empire. She helped Callonen constantly and gradually took on more responsibility. She enjoyed the work, and her insight into their people's feelings provided a valuable asset.

During one of their frequent sunset talks, Callonen cleared his throat and met her eyes. "Ana, may I ask you something important?"

"Of course," she said.

"I don't know what's going to happen in the next several years. We've tried to form alliances with our neighbors as much as we can. But Ara is still out there, growing in power and influence every day. We've already had many conflicts along our borders, and with the Shekkar on their side, I don't have the power to stop them. As I plan for the future well-being of our empire, I want to name you as my heir."

"Your heir?" Ana asked. All the breath had left her lungs. He couldn't be serious. She was nobody, just an orphan raised in a tiny farming village. She stared at him, waiting for him to laugh and admit he was joking. "Are you... serious?"

Callonen met her gaze with no trace of humor in his expression. "I have never been more serious."

"You want me to rule Sarine after you?"

"As much as I wish it could be, I'm afraid it won't be exactly like that," he said. "I don't have a child of my own, and the Warding can only pass to my firstborn child. When I die, it will vanish and there won't be an empire any more. Sarine will fall. My brother will send the demons, and within a few days, we will all belong to Ara. For your safety, you'll have to leave Sarine immediately if anything ever happens to me. The king of Paraman will offer you his protection. We discussed this when he was here." Ana stared at him with narrowed eyes. "You're not telling me this because you're ill again or expecting something to happen to you, are you?"

"No, but I want to make your rank and position official. You should have the recognition you deserve for your skills." Callonen put his arm around her shoulders. "And I want everyone to know that you are truly my family. You would make a wonderful leader for Sarine. If we can kill the demons, then you would become the first Empress of Sarine."

She looked up at him. "You really think that I could rule Sarine?" He nodded, and she could sense he meant what he said.

"I know you could. You're caring, kind and intelligent. The people already love you, and you love them too. Over the next several months, I will have General Gray teach you what you will need to know in order to lead our army."

"Callonen..." She hugged him fondly. "I think maybe you have too much confidence in me. I'm not sure I can. But if you ask, I will try my best."

"I know you can do it. But either way, be aware that someone will be ready to take you to safety if things should go wrong."

"What can go wrong if I'm here with you and I have the ring?" she asked.

His gaze was stern. "Your presence is a great source of protection, of course. But the ring is not a guarantee."

She thought about it. Of course, there were things that could still go wrong. If he were attacked and she healed him, what if someone attacked him again while she was still recuperating?

He had a point. "You're right," she admitted. "But if anything ever harms you, I'll be right here to heal you. I promise."

"And I intend to make sure you are safe. With this new position, there will be a need for more protection. I am assigning a guard to watch over you full-time. At least one of the guards is near me every moment. It's something you have to get used to."

"You mean he would go with me wherever I went?"

Callonen nodded.

"Is that really necessary?" she asked, her eyes widening.

"Yes. There is nothing more important to me than your safety."

Callonen assigned Captain Toren to guard Ana. He was one of Callonen's most trusted men. Tall, quiet and serious, and he had a formidable reputation among the soldiers. On the first morning of the new arrangement, he waited outside her door. When she left the room, he silently followed her. She stopped in the hall and turned to face him. "Did the emperor tell you not to speak to me?" she asked him. "You're just going to follow me wherever I go?"

"That's right, my lady," he said.

She looked back at him. "If you're going to follow me everywhere, you could at least say good morning."

The corners of his mouth twitched, and he bowed to her. "Good morning, my lady."

"I've never had a guard before," she said. "What if my routine disturbs you?"

"Emperor Callonen assigned me to see that you are safe," he said. "I will fulfill my duties to the best of my abilities."

"What if I go out into the market and go shopping, or sit in the garden for hours with my friends? Won't you be bored?" she asked.

"As the emperor ordered, I will follow you wherever you go. You don't have to consult me about what you do. It's my job to keep you safe."

"I appreciate that, Captain," she said.

He smiled then, and he didn't look nearly so intimidating.

It didn't take long for Ana and Toren to become friends. After Callonen's announcement that Lady Cirana was his heir, she received a lot more attention—especially from men. After her eighteenth birthday, a steady stream of suitors came, hoping to win her heart, from noblemen of assorted ages and foreign dignitaries to soldiers and tradesmen who worked in the city.

Some of Ana's admirers left her feeling uncomfortable, making her grateful to have Captain Toren constantly beside her.

On one occasion, she had dined with the son of a nobleman at his home. After dinner, they strolled in the garden under the stars. He took her hand in his as they walked. The stars glittered overhead.

"You are so beautiful," he murmured.

And just like that, she realized he intended to kiss her. Ana removed her hand from his. "I'm sorry," she said. "Dinner was lovely, and I've enjoyed our time together, but I don't want to give you the wrong impression. I'm not ready to..."

He did not understand her meaning. Instead, he put his arms around her and pulled her close.

"Stop," she ordered, shoving him away with all her strength and turning to make a quick departure.

He must have tried to follow because she heard a heavy blow, and when she whirled around, the young man was facedown in the dirt, Toren's boot in the middle of his back.

"I believe Lady Cirana made her wishes clear," Toren said courteously.

"I'm sorry," came the muffled reply.

"You should pay more attention to what she says." Toren applied a little more pressure. "You will improve your behavior in the future, won't you?"

"Yes," the young man gasped. "Get off me!"

Toren removed his foot, allowing the young man to scramble up, rubbing his bruised jaw. The would-be suitor and Ana stared at each other for a long, uncomfortable moment before he bowed awkwardly.

"Thank you for a lovely evening," he said.

"Thank you," she replied stiffly.

With a last glare at Toren, he departed.

In a moment, they were comfortably seated in the carriage, heading back to the palace.

❧

Busy months and seasons flowed by until a year had passed since Callonen named Ana his heir. One morning at breakfast, they were discussing her appointments for the day. Several of Ana's admirers had asked to see her.

"I didn't realize how many there would be," Callonen confessed. "I'm not prepared for this. What if you actually like one of them? I don't want you to grow up and marry. I want you to stay with me."

She reached over and gripped his hand fondly. "Don't worry yet," she said.

While there was no shortage of social occasions, few of her suitors were as easy to talk to as Zarek had been. Many were attractive, but none captured her attention until she met Gavin.

He was the youngest and newest member of the Emperor's Guard. The first time she saw him, he smiled at her as she passed him in the hall. He had dark eyes and dark, curly hair. Several days passed with no sign of him. At one of Callonen's banquets, he approached her and bowed. "I'm Gavin. Would you do me the honor of dancing with me?"

"I would." Ana extended her hand to him.

As he took it and led her toward the dance floor, her pulse quickened slightly.

He bowed, then smiled at her. "I'm flattered you would dance with me, my lady."

She couldn't help but notice he was an excellent dancer, and the pressure of his hand on her back made her feel warm. His build was athletic, his features attractive, and it was obvious that he was interested in her.

They shared several more dances that night, and he asked if he might see her again. "In five days, I have a break from my duties. Will you go riding with me?"

She hesitated for a moment. What should she say? Callonen probably wouldn't like it much, but she wanted to accept Gavin's invitation. Surely it wasn't wrong to enjoy herself a little? "Yes," she said.

The next morning at breakfast, she told Callonen about Gavin. He shook his head. "I was afraid this would happen. You sound as if you like this boy."

"He's nice," she said. And very charming. But she didn't say that out loud. "I'm almost twenty," Ana continued. "Many of my friends have married already. I've waited a long time to meet someone."

Callonen had to smile. "I know you have. I'm sorry. I'm just not ready to let you go. If he's one of my guards, isn't he too old for you?"

"He's twenty-four," Ana told him. "He just came to the city."

"The new one, with the dark hair? He seems like a nice young man. I don't sense anything from him that would cause me to worry. Where is he from?"

"Some town outside the Warding. I had never heard of it."

"Where does he want to take you?"

"He wants to go riding."

Callonen smiled. "Of course, you may go with him if you wish, but Captain Toren will still accompany you. He's the best man I have, and I trust him with my life."

Ana groaned. Toren was a good friend, and she appreciated his efforts to fend off unwelcome advances. But what would they do if there came a time when she felt ready to accept someone's attention? It would be awkward to get to know Gavin with a guard along. "It's not like we'd be going very far from the city."

"I know," Callonen said. "And I'm sorry, but I have to be sure you're safe."

On the day of Ana's ride with Gavin, Toren shadowed her. By now, Toren knew her well enough to know that his presence would be a little awkward. He said nothing as he joined them and tried to remain inconspicuous.

Gavin didn't look happy about the arrangement. He was a member of the Emperor's Guard, after all. But Callonen himself had assigned Captain Toren to protect Ana.

"I guess the emperor doesn't trust me," Gavin said sadly.

Ana's stomach sank with embarrassment. "I'm sure it's not that," she said. "He insists I always have a guard."

"So you're a prisoner?"

Ana was shocked for a moment. "No, of course not."

Gavin looked down at her. He touched her face with his fingertips. "I can see why he guards you so closely," he whispered.

Her heart beat faster.

CHAPTER FOURTEEN

ANA

A NA AND GAVIN RODE out of the gates with Toren following behind them. It was a fine summer day, and Ana hadn't ridden outside the city in a while. The emperor's lands were quiet, the farms and orchards well-tended, the fields green with young grain. They followed a trail that led into a forest.

"It's beautiful," Ana said, smiling at the dappled sunshine filtering down through the leaves. "It reminds me of how much I loved the woods when I was a child."

"I heard you didn't always live in the White City. Where did you come from?" Gavin asked.

"I spent my childhood in Bright Springs, a tiny village just inside the border of Kethel."

Gavin grinned. "I've never heard of it."

Ana returned his smile. "No one has. It's a long way from here. A beautiful grove of oak trees grew behind the inn where I lived, and when I wanted time to myself, that's where I went."

"Is that where you acquired your love of trees?"

"That must have been where it started," she admitted. "But this place is so beautiful, I don't know how anyone could disagree."

They rode along the bank of a little river. Deep shade covered the trail, and a few flowers bloomed beneath the wide trunks.

Zarek had shown her this trail years ago, before he'd left.

Ana heard the waterfall before she and Gavin could see it through the trees. For a time, their conversation paused as they listened to the water. They dismounted on the bank and took a short footpath to the edge of the pool below the falls.

"It's beautiful," Gavin said, leaning close to her ear so she could hear him above the pounding of the water. Ana sensed very little from him, only warmth. As they stood side by side, his hand found hers and held it. She had no desire to pull away. It felt good.

After a while, they returned to their horses and rode on, chatting about life in the White City and his training with the soldiers. He asked a few questions about her work with Callonen.

"Tell me more about your home," Ana said.

"It's a long way from here," he replied. "Just outside the Warding."

"Did you like it there?"

"Yes, but I always wanted to see the White City. Now that I have, I love it."

"Everything is wonderful here, isn't it?" she agreed.

They came out into the sunlight and paused in a meadow. Gavin had brought a meal for them, and they had lunch on the soft grass. Toren stayed back, saying nothing, becoming almost invisible.

The sun was setting as they rode back through the gates. Though the day had been pleasant, Ana breathed a sigh of relief to be inside the walls. She knew it was ridiculous since she was safe within the Warding, but she still didn't like to be outside the city gates after dark.

"I enjoyed being with you today," Gavin said.

"Me too," Ana answered. It was true. She'd had fun.

He bowed to her and smiled. "May I see you again?"

❧

Ana saw Gavin often over the next several days, and within a few weeks, she'd grown accustomed to seeing him daily. He brought her presents; beautiful things that she knew weren't easy to afford on a soldier's pay. Though she didn't sense much from him besides caring, he was always kind and attentive, and he seemed content to let their relationship move slowly.

They grew closer as time went on. One night, they stood on one of the towers watching the stars. She turned to look at him, and he kissed her gently.

Several weeks after that, Gavin told her he loved her, and Ana realized that the days of moving slowly had passed. She confided all this to Tess during one of their early-morning chats.

"And what do you feel for him?" Tess asked.

"I'm not sure," she said. "He's been sweet, and I like him, and he's so handsome..." Ana knew he was attracted to her, and he behaved as if she was very important to him. But did he love her? She wore the ring. If Gavin loved her, shouldn't she be able to sense the depth of his feelings?

"But...?"

"I'm not sure. What's love like, Tess? Is it when you know everything about someone, yet you still love them? When you've seen them happy and sad, and you want to be with them every moment? When they aren't there, you think about them all the time, and you're convinced they are the best person in the world?"

"That's right. Love means you would do anything for them." Tess agreed. "Is that what you feel for Gavin?"

"No," Ana confessed. "But I do like him. Should I stop seeing him?"

"I can't tell you that," Tess said.

Ana sighed. "When he says he loves me, I just don't know what to say."

"Well, you know that can't last. You're old enough to know your own heart and mind. It's time to decide."

"You're right, Tess. It's time to stop acting like a child. I can't keep hiding from this, and I won't lie to him." It would be difficult to tell him how she felt. She didn't know how he would react, but he would be upset, and she wasn't sure she felt ready.

Ana found Callonen in the dining room. He glanced up and smiled as she entered. "I hoped you would join me," he said, getting up to hold a chair out for her.

"Thank you," she said, taking a seat, placing an envelope beside her plate, and spreading the napkin over her lap.

"Did you miss me or is there something in particular on your mind?" he asked, looking pointedly at the letter.

Ana smiled at him. "Both, of course. I always miss you when I haven't seen you for a while. But I do want to ask you something. This message is from Rosie, who keeps the Blue Oak Inn at Hale Grove. She's become a good friend, and I've seen her many times as she's come to the city. She's invited me to come and stay with her for a week. With your permission, I'd like to accept her invitation."

"You met her when you first came into the Warding, didn't you?"

"Yes. Of course, she already knew Zarek, but she was so kind to me. It's been years now, and we've kept in touch. Her son and his wife will be there for some of the time, and she's invited me to see her first granddaughter."

"Hale Grove..." Callonen stared off into the distance, his eyes crinkled in thought. "It would take at least two days to get there."

"I know," Ana said. "It's been a while since I've ridden so far, but I'll be all right."

"If you prefer, you could take a carriage and stay at one of our outposts on your way there."

Ana nodded, hoping he would agree to it. She wanted to see more of Sarine, and she enjoyed spending time with Rosie.

"Hale Grove is a little close to the Warding," Callonen pointed out.

"It's still a long day's ride from the boundary," Ana protested. "And I promise I wouldn't go any nearer."

"What about Gavin? Would he be going with you?"

"I haven't told him anything about this yet," Ana said. "Callonen, I..." He met her eyes and waited for her to go on. She took a deep breath. "I don't love Gavin, however he feels about me. It's time to tell him I can't see him anymore."

Callonen's eyes widened in surprise. He let out a laugh that sounded relieved. "Even with the Warding, that's not what I thought you were going to say."

"I've spent a great deal of time thinking about this."

"So, he would not be going with you to Hale Grove?"

Ana shook her head. "He doesn't have enough leave saved to be gone that long. I expect he will ride to the inn and make the journey back with us."

"Is that when you're planning to tell him? Wouldn't it be better to discuss it before you go?"

Ana sighed. "I haven't decided what to say for sure. It's hard. I don't want to hurt him, but it's time. I plan on talking to Rosie about how best to tell him."

Callonen reached across the table and squeezed her hand. "You'll be all right. And so will he, in time."

"I hope so," Ana said. She could feel Callonen's worry about the trip. He would probably refuse to let her go.

Callonen regarded her. "You think I won't give you permission." She stared back. "Well?"

He sighed deeply. "I know I tend to be a little... overprotective. Please know it's just because I am worried about you being so near the edge of our lands. It's not because I think you would ever do anything inappropriate."

"That's a relief, at least," Ana said, one corner of her mouth lifting in an uneven smile. She picked up the letter, about to say that she would write Rosie and let her know she couldn't come.

"You can go," he said finally.

Surprise and excitement tingled inside her. She jumped out of her chair and circled the table to hug him and kiss his cheek. "Thank you! I promise I'll be careful!"

⁓

When Ana told Gavin her plan, he smiled, his expression happy for her.

"I know how much you wanted to spend time with her. I expected that she'd ask you to come and stay eventually. Rosie and I spoke of it during her last visit," he said. "She's wanted to invite you for a long time. But I'm surprised the emperor agreed to it."

"Me too!"

"I wish I could go with you," Gavin said, taking her hand. "I miss you every moment you're gone. With your permission, I will ride to Hale Grove to meet you. At least we will have the return journey together."

Being with her must be important to him. He would not take it well when she told him they were finished.

"I'm looking forward to spending time with you." He kissed her hand. "Even if it's impossible to get rid of Toren." A flash of annoyance crossed his face.

"He's only following Emperor Callonen's instructions." Ana had sensed from the beginning that Gavin didn't like Toren.

Gavin sighed. "I know. Be safe on the road, and I'll see you soon."

⁓

At sunrise the next day, Ana rode out of the city with Captain Toren and four guards. She had decided against traveling in a carriage, choosing to be outside in the open air where she could see the land as they rode. The autumn morning was peaceful, the weather perfect.

"Toren?"

"My lady?" he said, slowing his horse to ride beside her.

"I warned you when you began this assignment that it would be very boring for you." She looked over to meet his eyes. "I don't know if I've ever told you how much I appreciate your consistent work to keep me safe. Thank you."

"You're welcome," he said. "I realize that having a guard along is not always... convenient."

"Maybe not," she admitted, smiling, "but please don't take that as a poor reflection on you."

"Never," he replied.

"I should have asked if you minded riding all the way out to Hale Grove before I planned this trip."

"I don't mind, my lady," he said. "And you could have chosen the carriage. It might have been more comfortable."

Ana smiled. "I'd rather be out in the fresh air. Besides, I know you hate long carriage rides."

Toren opened his mouth to deny it, but then shook his head. "I didn't realize you knew that."

"It's all right," she assured him. "I chose to ride. We don't leave the city too often, and I want to look around."

"As you wish, my lady," Toren replied. "I can't help but notice the absence of a certain young man. Was he not able to join you?"

"He couldn't stay the whole time. He's coming in a week to meet us at the inn and ride back with us. Will that be all right with you?"

He nodded. "Of course, my lady. I know it's difficult to explore a relationship without having privacy, but I've been impressed by how gracefully you've handled it. Spying on you would never have been my choice, but I've been here the whole time, and I can't help but wonder if your feelings are the same as his."

She sighed. "You're right. They're not."

Toren met her gaze. "Gavin doesn't deserve you. This kind of thing doesn't get easier with time. It's better to get it over with."

Ana's week at the Blue Oak Inn passed more quickly than she had expected. Rosie made a charming hostess. They took walks and rides together and explored the market near the inn. They ate delicious suppers in the common room while everyone joked and laughed. Rosie proudly introduced her first grandchild, a warm little bundle with soft downy hair. The guests made a fuss over her and congratulated the new parents.

With all the smiling faces surrounding her, Ana's thoughts went suddenly to Zarek. He was the one who had first brought her here. Now he'd been gone a long time. Was he safe? Was he alone? Was there anyone to support him and laugh with him? Did he ever think of her?

He'd promised they would be friends forever.

As they finished their meal, Ana looked to where Captain Toren stood in his customary place near the door, keeping an eye on everything. "Will you please join us for a moment? Rosie's made pie. I know apple is your favorite."

His stern face relaxed into a rare smile. "You know me well," he admitted, "and I thank you for asking."

He joined them at the table to enjoy a piece of pie before resuming his post.

❧

The day arrived when Ana was to return to the city. Gavin hadn't arrived yet, but she and Toren could meet him on the road. Rosie shared a farewell lunch with her. They had nearly finished their meal when the stable master bent to whisper in the innkeeper's ear.

"Excuse me a moment, won't you? I'll be right back." Rosie followed him out the door.

A few moments later, the stable master came running in, his face white with shock. "There's been an accident!"

Ana jumped to her feet. "What happened?" She ran to the door. Toren was there ahead of her, his hand on the hilt of his sword, and they followed the man to the stable.

Inside they saw someone bent over Rosie's prostrate form. Ana saw the white uniform with a diagonal band of gold across the chest that identified the Emperor's Guard, and when he turned to look at them, she recognized Gavin.

"She's hurt!" he said. "One of the horses broke its tether. Something must have frightened it, and I think when it reared, a hoof struck her head. I didn't see what happened. I'm trying to slow the bleeding."

Ana knelt beside Rosie, finding her face white and her eyelids closed. Gavin held a wad of cloth against the side of Rosie's head. The injury was serious. Ana sensed the pain only faintly, as if it were far away. Her friend would not last long. Even if they could find a healer, what would he be able to do? Blood ran out from beneath Gavin's hand.

There was only one thing Ana could do. When she touched Rosie's forehead, she felt her head exploding and a heavy darkness. She couldn't see—she couldn't move. The pain faded into blackness.

CALLONEN

Callonen sat in his customary place at the head of the long table. General Gray and several of his officers had gathered.

"That will work, my lord," Gray said, pointing to a large map spread between them. "It will cover the east border well and—" he broke off, staring at Callonen.

Callonen had been focused on their discussion until the Warding became overwhelming. Usually, it was nothing more than a continual distraction in the back of his mind. Now it captured all his attention. A man had intentionally caused an accident, injuring someone. "Gavin!" Callonen jumped to his feet. He had trusted Gavin as a member of his own guard, allowing him to spend time with Ana.

In fact, he was with her now.

Nausea churned in Callonen's belly. Something horrible was happening.

He ran for the stables. General Gray followed him, gathering several of the guard as they went. They had nearly reached the gates when Callonen realized Gavin had attacked Captain Toren, intent on killing him.

Now Callonen couldn't sense Ana. Where was she? What had happened to her? She was the only reason anyone would attack Toren. Callonen seized the reins of a horse, mounted it, and made for the gate. His guards fell in behind him as he rode like a madman toward Hale Grove.

They rode for the rest of the day and throughout the night, switching horses at outposts along the way. Callonen couldn't pause, couldn't wait. When they reached Hale Grove, it was noon the next day. It wasn't hard to find the Blue Oak Inn. They reined in at the door.

Callonen jumped from his horse and ran inside. "Where is Rosie?" he demanded.

The startled waitress responded, "Your Majesty, follow me, please." She led him down a hall and opened a door. "It's the emperor."

A woman with gray hair got up from beside the bed and bowed to him. She had a kind face, only now it was taut with worry and marred by heavy bruising on one cheekbone. This must be Rosie.

With a shock, Callonen realized the man lying in the bed, swathed in bandages, was Toren. Callonen bent to one knee beside him.

"Toren?"

"I'm sorry, Emperor," Toren gasped, speaking only with great effort. "I should never have trusted him. I failed you, and I failed her."

"It's my fault," Rosie exclaimed. "I was hurt, and Lady Cirana healed me. It was a miracle. I woke up to see Gavin drive his blade into Toren, and when I tried to stop him, he hit me. I sent the stable master and all the grooms after him."

Callonen's eyes returned to the bruising on her face. Tears were running from Rosie's eyes. "He took her."

Callonen mounted a fresh horse and headed toward the border, sensing which way Gavin had gone. His guards hastily followed in his wake. They rode the rest of the day.

By the middle of the night, they reached the Warding. Gavin's trail led slightly to the north, bypassing the company of the emperor's army, heading straight for the border. Callonen followed him right up to the edge.

He would have continued. Ana was all he could think about. Nothing else mattered until he found her. But his horse snorted and sidestepped nervously. Callonen heard their voices before he saw them.

Shekkar. The demons stood in a line along the border, hissing and beckoning to him.

Callonen pulled his mount to a stop.

A man came up behind the demons, still wearing the uniform of the Emperor's Guard.

"Gavin!" Callonen yelled, "Why would you betray us? Where is she?"

Gavin laughed. "She's long gone, my emperor." Sarcasm dripped from the title. Gavin looked at the Shekkar, who stood on either side of him, as if eagerly awaiting his command. He turned to Callonen with an icy smile. "Go ahead. Please. Ride on. Take just one step outside the Warding."

Callonen yelled in frustration, and the demons shrieked back at him and reached out with their claws. His terrified horse reared and shied away from the border. Callonen dismounted and stood staring at them.

He confronted Gavin. "How did you hide from the Warding?"

"You think that nothing can deceive your precious Warding," Gavin sneered. "I've been planning this the entire time, and you never suspected."

Icy dread twisted in Callonen's stomach. "What about Ana? You said you loved her!"

Gavin smiled slowly. "Oh, I do. And now she will remain in my care. And there's nothing you can do to get her back. She will live the rest of her life in Ara, just like her mother."

"No!" The cry ripped from Callonen's chest. It felt as if his heart had torn in two, parting along the jagged, unhealed wound formed by losing Allia.

Callonen couldn't stand it. He lunged forward, but hands seized him from both sides, holding him back. He struggled against them with all his strength.

Gavin stood just out of reach, laughing at him, and the demons begged him to come. Only one thing mattered in his mind.

They had Ana.

Callonen screamed at them, all thought and reason gone from his mind, raging and struggling against the men who restrained him. He would kill Gavin. With his bare hands, he would rip the man apart. It didn't matter if the demons tried to stop him. He didn't care if the empire fell and they all died.

He had to save Ana.

PART TWO

BETRAYAL

CHAPTER FIFTEEN

YEAR OF WARDING 21, WHITE CITY, SARINE

ALLIA

Allia felt a quiver of excitement in her middle as the wagon rolled through the gates of the White City. The spring weather was warm, a cloudless blue sky arching overhead. She rode in the wagon beside Bend, an old farmer who had been a neighbor and family friend for many years.

"The palace won't be hard to find," he said. "Are you sure they'll give you a job?"

Allia patted her pocket. "I have a letter here for my mother's old friend Mara, who runs the place. I think they will. And if they don't, I'll remind them I am the granddaughter of Zarekathus, the most famous wizard in all of Sarine. And without him, our nation wouldn't exist. I've even met the emperor."

Bend raised his bushy eyebrows. "It's not nice to tease an old farmer. How does a girl from the country meet an emperor?"

"I'm not teasing you. It's true. Years ago, he came to help my grandfather, but by the time he arrived, it was too late."

Bend patted her shoulder awkwardly. "I'm sorry. Everyone respected Zarekathus. We all grieved when he died. And your mother. I'm sorry, Allia."

A moment of silence fell as they remembered lost loved ones.

Allia took a deep breath and squared her shoulders. "We miss them, but we have to go on."

"So, you're going to march up that hill and ask for an audience with the emperor? Are you looking for a job or do you expect them to polish a throne for you?" Bend teased, his heavy wrinkles deepening as he smiled.

"I'm not asking for an audience. He's the emperor, and I'm sure he doesn't remember me. But a job will be fine," she assured him. "It won't be any harder than the work I'm used to on the farm."

"Well, if it goes badly or you change your mind, meet me back here. I'll be on my way home as soon as I sell these." He gestured to the back of his wagon, loaded with spring produce.

"Thanks, Bend, but I'll be staying. I appreciate the ride, though." She jumped down from the seat as the old farmer pulled his horses to a stop.

Bend grinned. "I'll tell your brothers you got here safely."

Allia looked up toward the tall white towers that crowned the city. She left the farmer with a wave, slung her bag over her shoulder, and walked up the hill.

Horses, carts, carriages and people of all descriptions thronged the streets; everyone from farmers and tradesmen to elaborately dressed nobles traveling with impressive entourages.

Allia wore simple clothes, but she was eighteen and out on her own for the first time in her life. She would look for something new to wear after she'd earned some money.

Following the street up the hill, she came to the back entrance of the tall white palace. Several armed men dressed in spotless white tunics trimmed with gold guarded the gate, and Allia felt their eyes on her as she approached the nearest one.

He stepped into her path. "You have business in the palace today, my lady?" he asked. "I've never seen you here before."

"I'm here to see Mara, the head of the household. I have a letter for her." She held up the folded parchment for the guard to see.

His gaze moved from the letter to her face, lingering on the golden waves of her hair, and his smile became charming.

She could sense that he felt… attraction, and she felt her cheeks heat.

"Would you like me to guide you?" He smiled, bowing.

"You're very courteous, but no, thank you," she said. "I'm sure I can find her."

His smile faltered slightly. "Very well. Go through those doors to the end of the hall and turn right to the kitchens. If she's not there, the cook will help you find her."

"Thank you."

The guard watched disappointedly as she walked through the doorway.

Would all the soldiers be that… friendly? If so, she would have to be on her guard.

Allia walked down a long hall with several doors and side passages opening off it. She heard many voices and footsteps coming from behind her, and the space that had been empty became packed with people. The crowd carried her along until she stepped into an empty passage to let them go by. Many were soldiers in dark green uniforms, dusty and tired, and she guessed they'd been practicing their drills.

She realized she wasn't alone. A soldier stood leaning against the wall, one hand gripping his opposite arm.

"Hello," she said, still focused on the crowded hall she'd just left. "I decided to let everyone pass."

"Hello," he responded.

He had dark hair that fell in untidy waves over his forehead, but as soon as Allia looked at him directly, she noticed an uncomfortable tightness in his expression. And now that she was nearer to him, she could sense a nagging pain. Was he injured?

"What's wrong?"

He maintained the hold on his arm. "Nothing. I'm all right."

Her younger brothers used the same sort of tone when they didn't want anyone to know that something bothered them. "But you're hurt?"

He shook his head. "It's minor."

"It is hurting you," she pointed out. "Can I help?"

"All right." He held out his left arm, pointing to the strap of his armor. "The buckle is stuck. Will you loosen it, please?" He shook his head. "I can't believe I let him hit me that hard."

"Someone tried to hurt you?"

His dark eyes widened at the suggestion, and he shook his head. "It was only practice."

As he straightened up, she realized he was taller than she'd thought. Stepping close, she examined the armor covering his upper arm. One edge of the plate had been bent, driving the metal into his flesh. Allia quickly released the buckle and took the plate away. Blood soaked through the torn edges of the dark-green fabric of his sleeve. She pulled a clean handkerchief from her pocket, folded it, and held it against the wound.

"Keep pressure on it," she instructed, removing her hand as he put his in its place.

"That's an interesting ring." He nodded toward her finger and the ring set with a green stone.

"It was a gift from my grandfather." For the second time that day, memories of him flooded through her. She'd been only twelve when he died. She'd loved her grandfather deeply and spent every free moment with him. It had been a sound that had drawn her to his workshop that day, an explosion shattering wood and glass. Allia had run to him and found him bleeding on the floor.

The memory of holding her apron against the wound and feeling his warm blood soaking the fabric would stay with her forever. She couldn't forget the way he'd tried to speak, but barely managed to say her name. His last action had been to give her a small box containing the ring.

She had worn it ever since, cherishing it and her memories of him.

Now the crowd in the hall had dissipated and quiet returned. "Thank you for your help," the soldier said, taking a deep breath. "That's already so much better. It's very kind of you."

"Of course."

He felt better. She could sense his pain easing and felt his gratitude. He smiled at her, which made him even more attractive. Maybe it had been a good idea to come to the city. Hopefully, there would be another chance to talk with him. She opened her mouth to ask his name, but more footsteps approached.

"He's here," another armored man called, spotting them.

"I'd better go," the dark-haired soldier said. "Thank you again for your help."

He joined his friend and disappeared. Allia's eyes followed him, already looking forward to seeing him again.

In the vast kitchen, Allia found Mara, a stout woman with iron-gray hair, which she wore combed back and done up tightly.

"I'm not sure if you knew that my mother passed away four months ago, but she left you a letter." Allia handed the parchment to the head of the household.

Mara's stern face seemed sad as she read the letter.

"Your mother and I grew up together and were good friends for many years," Mara said. "I was sorry to hear of her passing. In the letter, she's asked me to give you a position here, and I can certainly use the help. Even so, you mustn't expect me to treat you any differently from the others."

"No, of course not," Allia said.

"Then welcome, Allia. I'll give you the usual wages. Tess!" Mara called to a red-haired girl passing by with an armful of linens. "Please show Allia around and then find her a room. Explain her duties and the rules."

"Yes, ma'am," Tess said. She handed the linens to another girl. "Follow me."

The palace seemed even bigger than Allia had first thought, and as she saw more of it, she felt a little bewildered. They climbed stairs, turned corners, and followed passages.

"Thank you for showing me," Allia said.

"It's no trouble," Tess replied with a welcoming smile. "It's more fun than making beds."

Allia smiled back, appreciating the friendliness she sensed from Tess and liking her immediately. "Have you been here long? Do you like it?"

"It's not perfect," Tess replied. "But I'm happy here. Where are you from?"

The two girls chatted happily as they walked along. Allia told Tess about the farm and her brothers, and Tess explained that she'd lived and worked in the palace since she was eleven, when her father had died, leaving her an orphan.

"Oh, I'm sorry," Allia said.

"Don't worry," Tess assured her. "Mara may seem a little serious and she does keep everyone on their best behavior, but underneath, she's really very kind. She's been like... like... Well, at least like an aunt to me."

Together, they laughed.

Tess showed Allia a small room containing a bed, a chair, and a tiny table. "The one next door is mine," Tess said, pointing.

There was a shelf for storage and hooks to hang her clothes. Tess brought sheets, a blanket and pillow, and together they made the bed. Allia put away the things she had brought. There wasn't much, only a few clothes, a beautiful hair comb that had belonged to her mother, and a ring her father had worn for years. Allia hid the comb behind her clean stockings, then threaded the ring onto a ribbon and hung it around her neck. When she changed into the dress Tess had given her, she tucked it out of sight beneath her collar. The dress was unremarkable. All the palace staff wore the same plain gray dresses and white aprons.

When Allia's bed had been made and her belongings unpacked, they went back out into the long hall, and Tess pointed up and down the corridor. "These are all the girl's rooms," she said. "Mara doesn't allow any men in here at all. If we ever want to have guests, we have to stay in the common room."

"Guests?" Allia asked, laughing. "Do many of the girls invite men over?" Unbidden, her mind rushed back to the memory of the young man she'd met earlier.

Tess shrugged. "Some do, but they don't invite them here. If Mara caught them, she'd dismiss them. And that's another thing to remember. She always knows everything that goes on here. Don't forget that if you meet someone and want some privacy."

Allia's cheeks warmed at the memory of the dark-haired soldier's handsome smile. She'd come to the city wanting to start a new life, and this was not something she had given much thought to before today. "I'll remember."

"Of course it can happen," Tess said. "There's an entire legion of soldiers, not to mention the Emperor's Guard. Most of them are young. Captain Talon is an admirable man, but he's married already. His second-in-command is well worth looking at though, big shoulders, blue eyes."

Allia stared at Tess. "Well? What's his name?"

"Harrow."

"I see," Allia said, nodding. "And are you thinking of... becoming friends with him?"

For a moment, Tess looked bashful and then she smiled. "Maybe." She blushed. "But don't tease me. I haven't even talked to him."

"Yet," Allia corrected.

"All right. I haven't talked to him yet. Now come on, I'll show you the common room."

The large room held a fireplace with a cozy hearth at one end. Several soft chairs clustered around it, pleasantly spaced for conversation. At the other end of the room sat several long tables and benches.

"We come here when we have free time," Tess said. "We usually have our meals here. The stairs to the kitchen are just through there." She pointed to a doorway on the far wall.

"It's nice," Allia said. Nothing fancy, but a pleasant room.

Together, they went back to work. Allia followed Tess, and they finished out the day together. By the time they had completed their tasks, they were fast friends.

Tess introduced Allia to the rest of the household staff in the common room while they ate dinner. When the meal ended, they played games and chatted for an hour. As the fire burned down, everyone appeared to realize that morning would arrive all too soon, and left to find their beds.

The next morning, Mara assigned Tess and Allia a list of cleaning chores, and they took their supplies and headed for the guest rooms.

As they turned a corner, Allia ran into someone coming the other way. He was tall, and her nose bumped awkwardly into his chest. "I'm sorr—" She reeled backward from the young man, who was dark-haired and richly dressed.

She'd never sensed anyone filled with such venomous anger. The heat of it almost knocked her down. He wore a calm expression, his face displaying none of what she perceived on the inside. He was the same soldier she had helped with his armor yesterday. Only now, he barely looked at her.

"My apologies. I hope you're not hurt?" His voice betrayed none of the anger he felt. In fact, there was no emotion in his tone at all.

"No," she managed to say. Allia felt frozen, terrified. It was the first time she'd encountered anyone feeling an emotion that intense.

How could he hide it? A person who felt that much hostility should be screaming, yelling, even attacking someone.

"Then may I get by?" His mildly irritated glance showed no trace of recognition or his inner feelings.

"We apologize, Your Highness," Tess answered for her, pulling Allia to one side. In a moment, the young man was gone.

She took a breath—her first since the encounter.

"What's wrong?" Tess stared at her. "You're white as a sheet. Are you ill?"

"I'm sorry," Allia said, taking another deep breath. "Who was that?"

"The prince, at least... one of them. The emperor has two sons."

Allia breathed again. "I'm sorry, Tess. I remember now." Even in the country, she'd heard of the emperor and his twin sons. "They're identical? So which one was that?"

Tess gave a small shrug. "They look exactly the same. I can't be sure. Prince Callonen is the elder, if only by a few moments, so he will inherit the crown and the Warding. Prince Haldreth is the younger."

To Allia, it seemed impossible that Tess hadn't felt the prince's anger. She didn't appear to have noticed anything unusual.

"I think that was Haldreth." Tess shrugged. "He's more likely to be annoyed by the staff. But I guess wrong sometimes."

"You've been here for years, and you can't tell them apart?"

Tess shook her head. "Just remember to always address them as Your Highness, and you'll be fine."

Realization flooded Allia's mind. The young man she met yesterday in the hall hadn't just been a soldier. He'd been a prince. At the time, Allia had no idea who he was. He'd been dressed exactly like all the other men she'd seen. Why hadn't he told her? He could easily have been angry because she hadn't treated him with appropriate deference. She hadn't curtsied or addressed him properly. Instead, he'd thanked her for helping him, just as if he were any ordinary guardsman. She'd sensed sincere gratitude and kindness from him, nothing like the scorching rage she'd felt a few moments ago. They couldn't be the same person.

She must have met both of the princes. Maybe some crisis had caused Prince Haldreth's feelings of anger today. She had no way of knowing where he had come from or what he'd just been doing. His rage felt dangerous. A person who felt that strongly would take action on their feelings. What could she do about it? Tell someone? She rejected that thought immediately. What could she tell them?

The prince is furious, and I think he will act violently? She had no evidence, and he was royalty, while Allia was only a servant in the emperor's palace. She couldn't just march into the emperor's audience chamber and accuse his son of—what, exactly?

Allia had no knowledge of wrongdoing. And in Sarine, if anyone did anything seriously wrong, the emperor would know about it because of the Warding. Wouldn't he?

She would keep this to herself, for now.

Allia settled quickly into her new life. The work was hard, but no more demanding than what she had done back home on the farm. She still found time for fun after finishing her work.

In the evening or on their days off, she and Tess went out into the city and shopped at the market. The common room always contained games, laughter and music, and Allia often joined in. She had no more encounters with Prince Haldreth, for which she was profoundly grateful.

One morning, when Allia had been in the city for two weeks, the household staff gathered in the wide kitchen so Mara could make the day's assignments.

"There's a royal banquet tonight," Mara announced. "I'll need extra help from everyone today."

Tess groaned under her breath. "We'll be working late," she whispered.

Mara went through an endless list of assignments for the event. She passed them out one by one until she came to Tess and Allia. "I want you two to attend to the drinks at the royal table," Mara said.

It seemed for a moment as if Tess wanted to object, but instead she said, "Yes, ma'am."

"I don't have to tell you both to be careful," Mara said, looking at them sternly. "Make sure your dresses are spotless, and I don't want to see a hair out of place." She eyed Tess's red curls as if looking for stray strands.

Allia felt anxious all day, and she pictured herself being dragged to a dark dungeon after spilling an entire pitcher into Haldreth's lap. "It will be all right," Tess reassured her. "Just make sure their cups are always at least half full, and don't spill. It's best if they don't even notice we're there."

"He will be there, won't he?"

"Prince Haldreth? Of course. Don't worry. He doesn't even notice the servants. He probably won't remember you."

"Are you sure?"

"Just don't draw attention to yourself." Allia felt a flutter of nervousness in her middle. Hopefully, nothing would go wrong tonight.

CHAPTER SIXTEEN

YEAR OF WARDING 21, WHITE CITY, SARINE

ALLIA

ALLIA TOOK HER PLACE in the grand hall with the other servants. The banquet began, and she stood rigidly—her face expressionless and her stomach tight. She wished she could move and stretch and wipe her damp palms on her apron.

Emperor Caldoreth entered, wearing a golden crown and flanked by his sons. Many members of his court and other guests followed them.

Allia remembered him. He appeared much the same as when she met him six years ago, except for the golden crown. Her eyes moved from him to his sons.

This was the first time she'd seen both princes together. Even after being warned, she was surprised by how alike they looked. How did anyone tell them apart? No one sat until the emperor was in his chair, then his guests seated themselves around him. Everyone at the table wore fine clothes, and their jewelry sparkled in the light of thousands of candles.

In her plain gray dress, Allia stood behind the high table, a pitcher in her hands. Others of the palace staff served the first course, a soup, and everyone started eating. Tess and Allia kept a sharp eye on the cups, and they did their job correctly and invisibly until one of the princes turned around and beckoned to Allia.

She couldn't tell them apart. Was he the angry one? She felt the urge to run. Handing the pitcher to Tess, she walked forward and curtsied, her heart pounding.

The prince addressed her. "Would you please ask Mara if she has any more berries? They are the ambassador's favorite."

"Of course, Your Highness," Allia said. She didn't sense anger from him, and relief flooded through her.

His dark eyes focused on her, as if he noticed her for the first time. "I remember you," he said. "You provided some timely assistance with my armor."

"Yes, Your Highness."

"Thank you." His dark eyes held hers with an expression she couldn't read. A quivery feeling began in her stomach, and Allia found it difficult to breathe. The room felt stuffy and hot. As if realizing he had held her gaze too long, he blinked and turned away, and Allia hurried to the kitchen.

While she still felt the pull of attraction, he had seemed so much more attainable when he'd been a soldier instead of the prince. She shook her head. He must think her an ignorant country girl.

Filling a big bowl with berries, she hurried back to the great hall and set it on the table.

"Thank you," he said, and unexpectedly, he smiled at her. She sensed the same gratitude she'd felt in the hallway a few days ago.

Smiling briefly back at him, she retrieved the pitcher and returned to her place.

The dinner stretched endlessly. Allia couldn't help but watch the prince, and since she stood behind the high table, she hoped this wasn't too noticeable. She wanted to see him smile again. But he never turned around, and she wondered if he wished he could. It would surely have attracted undue attention to have the prince look behind him.

The meal seemed to take forever, but finally it ended, and the emperor rose and walked past Allia toward the door. The prince who had asked for the berries followed him and, for the briefest of moments, their eyes met. Then he passed her and disappeared. Callonen. He was Prince Callonen. His brother passed Allia a moment later, and though it was not focused on her, she could still sense his carefully concealed anger. Haldreth.

Even if their faces looked identical, she could tell the twins differed greatly from each other.

When all the guests departed, the palace staff began cleaning up. The process took hours, but finally the room sparkled, the dishes had been washed, and Mara dismissed them all.

Tess and Allia hurried back to Allia's room.

"Well?" Tess exclaimed when they had huddled into the little room and safely shut the door behind them. "What was that?"

"What?"

"What about not being noticed? We aren't supposed to talk to them!"

"He asked me to bring more berries," Allia said. "What was I supposed to do, ignore him?"

"He was looking at you like—" Tess broke off, as if she wasn't sure what to say. "Like he couldn't look away."

"No," Allia protested. "That couldn't be it." She wasn't sure what to think. "I never thought I was that noticeable," she said.

"Oh, he definitely noticed you. He stared at you like you were painted green."

Allia laughed. "I probably had dirt on my face, food in my teeth, or something else like that."

Tess couldn't help but laugh.

"He certainly wasn't the same prince we ran into in the hall."

"No," Tess agreed. "I'm fairly sure that was Haldreth. He barely glanced at you that day. Prince Callonen was definitely looking at you."

"He... He is handsome, isn't he?" Allia asked.

"They're both handsome," Tess pointed out.

The next morning, Allia and Tess were busy cleaning the floor in one of the hallways. Looking up, Tess gasped. She nudged Allia, whispering, "Stand up." They stood against the wall.

A prince came down the hallway toward them. Which one? Resplendent in his formal clothing, he looked appealing. They bowed to him as he passed, and Allia caught a hint of carefully controlled fury before he walked by them as if they didn't exist.

No sooner had they gone back to work than footsteps returning down the hall interrupted them a second time. "He's back," Allia whispered, and they got up again. This time, the prince stopped in front of them.

Allia sensed uncertainty, a twinge of embarrassment, and an undercurrent of attraction, but no anger.

He cleared his throat. "Could I have a word with you?" She stared at him, not sure what to say.

Tess jogged Allia with her elbow and said, "Of course, Your Highness."

"I wonder if I might ask your names?" he asked hesitantly. Allia's eyes widened. Why would the prince care who they were?

She sneaked a sidelong glance at Tess, whose eyebrows were raised in surprise. But of course, they had to answer.

Tess spoke first. "I'm Tess, Your Highness."

He turned to Allia, his dark eyes meeting hers. Just like last night, the hallway felt much too warm. He waited for her to speak. "I'm Allia," she finally said. Why was he asking their names? She noticed then, while he wore clothing similar to the man who had walked by a few moments ago, it differed slightly. This had to be the other twin.

"I'm Callonen," he said, "But maybe you already knew...?"

Tess couldn't help but smile. Quickly wiping the expression from her face, she said, "We guessed that, Your Highness. Can we do anything for you?"

When his eyes met Allia's, it felt like her lungs had forgotten how to take in air. For just a moment, he smiled. Then he glanced up and down the hall. "It... appears that you are doing an excellent job here. I'll be sure to mention it to Mara next time I see her."

"Thank you, Your Highness," they said.

The sound of footsteps heading their way echoed down the hall. "I'm happy to have met you both," Prince Callonen said. Then he disappeared around a corner before several members of the emperor's court passed by.

When the hall was empty again, Tess exclaimed, "What was he doing?"

Allia giggled. "It was funny, wasn't it?"

Tess turned to look at her, her hands on her hips. "If I were to guess, I'd say he was looking for you."

"He was not," Allia protested, her face heating. "Don't tease me like that. You know I like him."

"I wasn't teasing," Tess said.

Allia remembered the warmth of his gaze. Would he find a way to meet up with them again?

Allia went to sleep that night thinking of Callonen and trying not to hope she would see him again soon. She woke up early the next morning and spent a little extra time on her hair. She sighed when she looked at the gray dress. Maybe if she wore something beautiful... "No," she told herself firmly. "He's the prince, and I'm... I'm just myself. No money, no fame, nothing unusual." But maybe that wasn't so bad. Allia smiled a little in her mirror.

"You look really pretty this morning," Tess said as they began their work.

"Thanks," Allia said gratefully. "But I'm sure it won't matter."

"We'll just have to see if he finds us again today," Tess said.

But Mara, with her uncanny awareness of everything going on in her domain, sent them to clean a series of storage rooms in one of the remotest corners of the palace. It took them a while to even get there.

"That's it," Tess said. "Pretty hair won't help. He won't be able to find us down here, even if he wants to."

"And he probably doesn't want to," Allia said. "He is the prince, and I'm cleaning his floors. Do you think Mara sent us here on purpose?"

Tess shrugged. "It doesn't matter if he wants to see you. He's supposed to marry some princess. The emperor has been begging him to get married for years. Everyone in the palace knows that."

"Why hasn't he?" Allia asked, trying to cover the disappointment burning in her chest.

"I don't know," Tess said. "Maybe he will. The emperor will probably make him."

"I'm sure you're right," Allia said, trying to put his warm, dark eyes out of her mind. "Princes have to get married, don't they?"

"Yes! Especially if they are going to inherit the empire and the Warding."

The day wore on slowly until late afternoon, when they were ready to start the last of the storage rooms. Allia concentrated on forgetting Callonen and focusing on her work. They entered a large room stacked with crates and boxes and began cleaning. She had nearly succeeded in putting him out of her mind when she heard footsteps in the hall outside. She drew in a breath and let it out slowly, reminding herself that it couldn't be him. He would be busy in the halls above, meeting important people, and...

The door opened, and Callonen entered. Allia felt a smile tickling the corners of her mouth.

"Your Highness." Tess and Allia bowed.

"Hello," he replied, one corner of his mouth lifting as he met Allia's eyes.

"Can we help you with something, Your Highness?" Tess asked.

"Well, I was actually looking for... I mean, I came to find..." he fell into an awkward silence. Then he glanced around at the barrels and boxes stacked everywhere. "There are so many..."

He took a deep breath, appearing to gather his thoughts. "I believe when I had some books put in storage recently, I included one I'd meant to keep. If we can find it, I'd like to take it back."

"As you wish, Prince Callonen," Allia said.

He turned quickly and stared at her. Startled, she froze for a moment. Had she done something wrong?

"You called me by my name. I am quite sure they instruct all the staff to address my brother and I as Your Highness. Few people can tell us apart confidently enough to use our names."

"We're sorry, Your Highness," Tess said. "We apologize for addressing you incorrectly."

"No," he protested, looking at Tess. "It wasn't incorrect. I am Callonen." He turned back to Allia. "How are you so sure which one of us you're addressing?"

She sensed him more strongly now. He felt... happy. He liked being with her and enjoyed that she knew for sure it was him. People constantly mistook him for Haldreth.

"You're nothing like your brother, Prince Callonen," she said.

He smiled at her. "Well," he glanced around at the stacks of boxes. "I'd love to find that book. Tess, would you please ask Mara if she knows where it might have been stored? I will search here, for now, if perhaps you would assist me, Allia?"

"Yes, Your Highness." Tess curtsied and left with a quick glance at Allia.

Allia's middle filled with butterflies as she realized she was alone with him.

"Are you nervous because of me?" he asked. "I didn't think you felt that way the first time we met."

"I didn't know who you were!"

He took a few steps nearer and met her eyes. "Does it really make such a difference? You don't know how refreshing it was to have someone treat me like an ordinary person," he confessed. "And you were kind. Not because you were doing your job or because I'm a prince. You were kind to me. Thank you."

"You're welcome, Your Highness."

The corners of his mouth turned down. "Please, you don't have to call me that when we're alone."

Allia's heart pounded. He made it sound like that might be often. "I... I don't?"

"No. In private, you may call me Cal."

Allia took a deep breath, trying to calm the butterflies. Except for the way his presence affected her and the fact that he was the prince, she might have felt comfortable with him. Talking to him felt natural.

"Very well then, Cal. Shall we find your book?"

He smiled, gesturing to the stacks of boxes. "It could be anywhere." He turned abruptly, looking toward the back of the room. "Did you hear something over there?"

"I don't think so," she replied.

He turned back to her and smiled. "What kind of imperial palace would this be if we had rats in the storage rooms?"

"We didn't see any sign of them in the other rooms," Allia said. "Let's try to find your book." She examined the floor. A thick layer of dust coated the room, but someone had left tracks. They led to the back wall where some dust-free containers had been stacked. "Why don't we look at the newest ones first, if they were stored here recently?"

"An excellent suggestion. I saw a pry bar near the door." He retrieved it, and they moved to the back of the room, selected a crate, and pried off the lid.

Allia's eyebrows lifted in surprise as she saw stacks of books inside. She'd assumed he had been making that part up. "Are they the ones you're looking for?"

Together, they examined the spines. "I don't recognize any..."

Allia drew in a sharp breath, as some of them were familiar to her. "Grandfather..." she murmured. Her grandfather had shown a few of them to her.

He looked at her, his eyebrows raised. "You know them?"

"Some of these were my grandfather's books. Zarekathus."

His eyes widened in disbelief. "Your grandfather was the wizard?" She nodded, running her fingers along the spines of the books.

"Did you know he was my father's best friend?"

"I knew they were friends, of course, and I knew he spent a lot of time here, but... his best friend?" Allia shook her head. "I didn't know that. I guess that explains why some of his belongings were left here."

He pointed to her hand. "You said that ring was a gift. Did Zarekathus make it? Does it have magical properties?"

"He did, and I'm not sure of everything it can do. I've noticed that I am more aware of what others are feeling around me since he gave it to me. I've never seen any other sign, except that it won't come off my hand, and it always seems to fit even though he gave it to me when I was twelve."

His eyebrows raised in surprise. "You can't take it off?"

"No."

"I wonder why that is? It's truly fascinating, as was all his work. I'm sure my father will want to meet you."

Her stomach clenched. "But... he's the emperor. There are much more important people who need his attention."

"Even so, how could he not want to see the granddaughter of his best friend?" Callonen put his hand over hers on the books for a moment and then took it away. "Maybe you'd like to keep your grandfather's books?"

"Your High—Cal, they're books of magic. They're dangerous."

"Spell books?" Callonen began opening the surrounding boxes and looking through them.

Allia heard him give an exclamation of surprise and wonder. She turned to see him staring into a wooden box. He pulled out a finely crafted dagger in a sheath. Strange symbols were carved into the hilt. Callonen held it up. "This should not be here. It should be safely locked up."

Moving to stand beside him, Allia looked closely. She thought the weapon had belonged to her grandfather years ago. Recognizing it, she brushed her fingers along the symbols on the hilt.

"Can you read them?" he asked.

Zarekathus had given her only the most basic explanation. "It's not really a language exactly, but the symbols have meaning. This blade is meant to defend against dark magic."

When Callonen drew the blade, it glowed a faintly green color. "Incredible," he murmured. "My father doesn't know what's down here. These things must be moved somewhere secure. I'll give this dagger to him at once." He replaced the blade in its sheath and stuck it into his belt.

Allia peered behind a stack of crates and found a large box with a wooden frame and glass sides. Across the top was a metal grate.

Something moved inside. Staring in horrified fascination, she crept nearer and reached out to touch the glass. As something inside struck the glass opposite her hand, she shrieked and pulled away. Looking inside again, she saw a grotesque, dark shape with a large, round body and too many legs.

Callonen was at her side at once. "Allia, are you hur—" He broke off, staring at the box. "What is *that*?"

No ordinary spider grew that large. It easily equaled the size of a dinner plate. What had they stumbled upon? How had it come to be here? Allia stared at its dark hairy legs, clustered eyes and fangs. Confirming that the creature remained firmly caged, Callonen turned back to the other crates and rummaged through them. He took out a book and opened it. "Look at this. A spell that will cause someone to die of old age in one year? All you need is a lock of their hair, two drops of blood, three drops of spider venom, and four—"

"Stop!" Allia's hand went to her mouth in shock. "Don't say any more out loud." She bent to look into the box and saw more spell books, strange objects, and pieces of bone and crystal. Some of the items she could identify, others she only remembered her grandfather describing to her. Things he would never use because they belonged firmly in the realm of dark magic.

She took a step back, her chest constricting.

Callonen placed a hand on her arm. "Are you all right?"

"I don't know much about magic," she said. "But enough to know that none of this is good. These things are used for spells that bind and control or kill. My grandfather never performed magic of that kind, but he told me a little about it. He kept many books and objects collected from other wizards so he could study them. But it's been six years since he died. Who could have put these things here?"

"I will find out at once," Callonen promised. "There would never be a good reason to perform magic such as this. Do the spells really work?"

Allia nodded. "I'm sure they do. There will be instructions in the book and necessary ingredients."

"I can't think of anyone who I would want to have die in one year."

"I hope not." Allia smiled at him.

He began replacing the lids. "Allia?"

"Yes?" She looked up into his eyes and felt her insides twitch. There was something about the way he said her name. It felt special, intimate. Why couldn't he be an ordinary man instead of the prince? They could have been friends without worrying about his rank... or hers.

"Please don't tell anyone about this for now. I will speak to Mara and to my father. These things are dangerous. We need to find out who is responsible."

"I won't say anything."

Out of the corner of her eye, Allia spotted motion. Her head whipped around in time to see something scuttle out of sight between the boxes. Callonen had seen it too. "Let's get out of here." Allia dashed toward the door. But a dark brown spider blocked her path. It was at least as big as the one in the container, only this one roamed free. It raised its front legs, displaying black fangs, and skittered a few steps toward her.

CHAPTER SEVENTEEN

Year of Warding 21, White City, Sarine

ALLIA

Allia stood frozen, her teeth clenched, staring at the spider. Callonen stepped protectively in front of her. When the spider came nearer, he took a swing at it with the pry bar. It retreated out of reach.

They paused, watching it warily. It rushed at them. Callonen waited until it nearly reached his boots, then struck it squarely with the metal bar. It twitched and struggled, but he kept it pinned to the floor until it finally stopped moving, and its knobby legs curled up under its body.

Allia clamped her jaws firmly shut to keep from screaming. Her eyes searched every corner of the room. Were there more? When Callonen offered his hand, she clutched it. They edged past the dead spider to run for the door.

They slammed it behind them and stood leaning against it, breathing hard.

"Thank you!" Allia gasped.

"Are you all right?" he asked.

"No! I'm never going to be able to sleep again!" She shuddered and felt his hand grip hers reassuringly.

"I'll send someone to take care of this immediately. We will make sure it can't escape, and that any others are destroyed. Please don't say anything about it."

He released her hand and walked with her back the way they had come. "I hope to see you again soon." He meant it sincerely. She could sense it.

"Me too, Cal."

He smiled at her as they parted, with him heading toward the stairs while she returned to the kitchens—her mind churning with questions.

CALLONEN

Callonen knocked on the door of his brother's study.

"Enter."

He opened the door to find his twin lounging in a chair, legs stretched out comfortably in front of him, feet on his desk. "Ah, it's my elder brother. To what do I owe the pleasure? Come in. Sit down."

Callonen crossed the room and took a chair across the desk from Haldreth. "Do I need a reason to spend time with my brother?"

Haldreth smiled. "Of course not. But lately, your visits seem to be occasions to point out my many failings."

This conversation already wasn't going well. Callonen felt his jaw clench. If his brother was already irritated with him, it would be best to be direct. "Have you been experimenting with magic?"

Haldreth's eyebrows raised in surprise. "Magic is dangerous. Why would you think that? And if I had, Father would know about it." Haldreth leaned back in the chair and laced his fingers together behind his head.

"I found the remains of a few of your... projects."

"And why do you think they're mine? We are inside the Warding after all."

"Are they?"

"You just can't wait for it, can you?" Haldreth broke in.

"For what?"

"To own the Warding. For the day when you have your own magic, and you know everything about everyone. For someone who craves control like you do, that will be the best day of your life." Haldreth put his feet down and leaned forward to look at his brother. "Isn't that what you really want? When the Warding is yours, you'll know everything I do without having to ask."

Callonen refused to let his brother divert his attention. "Don't you realize how dangerous magic is? If Father hasn't prevented you, you should stop on your own. I'm concerned about your safety."

"My safety?" Haldreth laughed. "Really? I thought you were just worried that I might wield a little power of my own someday."

"It's not worth it, Haldreth. Zarekathus knew a lot more than you do, and even with all his knowledge, a dark wizard killed him."

Haldreth slammed his hands down on the arms of his chair and jumped to his feet. "You have no idea what I know!" He circled the desk to face his brother.

Callonen stood and studied the face so very like his own, except for the bitter expression, which he hoped he never wore. Why did his brother have to be so difficult?

Maybe Callonen was wrong in his assumption. It was true that, through the Warding, the emperor should be immediately aware of anything like this.

"You might not believe it, but I care what happens to you," Callonen said. "You and Father are all the family I have. Please don't work any more magic."

"I'm touched by your concern," Haldreth said, the words edged with sarcasm.

His stomach churning with irritation, Callonen turned toward the door. "Even if you don't believe me, I really am concerned. I know you aren't content here, but Sarine isn't so bad," he said, turning back to his brother.

"Father is a tyrant!" Haldreth protested. "And you are just like him. Don't you think it's wrong to live in a place where he knows everything you think and do? Don't you ever want to be free of it?" He crossed the space between them and put his hand on Callonen's shoulder.

Callonen answered honestly. "Sometimes I do. But Father is a good man, and he needs our help."

Haldreth looked back at him and slowly nodded. "You're right. I'm sorry, Cal."

Callonen smiled. "You're the only brother I have."

Haldreth mirrored his smile, and Callonen felt a remnant of the bond between them that had been so strong when they were boys.

ALLIA

The next day, when Allia and Tess finished a morning of cleaning and got back to the kitchens, Mara handed them each a tray of food. "Take these to the private garden next to the north tower."

Allia was grateful she hadn't been sent alone. She didn't know exactly which garden Mara meant, but Tess led them confidently. When they opened the door and entered the garden, they saw no one.

As they walked farther in, Allia looked around, enchanted. Multitudes of beautiful plants surrounded them, and the scent of flowers filled the air. "This is amazing."

They rounded a large tree and saw a young man sitting at a table under an arbor covered with flowering vines. When he glanced up, they recognized one of the princes. By the time they placed the trays on the table in front of him, Allia had come near enough to be sure it was Callonen.

"Thank you," he said, leaving his chair to stand facing them. He wore a soft white shirt under a dark coat and a serious expression on his handsome face.

"Is there anything else you require, Your Highness?" Tess asked with a proper curtsy. Allia, distracted by looking at Callonen, belatedly imitated the gesture. Had he asked for the food specifically so he could see her? Or had it just been a coincidence?

"No, thank you. That will be all," Callonen said. They curtsied and turned toward the door. "Allia, wait!"

She turned back.

"May I speak with you for a moment?"

She nodded, not sure what to say.

Tess squeezed her hand and murmured, "I'll see you later." She slipped out the door, and Allia found herself in the middle of the garden with the prince.

For a long moment, they stared at each other. His serious expression vanished into a smile that caused her insides to shiver.

"I thought you might want an update after our adventure yesterday."

"Did you find out who's behind it all?"

"Not yet," he admitted. "We checked every room and found no more spiders. I wanted you to know that we haven't given up, and we're still looking for answers. My father forbids dark magic in Sarine. If someone is practicing it, he should know through the Warding."

"How does he not already know?" Allia asked curiously.

"I'm not sure," Callonen said. "Maybe he will soon." He gestured to the table and the two trays. "In the meantime, will you join me?"

"Join you?" He said it to her just as if she were an elegant lady.

How should she answer? How could she refuse?

Hardly daring to breathe, she took the chair he held out for her, and he took the seat across from her.

She sat very straight on the edge of her seat. "Your Highness, I'm sure I'm not supposed to be sitting in your presence. Mara would throw me out if she knew!"

But Callonen only smiled. "She won't. I asked her to send you here. And I told you yesterday to call me Cal. What makes you think that my company is any more valuable than yours? Maybe I shouldn't be sitting in *your* presence, Lady Allia."

She wanted to stay there forever, enjoying his smile. But she shook her head. "I'm not a lady. Despite who my grandfather was, I'm still an ordinary girl from a farm. You're the prince. Everyone here must obey your commands."

He met her eyes. "I wanted to see you again. You have complete permission to refuse if you don't want to sit here with me. Please don't interpret my humble request as a command. I only wanted to talk with you."

She could sense how worried he felt about this, but he wanted to be with her. Callonen could have the company of anyone he wanted. No one would refuse him.

His attraction to her was obvious. And that couldn't end well for her. A prince and a servant might have a few stolen moments, but that was all. Two people from such different stations never ended up together. But what harm could there be in talking to him?

"Will you dine with me?" he asked.

Allia couldn't imagine the tray of food she'd carried was intended for her. But she didn't want to refuse Callonen.

"Thank you very much... Cal," she said.

His smile lit up his face. He removed the covers on the trays and set a beautiful plate of food before her. Meals in the palace kitchen were casual, and Allia felt out of place sitting with him in her plain gray dress. She took the snowy white napkin and placed it on her lap.

"So you've been here three weeks already," he said, picking up a fork. "Do you like it?"

"Other than the spider!" And your brother's anger. It wasn't time to say that aloud.

"I didn't realize I'd need a weapon to enter the storage room," he said, grinning. "I never have before."

Allia shuddered at the memory. "Me neither. But I'm very grateful I didn't have to face that thing alone."

"If I hadn't been there, you would have had Tess."

Allia smiled. "She appreciates spiders even less than I do, if you can imagine. Have you ever seen anything like that before?"

He shook his head. "Never! And I've lived here most of my life. My brother and I explored every inch of the palace together when we were younger."

"Do you have any other family?"

"No. It's just my father, brother and me. Our mother died when we were seven."

"I'm so sorry."

"It was difficult to lose her. I know my father still misses her, but he's done a good job of raising us."

"Was she ill?" Allia asked.

Callonen stared down at his plate for a moment. She saw the muscles of his jaw tense, as she sensed a deep well of old sorrow and pain that made her wish she hadn't asked.

He lifted his eyes to meet hers. "We were attacked by the Shekkar."

Allia drew in a shocked breath. "I... I'm so sorry."

"Losing her was the reason my father went to search for the sword, Blackbane. Haldreth and I were very young. We'd just lost our mother, and when our father left, we were so afraid he'd never come back either. It was a difficult time."

Allia laid her hand over his on top of the table. "It must have been. It's never easy to lose loved ones. I understand how that feels."

Callonen nodded. "When Father came back with Blackbane, he used it to kill the Shekkar. Your grandfather helped him. Did he ever tell you the story?"

Allia smiled. "He did. But now that I'm grown, I feel sure the version he told left out many of the details."

Callonen's expression grew serious. "Some parts of it are very grim."

"I'm sure your father didn't tell you everything back then."

He shook his head. "He did not. But over the years, my brother and I have learned most of it."

"Do you... get along with your brother?" Allia asked, looking into Callonen's dark brown eyes. "I have three brothers, and I know they aren't always easy to live with."

Callonen rolled his eyes. "At least yours don't look exactly like you. When they do something wrong, they can't claim that you actually did it."

"Does that happen often?"

"Not anymore. When we were children, it did," Callonen said. "Haldreth and I can be... competitive. Even more so, lately. We're grown men, but I don't think he's happy that I will inherit the Warding. He's never liked it anyway. He feels it's a form of captivity."

"And what do you think?"

His brown eyes were very serious. "The Warding is like nothing else I know of. My father knows what's going on in his realm like no other ruler does. That's why we have such complete peace here. If anyone does anything really wrong, he knows about it. It is very difficult to have that kind of power and still judge fairly and kindly. I hope my father lives to be ninety, because I don't want the responsibility."

They'd finished their lunch, and Allia remained lost in conversation with him until she gazed up at the afternoon sun, realizing that she'd been away from her duties for hours. What would Mara say? "I need to get back."

Ending the time with him was difficult. She'd enjoyed it more than she wanted to admit. Reluctantly, she stood and stacked the trays and dirty dishes. Callonen helped her and then carried them to the door of the garden.

"I hope to see you again soon," he said.

"Me too." She took the trays from him and hurried back toward the kitchen. How had the time with him gone by so fast?

It had taken weeks for Allia to learn her way around the palace. When they had free time, Tess showed her around. After they'd explored the interior, they moved to the grounds.

"This is where the guard practices." Tess pointed to a large dirt field. "People come and watch." In the shade of the wall, chairs and benches lined the edge, and a grassy hill climbed up toward the palace wall. "Anyone is welcome to observe."

"Do you go often?" Allia asked.

"Only once in a while," Tess said. "Some of the girls go all the time, if they have a certain soldier who they want to notice them."

"I see," Allia said, tapping her chin as she considered. "Remind me the name of the one you wanted to meet?"

"Harrow," Tess said, her cheeks slightly pink, and for a moment, her gaze seemed far away. Then she looked back at Allia. "If you tell anyone about what I said—"

"Oh, I haven't told very many people," Allia teased. Tess smacked her arm.

Allia laughed. "I wouldn't tell," she said seriously. "Think—if you told all my secrets and I told yours, who would be in the most trouble?"

Tess laughed.

"So, do you want to go watch? Tomorrow we get off early."

"Maybe," Tess said, twisting a lock of red hair as she considered. "But I'm not coming here too often. If he notices, he'll think I'm desperate."

༄

The next afternoon, they both changed out of their work clothes as fast as they could and went down to the practice field. A crowd had already assembled, made up of palace staff, off-duty guardsmen, and members of the emperor's court. Some stood, others occupied chairs, and many sat on the grassy hill. Allia knew only a few of them, but everyone seemed friendly.

Halfway up the grassy hill, she and Tess found a place to sit where they could see the field. A noisy, dusty battle raged. As Allia looked closer, she realized the combatants fought with wooden weapons. The soldiers seemed to use some kind of system. When knocked down or struck in a certain way, they trudged off the field, apparently defeated.

After a while, fewer than a score of the men remained. Someone sounded a horn, and they all stopped. The watchers cheered and clapped their hands, and some of the remaining fighters waved back. "That's Captain Talon," Tess whispered to Allia, pointing out a tall, powerfully built man in the center.

"Is Harrow out there?" Allia asked.

"I think so," Tess said, peering out at the field. "It's so hard to tell when they're all wearing helmets."

The remaining men walked to a rack standing at the edge of the field and put away their wooden weapons, trading them for real metal blades. Allia sucked in her breath. "Won't they hurt each other?" she asked.

"Are you worried about them?" Tess asked with a grin.

"A little," Allia admitted.

"They know what they're doing," Tess said. "Watch." The men divided into pairs facing each other.

"They do this often," Tess explained. "The captain always wins."

Allia watched them. Some pairs were uneven, and the sparring between them quickly finished, as with Talon and his opponent. But others seemed evenly matched, and they fought longer.

At last, only two men remained. They moved back and forth, gracefully attacking and retreating, striking and parrying. Neither could gain any advantage, but neither appeared willing to give up. Finally, Captain Talon stepped between them. One of them drew back and lowered his sword, while the other tried unsuccessfully to push past Talon.

"Get out of my way!" the man demanded angrily. "We're not finished!"

"You are," Talon said, "You've had enough."

"I said, get out of my way." His voice was cold and angry, and Allia shivered, even though he didn't direct the malice at her. She couldn't sense it from this distance, but she could hear it plainly.

"Enough," Talon repeated, not backing down.

The other man still refused to listen. Instead, he raised his sword against Talon. Grinning, Talon drew his own blade so fast that Allia barely saw him move—but the blade was there to block his opponent's and steel rang on steel. The crowd hushed, and Allia held her breath. After only a few strokes, Talon knocked the man to the ground. A strained silence fell.

The man jumped back to his feet and yanked off his helmet, revealing Haldreth. She didn't wonder for even a moment if it was Callonen. She'd never seen him wear the expression of outrage now on his brother's face.

"How dare you refuse my orders?" Haldreth demanded.

"This training is under my command," Talon said coolly. "And you've had enough for today."

Haldreth stared at Talon furiously, but he said nothing, instead turning on his heel and stalking off.

"We're finished for the day," Talon announced. "Dismissed." The soldiers picked up their gear and headed back toward the palace. Only one remained on the field with Talon, the man who fought opposite Haldreth before Talon had separated them. Now, he took off his helmet as well. It was Callonen. The crowd had begun talking again—a low murmur at first, which rapidly became a confusion of many voices.

Allia watched from a distance. She knew she shouldn't run forward and speak to Callonen now. She hadn't realized he would be here today. When Tess had said that the soldiers practiced here, she should have realized he would be among them. Her memory went back to the day she'd arrived here and found him in the hall. *I can't believe I let him hit me so hard...* Had he been sparring with his brother on that day too?

"Well, Your Highness," Talon said loudly, clapping his hand on Callonen's shoulder. "We have just enough time to make it to that meeting with His Majesty." This statement stemmed the flow of questions from onlookers.

"Yes, please excuse us," Callonen said to the crowd as he swiftly followed in Talon's wake.

As Allia watched them go, she felt Tess's hand seize hers.

"That's Harrow!" Tess pointed to a man standing at the end of the field. He wasn't looking toward them.

With his dark hair and blue eyes, he made a striking figure in his armor. Allia could certainly see why her friend was interested in him.

She glanced at Tess, who sat momentarily frozen. "Go talk to him," Allia urged in a whisper.

Tess got up and took a step forward. But at that moment, another of the soldiers called, "Harrow?"

And Harrow vanished into the crowd.

CHAPTER EIGHTEEN

YEAR OF WARDING 21, WHITE CITY, SARINE

CALLONEN

CALLONEN PUT HIS HELMET under his arm and followed his brother up the stairs, Talon at his side.

"You know where he's going." Talon nodded toward Haldreth. Talon paused at the top of the stairs. "Maybe you two should see the emperor alone."

"Father won't take his side," Callonen assured him. "You might as well come with me to explain what happened."

They trailed behind Haldreth as he marched to the emperor's study and opened the door without knocking. He stormed into the luxurious room and up to the large desk. "I need someone sent to the dungeon!"

"Who?" Caldoreth asked. He glanced up from a stack of papers, first at Haldreth, then past him to Callonen, standing in the doorway. "Talon, former Captain of the Guard. He refused to obey my orders and tried to humiliate me in front of everyone."

"I see," Caldoreth said. "Before I have my captain dragged to the dungeon, may I ask what you ordered him to do?"

"He interfered with our training match. The rule is that no one can interfere. It was a fair fight, and I was winning before he stopped me! I ordered him to get out of the way."

"And who was this man you were so determined to defeat?"

"Callonen!"

"Wasn't this only a training match?" Caldoreth glared at his son.

"It's not about the match," Haldreth protested. "How can we trust the loyalty of our guard if they won't obey us?"

"I ordered Captain Talon to keep everyone safe as they practice. We've had very few injuries under his watch, but the last two have involved you. Can you explain that to me?"

"You've always taught us to do our best, to fight hard—"

Caldoreth broke in, "But never to forget that this is only training, and you are fighting with friends or your brother. You cannot lose control of your temper. I ordered Talon to stop any match that he feels is dangerous." Caldoreth looked toward the door. "Come in, Captain," he called.

Callonen moved out of the doorway to let Talon through.

"My emperor," Talon bowed.

"From what my son has told me, I gather you stopped the fight to preserve the safety of the participants?"

Talon glanced at Haldreth, who glared back at him. "That's correct, my lord."

"And no one was hurt?"

"No," Talon replied.

"And you don't even care that he tried to make me look like an idiot in front of everyone?" Haldreth protested.

"I trust Talon's loyalty." Caldoreth met his son's angry gaze steadily.

Haldreth lowered his eyes first. "You trust him too much!" He stalked out of the room.

Emperor Caldoreth rubbed his temples.

"I'm sorry, Emperor," Talon said. "After the last incident, I have made sure the two of them are not matched to spar. I apologize for missing that today. It won't happen again."

"Thank you, Talon," the emperor said.

Callonen had no idea his father had given those orders. He didn't know what to say about his brother's behavior. Haldreth was competitive. That had always been the case. But lately Callonen had felt a new seriousness to Haldreth's commitment to best him.

ALLIA

The next day, a guard handed Allia a note. She found a quiet corner and broke the seal.

> *I want to see you again. Please meet me after dinner in the garden by the north tower. -C*

Could it really be from Callonen? After dinner, she rushed back to her room and changed out of her gray dress into a gown of soft green. It was nothing fancy, but it was her favorite.

She found her way to the garden. He had been sitting on a bench, but he rose and smiled when he saw her. His face lit up, and Allia couldn't help but smile back. She didn't want to show her feelings too much, though. Every time she saw him, her heart leapt, and she was beginning to care for him far more than she should. He reached out and took her hands in his.

"I'm glad to see you," he said softly, and his smile seemed shy. "It's been two days."

She could sense that he meant what he said. He felt happy to be with her again.

"I saw you yesterday," she said.

"Were you there to watch us practice?"

She nodded.

"Then you must have seen Haldreth lose his temper."

"I saw," Allia said. "Does he act like that often? Why would it bother him so much to stop a practice fight?"

"I wish it didn't. I'd like things to be different," Callonen said. "My brother..." He took a deep breath. "My brother hates to lose.

In particular, he doesn't like to lose to me. And he really hates to lose to Talon."

"But doesn't everyone lose to Talon?" Allia asked. "That's what Tess said. If it happens all the time, shouldn't he be expecting it?"

"Haldreth has hated Talon for years. I've tried to help them make peace since the captain is my best friend, but I haven't had much luck. Haldreth resents the power my father has given Talon and his extraordinary abilities."

"And why would he act that way toward you?" Allia wondered aloud. Haldreth had been determined to win at any cost, and they had only been practicing.

"Sometimes his temper gets the better of him. He doesn't mean it. And he's competitive," Callonen said, as if that explained everything.

She had brothers herself. Many times, they had gotten into trouble because they were always trying to come out ahead of each other. Sometimes they fought, but they always seemed to work it out in the end. None of that explained Haldreth's actions. Allia knew what she had seen, and she worried about Callonen's safety. "Do you practice with the guard very often?" she asked, wanting to change the subject.

"Yes," Callonen said. "All the time. And every couple of months, my brother and I take turns riding with them when they patrol outside the Warding."

"Is that dangerous?" she asked.

Callonen laughed. "I don't think so. At least, not very much. And I have Talon with me. When he's around, I feel very safe."

Weeks passed, and Allia saw Callonen nearly every day. Notes appeared, asking her to meet him in obscure corners of the palace. As far as she knew, Tess remained the only person aware of their secret meetings. She hoped Mara didn't know. Allia didn't want to leave the palace now.

The moments spent with him were so much more vivid than the rest of her time. He occupied her thoughts constantly. The more she talked to him, the better she knew him and the tighter his hold on her heart became.

He treated everyone so kindly, thanking them for their efforts even when no one expected him to. Callonen never behaved as if he thought he was above anyone else, and Allia sensed that he genuinely cared about his people. He would make a wonderful leader for Sarine. Maybe there would be ways she could help him... Allia wrenched her mind firmly from that thought. It was only a dream. There was no future where she stayed at his side to love and support him in his work. But a future without him seemed bleak and lifeless. Instead, she dreamed he lived down in the city, as a tradesman or a soldier, someone she could share her life with.

CALLONEN

Callonen sat in the formal dining room pushing his salad idly around his plate as his father reminded him, yet again, that he wouldn't be around forever and Callonen must have an heir to pass on the Warding. The topic had become a favorite for mealtime discussion.

Private lunches for the royal family used to be an enjoyable event. But lately, they'd become a little strained. Callonen did not enjoy his father constantly pressuring him to get married.

"You're twenty-eight years old," Emperor Caldoreth exclaimed. "You could have been married ten years by now. Callonen, are you listening to me?"

Callonen looked up. "Sorry, Father. I am. And I understand. You're right that it's time to give my full attention to looking for a bride." He could picture it vividly... Someone with blond hair that fell in soft waves, her eyes a mixture of gray and green, the color of the hills in the spring rain. Someone smart and beautiful, who didn't only like him for his title or wealth, but who really saw him.

That first day he had met Allia in the hall, she hadn't known who he was. And she'd treated him as if he were... anyone. It had been so refreshing. She had known he was hurting and helped him. Allia. He needed to see her again.

"...and she's coming in a few days."

Callonen focused his attention back on his father. "Sorry, who?"

"Princess Elena of Paraman. The rumors say she is stunning. The king has already received a score of marriage offers, but his alliance with Sarine is important, and she's coming here to visit before they decide. This is it, Callonen. This is your chance."

"The king is hoping one of us will marry her?" Callonen asked.

Caldoreth still seemed annoyed. "Of course. You need to make this work. She's your last chance at a princess. Although, if this doesn't work out, a daughter of any of the nobles would be acceptable."

"What if she can't decide between us?" Haldreth asked. "So much charm. She'll be dazzled."

"You need to marry as well," Caldoreth said, "but Callonen's child will inherit the Warding. He needs to act immediately."

"You've never entertained the princess of Ara," Haldreth said.

"Ara?" Caldoreth turned his full attention to Haldreth. "We've never had friendly relations with Ara. You know this. So, why would you bring it up now? They hate us."

"Sometimes change is good, Father," Haldreth said. "Why shouldn't we try to open negotiations with them?"

"They are treacherous, Haldreth. I've invited them before, but they aren't willing to enter the Warding. They know if they do, I'll become aware of any deceit they might be planning."

"Maybe we should visit them," Haldreth suggested.

That was surprising. Haldreth had seldom taken any interest in diplomacy.

"I have a friend from Ara," Haldreth said. "He works closely with the king, and he could find out if they are open to receiving us. I can put together a delegation to accompany me."

Caldoreth stared at him, considering it.

"We can make it work, Father," Haldreth said.

Caldoreth took a deep breath. "Very well. As long as we can be sure of your safety."

Haldreth smiled. "I will get started on the details and keep you informed."

Taking advantage of his father's change in focus. Callonen rose. "Please excuse me," he said, making for the door.

"Callonen," Emperor Caldoreth said, "make sure you're prepared for Princess Elena's visit. You know how important this is."

"Yes, Father," Callonen said quickly. The lunch had taken too long, and now he'd have to hurry or he'd be late to meet Allia. He needed a way to change his father's mind.

ALLIA

When Allia returned to her room after the day's work, she found a note had been slid beneath the door.

> *Please dust the first of the guest rooms at noon tomorrow. −C*

The next day, Allia made sure her work took her near the guest rooms. She'd barely thought about anything else but seeing Callonen.

At noon, she slipped into the first room and found him sitting in a chair in front of the fireplace. He turned to smile at her. It made her feel very warm inside. She could sense his attraction, but also hesitation. Something was on his mind.

He rose and took her hand, then kissed it. "Welcome, my lady." The feel of his lips on her skin and the look in his eyes made her wish he would kiss more than her hand. "Will you join me?"

They sat down.

"Allia, I need to tell you something important," he said. "My father has invited a princess to visit Sarine."

Allia suddenly felt cold. "She's the one your father wants you to marry."

Callonen took a deep breath. "I'm twenty-eight years old. He's been trying to get me to marry for ten years now, and I understand why. If the Warding passes to me and I die without an heir, the Warding will fall and our land will lose its protection. Thus far, I have never felt ready, and I refused to do it."

"But he's not giving up, is he?" Allia asked. "He wants you to marry this princess." How had she let herself become so attached to him? She'd known all along this would happen.

"I won't do it," Callonen said. "I've managed to exercise my wishes in this so far."

"He'll force you." Allia averted her gaze, glancing down at her hands in her lap.

"I won't let that happen," he promised. "But I wanted to talk to you before she arrives. I have no choice but to spend some time with her."

Allia looked up at him. "Does your father know we are friends?"

"I have not told him yet."

"Will you get into trouble because of this?" she asked.

"I admit it's not very proper," he answered, "but I don't care. I enjoy being with you."

"But your father would be upset if he knew, and the princess is coming here to be with you. It's all arranged," Allia said, a sharp ache beginning in her chest. There was nothing she could do to stop it. After all, she was only a servant he met in secret, and she would never be anything more to him.

By the next day, gossip about the visiting princess filled the palace. Apparently, everyone knew about her arrival.

"I guess you've heard? I knew you wouldn't be happy," Tess said to Allia that night when they finished their work. "Everyone expects Callonen to marry her. And she'll be here in a few more days."

"I know," Allia murmured, trying to hide her sorrow with a smile.

"I'm prepared to hate her on your behalf," Tess said loyally.

Allia shook her head. "No need. It's all right. I didn't think that he... I mean, that we..." She fell silent. She couldn't bear the thought of Callonen married to someone else. He would never speak to Allia again, never look at her with those brown eyes, never put his arms around her. He cared about her, but his position would force him to marry someone else.

"I'll check with the stables. Maybe they can find us a snake to put in her bed."

Allia half smiled and hugged her friend. But that night, alone in her room, she cried.

By morning, she had dried her tears, determined that no one be able to tell she was upset. Putting on a smile, she went about her work. After all, how dare she be so bold as to think the prince cared for her?

⁓

Allia hadn't seen Callonen since their conversation about the princess. She tried not to think about him as she went about her work. They'd received word that their royal visitor would arrive at midday the next day. Last-minute preparations filled Allia's time. When she got back to her room, a note lay on the floor waiting for her.

> *I've been thinking of you constantly. I'm so sorry about our last conversation. I never meant to hurt you. Will you please meet me tonight? Midnight, on the west tower wall. -C*

Allia took the note and knocked at Tess's door. Tess was already in her nightdress, but she let Allia in.

"Look at this," Allia said, holding the note to the candlelight so Tess could see. She scanned it quickly and seemed surprised.

"What are you going to do?" Tess asked.

"I don't know." Allia felt tears on her face. "His guest arrives tomorrow. What can he possibly have to say to me? And midnight? Maybe he only wants too..." She took a deep breath. "I'm not going to bed with him!" Allia vowed, wiping her eyes. "I know he's gorgeous, and amazing, and tall, and—"

"Please stop!" Tess begged. "Listen to yourself."

"But his princess is arriving tomorrow! I still have some self-respect. I will not warm his bed tonight when he's going to propose to her tomorrow."

"You don't really think he's like that, do you?" Tess asked. "Maybe he only wants to talk to you."

"Maybe." Allia rubbed her forehead.

"You care about him," Tess said, putting her hand on Allia's.

"I love him, Tess! I can't help it." As she confessed it out loud, she knew it was true. Her life would never be the same after knowing him.

"You're not going to tell him 'no,' are you?"

Allia sighed. "No."

Tess knew her too well. Allia couldn't refuse Callonen's invitation. So, she put on her most attractive dress, brushed her hair smooth, and waited impatiently for midnight.

CHAPTER NINETEEN

YEAR OF WARDING 21, WHITE CITY, SARINE

ALLIA

GRADUALLY, THE PALACE GREW quiet until only a few people stirred. Allia crept out of her room and through the empty halls. She knew where the night guards were posted and avoided them. Higher and higher she climbed, past the level of the great hall and the audience chambers, past the elaborately furnished guest rooms, up to the west tower.

Darkness and silence covered the balcony. Allia saw no one. Her footsteps made no sound as she tiptoed from the top of the stairs to the edge of the wall. The city spread out beneath her, quiet and sleeping. Nervous quivers rolled through her middle. Allia crept over to stand beside the tower, where she waited, invisible in the shadows. What was she doing here? The princess would arrive tomorrow.

Her muscles tensed as someone approached.

A tall black shape walked silently from the top of the stairs and traced her steps out to the wall. The figure wore a cloak and hood, almost as if he didn't want to be recognized.

Allia stayed frozen in place, torn between hope that it was Callonen and fear that it might be someone else. Finally, she tiptoed forward until she was close enough to sense who it was. Allia whispered, "Cal?"

He turned to face her. "Allia! I was afraid you wouldn't come."

"I almost didn't," Allia admitted.

"The last time we spoke, I upset you. I'm so sorry. What made you come?" he asked softly, throwing back his hood.

"Because... if you have something to say to me, I'll listen."

"I wanted to see you," Callonen said. "The last few days have been so busy, and they watch me so closely. There's nothing I wanted more than to be with you for a little while."

He had gone to a great deal of trouble just to see her. But they were meeting at midnight because he wouldn't want to be seen in public with one of the palace staff, a mere servant.

"Callonen... there's no way anything could work between us. You can't even let anyone find out we've spent time together. I don't want to be the girl you only meet in secret."

"I am sorry," he said, his tone suddenly stiff and formal.

"I shouldn't be here." Allia started for the door.

"Allia... please," he begged, taking her hand.

"You know I'm right," she protested. "You should be with a princess."

"No! Allia, I can't help being who I am. I have been given power and responsibility that I would never desire if I had a choice. You don't know how many times I have wished to be just an ordinary man."

She pulled her hand away from his. "And I can't help being who I am. I'm not rich or powerful, and my father was not a king."

"It's not right to judge someone because of who their father was," he said. "If the world were perfect, every person would simply be who they are."

"But it's not perfect! In reality, royalty does not associate with commoners."

He shook his head. "No one could ever think you are common. And the difference in our stations does not matter to me."

Allia looked up at him without speaking. She couldn't make out his features in the dim light, but she sensed he was sincere. Maybe that was only because she wanted so badly to believe him.

"Will you do me the honor of walking with me?"

She took a deep breath and relaxed a little. "Do you always walk in the middle of the night?"

"Sometimes I do when I can't sleep. Tonight, I waited until everyone was in bed, then I snuck out."

She raised her eyebrows. "Aren't you a little old to be sneaking out at night?"

He grinned. "I admit it has been a long time," he said. "My brother always got into a lot more trouble than I did." Pausing, he offered her his hand. "Will you consent to accompany me?"

How could she refuse? She put her hand in his, and they strolled around the balcony. Where his hand touched hers, she felt hard calluses against her palm. Since he was a prince, she had wondered if his hand would be soft. Finding out differently made her wonder if she had misjudged him.

She had worked hard all her life, and it had been natural to assume that, as royalty, everything had been easy for him.

The rising moon bathed them in white light. They stood together, looking out over the city.

"It's beautiful," she whispered.

"Yes," he agreed. "The night is peaceful."

The white stone of the city gleamed in the moonlight. A cool breeze blew past, and Allia shivered.

"Here," Callonen said, taking the long cloak from his shoulders and wrapping her in it.

"Thank you," she murmured. The brush of his hands against her shoulders warmed her more than the cloak. But she couldn't afford to think like that—not with the impending arrival the next day.

"She's coming tomorrow," Allia said.

"Yes," he agreed. "I can't stop that, but just because my father wants there to be something between us doesn't mean that anything will happen. I told you before, I won't do it."

"He's the emperor," she pointed out.

"He's my father! I won't allow him to force me to marry her. I care about you."

He did care. Allia could sense it. But he hadn't discussed their relationship with the emperor. "If that's really true, Cal, then you'll tell your father about us."

"I will!" he promised. "I've just been waiting for the right moment. It will be soon." He offered his hand again, and Allia took it. Summer was nearing its end, and the night air grew crisp.

"It's getting colder," he said. "Follow me." They went down the stairs and through the halls. Allia couldn't tell where they were going in the dark, so she held his hand and allowed him to lead her. After a few twists and turns, Callonen opened a door, and they slipped through and shut it behind them.

"Just a moment," he said, dropping her hand. She couldn't see anything until he lit a candle. A few coals remained in the fireplace, and Callonen added fresh wood until a small, bright blaze burned.

Allia looked around the room. It was impressively furnished, with a throne on a dais at one end. She recognized it, though she'd only been here once before. "Your father's audience room?"

He grinned. "He never uses it at this hour." She had to laugh.

Callonen brought a small table and two chairs and set them in front of the fire. He held one out for her. "Will you sit, my lady?"

"Thank you, Your Highness." She curtsied and slipped into the chair.

When she spent time with him, Allia forgot everything else. She treasured every moment and hoped he was right about the future. They talked and laughed, and Allia had never enjoyed anyone's company so much.

"It's very late," he said, getting to his feet. He offered his hand and pulled her up.

The soft firelight only made him more irresistible. She reached up and brushed her fingers along his jaw.

"Allia," he whispered, pulling her close. His lips met hers in a gentle kiss.

The feel of his mouth on hers while he held her was the best thing she'd ever experienced. She slid her arms around his neck and returned the kiss. His embrace tightened, and she tangled her fingers in his hair and pulled him even closer.

The door opened, and the light of a lamp shone brightly in their eyes. Mara stood in the doorway, staring at them, her mouth slightly open in shock.

They hastily stepped away from each other. Without saying anything, she turned to go.

"Mara, wait! Please!" Callonen called after her. She turned back to face him, disbelief on her face. "Your Highness?"

"I need to discuss this with my father myself. Please, don't tell him until I've had time to talk to him!"

Mara's face twisted into a frown. "Your Highness, I cannot deceive my emperor, even for you."

"You don't have to deceive him," Callonen protested. "Just wait a little. I will talk to him about it immediately. I promise!"

"But... Your Highness, the princess is arriving today."

"Tomorrow," Callonen corrected.

Mara went to the window and pulled back the heavy drapes. The light of dawn shone in. "Today. You know what your father expects of you! Why would you do this now? And Allia! You know the standard of behavior I expect. You will leave the palace at once—"

Allia could sense Mara's anger and disappointment.

"No," Callonen broke in. "This was my fault. You will not punish Allia for my... indiscretion."

Mara took a deep breath. "She can't stay here as things are."

"I promise I will work things out with my father," Callonen said. "Please allow me time to do that?"

"As you command, my prince," Mara said, "but don't wait too long. He will not approve of this, especially with the princess arriving." Her mouth was set in a hard line. She went to the door and held it open. Callonen disappeared quickly into the dark hall. Mara and Allia returned to the servant's quarters. Allia didn't need the ring to sense the tension, and Mara didn't say a single word on the way.

She left Allia in the hallway and headed for the kitchen.

By the time Allia got back to her door, Tess appeared in the hall. After one look at Allia's face, Tess followed her into her room and shut the door behind them.

"What happened?"

Allia burst into tears. It had been the best night of her life. Callonen had kissed her. "It was wonderful. Every moment with him is... And he kissed me. I never wanted it to end... And then Mara caught us together."

Tess's mouth dropped open. "Is she sending you away?"

"She wanted to. Callonen told her she couldn't. He said he would explain everything to his father."

Tess gripped her hand. "But that's good, isn't it?"

Fresh tears flowed, and Allia wiped her eyes. "It won't be. Callonen will talk to him, but the emperor will be furious. He'll march down here himself and throw me out. Unless he sends the guards to take me to the dungeon."

"He won't do that," Tess said, hugging her. "You can tell me more later. I need to go."

Allia closed the door of her room behind her and curled up on the bed and cried.

Amid great ceremony and commotion, Princess Elena of Paraman arrived at midday. Tess and Allia went to the palace courtyard with everyone else to watch her ride in. Her entourage included many guards and attendants. Two ladies-in-waiting, dressed in matching red velvet gowns, their horses harnessed in red and gold, followed her carriage. The princess herself remained invisible behind the curtained windows of her carriage.

Tess and Allia watched the party ride into the courtyard to be met by Prince Callonen and Captain Talon, flanked by a formation of soldiers in crisp white-and-gold uniforms, their armor glinting in the sun.

Despair twisted in her stomach at the sight. Allia imagined arriving and opening the carriage door to see Callonen waiting for her, a smile on his face, his hand extended to take hers.

As the girls hurried inside to make a final check on the princess's room, they saw the entire palace bustling with preparations. Inside the finest guest room, Tess and Allia fluffed the pillows and made sure everything looked perfect.

"All we need now is the snake," Tess said as they surveyed their work.

Allia gave her a sad smile. "What do you think it would be like to have a room like this?"

"I'm sure that will never happen to me," Tess said. "Try not to think about it anymore. I know it isn't about the room, though. You want him."

Allia did not catch sight of the princess herself until the banquet that night in her honor. The finest food and drink were served, and the most skilled musicians played. The silver and crystal glittered in the candlelight.

Her expression stony, Mara had asked Allia if she were still able to fulfill her duties. Knowing the situation would be painful no matter where she was, Allia swallowed her heartbreak, promising she would do her job. With a stern warning not to speak to anyone during the dinner, Mara sent Allia and Tess to attend to the cups at the high table.

When the dinner began, Allia filled the pitcher and took her place, her face carefully free of any expression. As the royal family entered, she got her first look at the princess.

Elena was beautiful, her features delicate and her ivory skin framed by dark, almost black hair. She wore a silver gown, set with tiny gems that sparkled like stars. She seemed to float along with her hand resting gracefully on Callonen's arm.

Allia tried not to watch Callonen with her. He stood tall and straight, and she couldn't read his expression. Was he happy?

Annoyed? Did he like her? Maybe the sight of such a beautiful princess had made him entirely forget about Allia. He smiled, as politeness demanded, and Allia wondered if he really was happy. From this distance, she couldn't tell.

Emperor Caldoreth seemed exceptionally pleased, a smile on his face as he watched his son. The guests finished their meal, and the musicians began playing. Couples moved toward the dance floor, and Callonen stood and offered Elena his hand. They joined the other dancers, spinning in slow graceful circles.

Allia had to admit they made an attractive pair. Elena was slender and lovely, her manners perfect, and she gazed adoringly into Callonen's dark eyes. She obviously liked him.

Trying to look anywhere else, Allia glanced around the room. It didn't work very well. Her eyes kept sliding back to Callonen. She remembered what it was like to have his arms around her, his mouth on hers. Had it only been this morning when Mara had caught them together?

Allia couldn't wait for the evening to be over.

⁓

For the next three days, she saw Callonen only at a distance, and never alone. Elena constantly accompanied him. No announcement had been made, though rumors suggested an engagement was near. Gossip traveled quickly through the palace, and Allia dreaded hearing that the betrothal had become official. Everyone in the palace knew how badly the emperor wanted Callonen to marry and produce an heir.

Despite Allia's resolve to stay silent and give Callonen time to keep his word, it grew harder each day. At night, Allia couldn't sleep. The longer she lay in bed, tossing and turning, the worse it got. Finally, she pulled a robe over her nightdress and slipped out of the room.

Midnight had passed. Darkness and silence filled the palace, except for occasional lamps burning. The night guards stood in their places, but Allia made sure they didn't see her. She didn't want to explain to anyone why she was wandering the halls in her nightclothes. Her bare feet made no sound on the marble floors. The tower was the best place to look at the stars—the same place she had met Callonen just a few nights ago. He wouldn't be there now. Unless he slept, he would be with Elena. Her chest tightened at that thought.

Elena was a princess, the image of beauty and grace, exactly what Callonen needed to help him rule. They were perfect for each other. Perfect.

Allia felt tears sliding down her cheeks. If only Callonen hadn't been a prince. She could have loved him if he were a farmer or a soldier in Talon's company—anyone else.

She paused, leaning against the wall, wiping her eyes.

In the quiet, she heard voices in the distance. Two men were conversing. One sounded like Callonen. She crept nearer, turning down a hall she'd never been in before, and saw a door, unintentionally left slightly ajar. A thin line of light shone into the dark hall.

"How long will you remain here?" one of them asked. "Everything is almost ready." Callonen's voice. "Only a few details remain."

"You can't stay too long."

"But I won't leave before it's time. There are still possibilities here."

Where could Callonen possibly be going?

"There's one more thing I need from my brother."

Allia froze in alarm. Her mind had been on Callonen, and she'd assumed it was him. But he never spoke with the malice she heard now. It had to be Haldreth.

"The Warding is the source of their power. It will pass to Callonen unless he's dead, and I intend to make that happen. He and the Warding won't stand in my way forever."

Allia slipped silently down the hall, her heart pounding. If Haldreth found out she'd heard, he'd kill her.

Why didn't the emperor know about this? With all his power, how did he not sense his son's treachery? Haldreth planned to kill Callonen. No matter what, she couldn't let that happen.

Her heart racing, she ran through the palace. She had to find Callonen. He was the only one who would believe her. There might be others in the palace who were part of Haldreth's plot.

At last, she came to the hall where the royal family slept. She interrupted the stillness, and the guards blocked her way.

"Please, I need to speak with Prince Callonen! It's very important."

"Important?" The guard took in her nightgown and robe and snickered. "Aren't you a maid? You shouldn't be here."

"Yes, important! I need to talk to him."

"You can give me a message, and I'll tell him as soon as he wakes."

Allia shook her head stubbornly. "I can't do that. I need to tell him directly."

"You expect me to—" the guard's voice cut off at the sound of a door opening.

It was Callonen. His hair was rumpled, as if he'd been sleeping, but his eyes were sharp and alert. "What's going on?"

"Your Highness, I need to tell you something important," Allia said, curtsying.

"I told her I would give you her message when you woke," the guard explained.

Callonen looked back at her. "What's wrong? What is it?"

She couldn't say it in front of the guards. "Only you can hear it."

The guard shook his head, looking at Allia in her robe with her hair undone.

Callonen ignored him and came close to her. He bent his head. She put her hand on his shoulder and stood on her tiptoes to whisper in his ear. "Your brother is planning to kill you. I overheard him."

His eyes widened in shock, and he straightened abruptly. Allia's hand fell from his shoulder.

Princess Elena had come around the corner from the guest quarters in time to witness the scene and stood in the hall glaring at Callonen.

"Who is she?" She turned her gaze on at Allia. "In the daytime, you devote your time to me, but your nights—?"

In the shocked silence, Allia waited for Callonen to explain. He had to say something, anything. She needed him to defend her honor, to explain she had only been delivering a vital message. But he didn't speak. They all stood there for a long, uncomfortable moment until Allia fled.

Turning a corner, she cut them off from her sight and ran back to her own rooms. She closed the door and locked it behind her, breathing hard. It was over. If she had meant anything to him, he would have defended her. Why hadn't he spoken?

She realized what her presence must have looked like and hadn't meant to put Callonen in a difficult situation. But she had to tell him what she'd heard. He would explain things to Elena. He would tell her that Allia was only a servant with a message. The guard would support his story. Elena wouldn't be able to stay mad at him when he apologized.

When Callonen turned those brown eyes on the princess, it would be impossible for her anger not to melt away. Allia knew. Elena would forgive him, and they would be together.

Allia had warned Callonen of the danger from his brother. She'd done what she could, and now it was time to leave the city. The pain of staying here and watching them together would be too great. She had to get away.

❧

At the first glimmer of dawn, Allia went to Mara. "I have to leave," she said.

Mara's expression was stern. Finally, she sighed and her features softened. "I'm sorry, Allia. What I said the other night must have seemed harsh. I didn't mean it that way. Your mother was my friend, and I wanted to spare you this pain. For my part, you'll always have a place here if you choose to return."

"Thank you, Mara. I'm sorry I let you down."

"It wasn't your fault. I wish things could have been different for you."

Allia went back to her room to gather her things.

Tess came to her door and found her packing.

"What about waiting for Callonen to talk to his father?" Tess asked. "You're leaving? What happened?"

Allia couldn't bear to repeat the story. "I made a mistake last night. I had an urgent message to give to Callonen, and he came out of his room to receive it. Elena saw us talking and thought—"

Tess's eyes widened.

"It was nothing," Allia said, shaking her head. "Really nothing. I waited for him to explain, to tell her I hadn't done anything wrong. He didn't. I can't wait any longer. It's time to go."

Tears welled in Tess's eyes, and she hugged Allia. "I'm so sorry. Maybe he'll still fix things. I don't want you to go!"

Allia held her friend tightly. "I'm sorry, Tess. I can't stay and see them together. Callonen will work things out with her and with his father. Everything will be fine."

"Except for you," Tess said, wiping her eyes.

"But he'll be happy," Allia said. She finished putting the few last things into her bag, slung it over her shoulder, and gave Tess another hug. She left the little room, closing the door behind her.

Chapter Twenty

Year of Warding 21, White City, Sarine

Callonen

Callonen expected the summons from his father first thing in the morning. He went to Caldoreth's meeting room. As the guards opened the door for him, he saw Elena sitting across the desk from the emperor. She rose gracefully when Callonen entered, the folds of a stunning green gown falling around her. He couldn't deny her beauty, but no one could compare with Allia. He knew it now, and his feelings would never change.

Taking Elena's hand, Callonen kissed it briefly. Her expression appeared serene, but her eyes flashed with anger. They sat, and Callonen turned toward his father, whose brows were drawn together. Caldoreth looked furious.

His tone remained diplomatic for now. "Callonen, Princess Elena seems to have gotten the wrong impression last night. She has just informed me of her intention to depart immediately, and we don't want her to go. I'm sure you can provide an explanation." His dark eyes were hard.

An explanation desperately needed to be given, but not to them. Allia must have thought he didn't care, or that he didn't want to listen to her. He had wanted to follow her when she left, to explain. He'd seen the hurt in her eyes and that couldn't be allowed.

"I'm very sorry about last night," Callonen said to Elena. He turned to his father. "One of the staff brought an urgent message in the middle of the night. It was simply a misunderstanding."

"Some things cannot be misunderstood." Elena's tone was icy. "A beautiful young woman in her nightclothes came to your door in the middle of the night. It was obvious from the way she looked at you... What would you think if you were me?" Her cold expression softened, and a tear slid down her cheek. She wiped it away with a silk handkerchief edged with lace.

Callonen felt a twist of guilt. "The whole incident was my fault, and I'm very sorry, Elena."

"Maybe I would have thought it was only a misunderstanding if I hadn't seen the way you looked at her. I think it's time for us all to be honest." She dabbed at her eyes with the frilly square of fabric. "You don't want to marry me, do you?"

"Of course he does," Emperor Caldoreth broke in. "Callonen?"

Callonen turned to face his father.

Emperor Caldoreth seemed desperate now. "Please! Tell her it was all a mistake!"

He opened his mouth to speak, but Callonen couldn't say it. All he could think of was how beautiful Allia had looked with the soft waves of her golden hair unbound, how badly he wished she really had been sneaking into his chambers, and how it must have hurt her feelings when he didn't defend her. He never intended to make that mistake again.

Callonen took a deep breath and knelt beside Elena's chair, taking her hand. "I beg your forgiveness, Princess. You are beautiful and admirable in every way, and I apologize for the insult my behavior has been to you. But I cannot offer you my heart when it belongs to another. Please, forgive me."

He glanced up at her and wished he hadn't. Her eyes widened in anger and humiliation, and tears ran down her cheeks. She jerked her hand from his, stood up, and stormed out the door.

"Wait! Please!" Emperor Caldoreth jumped from his chair and followed her. But she disappeared out the door before he could stop her. "What in the name of—" The emperor flushed with rage and for a moment he couldn't get the words out. "What were you thinking?" he yelled. "Why did you do that? Don't you understand what will happen to Sarine if we don't have an heir? Would you leave our people unprotected? Go after her and try to change her mind!"

"No," Callonen said.

"No? Are you telling me that everything Elena said was true? How could you behave in such a way? It's unthinkable!"

"Nothing was going on last night. There really was an important message." *Your brother is planning to kill you.* How could Callonen tell his father that? He needed more information, some sort of proof, before he shared something like that.

"What could be so important in the middle of the night?" Caldoreth protested.

"I intend to investigate further," Callonen said. "Please trust me in this. It's enough to say that she had a concern for my safety."

Caldoreth stared at him, hard. "What threat to your safety?"

"I will look into it, Father, and bring you any information I find. The important thing is that she was trying to help. She did not intend to put either of us in a compromising situation. Two of the guards were on duty, standing right there the whole time. Absolutely nothing happened last night."

"Why didn't you tell Elena there was nothing to worry about? That she's only a member of our staff, and you don't have feelings for the girl?"

"Because I *do* have feelings for her. Elena could tell how I felt, and she doesn't deserve to be lied to. I can't marry her when I'm in love with someone else."

"So the last suitable princess disappears while you make a fool of yourself over a servant!" A vein pulsed on Caldoreth's temple, and he slammed his hand down on his desk. "How do you expect me to react to that?"

Callonen couldn't back down now. He faced his father squarely. "I love her! Do you really think that because a wizard created the

Warding and made you the emperor, that you are better than anyone else? If anything, we should bow to her. She belongs to the family of Zarekathus."

Caldoreth paused, his eyes widening in shock. "Really?"

"Allia is his granddaughter. She is good and kind and admirable in every way, and I love her!"

"You would give up this opportunity to strengthen our empire?"

Callonen didn't hesitate. "Absolutely," he said. "She would be well worth the trade. You married for love. Don't you want me to have the same chance?"

His father turned away and stared out the window. He took several deep breaths. When he turned back, he appeared calmer. "No matter what I do, the Warding will pass to you when I die. You know I can't disown you."

"I know," Callonen said. "But when Zarekathus made the Warding, he never asked me if I wanted it. Never. And now I can't escape it. I am bound to it for the rest of my life!"

Caldoreth was silent for a long moment. Then he sighed. "I'm sorry, Callonen. You're a good son, and you've always helped me. I should have considered your feelings more."

"Consider them now! I will rule your empire and take care of your people, and I can't escape the magic that will pass to me someday, but don't ask me to do it without Allia."

Calm had returned to the emperor's features. He turned to Callonen, rubbing his chin in thought. "All right." He shrugged in defeat. "I won't try to stop you. Marry whomever you want, but marry." Caldoreth shook his head. "What am I going to tell everyone?"

"Tell them the truth! Tell them that Allia belongs to the family of Zarekathus, the founder of our empire, and that I love her!"

Emperor Caldoreth stared at his son. "Are you sure about this?"

Callonen faced his father squarely. "I've never been more sure about anything in my life!"

"Callonen, I've watched you grow all these years, and I've come to believe you possess good judgment. Don't prove me wrong in this."

Hiding his relief, Callonen promised, "I won't." Then he grinned. "You'll love her."

Caldoreth nodded. "Very well. The decision is made, and I will support your choice, Son. You should have told me sooner. I will be happy to unite my family with that of my oldest friend."

Hugging his father, he exclaimed, "Thank you! You won't regret it!" He bolted out the door. Callonen wanted to run through the halls to find Allia, but he forced himself to maintain a dignified pace. Relief and excitement pulsed through his body. He was free to tell her how he felt about her, to ask her to be his wife. There would be no more secret meetings, no more hiding.

Callonen went directly to the kitchen.

Startled by his sudden appearance, Mara dropped her work and stood up straight. "Prince Callonen." She curtsied.

He took both her hands and kissed her cheek. Her eyes widened in shock, and she opened and shut her mouth wordlessly.

"It's done," he said. "My father and I have reached an agreement. Where is Allia?"

The blood drained from Mara's face. "She... She... She's gone, Your Highness. She left early this morning."

His exhilaration faded at once. "I told you not to send her away!"

"I didn't, Your Highness."

"Why did you let her leave? Where did she go?" he demanded.

"She went home to her family farm, Your Highness. If you head east, you might be able to catch up to her."

Callonen took a deep breath. "Thank you, Mara. I'm sorry I was rude." He left the kitchens heading for the gates.

Callonen borrowed a cloak from the guardroom and a horse from the stable. With the hood hiding his face and no escort to accompany him, he rode through the gates in the direction Mara had told him. Soon, he found that there were many people traveling along the road and paths branched off in different directions. He searched for her all day, and when darkness made it impossible to search anymore, he tended to his horse and wrapped himself in the cloak.

Shivering in the chill autumn night, Callonen's thoughts lingered on Allia. Where was she? Was she safe? Was she cold and hungry? He promised himself he would make sure she never suffered any of those things again. He had to find her. Impatiently, he waited for dawn.

ALLIA

As the sun set, Allia turned aside and settled into a sheltered spot against the trunk of a large tree up the hill from the road. She sat wrapped in her cloak, eating a cold meal from her bag.

Maybe she should have sought work in the city. The palace couldn't be the only option. Perhaps one of the shops? Or another household large enough to employ servants? She weighed the options. It would be better to arrange another job if she could. She didn't relish going back to her brothers after only a few months to confess that she'd made a complete mess of things.

Returning to the palace was out of the question. Her feelings for Callonen had become too deep. She cared too much, and it would break her heart to see him. She had left for good, and now she'd never see him again.

What had she thought would happen? The emperor was a powerful man, and he expected Callonen to marry the princess. That's the way it worked. There had never been any real hope that it would turn out differently. Why had she ever let herself fall for him? She wiped the tears from her cheeks.

A horse's hooves pounded against the road. She heard it coming long before the rider appeared around the corner. One man alone. The horse halted suddenly, and Allia tensed, wondering if she had something to do with it. But no, she was still, silent and hidden. She hadn't given herself away by moving, and the gray wool of her cloak blended with her surroundings.

The rider seemed familiar, but she couldn't be sure.

Another horse approached from the other direction, and the two riders met. The man who had been waiting turned his head, and Allia could see him better. It was Callonen! Had he come after her? Her heart leapt.

Firmly, she pushed the feeling down. No. That wasn't possible.

The two men left the road and steered their mounts into the trees on the far side, disappearing into the foliage.

Allia couldn't stop herself. She wrapped her cloak closely around herself and followed them. She heard voices long before she could see the men. Their two horses stood relaxed, heads down. Silently, she crept even closer.

"...the king of Ara sends his gratitude for your aid and is eagerly awaiting your arrival. Our people have been repairing the fortress at Hakvere. Without your help, the whole thing would continue to crumble away. It will take time to repair all the stonework." Allia didn't recognize that voice.

"How long will it take?" A very familiar voice demanded. Of course it was Haldreth. Callonen coming to find her had only been a daydream.

"I need more money," the other man said. "If you want it to go faster, I'll hire more men."

"You always want more money," Haldreth sounded irritated. "Take this for now and keep them working. Don't move forward with our plans until I say so. I'll take care of things with my father and brother. Then it will be time. Meet me back here at the next full moon to report."

Allia heard his heavy steps pass her hiding place. She froze, crouched down in the underbrush. He couldn't see her here.

He came close enough for her to sense him. Her stomach clenched, anticipating his malice and fury. Instead, she felt nothing from him except hopeful anticipation as he moved away. Not daring to look, she heard him mount his horse and ride back toward the city.

When Haldreth was gone, she heard the other man return to his horse and ride in the opposite direction.

༄

Allia spent the night well hidden. After her encounter, she slept little. Haldreth was obviously planning something big. Lots of people were involved in it, not just a single man jealous because he wasn't destined to receive the throne. There was much more.

She tossed and turned on the cold ground. Callonen didn't love her, and he never would. But he deserved to be warned, even so. She was very sure he did not know that his brother's treachery had gone so far, even if he'd believed her warning from the other night. Did he truly understand the danger? What if Haldreth succeeded in murdering Callonen?

But Allia couldn't ignore what had happened the last time she'd attempted to warn him. He'd allowed everyone to think she had come to his room in the middle of the night only to throw herself at him. How humiliating. He'd gotten all the warning he would get from her, and he probably didn't believe her anyway.

When the sun finally rose, she was still arguing with herself. But she started walking back toward the city. Carts and wagons passed her on the road, along with a few riders. She doubted whether she'd recognize the man Haldreth had been talking to. It had been dark, and she hadn't gotten a good look at him.

She stopped, frozen in the middle of the road. Haldreth was coming back, riding directly toward her. And the road ran through open fields just then, with nowhere to hide. How had he found out that she heard?

No. Allia knew they hadn't seen her last night. Even if they had seen someone, it had been too dark to make out her face. Haldreth couldn't know she'd overheard.

A powerful urge to flee swept over her, but running would only attract more attention. She kept walking, waiting for him to pass by. As his horse pulled up beside her, relief flooded through her as she realized it was Callonen.

He jumped to the ground. "Allia?"

She felt the sharp prick of sorrow. "Your Highness," she said coolly, curtsying.

"Allia, please. I must speak with you."

Callonen. It really was him, but she couldn't believe it. "It can't be you," she muttered, shaking her head.

"Why can't it be me?" He seemed confused.

"Prince Haldreth traveled this road last night, and Prince Callonen is in the city with Princess Elena." She couldn't get her mind to catch up to her eyes.

"My brother was here? He was scheduled to visit the estates of several of our friends out near the Warding. Allia, can we please talk? I came to beg your forgiveness. I'm so very sorry about my behavior. Will you allow me to explain?"

His brown eyes were earnest as he looked at her. It was really Callonen. And he'd come to apologize to her? "I don't expect an apology," she said. "You're going to marry Elena. That's what your father wants. I know you have to get married. Don't worry. I understand. I only came back to tell you something important."

"Wait! Before you do, can I explain?" He reached for her hand and held it.

She felt tears welling in her eyes and willed them to disappear.

Having him so close made her want him closer still, and—

He loved her. All of his doubts had disappeared. She could sense the overwhelming feeling clearly, and it took her breath away.

"I'm sorry I didn't defend you when you came to my room. I know you had nothing in mind but my safety, and I'm so grateful you care enough to come to me with something like that. But I violated your trust by not defending you."

"Elena was angry when she saw me, and I'm sure your father was too when he found out."

"They were both angry—"

Allia pulled her hand from his and turned away again.

He reached out and took it back. "They were angry because I told Elena I couldn't marry her since I was already in love with you."

Chapter Twenty-One

Year of Warding 21, Sarine's Countryside

Allia

Allia stood in the middle of the road and stared at Callonen, positive that she had heard him wrong. "You said... what?"

"Elena was upset because she saw the way I looked at you. She could tell that I cared for you deeply and was jealous. When she saw how much I wanted you, she lost all interest in me."

"Why didn't you tell her we were only friends? I didn't mean to cause trouble for you. I'm sorry, Callonen. If you explained the whole thing to her, she would forgive you. Why didn't you?"

"Because what she said was true. When I look at you, I can't think of anything else. I could never feel for her the way I feel for you."

"But that only makes it worse," Allia exclaimed, the traitorous tears spilling over and running down her cheeks. "You have to marry her! Your father is still the emperor."

"He's my father first. And I'm going to rule after him. I told him I needed you, that I never wanted to marry anyone but you."

Allia looked up at him in disbelief. "And then he threw you out for defying him?"

Callonen smiled and brushed her tears away with gentle fingers. "No. He can't, and he knows it. I made him agree with me in the end. He promised to support my choice."

She still stared back at him with her mind spinning in circles. Callonen bent to one knee. "Allia, will you please do me the honor of becoming my wife?"

His wife.

Callonen was on one knee before her, asking her to marry him. Shock bound her tongue. She stared at him in disbelief as the silence grew longer.

"I—"

"Please say that you'll forgive me? I will defend you for the rest of my life. Please?"

She reached down and touched the side of his face. "Yes," she found her voice at last. "I will." She threw her arms around him. "I will!"

He laughed and got to his feet, still holding her. "You said yes!" He sounded amazed.

Allia had waited and dreamed of this moment, thinking it would never come. She smiled at him, and he pulled her close and brought his lips to hers. She tangled her fingers in his hair and kissed him. His mouth was warm and wonderful.

Finally, he took a breath. "Can you forgive me?" he asked again.

"I forgive you," she murmured, her lips against his ear. "But please tell me why you didn't say anything."

"When Elena saw you there in your nightclothes, and she assumed that you—that we—"

Allia shook her head. "I know how it must have appeared, and I wouldn't have done it if I hadn't heard—"

"I need you to tell me everything you found out about my brother. And I promise I'll listen, but let me finish first. The truth is, I hadn't been sleeping when you came. I'd been lying awake thinking of you, and when I saw you there, you looked so beautiful. I wished with all my heart that you had been sneaking to my door to see me. Elena could tell how much I wanted you. It didn't matter what I said to her, she could see it. And I knew it was time to tell her the truth, and my father. But I'm so sorry

I hurt you. I should have defended you anyway. I didn't mean for you to feel that I didn't care."

He kissed her again. "Forgive me?" he whispered, his lips still pressed against hers.

"Yes," she murmured breathlessly.

"Good," he grinned. "Now tell me about my brother."

They headed back toward the city at a slow walk, hand in hand with Callonen leading the horse, while Allia explained what she'd heard.

"How is it possible?" Callonen asked. "My brother told everyone he would be away, taking care of business with some of the noble families. How does my father not know what he's really doing?"

"I'm not making this up!"

"I'm sorry," he said. "Of course, I didn't mean that I don't believe you. I believe everything you told me. It just seems my father should already know about this."

"And you don't think he does?"

"No." Callonen shook his head. "He would have told me."

"What can we do?"

"I'll talk to him alone when we get back and explain everything."

"Do you think he'll believe you? He has no reason to trust me. What are we going to do if he doesn't?"

Callonen knit his brows in deep thought. "We need to find some sort of evidence. This is a very serious accusation. I want to know how Haldreth can trick the magic. My father should be able to sense any treachery. It's part of the Warding."

That meant someday Callonen would be able to sense his subjects' intentions too. That would be a heavy weight to carry. But maybe she could help him carry it, especially since she had some understanding of it herself. But in the meantime, they had to keep him safe. "Please promise me you won't trust Haldreth anymore, not for a moment."

"I promise," Callonen said.

"Don't give him any opportunity to hurt you. You can't put yourself in danger, and you shouldn't have come out here alone.

He was just here last night, and he has several people working with him. If he should get them to ambush you—"

Callonen squeezed her hand reassuringly. "He doesn't know I'm out here. I didn't tell anyone I left the city."

"Aren't they looking for you?"

He looked a little guilty. "I didn't think about anything but finding you and begging you to forgive me. And besides, if there were a troop of violent men waiting to attack, I'm sure my father could tell."

"That doesn't mean he could get here in time to stop them," Allia pointed out.

"All right then," he conceded, "We'll go back." He mounted the horse and offered his hand. She took it, and he pulled her up behind him. She slid her arms around his waist.

Allia hadn't even imagined what it would feel like to be so close to him, to feel the warmth of his body through his shirt. And she could feel his love. He wanted to be with her. She meant more to him than anything else. Her eyes welled with tears. She'd never expected to be so happy.

Their ride back to the city was the longest time they had been truly alone together, and Allia enjoyed it completely. No one could interrupt them, and no errand could call Callonen away from her side.

"We should turn around and ride away," he said. "No one would ever know what happened to us. We'd see the world together."

The idea tempted her more than she'd like to admit. But so many people depended on him—everyone who lived in Sarine. Callonen could not throw his duty aside so lightly. He had promised his father.

Allia said, "You wouldn't really do it." She gave him a quick kiss on the back of his neck.

"Right now, I wish I could," he said.

"And I would go with you," Allia said. "But you wouldn't leave Sarine to your brother."

"No. I will keep the Warding."

They rode in silence for a few moments until Allia laughed suddenly.

"What is it?" Callonen asked.

"How long has it been since you've eaten? I can feel your stomach growling."

"Breakfast... yesterday," he admitted. "I left without bringing anything with me. I was in a hurry to find you."

"That's very sweet," she laughed, "But not very practical. I have bread and cheese in my bag."

Stopping beside the road, they sat together on the grass and shared a simple meal.

They spent all that day together, and it was the best day of her life. Callonen didn't ride as fast as he might have, but she knew he dared not delay too long.

"I don't want to go back yet," Callonen confessed. "I love being out here with you."

All too soon, they came within sight of the city. He took his cloak from behind the saddle and put it on as they rode. They entered the gates without being questioned and rode up the hill to the palace.

Outside, they dismounted and walked hand in hand through the doors, Callonen with his hood up and his head down. They passed most of the guards without being questioned, but then Captain Talon stepped deliberately in front of Callonen, forcing him to look up.

Allia held her breath and clutched Callonen's hand. Up close, grim-faced and bristling with weapons, Talon was thoroughly intimidating.

But Callonen only smiled, looking up to give Talon a clear view of his face.

"What are you doing?" Captain Talon growled in a low voice.

Callonen grinned. "Just let me in, Talon. Quietly."

"Go straight to your father, Cal," Captain Talon ordered. "He almost rode out after you himself. And he's assigned you to join the patrol. Don't forget. We're leaving tomorrow at dawn."

"Thanks for telling me," Callonen said. "I've been a little busy."

Glancing at Allia, Talon replied, "So I see." His harsh expression melted into a smile, and he shook his head and moved aside.

As they passed him, Allia sensed he wasn't really angry, only glad that Callonen was safe.

She sighed in relief and relaxed. Callonen's hand tightened around hers.

"Talon may look frightening, but he's one of the kindest people I know."

"I was afraid of him at first," Allia confessed. "He is intimidating, and I've seen how well he can fight."

"If you were his enemy, you should be afraid. He's very dangerous," Callonen said. "But you have nothing to fear. Now, are you ready to meet my father?"

"Now? Shouldn't I put on my best dress or something?" Her one comfort was that, though her dress was simple, it was one of her own she had brought from the farm and not the gray dress she wore when she worked in the palace.

"Don't worry about that," Callonen said. "I told him everything before I left, and he agreed to support our betrothal. He wanted to meet you immediately."

"You told him I've been a servant in his palace, and that I come from a farm in the country?"

"Yes, and that Zarekathus was your grandfather," Callonen said. "He's excited to meet you."

"I met him once before," Allia said, "on the day my grandfather died. He might not remember me."

"Either way, it will be fine. Don't worry."

Don't worry. Allia shook her head slightly and tried to breathe evenly to calm the twisting nervousness in her stomach. They were headed up the stairs to meet the man who ruled the empire of Sarine, the man who knew the hearts of everyone in his realm, the man who would prefer his son to marry a princess. No one in the palace stopped or questioned them until they reached the emperor's audience chamber. It was the same room where Mara had interrupted their kiss.

The guard bowed to Callonen. "Your Highness."

"Is my father in there?"

"Yes, Your Highness," the guard replied. "He should be finished any moment."

Callonen nodded. "We will wait, rather than interrupt him."

They stood in the hall. Allia's heart pounded. Callonen gripped her hand reassuringly. "Don't worry," he whispered. "Everything is going to be fine."

She heard a voice approaching the other side of the door, and it opened. A nobleman came out.

"Thank you, Your Majesty," he said to the emperor. Seeing Callonen, he added, "Good day, Your Highness." Then, glancing briefly at Allia, he nodded and departed down the hall.

It was time.

Hand in hand, they entered the room. It appeared grander in the daylight than the last time she'd been here. The emperor sat on his throne, powerful and stern, flanked by white-uniformed guards. She had seen Emperor Caldoreth many times from a distance, but she'd never spoken with him since she came to the city. Now his attention focused entirely on her and Callonen, and her stomach churned. He looked like Callonen, with brown eyes and dark hair beginning to gray. She remembered him well from that terrible day six years ago. When her grandfather was in trouble, he'd come to help.

Caldoreth rose from his throne and came to meet them, frowning. "I almost sent the entire guard out after you," he glared at Callonen. "You should not leave the city alone. If not for the Warding, I wouldn't have known where you were, and I would have searched for you myself."

"I'm sorry," Callonen said. "I didn't plan to. When I learned Allia had left, I went after her. I apologize for worrying you. Father, this is Allia."

Emperor Caldoreth turned his attention to her. His dark eyes were penetrating. Allia returned his gaze, sensing that he wanted to know more about her. Did she really love Callonen? Did she keep secrets? If he could tell her intent, then he would realize she loved Callonen with all her heart. For a long moment, they met each other's gaze.

Emperor Caldoreth's expression softened into a smile, and he took Allia's hand and kissed it. "I do remember you," he said. "We met on the day Zarekathus died. You ran to help him."

Allia nodded. "Yes." She could sense that the memory of that day was a bitter one for Caldoreth too. He felt guilty. He'd tried to protect his friend and failed.

"I rode as hard as I could," Caldoreth said. "As soon as I knew that our old enemy had entered the Warding. I tried to get there in time to stand with your grandfather. Instead, I arrived to see him on the ground, dying. You were beside him."

Sudden tears filled Allia's eyes. She felt Callonen's arm tighten around her. It had been one of the hardest moments of her life. She'd tried frantically to save her grandfather, but in only a few moments, it had been too late.

Caldoreth took her hand again. "I'm very sorry to remind you of that day."

"It's all right."

"Please forgive me, my dear. I didn't realize you were here, and you've grown up so much since I saw you. I didn't know who you were until Callonen told me. Instead of allowing you to work in the palace, I would have offered you a place as my honored guest for as long as you wanted. With all my heart, I will support my son's choice of a bride." He smiled at her.

Now Allia could see where Callonen's charm had come from. And she sensed that he sincerely meant what he said. "Thank you," she replied, and her stomach relaxed.

"My son has told me how highly he thinks of you," the emperor said. "I trust his judgment."

"You are too kind, Emperor," Allia said, glancing quickly at Callonen.

The emperor's gaze became searching again. "Allia, are you prepared to live with the challenges that accompany my son's position? He will have many demands on his time and duties to fulfill. And you must be aware that there are those who might disapprove of your marriage?"

"I understand," Allia said. "I am not of noble birth."

"My son has reminded me that other things are more important."

"Thank you, Emperor."

"You belong to an honorable and talented family, one that has already proved its loyalty. I can tell that you sincerely care for my son. I agree with his decision to see you as a princess," he said graciously, smiling at her. "Your grandfather always stood by me. And we will stand by you."

"Thank you," she exclaimed, hugging him impulsively. Then she stepped back. What had she been thinking? He was the *emperor*. "I'm sorry. That wasn't proper."

But the emperor only laughed, and Allia's distress melted away. He accepted her, and she felt it. Gratitude rushed through her, taking the last of her nervousness with it.

"I'm delighted to welcome you into our family. Now that I've met you, I can understand why you are more important to Callonen than anything else."

"He said that?" Allia whispered, her eyes widening as she looked up at Callonen. She could see love and commitment in his eyes. He reached out to take her hand and kissed it.

"He and I cannot afford to be at odds," the emperor said. "Even if he's stubborn at times, I need him. He has spent his whole life preparing to lead Sarine."

"I need him too," Allia murmured, tightening her hand on Callonen's.

The emperor smiled. "Then marry him, *please*. No one else will."

Allia couldn't help but laugh. "I will."

"I'm glad that's settled," the emperor said. "Now, as soon as you get back from your patrol, Cal, we'll have a party and announce your betrothal officially."

"That's right, I have to ride with the guard." Callonen nodded ruefully.

"I'm afraid that's my fault," Caldoreth said, turning to Allia. "After the princess departed unexpectedly, I assigned Callonen to go out with a patrol. He'll be gone for about ten days."

"I understand," Allia said. She'd just agreed to support the demands of Callonen's position, and it would be foolish to break that promise a moment after making it. Still, she didn't want him to go. She'd only just gotten him back. Ten days without him seemed an eternity.

"But I agree the schedule isn't convenient for you." Emperor Caldoreth turned to his son. "With things as they are, perhaps Allia would consider accompanying you, if the traveling conditions wouldn't be too rough for her?" the emperor asked. "Captain Talon will meet his wife and son on the road anyway, and there will be plenty of men to escort you."

Callonen's face brightened. "Would you like to come?" he asked Allia. "You would see more of our empire."

She smiled. "Of course I would come. But will it be all right? It won't cause trouble?"

"No," Callonen said. "You can bring Tess with you. Talon won't mind, and he's in command of all the guards. Meet me by the palace gate at dawn."

"It's all settled then," Caldoreth said. He took Allia's hand and kissed it. "I wish you happiness." He embraced his son. "And you, Callonen. We will speak more when you return."

"Thank you, Father." Callonen grinned, taking her hand in his, and they slipped out into the hall. He pulled her around a corner into an empty passageway. "You did it!"

"It wasn't me," Allia protested. "Whatever you said must have won him over."

"You won him over." Callonen put his arms around her and held her. "Are you sure you want to go with me tomorrow?"

"I would go anywhere with you," she said. "But I'd better get some rest if I need to be ready at dawn."

"Shall I speak to Mara about a guest room for you?"

Allia smiled at his concern. "No, thank you. I'll speak to her. I was going to anyway."

"Is there anything else you need?" Callonen's brows lowered in concern.

Allia shook her head.

"Then I'll be counting the hours." Callonen left her with a kiss that ended far too quickly.

CHAPTER TWENTY-TWO

YEAR OF WARDING 21, WHITE CITY, SARINE

ALLIA

WHEN ALLIA WENT DOWN to the kitchens, Mara spotted her at once.

"I'm very sorry for all the trouble I've caused you," Allia said.

"What are you doing back here? What happened?" Mara asked urgently, pulling her into a pantry where they could talk privately.

"I've just come from meeting with the emperor. Prince Callonen asked me to marry him, and his father has given his full support."

Mara's features froze in shock for a moment. "I—" She shook her head and smiled in astonishment. "I didn't think it was possible. Allia, that's wonderful news!"

"You're not upset about it?" Allia hadn't thought Mara approved.

"I was upset because I thought the emperor wouldn't allow it. You're a good girl, Allia, and I think you'll make the prince very happy. Do you need your room back?"

"Just for tonight. After that, I don't know what will happen," Allia confessed. "But with your permission, I will ask Tess to come with me when I ride with Callonen in the morning."

"Very well," Mara agreed. "Two more girls came yesterday looking for work. I will find out if they can start tomorrow."

"You won't move Tess out of her place?"

"No, but if you really plan to marry Callonen and become a princess, you'll need her help. I have a feeling both of you will be very busy in the coming months."

"Tess!" Allia knocked on her friend's door.

After a moment, Tess opened it, her eyes wide. "You're back! What happened?"

"You'll never believe it!" Allia suddenly hushed her voice and glanced up and down the hall. No need to start any more rumors.

"Come in and tell me everything," Tess said, pulling her inside.

They sat side by side on the bed.

"It happened, Tess. It really happened!" Allia whispered excitedly. "Callonen asked me to marry him and then took me to meet his father. Emperor Caldoreth said..." She paused. For a moment, the whole thing seemed unreal. She took a deep breath. "He actually looked at Callonen and said to me, 'Marry him, please. No one else will.'"

"The emperor said that? I don't believe it," Tess exclaimed. She hugged her friend, and they both laughed in joy and surprise. "Oh, Allia. It's wonderful."

"I thought it could never happen, that he would never approve. It's so much more than I ever hoped for. I didn't expect the emperor to be so kind. He said he would support us."

"That's wonderful, Allia. When is he going to announce it?"

"Callonen has to go out on patrol with the guard. The emperor said when he gets back."

"He's leaving now?" Tess asked. "Are you upset that he's going?"

"Not if we go with him," Allia looked pleadingly at her friend.

"You and I... go with him? You mean ride with the soldiers? Out in the dust? Sleep on the ground, and cook over a fire? All that?" Tess asked in dismay. "But you would be with him, and you don't care about the rest."

"I don't," Allia admitted. "But I don't want you to be unhappy. Mara has given her permission, though."

"There are bugs out there," Tess protested. "And snakes and spiders."

"If we see a spider, I promise I'll get Callonen to kill it for you." Allia's mind rushed back to that day in the storage room. He had more than proved his skills.

Tess shuddered. "Promise?"

"Promise," Allia vowed. "Please say you'll come? Please, please! I think Harrow will go too. This is your chance to get to know him."

"He is usually with Talon," Tess said, twisting one of her red curls as she thought. "We'll be riding. What would we wear?"

"Have you got a pair of boots?" Allia asked.

"Yes, but I can't ride as well as you. How are we supposed to ride all day in a dress? Do you want to give Callonen the chance to admire your legs?"

"Not that I wouldn't enjoy his attention," Allia confessed, "but we do want to be proper. Back on the farm, I wore a divided underskirt for riding. I have an extra one you can borrow. Just slide it on under your skirt."

Tess seemed relieved. "I think that might work."

"Of course it works. Will you come, please?"

Tess shrugged as she gave in. "Who knows, maybe it'll be fun."

Allia was so excited she barely slept that night. Callonen had *really* asked her to marry him. They would spend several days together, and when they got back, the emperor planned to announce Callonen's engagement. Her life would never be the same. Not even close.

When morning arrived, she dressed by candlelight. Allia had already decided she wouldn't appear anywhere with Callonen wearing the gray palace uniform. Putting on her favorite green dress and a green cloak, she stuffed a spare outfit into her bag.

In the gray light of dawn, Allia and Tess went down to the gates, each with a couple of rolled-up blankets and a small satchel of belongings. The girls felt conspicuously out of place as the soldiers and horses assembled. The men all dressed alike in dark-green uniforms topped by chain mail, assorted armor and weapons. Captain Talon was giving orders, and he looked as dangerous and intimidating as always. In addition to his sword, knives and axe, he wore a bow and quiver of arrows over his shoulder. Allia had hoped to escape his notice, but he headed straight for them.

"What are you two doing here?" he asked. "Don't tell me that Prince Callonen invited you to come along?"

Allia nodded mutely.

"Can you fight?" Talon asked, offering her a short sword.

"I..." she faltered, horrified by the thought until she sensed Talon was joking. He was enjoying himself. She met his eye and took the blade from him. "I'm glad you asked, Captain. Perhaps not as well as you, but I learned a few tricks from my brothers."

His eyebrows raised. "I'll remember that, if we run into any action."

Callonen appeared just then, dressed in the same uniform as all the soldiers. "Don't let Talon tease you," he said, glaring at his friend. He took the weapon from Allia and returned it to Talon. "I brought horses for you. These two are very gentle."

He gave Allia and Tess each a horse's reins, slipped their satchels into the saddlebags, and buckled their blanket rolls behind the saddles. "Can I get you anything before we go?"

"No, thank you. We're ready," Allia said, looking at Tess for confirmation.

Tess nodded, but looked at the horse uncertainly.

A soldier appeared at her side. "May I help?" he asked. It was Harrow.

"Yes," Tess said, allowing him to assist her into the saddle. "Thank you." She rewarded him with a smile.

Allia accepted Callonen's help to mount. The other men were already on their horses and prepared to go. She counted fourteen uniformed men.

"Move out," Talon called, and they rode out of the gates.

It was a beautiful early autumn morning. The forests were green, while the fields had turned golden. By the time the sun rose over the hills, the city lay far behind them. Tess had fallen a little behind, but when Allia turned to look for her, she saw Harrow riding beside her. Callonen gradually slowed his horse to let the others pass him until he rode beside Allia.

They had plenty of time to talk, and they could enjoy each other's company with no meetings to attend, no diplomats to deal with, and nothing to interrupt them.

The group traveled all that day until the sun hung low in the west. Allia was tired and dusty, but she could see that Tess felt even more weary than she was.

"We'll stop here for the night," Talon announced as he found a suitable spot under a grove of trees at the bottom of a grassy hill. Callonen and Harrow helped the ladies off their horses. "Would you like to rest a little?" he asked, and the girls sat down, savoring the feeling of not being on a horse.

The soldiers seemed used to this kind of expedition. They appeared to have a familiar routine of working together to make a fire, haul water, tend to the horses, and prepare an evening meal. Callonen helped the rest with their work, and if it was unusual for a prince to collect firewood, no one said anything.

As darkness fell, Allia and Tess joined the others as they gathered around the fire and ate. Soon, Callonen took a seat beside Allia.

"May I sit here?" asked a voice from behind them.

Allia saw Tess's cheeks flush as she realized it was Harrow.

Tess swallowed quickly. "Please do," she said, as he took a seat beside her.

Allia sat with the others, talking around the fire as it burned down. One by one, the men dispersed and rolled themselves into their blankets to sleep.

Harrow stood up and stretched. Looking at Tess, he said, "Thank you for your company today. Good night."

She smiled. "Good night, Harrow. I'll see you in the morning?"

"I'll be here," he replied with an answering smile as he left to find his bedroll.

"We should get some rest too," Callonen said. "It's been a long day." He got to his feet and offered his hand, pulling Allia up. "Good night."

"Good night, Callonen." He kissed her cheek and went to find his blankets.

Tess and Allia wrapped themselves up in their bedding, side by side, and tried to get comfortable.

"Something's crawling on me," Tess whispered, sitting up to brush vigorously at her hair.

"A bug?" Allia asked.

"I'm trying not to think about what it was," Tess groaned, lying down again. "You owe me."

Allia smiled at her. "I know. Thanks for coming with me." Then she leaned close and whispered, "Do you want me to go ask Harrow to come and check for spiders?"

Tess elbowed her in the side in reply.

The night deepened, and the camp grew quiet. But Allia couldn't sleep. She lay there for hours, listening to the breeze whispering through the trees and watching the stars turning slowly above her. Even Tess had finally dozed off. Allia raised herself on one elbow and looked around at the dark sleeping forms. Which one was Callonen? She couldn't tell for sure. Someone was snoring faintly. It must have been past the middle of the night when she finally left her blanket and tiptoed through all the sleeping bodies to the edge of the camp and a little way up the hill beyond. She sat down on the grass, pulled her knees up under her skirt, and wrapped her arms around them. There was no sound except for the night breeze in the grass and the sleepy chirp of crickets.

She heard something behind her. Turning to see a large black shape, she gasped in fright.

"Allia?"

It was Talon. She let out a deep breath. "You scared me."

"Sorry," he said. "I was on guard, and I didn't know you would be out here. Is something wrong?"

"No, I'm fine. I just couldn't sleep."

"Worried about something?" he asked, sitting down beside her. His voice was kind. She could sense he wasn't as mean as he seemed. "Or maybe you were thinking about someone?" he prompted.

"Maybe," she admitted.

"I remember how I felt when I first met my wife," Talon said. "I couldn't think about anything but her. She was so beautiful. I couldn't help hoping that she felt the same."

"What's her name?" Allia asked.

"Mirithel," he replied. "I've loved her for almost eight years now. Our son, Zarek, is six."

"You must be proud of him," Allia said.

"Any father would be," Talon replied. "He's smart and brave and strong. He says he wants to lead the guard someday, but Mirithel is against it. She wants him to be a scholar."

"You still have time before he has to make that decision," Allia said, smiling in the dark.

"True," Talon said. "He will have to choose, and I'll be proud of him no matter what he does. There are other, less dangerous things he could do. I'm sure he will have the skill for almost any occupation." Talon yawned. "I've taken my turn on guard, and now I think I'll sleep. Are you ready to go back now?"

"May I sit here and watch the stars a little longer?" she asked.

"Better not to stay out here alone. I'll send someone to join you. Good night then," he said, returning down the hill. Allia had definitely misjudged him. Captain Talon was nothing like he appeared to be.

A little while after he had left, she saw someone else coming up the hill in the dark and hardly dared hope that it would be Callonen. When he came near enough, she could see his face in the starlight. She felt a spark of excitement as he sat down beside her. "Cal," she whispered.

"Why aren't you asleep?" he asked. "We had a long ride today."

"I just couldn't sleep," she said. "Talon came and talked to me. He told me about his family."

"He's missed them while they were gone. They've been away from the city, visiting her parents, and they're on their way back. They will meet us on the road. Does he still frighten you?"

"No," Allia said. "He is so much kinder than he seems at first."

"Yes."

For a moment, they sat in silence. The night was cooling off, and Allia shivered. Callonen put his arm around her and held her close. He had shed his armor and chain mail for the night. Now she felt the warmth and strength of his body against hers. She turned to look at him, and his mouth found hers. She put her arms around him and pulled him closer. They were in love, and when they got back to the city, everyone would know it.

The next morning, they prepared to ride as soon as everyone had eaten. Tess groaned as she got back into the saddle. "Aren't you sore too?" she asked Allia.

"A little," Allia said. "It should get better soon."

Tess rolled her eyes.

The company continued their trip, stopping now and again at guard stations or villages. Allia saw much of the country that she had never seen before.

In just a few days, they had passed beyond the Warding. The farms and villages outside seemed peaceful, but reports of bandits or other dangers in the area had reached the White City. Emperor Caldoreth had sent them to investigate.

The company kept a vigilant watch, especially at night. Talon doubled the number of guards at the edge of their camp, and Allia and Callonen did not wander outside it, as much as they would have enjoyed the time to themselves.

CHAPTER TWENTY-THREE

YEAR OF WARDING 21, VARDA, SARINE

ALLIA

THE MIDDAY SUN SHONE high above as the company passed through a village called Varda and came to the edge of a forest. They stopped on the road.

"The trees look thicker since the last time we came this way," Callonen said.

"Your brother passed this place on his way back to the city a couple of weeks ago," Talon informed him. "He told your father we should check the forest. There were some strange rumors in the village about two missing people. The road goes right through it, and Mirithel will travel this way, coming toward us."

Talon rode into the forest, and the rest of the company followed him. It was cool under the trees, and the shade deepened as they went along.

Allia loved trees, but she didn't like this place. There was something unpleasant about it. She couldn't describe what bothered her, but the soldiers seemed uneasy too. They kept their hands close to their weapons and watched the surrounding undergrowth. The light of the afternoon faded, especially under the thick cover of leaves.

Callonen turned to Talon. "I think we should go back. It's getting late, and this isn't a good place to spend the night."

"I agree," Talon said. "But there's a horse lying beside the road up there. Let's check it before we go."

When they got closer, Talon leapt to the ground and ran to it. "It's my wife's horse," he exclaimed. "Spread out! Find her! And be careful!"

Everyone dismounted and began a hasty search, which revealed another dead horse and one of the guards who'd been escorting Talon's wife.

"Is he alive?" Callonen asked.

"No," Talon said in a tight voice. "Look at this." He pointed to dark lines radiating from two puncture wounds on the man's neck.

"What could have done that?" Callonen asked.

"I have to find my family!" Talon resumed his desperate search and soon found footprints in the soft earth. "This way!" he cried. Holding their weapons ready, the soldiers followed him into the woods. Allia and Tess kept close to the men as they moved through the thick trees. Sticky gray lines trailed from the branches overhead.

Talon followed the footprints. "Mirithel!"

They heard a faint reply and hurried through the brush and trees until they found a woman lying on the ground in a small clearing. She must be Talon's wife.

Another of her guards lay nearby. Two soldiers went to help him while Talon ran to the woman who was pulling at a bundle wrapped in the same gray fibers. "Let him go!" she moaned.

At first, Allia couldn't tell what the woman clung to until Talon began pulling back the cords to reveal a child, wrapped from head to toe in sticky threads. This must be their son. Talon cut the strangling cords and freed the boy. His skin was white, and he barely breathed.

Talon just had time to see that his son still lived before one of the men yelled, "Spiders!"

Allia felt Tess clutching her arm. All the color had drained from Tess's face, and her green eyes were round in terror.

Spiders. And from the condition of Mirithel's party, their bite was toxic. Allia searched her memory. Her grandfather had showed her an herb called redleaf, which could cure poisons. The plant grew almost everywhere. She needed to find some.

A spider dangled from the leaves overhead and Tess shrieked. Before Allia had a chance to do anything, Harrow struck it with his sword.

"Thank you!" Tess gasped. He kept his sword ready, but offered her his other hand, which she took.

Allia looked around. Spiders crept toward them from all sides. They were just like the ones she and Callonen had discovered in the storage room, except now there were dozens. Allia picked up two fallen branches and gave one to Tess. "Don't let them get too close." They tried to watch in all directions at once. Three more spiders dangled from above, and when Harrow turned to strike at them, Allia saw a horrible dark shape already clinging to the chain mail on his back. He grunted in pain.

She used the stick to pry the spider off him. When it fell to the ground, Harrow stomped on it. The spider's body was nearly the size of his foot, and it required several heavy blows from his boot before it stopped twitching.

Talon grabbed his bow from his back and started shooting. His arrows pierced several spiders.

Callonen used his sword, striking as many as he could reach. "We have to get out of here!" he yelled, picking up the little boy. Talon returned the bow to his back and lifted his wife. Two men carried the unconscious guard. The rest of the men formed a rear guard as they retreated the way they had come.

As everyone moved through the woods, Allia spotted a familiar, low-growing plant near her feet. Redleaf. She dropped to her knees and gathered handfuls of it, stuffing her pockets full of the leaves.

"Hurry!" a soldier urged her, slashing at spiders that crept closer.

"I'm coming!" Allia got to her feet, and they hurried toward the road. Harrow sheathed his sword and pulled Tess forward. Soon he stumbled along, leaning heavily on Tess. Allia took his arm to support him from the other side.

When they reached the road, they found four of their horses dead. "Double up," Callonen ordered. "Single riders guard our retreat."

The girls supported Harrow toward his horse. They got him that far and put his foot into the stirrup, but they couldn't push him into the saddle. The other soldiers hurried to help. They shoved Harrow into his saddle, and one of them jumped on behind him, holding him in place as he slumped.

Callonen still held the little boy in his arms. Allia ran to him. "I found something," she gasped. "This plant should help the poison." She held out a handful. "Crush the leaves and rub it into the bite."

Callonen's brows pulled together in worry. "I can't hear him breathing! Is it already too late?"

"It's not," Allia insisted. The boy was nearly gone, but she could still faintly sense his pain. "But we need to hurry!"

Setting him on the grass, Callonen pulled off the boy's shirt to reveal a red, festering bite plainly visible on his shoulder. Black lines had already spread from it, all across his small body and up his neck. The boy needed help immediately. He might die at any moment.

Allia could sense his injury, the pain and poison seeping through his veins. It wasn't right. The boy was so young, he'd barely experienced life. He should live. He needed to live. Allia wanted him to live.

She crushed the leaves between her fingers and applied them to the bite. When her fingers touched his skin, she saw a burst of green light and felt a stabbing pain in her shoulder before everything went black.

CALLONEN

Callonen saw a sudden flash from Allia's ring. She cried out in pain and crumpled to the ground, where she lay face down and didn't move.

"Allia!" He knelt beside her. "Allia, what happened?"

She did not respond, even as he tried to wake her. He turned her over, finding her body lifelessly limp. Terrified, he put an ear to her lips. She still breathed, slowly but steadily, as if she were only in a deep sleep.

Allia was alive. Relief flooded through him. His muscles, which had tensed in shock as she collapsed, loosened a little. He did not know what had happened, but at least she was alive.

The little boy sat up suddenly and stared around in alarm. "Mother! I'll keep the spiders away—Mother?" He stared at Callonen with wide eyes. "Prince Callonen? What happened?"

"Zarek, you're all right?" Callonen asked, astounded. The dark festering wound on the boy's small shoulder was no longer visible.

"I'm fine." Zarek jumped to his feet. Callonen handed the boy his shirt, and he pulled it on over his head.

Talon was already on his horse, Mirithel in his arms. He stared down in disbelief. "Zarek!"

Callonen lifted the child, who threw his small arms around Talon's neck. "Father! I tried to keep them away. She's scared of spiders, and I told her I'd protect her."

"You're alive, you're all right," Talon said, his voice choked. "I don't know how, but I'm so grateful. Hurry! We need to get out of here." Zarek climbed agilely to a seat behind Talon and held onto his waist. "Was Allia bitten?" Talon asked.

"I'm not sure what happened," Callonen said.

"Can you move her? We need to go!"

Two of the soldiers came forward to help. "Can you hand her up to me?" Callonen asked. He mounted his horse, and they settled her into his arms.

Darkness was falling when they reached the edge of the forest. None of them wanted to linger too near the trees, so they kept riding until the light was gone and they found a large open field.

"Let's stop here," Talon said, reining in beside Callonen. "We have to do what we can for them."

Callonen nodded.

"Halt!" Talon called, and the soldiers stopped around him. "Keep everyone close," he ordered. "Don't go anywhere alone. You two start a fire. Everyone else, create a perimeter. Make sure there's nothing hiding in the grass. I need two men to help me here."

The soldiers spread out to follow his instructions. Two of them dismounted and came to him. "Find some blankets, please. Spread them on the grass." When that was done, they moved Mirithel carefully and set her on a blanket. Talon dismounted and swung his son off the horse.

Taking Allia from Callonen's arms, the soldiers set her gently down. One of the men took the horses and led them away.

Tess came running over to them. "Did a spider bite her?" She stared at her friend, lying unconscious on the blanket.

"I don't know," Callonen answered.

By the time they laid Harrow on the ground nearby, he appeared nearly lifeless. Mirithel's guard was even worse, barely breathing.

As the two men started the fire, Callonen could see a little more in its light.

"There has to be something we can do." Talon held his son close and stared at the motionless form of his wife. "Allia helped Zarek. What did she do?"

"She found an herb that would cure the poison. It was in her hand. She told me to crush the leaves and rub them into the wound. We have to find out where they were bitten," Callonen said. "Check Mirithel."

He turned to Tess. "Would you please examine Allia and make sure she wasn't bitten?"

Tess knelt beside Allia to do as he asked.

"Will you check on the others?" Callonen asked the two men nearest Harrow and the guard, and they began pulling off the soldiers' weapons and chain mail.

"I don't see anything." Tess had finished her inspection. "There's not a mark on her skin."

What had happened to her? Would she recover? Had he lost her? Callonen felt his stomach clench. He knelt beside Allia and began pulling the redleaf out of her dress pocket.

Talon's examination had revealed a wound on Mirithel's arm. He pulled out his knife and cut the sleeve of her dress away so he could see the injury.

The soldiers had finished checking the two unconscious men. "We found one bite on each of them," the nearest man reported, pointing to a wound on the guard's shoulder and another on the back of Harrow's neck.

Callonen held out a handful of leaves to Tess. "Will you please treat them?" He turned to Talon with another bunch. "All I know is to crush them and apply them to the bites."

Harrow lay on his stomach. The others had removed his armor and shirt, and the angry red bite stood out on the back of his neck just above where his chain mail had protected him. Dark lines spread from the twin punctures. Tess rubbed the crushed leaves liberally into the wound. Then she moved to the guard, repeating the process. Neither of them moved or responded at all.

Callonen took Allia's hand in his. He could see the pulse beating in the hollow of her throat. He touched her forehead and found her skin warm. She seemed unharmed, except that she didn't respond to his voice or touch. Would she recover? He brought her hand to his lips and kissed it. She would be all right. She had to be.

The remaining soldiers set up a rotation to guard the edges of the camp. Those not on watch settled down to sleep. Callonen, Talon and Tess waited nearby while the stars brightened above them. Talon held his son close.

"Zarek, do you mind if we look at your shoulder?" Callonen asked.

The boy leaned forward and pulled his collar aside to show where he'd been bitten.

"You can see it." Callonen stared at the place that had been a red, swollen wound earlier. Now nothing remained but two round white scars.

"That's where it bit you?" Talon asked.

The boy nodded. "It doesn't hurt anymore. The lady made it better."

"When Allia touched him, I saw a flash of green light. It sounded like she was in pain, and then she collapsed. I can't wake her."

"Have you ever seen anything like this before?" Talon asked.

"Never," Callonen said. "It's a miracle."

"Magic," Talon whispered.

The time dragged. Little Zarek curled up beside his father and fell asleep. Talon tucked a blanket around him. Tess had dozed off between Allia and Harrow. Callonen sat beside Talon, watching.

In the middle of the night, Harrow groaned and shifted. Tess woke up. "He moved! Maybe he's getting better." She took more of the redleaf and applied it to Harrow and the guard. Talon did the same with Mirithel.

There was nothing else Callonen could do for Allia. He made sure she was covered warmly and returned to his vigil.

TESS

Tess heard a groan and opened her eyes to see the gray light of dawn. Harrow stirred beside her. She sat up. He lifted his head a little, turning to look at her. "What happened?"

"A spider bit you," she explained.

"I remember that," he mumbled. "We were going back to the horses... That's all."

"We rode out of the forest and camped here. Do you want some water?"

He nodded.

She helped him drink, and then he closed his eyes again. Tess pulled the blanket around him.

"Thank you," he whispered.

CALLONEN

Callonen realized he must have dozed. When he opened his eyes again, Talon still sat, watching his wife. Callonen rubbed his hand over his face and sat up. He checked Allia. She lay unmoving, exactly as she had before. But she was breathing, still alive.

"How is she?" Talon asked.

"The same," Callonen said. "Mirithel?"

"She's beginning to stir. Harrow woke up a little while ago, and I hope she will soon."

The sun was high when Mirithel gasped. "Zarek?"

"He's all right." Talon bent over her immediately.

"How? I thought I lost him."

"He's well now."

Mirithel took a deep breath, calming herself. Opening her eyes, she recognized her husband. "Talon? How did you find us?"

"We found you in the forest. We're doing everything we can to help you feel better. What can I do?"

"My arm hurts," she murmured.

Callonen offered him more of the redleaf. "Try this."

Talon rubbed the leaves between his fingers and applied them to her arm.

"That helps," she whispered.

He gave her a sip of water, and then she slept again.

CHAPTER TWENTY-FOUR

Year of Warding 21, Varda, Sarine

TESS

At midday, Tess knelt beside Harrow. He lay on his side and seemed considerably more alert than he had the previous night.

"How are you feeling?" she asked.

"Not good," he confessed. "But I'm alive. Last night, I wasn't sure I would make it."

"You're already improving," she observed.

He tried to push himself up and made it about halfway before he fell back. He shook his head. "I can't even sit up. Please don't tell the others."

"Don't worry," Tess said. "You'll feel better soon. Can I look at the bite?"

"Yes."

She moved to kneel behind him and removed the bandage covering the wound. It remained swollen and oozing, but the red lines radiating out from it were fading. "Does it hurt much?" she asked. It looked awful.

"A bit," he admitted through gritted teeth.

Tess left their camp and searched through the surrounding brush until she found more of the redleaf. After harvesting it, she mixed the leaves into a poultice and spread it over the bite.

"Does that help?" she asked.

"Yes," he sighed. "Thank you."

The company remained in their camp that day. Tess and those who were healthy cared for the sick. The others who had been bitten were weak and dizzy—except for little Zarek, who was full of energy and constantly running around. Finally, Callonen asked him to gather firewood, and the boy dashed back and forth collecting sticks. Tess offered Callonen food as he watched over Allia through that day. He was so focused on her that he barely ate anything. Allia didn't stir. There wasn't much Tess could do other than check on them frequently.

At midday, Tess took food to Harrow, but he ate only a few bites. "My stomach," he muttered, holding it. "And if I move, the world spins."

"Just stay quiet then." She put her hand on his shoulder. Covering her hand with his own, he looked up at her, his blue eyes meeting hers. "Thank you for helping me."

ALLIA

Allia opened her eyes to see dark vegetation and the night sky. Where was she? What had happened? When she tried to move, she couldn't. She gasped, terrified. It felt like her limbs were bound.

Callonen bent over her. She could see him in the flickering light from the campfire. "Are you all right?"

Fear twisted through her. "I can't move. What happened?"

He took her hand. "Can you feel that?"

"I feel it, but I can't move my hand."

He gripped her hand reassuringly. "What can I do?"

"May I have some water, please?"

He brought the water, but she couldn't raise her head. Callonen lifted her so she could drink.

"Thank you," she murmured, her eyes closing. "I'm so tired."

"Rest," he whispered.

She felt his lips brush her forehead.

When Allia woke again, the sun was high and her thoughts were clearer. Callonen sat beside her.

"What happened?" she asked. "I remember looking at the boy. They said he was dead, but I watched him take a breath, even though you could barely see it." Just as she spoke, Zarek ran past where she lay. Allia stared after him in amazement. "He's alive?"

"Yes," Callonen said. "When you touched him, he became well again."

"How?"

"I saw green light flash from your ring, and you sounded like you were in pain. Instantly, the boy was whole. Did you know the ring could heal?"

"No! It's never done anything before," she said.

"As soon as it happened, you fell unconscious."

"I remember looking at him. When I put my hand on him, I felt a terrible pain in my shoulder."

"That's exactly where the boy was bitten," Callonen said. "You... felt his injury... and then you healed him."

"I'm so happy he's well," she said.

"But what about you?" he pointed out.

"I feel stronger than I did." Her fear receded a slightly, but she had no way of knowing if she would improve. What if her strength was permanently gone, dooming her to be an invalid forever?

Callonen squeezed her hand as if he could tell what she'd been thinking. "You'll be all right," he insisted. "I'll take care of you until you're strong again."

His devotion warmed her heart, and she felt tears welling in her eyes. "What if I don't get better?"

He bent to kiss her forehead. "I would still be in love with you. But don't worry. You will get better."

⤸

The next day, when Allia woke, she discovered to her profound relief that she could move her hands and arms a little. Gradually, her strength returned. That afternoon, they began their slow journey back to the city. Allia couldn't walk or even stand. Two of the soldiers lifted her into the saddle in front of Callonen. He put his arms around her to hold her in place.

"I can usually get on a horse by myself," she murmured.

"You'll be able to soon."

She hated feeling weak, but Allia loved being in his arms. She felt so safe there, and his hands were strong and gentle.

Mirithel rode in front of Talon, complaining of dizziness.

The soldiers helped the unsteady guard into the saddle, while Harrow mounted his horse without aid or protest. After a moment, he got off again to lean over some bushes and vomit. When he finished, he wiped his mouth and took a sip of water, then got back on his horse without a word.

They rode at an easy pace until they stopped at sunset to make camp.

Tess spread a blanket on the ground before Callonen set Allia gently down. "Here's some water," he told her, helping her drink from the waterskin. "Do you need anything else?"

"No, thank you," she replied.

"I'm going to help gather firewood," Callonen said. "I'll be back soon." He joined the other soldiers in setting up camp.

"How are you feeling?" Tess asked, coming to sit beside Allia.

"I am getting better," Allia replied, from where she lay on the blanket. "I can move my feet a little now." She demonstrated. "But I hate needing help with everything. I feel silly, but I'm too weak to do it on my own."

"But you saved that boy's life," Tess said, pulling another blanket up around her. "Can I bring you anything?"

Allia shook her head.

Gripping her shoulder reassuringly, Tess moved to check on Harrow. She uncovered the spider bite and applied more redleaf to it. When she finished, they sat near each other for a long while, murmuring quietly.

After they prepared and ate a meal, the company settled down to sleep. Allia saw Talon lay his son beside his wife and wrap them both in a blanket.

As if he sensed her watching him, Talon turned and met her gaze. He came over and sat beside her. "I owe you my thanks. You saved my family."

She shook her head. "It wasn't me," she protested. "The ring is enchanted."

"But you are the only one who knew about that plant. Without it, the others would have died. I love my wife, and Harrow has been my friend for many years now. He's a good man. How can I possibly thank you?"

"You don't have to thank me. I'm glad I could help them."

"I'll never forget this," Talon promised.

In three more days, they reached the city, relieved to be home. Allia had improved enough to be able to walk with support. They entered the palace with Allia leaning heavily on Callonen's arm. He led her to one of the large formal bedrooms—the very room she and Tess had prepared for Princess Elena, the finest guestroom in the palace. Allia remembered changing the sheets and dusting the mantle. Now he helped her to a seat in one of the beautiful chairs in front of the fireplace.

"This will be your room for now. My father ordered it prepared for you. They will bring you hot water for a bath, and anything else you need."

"I could go back to my old room," Allia suggested. The luxury of the room felt overwhelming.

"No," Callonen said. "This room suits you much better. Don't forget," he whispered. "You promised to marry me, which will make you my princess. Use this room until we're married, and I can take you to my room."

She felt her cheeks coloring, and he winked at her on his way out.

As Callonen left, the servants brought hot water. Tess remained to assist as she bathed and dressed. When they had finished, Tess supported her as she climbed into the enormous soft bed.

"Do you mind helping me?" Allia asked. "I know this whole situation is crazy. I never thought any of this would happen."

Tess looked at her, then around at the luxurious bedroom. She sat down on the edge of the bed. "I have to admit, I was jealous for a moment, but none of this was your doing. You saved four people's lives. And one of them is a particularly good-looking soldier who now owes me his undying gratitude."

Allia smiled as Tess blushed, obviously thinking of Harrow. "Maybe you need to go see if he needs help," Allia teased. "I think he would be happy to see you."

Tess smiled. "Maybe I will. And I have you to thank for getting to know him. Really, it worked out well for both of us. Can you believe they gave you the same room the princess stayed in? You and I cleaned it!"

"I hoped you'll move next door." Allia pointed to the adjoining room.

"Me?"

"I'm going to need someone to help me more often, if you're willing."

Tess hesitated momentarily, then said, "Yes."

"Thank you. I'm glad now that we never put a snake in here," Allia exclaimed, laughing. "Do you need help to bring your things from your old room?"

"I can manage," Tess replied.

They talked and laughed for a while, but Allia couldn't stay awake for long. "Thank you, Tess," she murmured, feeling her eyes drift closed.

⌁

Allia's weakness following the healing passed slowly. For a few days after they arrived in the city, she still tired easily. She spent much of her time resting and had hours to think about Callonen and their future together. In a few more days, the emperor would announce to the world that his son had chosen a bride.

She had been excited when Callonen told her about the banquet, but later nervousness took over. So many people, and they would all be watching her. She hadn't completely regained her strength. What if she collapsed, right in the middle of everything?

⌁

The next evening, Callonen brought a tray of food, and they had dinner in Allia's room. "Only two more days," he said, as they finished eating. "Then our entire empire will know that you have agreed to be my bride."

Allia tried to hide her nervousness. "I'm not used to being in front of people all the time like you are."

"You will get used to it after a while."

"Cal, I..." She paused and took a deep breath. "I don't have anything to wear to the banquet."

He smiled. "You're now betrothed to a prince. One of the worst things about ruling a nation is that people expect to see you in formal clothes more often than you might want to wear them. Is that something you think you can adjust to?" He seemed worried for a moment.

She smiled. "I'll be fine."

He looked relieved. "I'm glad. Then I will make sure you and Tess both have something to wear. She should have a nice gown as well. I will have the seamstress and the cobbler come to measure you."

"And you haven't changed your mind either? Knowing I've never worn a ball gown before?"

His eyebrows shot up. "Why should that make me change my mind? They're only clothes. It's you I love, not your wardrobe."

Allia laughed. "I love you too."

The day before the banquet, Allia rested in one of the comfortable chairs near the fire, with Tess sewing beside her. Someone knocked on the door.

"Are you expecting anyone?" Tess asked. She got up and went to answer it.

She opened the door to see Harrow. He appeared to be strong and healthy again.

"Harrow," Tess said. "How are you?"

"I am well. Much better, thank you." He sounded a little stiff.

"Will you come in and sit down?" Allia asked from her chair.

"No, thank you," he said politely. "I actually came to..." He paused and looked at Tess.

She returned his gaze, waiting for him to go on.

After a moment, he took a deep breath. "I rarely go to these things because I can't dance well. But I wondered if you would..."—he glanced down the hallway, then back at Tess—"go to the emperor's banquet with me?"

Tess smiled, and suddenly Harrow seemed much more relaxed.

"I'd like that very much," Tess said.

"Shall I meet you here?" he asked.

Tess looked at Allia, who nodded.

"That would be wonderful," Tess said.

"I'll see you tomorrow then," Harrow promised, bending to leave a light kiss on Tess's cheek. He bowed to them both and strode off down the hall.

The day of the banquet finally arrived. Tess and Allia had planned to help each other get ready, and it was almost time to dress for the evening. Allia hoped Callonen hadn't forgotten his promise. If he had, she didn't know what she would wear tonight.

A knock came at the door. Tess opened it to see Mara. "Please, come in," she invited. "Let me help you." Mara's arms were full of yards of fabric. Tess helped her lay her burden along the edge of the bed.

"Thank you," Mara said, taking a deep breath. "I could have sent someone, but I wanted to bring these myself."

Her hands now empty, she smoothed the front of her dress. Allia and Tess faced Mara, waiting. She looked as though there was something she wanted to say.

"I've been close to the royal family for a long time," she finally said. "I care for them deeply. When Emperor Caldoreth lost his wife, and he had to raise those boys alone..." She shook her head and sighed. "Maybe I came to care for them more than I should—especially Callonen. He has such a good heart."

Mara met Allia's gaze. "And I've never seen him as happy as he is with you."

"Thank you, Mara." Allia hugged her impulsively.

Mara held herself stiffly at first, and then softened to return the hug. "He deserves to be happy. And so do you. I wish your mother were alive to see this day. She would be proud of you." Mara drew back and turned away to wipe her eyes.

"And Tess," she went on, hugging her as well. "I won't deny how much I have missed you downstairs the last several days. No one else manages things as well as you do. But I know you are needed here." Mara turned to the bed, where she had left her armful of gowns.

A wooden box had been hidden in their folds. Mara took it out and looked at Allia seriously. "Emperor Caldoreth would like you to wear these tonight. They belonged to his late wife. Please, make sure they are returned to him afterward." Her gaze had never appeared sterner.

Allia took in a deep breath. Mara opened the box, and Allia felt light-headed. The jewelry inside appeared priceless. A necklace, bracelet and matching earrings set with pearls, sapphires and glittering diamonds. "He... He wants me to wear them?"

Mara nodded, then set the box aside. Unwrapping the fabric, she held up a long gown that was a deep blue velvet, trimmed with silver and gems. The skirt flowed around it like a waterfall. Allia's eyes widened, and she glanced at Tess, who stared at the gown in wonder.

"Oh!" Tess exclaimed. "That's the most beautiful dress I've ever seen."

Mara draped the blue dress across the bed and pulled out a green one, which was the exact shade to complement Tess's coppery hair and highlight her green eyes.

Tess's mouth fell slightly open in shock. She stared at Mara in disbelief. "F-For me?"

Mara smiled. "Of course." She laid out the dress on the bed and brought out two pairs of gorgeous shoes.

Turning back to the girls, she hugged them both in turn. "Have a good time tonight. Enjoy sitting at the high table instead of standing behind it." She slipped out, leaving them too shocked to speak.

Finally, Tess picked up the green dress and held it in front of herself, looking into the tall mirror. "I don't believe it!"

Allia laughed. "Callonen said that you must be appropriately dressed."

"I think he went a little beyond appropriate."

"Try it on," Allia urged.

Tess obeyed, and the fit was good. She looked lovely with her long red curls against the rich green fabric.

"It looks wonderful on you," Allia said. "Harrow is going to fall over when he sees you."

Tess's cheeks colored.

Allia put on the blue gown, and they took turns arranging each other's hair. With great care, Tess removed the necklace and bracelet from the box and put them on Allia.

Looking into the mirror to put on the earrings, Allia almost didn't recognize herself.

"You really look like the Empress of Sarine now," Tess said, examining her critically.

Allia stared back at her reflection. "Tess... What am I going to do? Do you think everyone will accept me as Callonen's bride? I may look like an empress, but I'm still just me inside. I've never even gone to a formal party before. The farm was the only life I knew before coming here. I don't know how to behave in front of nobility, let alone royalty. What if I do everything wrong and embarrass the emperor? Or Callonen?"

Tess hugged her. "I've worked with royalty for years. They're just people, Allia. Callonen chose you. He loves you. You're brave and kind and quick-thinking."

"Thanks, Tess."

"Just remember us little people when you are Empress of Sarine." Allia peeked down at the gorgeous blue-and-silver dress and the pearl and sapphire bracelet on her wrist. She took a deep breath and nodded.

Another knock interrupted their talk. They opened it together to see Harrow wearing a snow-white shirt and a dark-blue coat that complemented his eyes. He seemed a little uncomfortable, but he smiled when he saw them.

Harrow's eyes widened when he took in Tess, as if just noticing her for the first time. "You look wonderful."

"Thank you," Tess said. "And you look very handsome."

Bowing to Allia, he said, "Thank you for saving my life. If not for you, that spider bite would have killed me."

"I am happy I could help," Allia said.

Harrow offered his arm to Tess, his eyes meeting hers. She took it and gave Allia a quick smile over her shoulder as they left for the banquet hall.

CHAPTER TWENTY-FIVE

YEAR OF WARDING 21, WHITE CITY, SARINE

ALLIA

Allia waited in the doorway for only a moment before Callonen appeared. He stared at her with obvious admiration. His eyes slid from her hair along the gown down to the beautiful silver shoes that went with it.

"They'll have to cancel it," he said, shaking his head.

"What?"

"The party. I can't go... because when I look at you, I forget how to speak. Everyone will think I've lost my mind. You... You look amazing."

She felt her cheeks warm a little. "You are too kind," she said.

"I've never seen anyone look more beautiful. I can't believe you would spend the evening with me."

He must have that reversed. She could have stood staring at him for an hour. Callonen appeared every inch a prince in his dark coat with polished buttons and gold braid trim. He looked elegant and powerful, and Allia couldn't believe she was going to be with him. But underneath the fine clothes, he was just Callonen. He cared about her, and he had chosen to make her a part of his world. He had even been willing to leave all this behind for her. His presence made her nervousness about the evening's events fade into warmth.

"I love you," she said.

"And I love you." He slid his arms around her and kissed her. For a moment, she forgot everything else besides him, but her nervousness came back as she thought of standing in front of all those people.

"Are you ready to go?" he murmured in her ear.

Allia smoothed the gorgeous blue-and-silver skirt and said nothing of her fears. Instead, she tried to focus on the hope that everything would work out. "Before we do, I want to give you something."

"Your presence is more than enough."

"This is important to me, and I want you to have it." Allia took out a tarnished silver band. "My father died many years ago. This was his, the only thing I have that belonged to him. He wore it every day for many years, and I loved him very much. He was a good man, and he would have been happy to have you as his son-in-law."

Callonen smiled and took the ring. "Thank you for honoring me with something so close to your heart. I will treasure it. With your permission, I will wait and allow you to place it on my hand when we wed."

"Don't you want something finer as a wedding band?"

"What could be more precious than something of yours?" He brought the ring to his lips and kissed it, then slipped it carefully into his pocket. Thank you, Allia."

She smiled up at him. "You're welcome."

He offered his arm. "It's time to announce to everyone how much I love you."

She extended her hand, glittering with jewels, and took his arm.

Everything would be all right as long as she was with Callonen.

They walked to the door of the great hall, and a herald announced their entrance. "Prince Callonen and Lady Allia." She waited for him to add "she used to be a servant here"—but he didn't, of course.

Callonen and Allia entered the hall. The room seemed alive with whispering voices, but perhaps she was only imagining them. Time seemed to stop as they made their way toward the front of the room. She felt as if every person there stared at her. It was a relief when they reached the table and sat down.

Allia found herself at the high table, from which she could see the entire room. She carefully avoided looking behind her, not wanting to turn around and see someone she knew standing back there with a pitcher. Allia resolved not to empty her glass, so whoever it was wouldn't be forced to come and fill it for her.

Callonen sat at her side and held her hand under the table. Next to him sat Emperor Caldoreth, and beyond him, Prince Haldreth. Allia avoided looking at him.

On her left were Talon and his wife. Allia felt relieved to have Talon there. She no longer feared him. Now she found his presence comforting.

Harrow and Tess sat at a nearby table. They appeared to be deep in conversation and were both smiling.

Allia took in the ridiculous array of silverware spread on both sides of her plate. She had often washed all the utensils, but never learned how to use them properly.

"I'm the second son of a blacksmith," Talon whispered from beside her. "Just act confident and start from the outside."

"Thanks!" she replied. She had been so afraid that all these important people would laugh at her or look at the prince and pity him.

Despite that, she had a wonderful evening. The food was glorious, made even better by the knowledge that she didn't have to wash the dishes, and Callonen guided her through the evening gracefully. With that and a couple of tips from Talon, she did fine. After dinner came the dancing. Allia didn't have much practice, but Callonen led expertly, and it didn't seem too difficult. She spotted Harrow with Tess a few times, but though Tess danced well enough, Harrow displayed more grace handling weapons.

Then came the moment Allia had been nervously waiting for.

Complete silence fell, and the emperor spoke.

"Crown Prince Callonen," he said, looking out at everyone, "has an announcement."

Callonen and Allia walked to the front of the room, and everyone stared at them expectantly. Her insides twisted into a knot with all those eyes on her, but he didn't seem concerned. He simply smiled at the crowd. "Thank you all for being here tonight. I know this is an announcement you've all been anticipating for many years. It is my pleasure to introduce Lady Allia, granddaughter of the wizard Zarekathus. You might have already heard a rumor or two about how brave and talented she is. Because of her efforts, four people live who would have otherwise died. I have come to care for her with all my heart." He turned to gaze into Allia's eyes. "I'll be forever grateful that she has consented to become my bride." He took her in his arms and kissed her as everyone applauded. Even all those people could not distract her from this moment. Allia let out a breath she hadn't realized she was holding. The moment had come and gone, and she was officially engaged to the prince.

Even before the engagement was announced, in the days after Callonen and Allia had returned to the city, the story of the strange healing had spread. Like all rumors, the story grew as it traveled, until they heard scraps of it that were nothing like the actual events. Now, in addition to the rumors about the healing, Allia was notable for her betrothal to Prince Callonen. Crowds of people came to the palace wanting to meet Allia and to beg for her help. They suffered from maladies ranging from sprains and broken bones to people who were lame, blind or seriously ill.

Two weeks after their announcement, Callonen met Allia at her door, and they walked to the royal dining room for breakfast. As servants set out food for them, he took her hand. "Allia, I've received word that there are people at the palace gates who wish to ask for healing." Allia's eyes widened. She'd gone through her life never being particularly noticed before. Of course, it made sense if these people were in need and were searching for a miracle. "I want to help as many as I can."

Callonen nodded. "I understand. But when you healed for the first time and collapsed, for a moment, I thought you were dead. And then I thought you might sleep forever, never regaining your health. Even now, you're still tired. Do you know what the long-term results of using this ring will be?"

She shook her head. "I've never heard of anything like the ring before. I'm sure my grandfather would have told me more about it if he hadn't died so unexpectedly."

Callonen met her gaze and held it. "I know you want to help as many as you can. That's one of the things I love about you. But there's no way you can cure everyone. You must reserve space for your life and protect your own health."

"But how can we turn away people in need?"

"I suggest this," he said, rubbing his chin. "I will assign someone to talk to the petitioners and learn more about them. If they're here asking for help, none of them can be dying at this moment. You must have time to recover fully before you try to do this again. I will have them select the person most in need, and we will arrange to have them come back in two weeks. If you feel strong and well, and you choose to do it, you can attempt to heal them then."

Allia agreed to his plan.

$$\backsim$$

Allia's new position put so much attention on her that she couldn't leave the palace without guards. The one time she and Tess decided to go to the market, crowds of people gathered around her, and the six guards who had felt like too many when they left the gates, now didn't seem nearly enough. Everywhere, people called to her, spoke to her, asked her questions. She briefly met the eyes of a young woman who seemed filled with worry and desperation. Allia suddenly stopped and turned back to her.

"My son," the woman said, and Allia glanced down to see a little boy with large dark eyes. Instead of standing straight, he bent to one side and stood with the aid of a crutch. "His lame leg causes him great pain, and he's been very ill. He falls unconscious often, his limbs shaking and jerking. There's no way to control it."

Allia could sense how much the woman loved her son, how worried she was. She only wanted him to grow up and be strong and happy.

"Please, help us," the woman pleaded.

Allia couldn't refuse. She beckoned one of the guards near. "I'm going to try to heal the child. I might not be able to walk after. Will you make sure I get home safely?"

"I will, my lady," he said.

Allia had only done this once before. As when she'd healed Talon's son, she could sense the child's pain. She put her hand on the boy's curly head.

TESS

Tess stood beside Allia as a flash of green light came from the ring. Allia crumpled, and the guard caught her. Exclamations of wonder came from the crowd.

The little boy dropped his crutch and bounced around in excitement. He threw his arms around his mother, who embraced him tearfully. Still holding the child, she stood and looked at Allia's unresponsive form. "Thank you!" She turned to Tess. "Tell her thank you! This is a miracle for us!"

Tess and the guard holding Allia pushed their way through the crowd with the rest of the soldiers behind them and walked back up the hill to the palace. Callonen must have already been near the palace gates. As soon as they were inside and away from the crowd, he appeared beside the guard who carried Allia and bent over her, checking her breathing and pulse.

"What happened?" Callonen demanded, looking at Tess.

"A woman came to her with a little boy who was very ill. Allia healed the child."

"Couldn't someone have at least brought the boy here?"

Tess exchanged a look with the guard. "I'm sorry, Your Highness. I should have advised her to wait."

Callonen had a point. Allia was defenseless after she healed, and it wasn't a good idea for it to happen out in the crowded city. None of them had anticipated the reaction people would have when they discovered what Allia could do. Their days of shopping unnoticed at the market were gone.

ALLIA

When Allia woke in her room, she found Callonen watching over her. As soon as he saw her eyes open, he reached out to take her hand.

"I owe you an apology," she murmured. "I failed to keep our agreement."

"We made it for a reason," he said. "Can you imagine the panic I felt when I saw a guard carrying you home? I didn't know what had happened." He brought her hand to his lips and kissed it. "Although, I should have guessed. I'm sorry I was so worried. Your safety is very important to me."

Weeks passed, and one night an urgent plea for help came to the palace. The man was a young tradesman who loved his wife dearly, and she was in danger of dying during the birth of their first child.

Allia looked at Callonen.

"You wish to go?" he asked.

"Yes. He feels the same way for her that I feel for you. I want to help."

"Then we'll go together."

Callonen had taken four guards with them, and he and Allia had worn cloaks and hoods, trying not to be recognized on the way.

When they reached the little home, Allia could tell at once that the situation was dire. The woman had delivered the child, which seemed to be doing well. But the mother was nearly gone by the time they got there. Allia's last memories were Callonen beside her and the pain as she reached out to touch the woman.

Sunshine streamed through the tall windows of her room in the palace when Allia woke. She recalled nothing after healing the tradesman's wife, but hoped the woman and her baby were both doing well now.

Allia ached in every bone and couldn't get out of bed. Still, this would go away in a few days, and a life had been saved. She slipped back into a doze.

"Wake up, Allia." It was Tess. Allia opened her eyes to see her friend's concerned face above her. "Prince Haldreth is here to see you."

Her eyes widened in surprise. What could he possibly want? Had he somehow discovered she'd eavesdropped? Could he tell that she knew about his plans? Her heart beat faster.

Prince Haldreth came to her bedside, a bunch of flowers in his hand, and smiled pleasantly at her. She hadn't spoken directly to him since her first few days in the palace when she had run into him in the hallway.

He had looked exactly like Callonen at first, but she could tell them apart. His eyes were the same dark brown, but the expression in them was different. They held secrets, which Callonen didn't keep from her. The first several times she had been near Haldreth, she'd been able to sense the darkness he concealed. Now, she didn't feel anything except that he was glad to see her.

He smiled.

Allia stared back at him, scanning his eyes for the anger she could usually sense. "I apologize for not getting up, Your Highness. How can I help you?"

"My lady." He bowed low enough to take her hand and kiss it. "Are you well this morning?"

"I will be. Thank you, Your Highness." She kept her tone calm, even though she felt uncomfortable in his presence.

"I heard about the carpenter's wife and her child," he said. "I felt it was appropriate to thank you for the work you've done for our people. It doesn't seem to matter what sort of ailment afflicts them. At your touch, they are whole again. Can you really heal any sort of injury?"

"As far as I know."

"You are very caring to do it." The pleasant expression on his face almost made him look like Callonen.

"I want to help those in need," she said.

"You have already helped many people," he said smoothly. "I brought you these." He held the flowers out to her.

"That's very kind of you," she said, motioning to Tess to take the flowers.

"Since my brother plans to marry you, I felt you should know that I support his choice. You have already more than earned your place in the palace. Rest well." His dark gaze was unsettling. He kissed her hand again and then departed.

As soon as he'd left, Tess returned. "What was he doing here?"

Allia couldn't shake the uneasiness growing in her belly. "I don't know."

CHAPTER TWENTY-SIX

YEAR OF WARDING 21, WHITE CITY, SARINE

ALLIA

OVER THE NEXT FEW weeks, Allia saw much more of Haldreth. He still gave no sign that he knew she had overheard his plans. But his presence made her very uncomfortable. She had vastly preferred being ignored by him. Now he treated her with flawless courtesy, only appearing when Callonen was not with her. Apparently, Haldreth knew his brother's schedule and arranged to turn up when Callonen was away.

Allia didn't know what to do. Her first impulse was to accuse Haldreth of pursuing her and demand he leave her alone, but she had no proof. He would surely claim that they had only run into each other by accident.

Haldreth wanted something from her. Even though she couldn't sense it, her heart told her he hadn't changed. But what could it be? He was still jealous of Callonen, but she'd thought that involved the crown and the Warding, not her. Haldreth had another reason for his sudden interest. Allia needed to know what it was.

One evening, as Allia stood on the tower watching the sunset, she heard footsteps behind her and turned to look. Her heart leapt thinking it was Callonen, until he came to stand beside her, and she realized it was actually Haldreth. A sliver of unease slid through her.

"Your Highness," she said, curtsying.

"My lady," he said, bowing and kissing her hand. "I'm sorry to disturb you. I didn't know anyone else would be up here."

"Did you want something, Your Highness?" She didn't want to spend time with him, but this could be her chance to discover his motives.

He rested his arms on the railing, looking out over the city. "I hoped we might share a conversation."

She couldn't help but wonder what he really wanted. "What do you want to talk about?"

"Have you lived inside the Warding all your life?" he asked.

"Yes."

"Of course, I have lived here since Sarine was founded, but in the last few years, I have had the opportunity to travel and visit other kingdoms. They are very different."

"Sarine is unique," she agreed.

He smiled. "That's one way of putting it. Haven't you ever considered how disturbing it is that my father knows what everyone is doing? He's more than just a ruler. He's tried to make himself a god, setting himself above everyone and judging their actions."

"Your father is a good man, Your Highness," Allia protested.

"Is he? Would you still think that if you tried to do something he disagreed with?"

Allia didn't know the answer to that. "I believe he tries to rule fairly."

"Fairly?" Haldreth raised his eyebrows. "Maybe, but he rules in absolute power. No one can even think of opposing him. What would any of us do if he oppressed us? Or oppressed us more than he already does by spying on our feelings and actions. Haven't you ever wanted to escape that? It would be freedom, Allia. Isn't that an amazing idea?"

"Of course. But I have no desire to leave Sarine."

He nodded. "I understand. You've allied yourself to the power of the Warding."

"That's not why I promised to marry Callonen!" she protested.

One side of his mouth lifted in a sly smile. "No? You're an intelligent girl. You identified the man who will rule this nation and found a way into his heart."

Fury burned through her. "That is not what happened!"

His smile widened. "You don't have to explain yourself to me. But Callonen isn't the only one who is powerful. If control is what you really want, you should consider getting to know me better."

Her mouth dropped open in surprise. How had he expected her to react to that? "I'm very sorry, Your Highness, but I'm afraid I have another appointment." She stepped away from the wall.

He caught her hand. "Don't go yet," he protested.

"I can't stay," she insisted, pulling her hand from his.

His dark eyes hardened. "And if I *order* you to stay? What harm is there in spending a few more moments with me? I offered you the opportunity to become better acquainted."

When she met his gaze, he stared back, challenging her, waiting to see what she would do. The ability to tell what others were feeling, never absent before, seemed to have deserted her. Now, when she needed to know what he felt, she sensed nothing from him. She retreated a step toward the staircase.

"You came here as a servant. It's your place to do as I command." His voice was hard.

"No. I am no longer a servant. I am the future Empress of Sarine." She took another step backward. The sound of footsteps interrupted them. Someone was coming.

Haldreth lifted his head and turned toward the top of the stairs. He heard them too. In a moment, five members of the emperor's court appeared.

Allia walked swiftly toward them, forcing herself to smile and nod at them, while wishing them a pleasant night. She hurried down the stairs and through the halls as fast as she could without attracting attention. Worried that Haldreth might follow, she headed for her room, intending to bolt the door behind her.

He hadn't revealed the details of his plans to her, but he had made it clear he wanted her to participate in some way. That would not happen. She wanted no part of Haldreth's schemes, no part of him. How could he think that she only wanted Callonen because of his power?

She paused at the door to her room. Someone was coming along the hall from the other direction. She started. It was him! She fumbled with the door latch, but her hands were all thumbs, and he was already beside her. Panic welled up in her.

"Allia? What's wrong?"

She stared up at him with wide eyes, every muscle tensed for flight. Her sense of his feelings slowly penetrated her fear. He was worried. Callonen. Her shoulders sagged in relief.

"Allia, what's wrong?" Callonen asked, putting his arms around her.

"I'm all right," she said, trying to regain control of herself.

"You're shaking. What happened?"

She clung to him. "I'm all right now."

"You looked at me as if you were terrified," he said slowly. She could sense how much that had hurt him.

"My love, why would you ever be afraid of me?"

"Not you," she whispered. "Your brother."

"What has he done?"

She tightened her arms around him. "He's everywhere I go, paying more attention to me than I'm comfortable with. I didn't know how to tell you. I've never done anything to encourage him. I only wanted him to go away. You must believe me!"

Callonen's embrace felt warm and comforting.

"Of course I believe you," he said. "When you saw me just now, you thought I was him?"

"Only for a moment. I'm sorry."

"You have nothing to apologize for. It's all right," he said, stroking her hair. "What has he done to make you afraid?"

She took a deep breath, savoring the safety she felt in his arms. "Other than threaten you? The more I learn about his plans, the more frightened I am. There is something he wants me to do for him, and I don't know what it is. But there is terrible darkness in him, Callonen. Even though I can't sense it anymore, I know it's still there. Your father would be wise to lock him up."

"But... he's my brother." Callonen shook his head sadly. "My father and I have already spoken many times about Haldreth and his plans, but I'll speak to him again."

Two days later, just after breakfast, somebody knocked at Allia's door. As she rested her hand on the knob, she could sense that Callonen stood on the other side. When she opened the door, he smiled.

"Are you ready to go out?" he asked eagerly.

"I guess I am. Why?" she asked, sensing his excitement.

"Quickly," Callonen took her hand, pulling her from the room. "I have something to show you."

She couldn't help but smile. "What is it?"

"A surprise," he replied, and she went with him out through the gate and along the palace walls, where there were many gardens. Callonen led her along a stone path bordered by green grass.

They came to a wall about twelve feet high that extended out from the soaring height of the palace wall. Callonen took out a large ornate key and unlocked a door.

"Close your eyes," he whispered in her ear. Her heart sped up at the feel of his breath on her skin.

Allia heard the door creak, and Callonen led her through it. "Can I open them now?" she asked.

"Now," he said.

They stood in a beautifully tended garden. A fountain bubbled in the center with a large tree nearby. A table and chairs sat in the shade of its branches.

"It's beautiful!"

"It's yours," he said, smiling at her.

"Mine?" she asked in wonder. "The entire garden?"

"Your very own!" He handed her the key. "You can plant whatever you wish here and entertain whoever you want and come here whenever you please. You don't have to let anyone in here who you don't want to see, including Haldreth. No one will enter without your invitation. And, with your permission, I will keep the only other copy of the key. No one else will be able to come in without your knowledge."

"Then you can come and find me here anytime you want." She threw her arms around his neck, laughing. Her own garden. Amazing. He knew she loved growing things. How thoughtful he was. "I am so lucky."

"To have such a place?"

"No. To have you."

⌇

A few days later, Allia and Tess decided to have lunch in the garden. They could have ordered food served to them there, and someone would have come, bringing their meal on a silver tray. But Allia just couldn't ask for that. The person serving them would be someone they knew, one of their friends. So, they went to the kitchen themselves and made their own lunch, packing everything into a basket and carrying it to the garden.

"When you are empress, will you still run to the kitchen yourself every time you want something?" Tess asked as they set everything out on the table under the tree near the fountain.

"I don't know," Allia confessed. "I haven't figured that out yet. But I feel awkward ordering anyone around, especially Mara. I don't want to give the impression that I think I'm better than they are."

Sitting comfortably in the shade, Allia and Tess lingered over the last of their lunch. They sat, enjoying the autumn sunshine, laughing and talking.

Finally, Tess left, remembering a few tasks remaining undone. Allia remained alone in the garden. She wanted to see Callonen this afternoon, but he was stuck in a long, necessary meeting. They would have a late dinner together when it was finished.

In the meantime, Allia enjoyed the quiet of her garden. The peace and beauty of it relaxed her, and she leaned back in her chair and put her feet up. Before she knew it, she had dozed off.

Allia drifted into a dream where she and Callonen were together.

They walked through the palace hand in hand. "I don't want you to go," Callonen said.

"I would never leave you," she assured him.

"No," he said. "You can't leave." He pulled her close.

Allia felt a gentle kiss, and still lost in the dream of Callonen, she responded without opening her eyes. Fingers caressed her face, and a mouth wandered across her cheek and down her neck.

Her breathing quickened.

He kissed her on the lips again, hard and hungry, and, suddenly, it felt very wrong. Kissing Callonen didn't feel that way.

Allia sat up with a start, staring in horror at the man who'd been kissing her.

"Haldreth!" she cried.

He stared back at her, an insolent smirk on his handsome face. "What's the matter?" he asked.

She jumped to her feet and backed away from him. "What are you doing?" she demanded. How had he even gotten in here? She had watched Tess close the door on her way out, and from the outside, it was locked. Glancing at the door, she saw it was still closed. How had he gotten in? And why?

"I came to see you," he said, as if answering her unspoken question. "This is an important day." He stepped nearer.

"What day is that?" she asked.

"My future begins," he said. "Today I will start a new life and come into my birthright."

Allia moved away from him. The look on his face sent a chill down her spine. She retreated until she bumped into the tree trunk. "Leave now," Allia ordered in her most commanding tone, pointing at the door.

He laughed derisively. "You think a serving girl can tell me what to do? I am a prince, and soon I will be a king. There's only one more thing I need."

"And what is that?" she asked, her heart pounding. She dreaded hearing his answer.

He came closer until he stood uncomfortably near. Then he reached out to take her hand. She tried to pull away, but he tightened his grip until it hurt. Leaning nearer, he whispered in her ear. "I need the power of your ring. And you'd be wise to join me yourself." He pulled her closer still and put his arms around her.

She shoved him back. "Get away from me!"

As she tried to flee, he grabbed her arm, pulling her against him and drew a knife from his belt. Allia felt the blade against her throat.

"Don't struggle," he commanded. "I'll kill you if I have to and chance that the ring will work the same on someone else."

Her heart pounded in her throat and her breath came in gasps. "But... the Warding... Your father will know what you've done. You won't get away!"

"It's true. If I go that far, my father will finally realize. The veil concealing my actions can only cover so much. But after today, it won't matter anymore. I will be long gone before he can stop me. I've been preparing for this day for years. He won't be able to act fast enough to keep me inside the Warding."

The cold steel was sharp against her neck. Icy fear flooded through her. Would he really kill her?

"You have a choice, you know," he whispered. "I told you before that you don't have to take Callonen. I can give you a throne too. Anything he can give you, so could I. My empire will be greater than his. Join me. When you kissed me, I could tell you wanted me."

"No!" Allia cried, "I thought you were him."

Haldreth pulled her closer. "I don't believe you."

"Let me go!" Allia yelled. She tried to gouge him with her fingernails.

"Stop!" he commanded. He pushed the knife harder against her neck, and the keen blade cut into her skin. She froze.

"That's better." He dragged her to a chair, sitting down and pulling her onto his lap.

"I know you want me." He caressed her neck. "You liked it before. I could tell."

"No!" she protested. "Please stop." But the knife edge bit her neck.

"If you do what I want, you won't get hurt," he promised, sliding his hand beneath the lavender silk of her skirt and running it along the inside of her thigh.

"Don't touch me! Your father will know what you're doing!" she said in desperation.

Haldreth laughed, and Allia felt a wave of nausea roll over her.

"I can hide my darker intentions from him," Haldreth said. "Besides, he's not here. The emperor doesn't leave the city very often. But once in a while, he rides out to visit the holdings of some of his nobles. By strange coincidence, he's gone right now."

Her stomach churned, and Allia wanted to throw up. When she pulled desperately away from him, she felt the sharp blade against her skin. But his hand crept higher, and she couldn't stay still. Driving her elbow hard into his ribs, she jerked away from him, springing to her feet.

Haldreth rose to face her, the knife still in his hand. "Don't do that. I don't want to hurt you."

"Yes, you do," she said, her eyes on the blade. "Otherwise, you wouldn't be doing any of this."

"It isn't about you."

Why then? "It's Callonen, isn't it? Why do you hate your brother?"

His eyes narrowed and his lip curled into a sneer. "You think just because you love him, everyone does. You don't see how he enjoys commanding every man in the city, how he craves power. He thinks he is the best thing that ever happened to Sarine. He is convinced he's—"

Allia met his eyes. "Better than you? He is better than you! In every way. And nothing you do to me will change that. Nothing!"

His knife ready, he lunged forward. She dove to one side to avoid his blow, landing on the grass. Before she could get back up, he dragged her to her feet, holding her against his body.

"Never say that again," he hissed, returning the knife to her throat.

She gasped, trying to get her breath back.

At that moment, something seized Haldreth's hand, wrenching the knife away from Allia. Callonen. He must have come to find her. But now he was locked in a deadly struggle for control of the weapon.

"What are you doing?" Callonen demanded of his brother.

"What's wrong?" Haldreth snarled. "Are you jealous? You think she might change her mind? She only wants you for your power."

"Never touch her again!" Callonen yelled. His eyes blazed, and Allia sensed a fury she had never felt from him before. They twisted and fought back and forth until Haldreth knocked Callonen to the ground and drove his knife to the hilt in his brother's chest.

"No!" Allia screamed. She ran to his side, seeing his eyes wide with disbelief. "I love you," he said in a choked whisper.

"I love you too!"

His breathing became labored, his skin ashen, and his eyes closed. She grasped the hilt of the knife in both hands, wrenching it from his body and throwing it away from them. Blinded by tears, she put her hands on him. Callonen couldn't die, not like this. He would live. He had to live.

As the green ring glowed, Allia screamed at the pain of a knife in her heart. Then everything went black.

CHAPTER TWENTY-SEVEN

YEAR OF WARDING 21, WHITE CITY, SARINE

CALLONEN

YELLING IN OUTRAGE, CALLONEN jumped to his feet, tackling his brother and slamming his fist into Haldreth's face. Haldreth twisted and bucked, trying to throw him off, then rolled to the side, pulling his brother with him. He was searching for the knife, and Callonen couldn't let him find it, knowing if he did, his brother would hurt Allia. He struck Haldreth's jaw. They rolled as they struggled for control. Finally, Callonen pinned his brother.

At the same moment, he caught a flash of movement out of the corner of his eye. Allia. A man carried her toward the door.

"Stop!" Callonen commanded, but his brother's fist struck him, and for a moment, all he saw was light. Another blow followed the first, and he realized he was on the ground.

They were taking her away, and he had to stop them. When he attempted to rise, pain exploded in his side, and a second later, something struck his head. Everything fell away.

Callonen felt something cold on his forehead. Water? He blinked. "Where is Allia?" He opened bleary eyes to see Talon. "He took her! We have to stop him!" Callonen struggled to sit up, and Talon helped him. His head felt like it was splitting apart. Now upright, the world spun wildly around him.

"Stay still," Talon advised. "You need the healers."

"You don't understand," Callonen exclaimed. "Haldreth took Allia. We have to go to the gates. Now!"

Talon didn't argue further. He helped Callonen to his feet, and they headed for the palace gates.

Soon, Talon had them mounted. It was faster that trying to walk, but Callonen's head throbbed wildly at the pounding of the horse's hooves. They rode straight to the city gates where a group of guards were stationed.

"Your command, Prince Haldreth?" their leader asked, saluting him. "Prince Callonen was just here. He said that Lady Allia was ill, and he was carrying her to a healer outside the city."

"I'm Callonen! That was Haldreth, and he's abducting her. We have to stop him!"

Several of the guards mounted their horses and followed Callonen and Talon.

Just outside the city, a detachment of the Emperor's Guard in their white uniforms approached. Callonen recognized his father among them. They all reined in, and Emperor Caldoreth came forward.

"Callonen!" his eyes seemed desperate. "He tried to murder you! For a moment, I thought he had succeeded. This is my fault! You tried to warn me. I was a fool." His gaze locked on the blood-soaked front of Callonen's shirt.

Callonen shook his head. "There's no time for that now. We have to help Allia!" He urged his horse into a gallop and raced off, trusting the others to follow.

They rode with all speed toward the edge of the Warding. The emperor knew exactly where Haldreth had gone. After half a day's ride, they realized Haldreth must have planned this day well in advance, for he had fresh horses waiting along the way.

Their own horses grew tired and slowed as the day wore on. At the next outpost, they traded mounts and continued the pursuit.

"He's getting away from us." Emperor Caldoreth's voice sounded agonized. "The Warding is mine, and he should not have been able to deceive me. When you wanted to lock him up, I should have listened to you. I can't believe he's done this."

Callonen and his company did not stop at nightfall. By dawn, the emperor bowed his head in despair and reined in his horse.

"Don't stop," Callonen pleaded, pulling up beside his father. "We have to be getting close."

"He's gone," Emperor Caldoreth said. "He's outside the Warding now, and I can't tell where he's going."

"But we can't give up!" Callonen protested. He dreaded what Haldreth would do to Allia. After what he had seen in the garden, he realized his brother was capable of anything.

Callonen urged his horse on, heading toward the Warding. The pounding of its hooves failed to clear away the images of Allia from his head. She was young, ten years younger than Callonen, so pure and innocent. And she had trusted him completely. Yet he had failed to protect her from his brother. Callonen's hands clenched into fists around the reins.

Allia had known. She had been terrified of Haldreth and suspected what he would do.

If only Callonen had done more to protect her. He could have assigned guards to follow her every moment, or he could have stayed himself, never left her side. Now, it was too late. He urged his horse to greater speed.

ALLIA

When she opened her eyes, she saw Callonen's face above her. He held her, and they were moving. It felt like they were on horseback.

"You're alive. You're safe," she whispered weakly.

He glanced down at her when she spoke, and she realized in dismay that he wasn't Callonen at all, but Haldreth. She felt his usual undercurrent of anger.

Her heart froze to ice in her chest. "No!"

"What's wrong?" he asked sarcastically.

"No. Please let me go!" She wanted to push him away, to run from him, but she could barely move. "Where's Callonen? Is he all right?"

"You should have let him die," Haldreth said. "Now he will live knowing I have taken what he wanted most in the world."

When he laughed coldly, Allia shivered. She could sense his triumph and how much he hated his brother. Her body ached with the exhaustion that followed a healing, and her heart broke for Callonen. And for herself.

There had to be some way to escape Haldreth. But how? It would be days before she could even walk again. Even now, without him holding her, she would have fallen off the horse. She closed her eyes and tears slipped from beneath her eyelids.

Allia and Haldreth rode for several days. Along the way, two dozen men joined them. None of them spoke to Allia. She sensed their disdain for her and loyalty to Haldreth. Asking any of them for help would be useless.

The weather grew cold. Only the last few golden leaves still clung to the trees. Gradually, Allia's strength returned, but Haldreth guarded her relentlessly, forcing her to ride double with him even after she could have ridden by herself. At night, he tied her hands and feet.

One day, the faint path they had been following joined a larger road that brought them to the edge of a canyon, narrow, deep and sheer. Allia gasped when she looked down into it. A slender bridge spanned the chasm, leading to a dark stone fortress on the other side.

Armed men streamed across the bridge toward them, but they didn't attack Haldreth. Instead, they cheered in greeting and bowed respectfully.

As they crossed the bridge, Allia stared straight ahead, not daring to look down.

More soldiers surrounded the gate. They wore dirty, ragged, royal-blue uniforms and black armor.

"Welcome to Hakvere, the most powerful fortress in Ara," Haldreth whispered in Allia's ear.

In the courtyard, he dismounted, pulling her down with him. He seized her arm, leading her through halls and up stairs. He took Allia into a room and shut the door behind them.

"I apologize for the roughness of your accommodations, my lady." He gestured around the dirty room, furnished with a moth-eaten bed and a few rickety chairs. A single window, bare of glass or any drapery, opened to the outside. "You will learn to appreciate what I choose to give you."

Allia stared at him silently.

"So, how do you like Ara?" he asked. "Our new friends have been waiting to make you comfortable. I know Hakvere doesn't look like much yet, but it will. I will make it great. For now, I have the support of the king of Ara. But he won't last long. Soon all of Ara will be mine, and then I will conquer Sarine. And you..." He stepped near her, and she backed away until she pressed against the wall. "You will help me."

He caressed her cheek with his fingertips, and Allia shrank from his touch. "You would be wise to submit to me willingly," he said. "It will save you a great deal of pain."

She raised her chin to meet his eyes. "Leave me alone!"

He gazed down at her. "I can see why my brother fell for you," he said, putting his arms around her and kissing her roughly as she struggled against him. "I'll be back soon." Haldreth released her and left, locking the door behind him.

CALLONEN

As Callonen and Talon pursued Haldreth, the tracks indicated that many more men had joined him as he rode. If they caught up now, their little group of ten guardsmen would be terribly outnumbered.

Emperor Caldoreth and the rest of the company had turned back at the edge of the Warding. But Callonen couldn't give up and go home. He and Talon had followed the tracks, crossing the river above Iron Bridge. The outpost there housed the last of Sarine's soldiers. Now the trail left the North Road and headed straight toward the border of Ara.

Warily, Talon and Callonen followed the trail through bare, rocky lands to a river that ran through a deep canyon. The fortress of Hakvere guarded a bridge spanning the precipice. They considered their options.

"From the tracks, Haldreth and his men went across. But we can't follow." Talon shook his head. "If we try, they can take us any time they want. None of us would make it to the other side."

They saw several guards at the far end.

"But we have to do something!" Callonen protested. "We can't just leave her in Haldreth's hands."

"I agree," Talon said. "But we need a plan and a lot more men to get into Hakvere."

ALLIA

Allia searched every corner of the room for a way out. She tried the solid wooden door, finding it locked. Leaning out the bare window opening, she looked down at a rough stone wall. Below it a bridge spanned the deep canyon. She quickly discarded the idea of using the moth-eaten bed linens to lower herself to the ground. But the stones were set unevenly, allowing for hand and footholds between them. She waited, hoping the darkness would come before Haldreth did. She gathered her skirt and tied it into a knot to keep out of her way.

Eventually, darkness fell and Allia scrambled out the window. She tried not to look at the yawning space below her. The canyon was deep, but she wouldn't be climbing down there. She hoped to descend the stone blocks of the wall. By her estimation, it was about twenty feet to its base. The spaces between the stones were wide enough to fit her toes. Gripping the windowsill, she lowered herself until her feet found a ledge. Clinging to the top of a stone, she searched for a lower toe-hold.

Working carefully, she made her way down to the narrow ledge between the fortress wall and the sheer edge of the canyon. She could see over the bridge, but it was well-lit and heavily guarded. Allia turned away from it, moving in the opposite direction.

Guards would patrol the battlements, and she hoped to stay out of sight along the base of the wall. Allia turned the corner and followed the south edge of the building. From this corner, she saw a village standing in the fortress's shadow. A few little lights glowed from windows. Another corner turned her path north again. Hakvere was large, and it felt like it took hours to walk around it. This side of the wall had a gate in it as well, now closed fast, with no guards on the outside. She hurried past, continuing north. Allia saw no lights or sign of guards here. This path would not lead her immediately toward Sarine, but for the moment, any route that led away from Haldreth was a good one. If she made her way north following the river, eventually there would be a place to cross. Once that was done, she could find a way back into Sarine. It would be a long journey, especially with no provisions. Hopefully, she'd be able to find supplies along her way. But anything was better than staying here.

The night was chill, but walking at a brisk pace, Allia wasn't too cold. The land was barren and rocky for some distance from Hakvere until she came to the edge of the hills. They would provide cover. Allia walked all night. When the first light of dawn lit the sky, she searched for a place to hide. She found a thick patch of brush with a space beneath it and crawled in. The land was silent around her. The air was chilly, and when she stopped moving, she began to shiver. For a little while, she dozed until the distant sound of horses woke her. She huddled a little deeper beneath the brush. They weren't too close yet. Allia listened, still and silent.

Anxious moments passed, and the horses drew nearer. If she stayed here, they would find her. Forced into motion, she slipped out the other side of the thicket and into the rocks. Staying low, she moved away. The pounding of hooves sounded loud and near. She turned and bolted away from it. A shout behind her told her she'd been spotted.

Allia dodged between the rocks, choosing a path too narrow for horses to pass. She slid into a crack between two boulders and stopped there, trying to calm her rapid breathing.

All was quiet for several moments until a shadow fell across her and her breath caught in her throat. One of the blue-uniformed soldiers stood there, staring at her with wide eyes. He was young, maybe about her own age, with boyish features. He had brown eyes and curly hair that fell over his forehead. For a long moment, they stared at each other. She sensed that he felt sorry for her. He didn't want to hurt her.

"Please," she whispered. "Don't tell them you found me."

He said nothing and disappeared. Allia breathed a sigh of relief.

The respite was short-lived. She heard the sharp crunch of boots on the gravel and a shout. A hand seized her arm and dragged her out of her hiding place. "She's here," the man yelled.

Allia struggled, trying to wrench her arm from his grasp. He pulled her toward the other horses. She jerked her arm away, escaping his grip, and ran. After only a few steps, his shoulder slammed into her, his weight pinning her against a boulder. He twisted her arm behind her.

"Let me go!" she cried. He laughed.

Two of his friends came to help him, and they dragged her back to the horses. She twisted and struggled, trying to get away from them. "Tie her hands." One of them held her wrists together while another bound them.

They shoved her into the arms of a man on a horse, and he urged the horse into a gallop in the direction of Hakvere.

"No!" Allia cried. "I can't go back there."

The man ignored her, his grip on her tight enough to bruise. Any scrap of sympathy he felt was buried deep under his determination to serve Haldreth.

CALLONEN

Callonen strained his eyes, staring into the last of the fading light. At this distance, all he could see was a tiny flash of lavender, the exact shade Allia had been wearing that day in the garden. It had to be her.

At first, he could see her in the window. Then she climbed slowly down the wall. Her hold seemed precarious, with the height of the fortress wall and only a narrow ledge above the sheer depths of the canyon.

Allia was trying to escape. She wouldn't try to cross the heavily guarded bridge, would she? She'd know that course was futile. Callonen held his breath as he watched her descend, his eyes following her progress. There must be some way to help her. He scanned the canyon walls desperately. How could they get across?

His eyes found no other way but the bridge.

Would she try to go north or south? Going south would mean crossing more populated areas of Ara and many miles until the canyon opened into a wide valley. North?

The lands north of Hakvere were rocky and barren, but sparsely inhabited. Many miles to the north, the deep canyon walls grew lower and lower until it was possible to cross the river without much trouble. If Allia was going to run, she'd run north.

Callonen and his friends gathered their things and slipped quietly into the darkness.

They walked north along the rim of the canyon all night. In the first light of dawn, Callonen hoped and dreaded to catch a glimpse of her. She would do everything she could to stay out of sight.

The morning light illuminated a rocky landscape dotted with riders in blue Aran uniforms. Callonen felt his stomach clench into a knot. How were there so many? He glanced at Talon, who stood beside him staring in disbelief at the endless patrols searching.

"I'm sorry, Cal."

"We have to find a way across. There must be something we can do to help her!"

Talon's eyes scanned the east rim of the canyon. "We could scale the cliffs. Not quickly, but it's possible. But if we reach the other side, there won't be anything we can do. There's too many of them."

Callonen clenched his hands into fists. "I'll bring all of Sarine's army and burn Hakvere to the ground!"

"Our soldiers are several days away." Talon's voice was grim. "And many lives would be lost if we try to attack that bridge."

Callonen knew he was right.

It was agonizing to watch the patrols combing the landscape, searching every inch. Even across the distance, Callonen saw a group of horsemen galloping back toward the castle. One horse carried two people. He could just see a bit of lavender. Unable to stop it, his hand reached out toward her. It was futile. There was no way to help her from here.

His heart felt as if it had frozen into solid ice. They were taking her back to Hakvere. On weary feet, his heart breaking, Callonen started back toward their camp.

CHAPTER TWENTY-EIGHT

YEAR OF WARDING 21, HAKVERE, ARA

ALLIA

THEY RODE FOR WHAT seemed hours, but it wasn't nearly long enough. In the light of day, Allia had a view of the surrounding land. In all directions, she saw men on horseback searching. There must have been a thousand of them. All hunting for her?

A familiar figure rode to meet them. Her captor passed her into Haldreth's arms, and he pulled her across his lap, gripping her tightly as they turned back toward the fortress.

Allia was glad she couldn't see his face from this angle, but she could sense him. Being near him was painful. The ring allowed her into his heart, and that was not somewhere she wanted to be.

He was relieved they had found her. Haldreth considered Allia a possession, and he cared nothing for her as a person, only about how she could further his ambitions. Any worry for her well-being was absent, but she remained essential, and the thought of her escaping terrified him.

Maybe there would be another chance for Allia to get away. There had to be some way to stop Haldreth. His schemes must be larger than just his desire to destroy Callonen. Panic and despair rolled through her stomach.

"If you do anything like that again, I will make you regret it." His voice was icy.

Allia shivered. Not only from his words, but because she could feel his determination to bend her to his will. No, he wouldn't mind if she suffered. He would enjoy it.

They reached the back gate of the fortress and rode inside. Haldreth escorted her to the same room he had locked her in before. Nothing had changed except for the addition of a heavy iron grate bolted to the wall to cover the window opening.

Haldreth dragged her into the room and shut the door behind them. The sound echoed in the sudden silence, and Allia realized they were alone. Her eyes darted around the room, seeking any possible means of escape.

Observing her distress, Haldreth smiled. "It's good to be home again." He took off his coat and threw it over the back of a chair.

Allia stared at him; her limbs frozen.

"You don't need to be afraid of me," he said. "I don't want to hurt you. All I ask is a little cooperation." He spread his hands to indicate the room. "I've already made Hakvere much more than it was. I'm going to do the same for the entire land of Ara. It will become the most powerful nation of all. I have undertaken a great work. All I ask is a little help from you. Is that so bad?"

He sat down in a chair beside the empty fireplace and removed his boots. Standing up, he met her gaze, then pulled off his shirt. Allia dropped her eyes at once, heat rushing to her cheeks.

"You enjoy looking at me," he said. "Why do you fight it so hard? You don't have to. And it won't change anything. You can't get away, and now you need to make the best of the situation. Am I really so different from my brother? You wanted nothing more than to share his bed. Stories about you were everywhere in the palace. You were caught sneaking into his room in the middle of the night. I guess you wanted him so badly you forgot the guards might see you."

He laughed derisively, and Allia felt the color in her cheeks deepen.

"Don't be embarrassed. I understand. I can help you get what you want, and you don't have to fight me. If you accept me, I'll make sure you enjoy it."

Allia raised her eyes to trace the smooth skin and hard muscles of his chest and shoulders. There was nothing wrong with his appearance. She'd never gotten the chance to see Callonen undressed, and she couldn't help but wonder if he looked the same. But even though Haldreth was every bit as attractive as Callonen on the outside, the ring lent her the ability to see inside, and Callonen's mind and heart were even more appealing than his appearance. He was kind and cared for his people, even strangers he didn't know. He was a good man. It wasn't necessary for him to keep secrets or lie or deceive anyone. He simply was who he was.

In contrast, Haldreth was a well of secrets and lies. Somehow, he had prevented his father from seeing how dark his ambitions were or how little he cared for anyone except himself. His pride, cruelty and lust for power grated on Allia any time she was near him. He never cared about her, except for how he might use her power. All the people around him existed for him to use in order to reach his goals. More power, more control.

Though it had been hidden from her too, back in Sarine, Allia could feel it now, and she shrank from the evil she felt. His plans would mean suffering for everyone around him. She needed to stop him. Her eyes flicked to the dagger on his belt. There might be just one chance. But she needed to distract him. She took a calming breath and looked up at him through her lashes. "Will you take care of me if I help you?"

He took a step nearer. "Of course I will." His expression became so much kinder as he said it, that she couldn't help but think of Callonen. She met his gaze, trying to appear bold. "You understand what an advantageous position I would have had in Sarine, with your brother."

He smiled slightly and nodded. "I knew that was important to you. Why else would you like Callonen so much?"

It went against everything inside her, but Allia took a step toward him. "Perhaps it is time to reconsider my options."

Haldreth closed the distance between them and softly touched her shoulders. Everything inside Allia demanded that she shrink from his touch, but she forced herself to remain still, not even breathing. Her hands brushed his waist, and he drew in a breath as he felt her touch. He caressed her neck, sliding the neckline of her gown down off her shoulder.

She only had a moment. Her hands found the dagger he wore at his waist, and her heart pounded wildly in her chest. This was the only way out.

Allia slid the knife from his belt and raised it. As Haldreth saw the stroke falling, he twisted to one side, and the blow intended to pierce his heart slipped between his ribs, too low to be immediately lethal. For a long terrible moment, they stared at each other, Haldreth's eyes wide with shock.

Horror swept over Allia. She saw blood welling and sensed the terrible wound. With her own hands, she had inflicted this pain. Haldreth sank to his knees, dragging her down with him, clutching her arm in an iron grip.

"Heal me!" he commanded. "Or you'll die with me." With his other hand, he wrenched the knife out of his flesh, his teeth clenched, his skin unnaturally white.

Allia stared into his terrible eyes and clawed at his hand, trying to escape his grasp. He took the knife, already dripping with his own blood, and held it to her throat.

The blade bit into her flesh and she felt a searing pain, blood running down her skin. He would kill her. There was no uncertainty. He had already stabbed his own brother in the heart. The blade cut deeper.

"Don't!" Allia cried. She put her hand over his. Before, she had sensed his pain. Now she claimed it for her own, a shaft of burning agony. The familiar darkness closed in around her.

Allia woke in the dark, lying on the cold floor where she had fallen, feeling the familiar aching weakness following a healing. She was alone, still a prisoner, and she couldn't rise. Haldreth undoubtedly felt whole again. And she wouldn't get another chance to kill him. She'd failed.

By the next night, she could move her arms and legs, but she remained dreadfully weak. They had brought her a little food and water, but the door remained locked, and she had seen no one. When she could get up again, she crawled to the window.

The heavy iron grate covering the opening didn't yield at all when she pushed at it. Outside, she saw guards at the gates and patrols of blue-uniformed men crossing the bridge.

Was Callonen still out there somewhere? Maybe the Aran soldiers were hunting him. Maybe they'd killed him.

Allia awoke to the light of a candle shining in her eyes. She wasn't alone. Someone slid beneath the covers beside her. In the candlelight, she recognized Haldreth. Sensing his lust and desire to control her, she shrank away from him, longing for the strength to run or fight him.

When he saw her fear, he laughed and pulled her close against him. He was strong, his bare skin showing no trace of his wound except for a thin white scar on his ribs.

Allia pushed at him, but the healing had left her weak. "I saved your life, and this is how you repay me? Get away from me," she demanded.

"You don't mean that." He kissed her.

When she bit his lip, he pulled back for a moment. A few drops of blood stained his mouth, and he wiped it away with the back of his hand.

"Don't try to convince me you hate me. You couldn't stand to let me die." He ran his hand gently down the side of her face. "I think you're relieved that you don't have to pretend to like Callonen anymore. He's so pompous and full of himself. It must be a relief to get away."

"No. Leave me alone!" She struggled in his arms, but so soon after healing, she lacked the strength to fight him. "You would take advantage of my weakness?"

He laughed again. "I will do whatever I want." His hands slid beneath her skirt.

She cried silently as Haldreth took her. She and Callonen had shared so many hopes. Now Haldreth was destroying them all. If only she had been strong enough to die with him after she had stabbed him. "I should have let you die!"

"But you didn't," he replied, his lips against her neck. "You saved my life, and I saved yours. We belong to each other now."

"No!" she cried, trying again to shove him away, cursing the weakness in her limbs. "I will never belong to you. Someday you'll lose your power. And then, I'll kill you."

"No, you won't."

"I promise you I will!"

His laugh was bitter. "Sweet Allia, a killer? What would your precious Callonen think of that?"

It hurt, and Haldreth knew it. She was a healer, and it went against her very nature to cause harm. But maybe he was right. Maybe Callonen would hate her for what she had done. But something had changed within her. She would not fail again if she had another opportunity. She didn't know how long Haldreth stayed with her. Allia loathed the feel of his hands on her body and every touch of his skin, and she hated him for taking her freedom. At last, he got up to leave. "I will come back whenever I choose," he said, kissing her. "Allia," he whispered her name almost gently, "our fates are bound together, and we will never be free of each other."

Allia dreaded the nights. She could not predict when Haldreth would come, and she hated being startled out of sleep by the sound of the key turning in the lock. Her strength returned in a few days, and sometimes she fought him. She sensed that he enjoyed her attempts to hurt him. Still, he had not worn a blade again after that first night and was careful to prevent her from seizing any potential weapons. With her bare hands, she couldn't inflict much damage on him.

As he had repeatedly reminded her, he had the advantage of size, strength and fighting ability.

One night when she heard the sound of the door, she jumped out of bed and stood with her back to the wall. Haldreth came in with a candle and smiled when he saw her.

When he put his hands on her, she tried to drive her knee into his groin. He twisted his hips to avoid her blow and encircled her throat with his fingers, cutting off her wind. She twisted and clawed at his hands, trying to break his grip. As she saw spots of light, he hissed into her ear, "This is a reminder to cooperate."

Her struggles weakened until, just as everything began to fade, he released her.

CALLONEN

Callonen lay full length on the rocks where he could monitor the gates of Hakvere without being seen. He and his men had been watching for three weeks. Low in the sky, the fading autumn sun did little to warm him.

He watched companies of soldiers coming and going. How did the Arans have so many troops? He hadn't realized that Ara had grown into such a powerful nation. It had been Haldreth who wanted to establish relations with them.

Callonen shook his head. How had he and his father been so blind? He tried to swallow the guilt that rose in his throat. Allia had warned him. *Your brother is trying to kill you...* And he hadn't truly believed it until Haldreth drove a knife into his heart. Now Allia was paying the price.

"Cal!" Talon hissed. "Trouble! There are soldiers riding toward the bridge, and we're in the way. Forty men, at least."

Callonen slipped from his hiding place to see for himself. The men approaching the bridge were well-armed and greatly outnumbered them.

"Prince Callonen." Harrow pointed to the fortress in the east. The gates were open and another column of soldiers was crossing the chasm.

"They're coming this way," Talon said.

If they stayed where they were, the two groups would converge on their hiding place.

"We have to go. Now." Talon gripped Callonen's shoulder. "I know you love her, but none of us can help her if we're dead."

Hastily, they gathered their men and mounted, riding away from the approaching soldiers. The Arans shouted when they spotted them and raced in pursuit.

Callonen and his companions galloped through the bare, stony hills. Haldreth's men couldn't catch up, but didn't stop trying. A chill night fell, and Callonen could no longer see them. Had their pursuers gone back? Made camp for the night?

His company dismounted to rest their horses for a few moments. Small patches of trees dotted the hills, and at Talon's orders, they gathered fallen wood into three piles.

"We're turning south," Talon said. "Ride where the ground is rocky, so you won't leave tracks."

Lighting the three large fires to attract the attention of their enemies, they slipped away into the dark. They followed the course of a little river, and before dawn, gathered their horses and turned to one side, climbing up into a narrow draw above the flowing water. If they stayed behind the rocks, they were out of sight.

"I need two men on guard with me," Talon said. "The rest of you, take care of the horses, eat and then get some sleep. Keep your weapons close in case they find us here."

Callonen caught a few hours of restless slumber. When he woke, he saw Talon asleep, wrapped in a gray cloak, his hand still on the hilt of his sword.

Harrow and two others guarded the entrance to the gully. They had positioned themselves in the rocks where they could look down toward the river without being seen. Callonen slipped down beside Harrow. Several mounted men in black armor were riding along the water.

"They've been riding past all day," Harrow said. "It looks like there are more than we thought."

Callonen's heart sank. There had to be a way to save Allia. Maybe his brother had killed her, but he didn't think so. She was alive, a prisoner, alone and miserable. There was no way to know what Haldreth had already done to her, but the thought of it made acid rise in Callonen's stomach. He wanted to gather every man in Sarine to ride back and take that fortress apart stone by stone. But how many people would die if Callonen did that? If saving Allia demanded his own life, he would give it willingly. But how could he send Sarine's armies into a full-scale war? Sarine had always been a peaceful nation. His father was no warlord. His soldiers were good men. They had families, lives of their own. What kind of man was he if he offered them up in exchange for Allia?

CHAPTER TWENTY-NINE

YEAR OF WARDING 21, ARA'S COUNTRYSIDE

CALLONEN

FOR THREE DAYS, CALLONEN and his friends remained in their hidden hollow. The entire third day went by without them seeing a single Aran soldier. "We need to move," Talon said, looking down at the open area where the horsemen had passed.

Callonen nodded in agreement. "I'll tell everyone to get ready."

"As soon as it gets dark, we'll ride for Iron Bridge," Talon said. "There's a company of our soldiers there, and they can help us if the Arans follow."

Under cover of night, they led their horses down through the rocks onto the level ground. When they reached smoother footing, they mounted. Talon set a slow pace, keeping a close watch on the surrounding woods. The quarter moon provided only a little light. All was silent except for the soft sound of hooves against the ground. Talon halted them, and they all hushed to hear the distant murmur of voices. Several fires gave away the position of a large camp. They altered their course to steer clear. The night passed slowly, and their progress felt painfully slow.

The moon had nearly set when Callonen heard a shout of alarm from behind him. Harrow had been guarding the rear of their group. Now there was barely time for Callonen to put his hand to his sword before something struck him. He turned in the saddle to meet the attack of a group of men on foot. For several moments, he held his own, until a blow came from behind, knocking him off the horse.

With his back throbbing in pain and trying to catch his breath after the impact, Callonen raised his blade to defend himself. All around him were cries and the clash of weapons. He swung his sword, but the group of attackers broke through his defense and struck him twice. The cuts weren't too deep, but his adversaries were attempting to surround him. If they got behind him, he wouldn't last long.

With a shout, another man knocked several enemies away. Talon. Working together, the two friends drove the Arans back until they broke and fled.

"This way!" Talon pulled his arm, and Callonen followed him into a patch of woods.

They weren't sure if they had been followed, but hurried away from the worst of the fighting.

"What about the others?" Callonen protested.

"If they can't find us, they will run back to the border," Talon said. "Come on."

They slipped quietly between the tree trunks, until cries and shouts surrounded them a second time, and they raised their blades to defend themselves. When they had driven away the Arans again, they fled.

For hours, they ran for their lives, fighting their way through any soldiers who tried to stop them. Both had several minor wounds from the fray, but they were alive and free for the moment. At last, they heard only silence around them. Just as the first light of dawn lit the sky, they hid in a thick patch of brush. Staying silent between the leaves and branches, they helped each other bind their cuts. None of them were too serious. Now that the adrenaline of their flight had worn off, pain settled in. Talon had saved his life last night. He turned to his friend. "Thanks."

Busy tying a bandage in place, Talon nodded without speaking.

They waited out the daylight in their hiding place, not seeing or hearing anyone else, and slept a little in turns.

For two more nights, they made their way toward the river, hiding during the daylight. They hadn't seen any of their friends, and Callonen hoped with all his heart that he hadn't gotten them killed. Waiting until it was fully dark and keeping under cover of the trees, they hurried through a draw between two hills, heading southwest.

In the dark, they heard the river before they saw it. They had to get across before any more Arans spotted them. If they reached the Aran encampment on the far side undetected, they could steal horses. Once mounted, they would ride for Iron Bridge.

Creeping from the cover of the trees, they approached the water. Callonen heard shouts behind them and the hiss of an arrow flying past his ear.

"Hurry!" Talon stood at the water's edge.

A point of white-hot pain exploded in Callonen's leg just below his knee. He found himself on the ground, trying to make his leg work. If Talon kept going, he could get away. But his friend wouldn't leave him and was beside Callonen in a moment.

"Go without me," Callonen ordered through gritted teeth. Talon ignored him. He seized the arrow shaft protruding from Callonen's leg. "Get ready," he warned. He swiftly snapped the shaft.

Pain radiated from the wound until Callonen felt it throughout his body. His vision faded, and he nearly lost consciousness.

"Stay with me," Talon commanded. "We're crossing the river."

Talon pulled him upright, and leaning on his friend, Callonen stood on his good leg. They heard shouts behind them. But they had almost reached the water. It was difficult to move, but Talon half-supported, half-dragged him along.

They staggered through the rocks at the edge and into the water. The swift current was brutally cold, dulling Callonen's pain a little and forcing him back to alertness. As they plunged ahead, the water grew deep quickly. Callonen could swim more effectively than he could walk at the moment. Talon reached the other side first. As soon as he had his footing, he turned back to pull Callonen out.

"Wait here while I get horses," Talon ordered, leaving Callonen shivering between the rocks, while he disappeared into the dark. A few moments later, he heard the neighing of frightened horses, shouts, the clash of weapons, and the pounding of hooves. Talon came galloping back, pulling another horse behind him.

Dragging himself to his feet, Callonen took the reins. Talon stopped beside him, grabbing Callonen's belt to hoist him into the saddle. They dashed away into the night, riding hard. Several arrows flew past them. One struck Talon's shoulder, and he jerked in his seat but kept going. A shaft like burning fire struck Callonen, below his ribs and off to one side. His vision blurred, and the pain made it impossible to think. But he had to follow Talon.

They pulled away from their pursuers, and no more arrows passed by them. Talon paused to allow Callonen to catch up. "Can you keep riding?" he asked through clenched jaws. "It's only twelve more miles to Iron Bridge. You can pass out when we get there, but not before."

His jaw clenched, Callonen nodded. "I'll ride."

The pounding of the horses' hooves jarred their wounds with every stride. But they had to keep going. Callonen stared straight ahead. If he turned to look behind them, either he'd see the Arans getting closer or he'd fall off his horse.

He lost all sense of time, but he could have sworn they'd been riding for a week. The night was dark around them. Ahead, he could barely see Talon, and he hoped they were going in the right direction. Eventually, he heard a shout ahead, hailing them. Talon slowed his horse, and Callonen did the same.

"Halt! Who are you?" the guards yelled.

"Captain Talon and Prince Callonen!" Talon replied.

"Come through, Captain."

The guards opened the doors of the fort. Callonen slumped in the saddle. They had made it. These soldiers served Sarine, and they would help.

As Callonen and Talon entered the outpost, several men hurried forward to assist them. Callonen felt himself being lifted down from the horse. He heard Talon's voice and was dimly aware of being carried into a building and laid face down on a cot.

Other voices surrounded him, but he didn't have the energy to pay attention to what they were saying until he heard Talon. "Take it out now while he's unconscious."

"No," Callonen muttered into the pillow. "I'm not unconscious. I'm not—" No one heard his protest. The pain of them pulling the arrow out was worse than getting shot. He screamed. That was all he remembered.

❧

Callonen woke to see lantern light in his eyes. He blinked. Looking around, he saw the infirmary of the Iron Bridge outpost. The lantern rested on a small table nearby. Talon lay on the cot next to him. His friend no longer had an arrow protruding from his flesh, and someone had bandaged his shoulder and several other cuts.

"Talon," Callonen whispered. Talon opened his eyes.

"The whole thing was my fault," Callonen said. "I'm sorry you were injured."

"Don't worry." Talon grimaced in pain as he shifted. "Nothing too serious."

Callonen rubbed a hand over his face. "I screamed like a little girl when they took it out."

Despite his discomfort, one side of Talon's mouth lifted. "I heard. Don't worry. I think I did the same."

"No, you didn't!"

"You passed out and couldn't hear me," Talon said.

"I don't believe you." Callonen shook his head. "Are the others safe? Have they come back?"

"Four of them are here already. More will come. Give them a little time."

Guilt for the pain he had caused twisted in his belly. "I can't put them in danger again. Next time, I'll go alone."

"You can't go back there!" Talon protested. "They have every man in their army looking for you. Do you realize how close we came to dying? You're not going anywhere for a long time."

The pain he was in forced Callonen to admit that Talon might be right.

"Your father ordered me to keep you safe. Cal, we have to go home."

"No!" Callonen protested, trying to push himself up. Agony exploded from the wound when he moved, and he sank back into place with a groan. It was a few moments before he could speak again. "I can't go home, Talon. Not until I find her."

ALLIA

One morning, when Allia had been locked inside the fortress of Hakvere for two months, Haldreth entered her room.

"I want you to take a walk with me." For the moment, his tone was friendly.

Of course, with Haldreth, nothing was simple or easy. "Where?" she asked warily.

"Does that matter?" His tone remained casual on the surface, but now had an edge. "I asked you to come, and you know what happens if you don't cooperate." Today, he wore his knife, caressing the hilt as he spoke. "Come with me."

She hesitated.

He gripped her arm and yanked her to her feet. When she resisted, he drew the weapon and held the point against her throat. "I said, come with me," he repeated through clenched teeth.

She didn't try to stop him as he dragged her to a long, dim room. Glass cases and shelves lined the walls, filled with strange items she dared not guess the purpose of. She stared around in horrified fascination.

"The wizard was your grandfather. I need you to help me find something of his." Haldreth gestured to the piles of unusual objects.

"What?" Allia asked. She forced her voice to sound casually curious.

His cold eyes met hers. "I need the gate pin."

"The what?" Allia kept her expression carefully blank. Her grandfather had showed the gate pin to her, warning her several times how dangerous it was. And powerful.

"The gate pin," Haldreth repeated, his tone hardening.

"What's a gate pin?" she asked.

"I'm sure Zarekathus would have told you about it, and I need to find it." Haldreth grabbed her arm and pulled her to the end of the room, stopping before a large glass box. Dark foliage filled the case, hiding whatever occupied it. She shrank away as soon as she saw it, realizing what must be inside.

"Yes," Haldreth whispered in her ear. "You already know what this is. You found her back in Sarine, before I had a chance to transport her to safety. She's my favorite pet. She's shy, though. We have to coax her out." Haldreth uncovered a small hole in the box's front. He grabbed Allia's arm and forced her hand and forearm into the opening. She struggled against him, trying to pull away. Her heart raced, and her chest constricted.

"Go on," he said. "Move your arm a little more. The motion signals her it's time to strike."

Allia stopped struggling and froze, staring in horror as a dark brown shape moved in one corner of the box. "Please... No..." she begged. "It's coming."

"Yes, and there are no plants here that can cure her poison. I wasn't aware an antidote existed until you found it. How did you know? I suppose your grandfather taught you. What else did you learn from him?"

"Nothing... It's coming!" The spider inched forward, hesitant at first, but at any second, it would strike. The pale skin of her forearm stood out even through the dingy glass of the tank. She shook uncontrollably now, and the spider came nearer.

"If it bites me, within a few moments, I won't be able to tell you anything," she protested.

His expression remained impassive. "Yes, the venom is quite deadly. I believe I improved on nature there. One of my early experiments, but still a favorite. You don't have much time left." He bumped her elbow so her hand moved.

"No, please!" She felt one of the spider's legs tentatively probe at her finger. Tears ran down her cheeks, and she held her hand perfectly still. If she moved at all, it would bite.

The moment lasted years, until Haldreth rapped sharply on the glass, causing the spider to retreat a few steps. He pulled Allia back, and she sank to the floor, shuddering in horror. He disappeared for a moment and returned with a mouse in his hand, which he carelessly tossed through the hole and redid the latch. The waiting spider pounced, driving in its fangs to prevent the struggling rodent from escaping.

Allia clenched her teeth to hold back a scream.

Haldreth dragged her to her feet, pulling her to him. She couldn't stop shaking.

"Are you ready now?" he asked. "Or must I use more persuasion? It's up to you. If you like, I can arrange for you to spend the night in a room with her..."—he nodded toward the spider—"and some of her children. They do seem to multiply quickly. At first, there was only one in the forest—one of her sisters."

"You put them there?" she whispered, horrified.

"A present for my dear brother," Haldreth said. "I hope he enjoys them."

Allia thought of Talon's little boy lying lifeless after being bitten.

And Haldreth didn't care.

"Now, unless you want to feel it walk up the bare skin of your back..." His fingers tugged at the laces of her dress.

"No!" she cried.

"Then help me find the gate pin!"

Allia looked around the large room desperately. "What if it's not here?"

"Find it!" Haldreth ordered. Tears stung her eyes.

Haldreth seized her wrist and dragged the point of his knife along her forearm, a line of red blossoming behind it. "Start looking," he demanded, pulling the knife back.

Allia clamped her hand over the cut, trying to stop the bleeding. Her arm throbbed and burned with pain.

He would kill her if she didn't help him. So, she walked to the nearest shelf and began looking through the strange objects. The collection held a unique mixture of ancient junk, heirlooms, and a few magical artifacts. Haldreth followed her as she searched the room. She didn't know how to use the gate pin. Grandfather had never told her how, only warned her it was dangerous. Haldreth's plans for it couldn't be good. What was he going to do if she pointed it out to him?

But what choice did she have, really?

On their third circling of the room, Haldreth seized her shoulder. "You're stalling," he hissed in her ear. "Is one cut not enough? What's it going to take for you to cooperate?" He seized her arm and made a second slice beside the first. This time, she couldn't hold back a cry of pain.

With the knife point pricking her side, they went back through the room, and finally, Allia pointed to a cylinder of dark iron lying at the top of an open box. It had six sides and was about the length of her hand and the thickness of her finger. He reached for it.

"Are you sure it's the one?"

Allia nodded.

He put the knife point against her arm again. "Tell me how to use it!"

She tried to pull away, tears running down her face. "I swear, that's all I know. That's all he told me. I don't know how to use it. I don't even know what it does!"

He appeared to believe her at last because he took her back toward the door. Pausing beside a bucket of water, he picked up a piece of cloth and started washing the blood from her arm. His fingers were gentle now.

"It's a shame you're so stubborn," he murmured as he worked. After cleaning the cuts, he bandaged them. Taking her other hand, he washed it too. "It doesn't have to be like this. You could choose to help me. If you did, I'd make sure you were more comfortable."

Allia did not reply. When he finished, Haldreth took her back to her room and left her there.

CHAPTER THIRTY

YEAR OF WARDING 22, HAKVERE, ARA

ALLIA

FOUR MONTHS HAD PASSED in Haldreth's fortress. A bleak late-winter snow covered Ara. Allia remained locked in her room, where a guard brought her food and water twice a day. What was happening back in the White City? Did they miss her? Had they sent some explanation to her brothers? Would she ever get home? One morning, as she looked at the food, nausea overwhelmed her. A few hours later, it passed, and she ate. But the same thing happened the next day. It was the last of a list of physical changes she couldn't ignore.

She was going to have a baby.

At the realization, Allia sank onto the bed and cried. What was she going to do? Haldreth had fathered this child. What would he do when he found out? Allia was a prisoner, trapped in this room. Would he continue to hurt and manipulate both of them? Or would he take the baby away from her and raise it to be just like him?

Allia sat in a chair, looking out the window. Spring was passing, and her condition had become obvious. Despite the circumstances, she loved the baby growing inside her. She hadn't seen Haldreth since she had showed him the gate pin months ago, before the snow melted. The absence of his visits to her room had been a blessed relief.

The sound of the door being unlocked startled her out of her thoughts. Haldreth entered her room, unannounced as usual and without knocking. She pulled a blanket into her arms, clutching it against herself as she stared at him. He came nearer.

"Get up," he ordered, pulling her to her feet.

Haldreth pulled the blanket away and stared at the curve of her belly. He laughed. "So it's true. I heard from the guards. Didn't you want to tell me the good news yourself? This is... perfect."

Allia stared back at him, saying nothing. If he was happy about her pregnancy, that couldn't be good for her.

"Don't worry," Haldreth said. "People have babies every day. There's an excellent midwife in the village. I'll send her to see you." When he'd gone, Allia couldn't think of anything except what Haldreth was going to do to them. Of course, he would weave this into his plans.

To Allia's surprise, Haldreth kept his word. A few days later, he sent the midwife to see her. She was a tall woman, wearing the plain dress of a villager. Her hair was dark, streaked with gray, her face lined with experience.

After spending some time with Allia, she reassured her, "Everything's going to be fine, my dear."

The midwife's gentle expression and calming presence made Allia's eyes fill with tears. How long had it been since anyone had been kind to her?

"You don't understand. Everything is not fine. I'm a prisoner here, and I need help."

The woman's eyes widened. "I didn't realize…"

"Please, is there anything you can do?"

The midwife put her hand over Allia's, giving it a reassuring squeeze. "I will try."

Allia watched her leave, feeling the first spark of hope she'd felt since coming to Hakvere.

Over the next few weeks, the quality of the food Haldreth provided improved. He must want Allia to have a healthy child.

❧

The long weeks passed slowly, and the time for the baby to arrive drew near. Allia wished bitterly for some means of escape, but she was in no condition to run away. The sympathetic midwife was a comfort to her, but had found no way to get Allia away from the fortress.

"Can you take the child with you when it's born to keep it out of Haldreth's hands?"

Shaking her head, the midwife said, "He'll find me and kill my family. I'm sorry. I wish there was more I could do."

Giving birth to the child would only make Allia and the baby both more vulnerable to Haldreth. But what else could she do?

❧

One summer morning, she woke to feel a pain in her belly. It eased after a few moments, but then it returned. As the pains came and went, ever closer together and increasingly more intense, Allia knew the baby was coming. She went to the door and pounded on it. There would be a guard there. She had never tried to ask Haldreth's men for anything, but now she called for them to bring the midwife. No one answered, and she waited a long time as the pains came and went.

The midwife arrived in the middle of the worst pain so far. Allia sat panting, her hands clutching the bedding. The woman came through the door and walked to her bedside. After checking her over, the midwife put a comforting hand on her shoulder. "Breathe. Just breathe, my dear. It will be all right."

Allia did her best to obey.

The woman walked back to the door and knocked for the guards again. "Bring hot water," she instructed them. She returned to Allia's side. "It won't be long now."

The labor pains came and went, ever increasing in magnitude and frequency. Allia had used the ring enough to know what life-threatening pain felt like. "Am I dying?" she asked the midwife.

"No, dear," the woman said. "But the baby will be here soon, and then it will be over. Keep breathing. Try to relax."

Relax? She couldn't be serious. Allia clutched handfuls of the blanket in her fists as she pushed. Everything seemed to happen from a distance, except the pain. It shoved other things into the background and continued to worsen until it suddenly eased. As Allia lay back, trying to catch her breath, she heard a baby crying. Her baby. She struggled to lift herself and saw the midwife cleaning and wrapping a tiny wriggling body.

"You have a daughter."

When the midwife wrapped the child and put her in Allia's arms, Allia felt the first scrap of joy she had known since she came here. The baby was so beautiful. Her tiny fingers were perfect, her face lovely. Soft, downy hair covered her head. She looked up at Allia with wise, calm eyes, and when Allia held out her finger, the baby seized it with a surprisingly strong grip.

"You're beautiful," Allia whispered. "Cirana. My Cirana."

For several days, Allia rested and enjoyed caring for her baby.

Haldreth had not appeared yet, but she knew he would come.

When Cirana was two weeks old, Haldreth entered Allia's room, unannounced as always. A stout woman with a grim face followed him. "I am working on something important," Haldreth said. "And I will require your services."

"My services?" she asked, holding her baby a little closer. This was exactly what she'd feared. What was he working on?

"Come with me," he commanded. "Give me the child."

She didn't want to do it, but he would only force her if she refused, and tiny Cirana might be hurt. Reluctantly, she handed him the child. He looked at the baby with interest for a moment. "Is it a boy or a girl?"

"A girl. I named her Cirana after my grandmother."

"How touching," he said sarcastically. He brusquely handed Cirana to the grim-faced woman. "She will be taken care of while you are gone. Come with me."

With her stomach clenched in fear, Allia followed him out the door. He led her down many stairs and dark passageways, past what appeared to be dungeons and caverns, until they came to a large, dim room. She had never seen this part of the fortress before. A fire lit one end, and someone had pushed the furniture back against the walls. Flickering candlelight created shadows around the room, which was dominated by a large black circle, four or five paces across, painted onto the stone floor.

It was an unpleasant place, and fear rushed through Allia when they entered, even though everything was quiet for now. Haldreth shut and locked a heavy wooden door behind them, then pointed to a chair against the wall. "Sit down. It will be nightfall soon. Everything is almost ready."

She sat down in the chair. "What..." Her voice faltered. "What are you going to do?"

"I am about to achieve power beyond imagining, power to defeat anyone who stands in my way. And you're going to help me."

Allia jumped to her feet. "No! I won't!"

Haldreth reached for her shoulder and pushed her back into the chair. "Yes, you will."

"No!"

"Remember your child upstairs, and you *will* do as I ask." The threat behind his words was plain.

"Haldreth, she is your child too. You wouldn't hurt her?"

His cold expression betrayed no hint of emotion. "I will do what I must to convince you to help me."

"But she's an innocent baby!" Allia cried. How foolish she had been to think he might care, even a little, for the child he had fathered.

"I will do what you force me to do," Haldreth said. "No one will stand in my way. Not you, not the child. I need the power of the ring. If you refuse to help me, you are expendable. I am prepared to find out what happens when someone else wears it."

He had won. Allia knew it, and so did he. She couldn't bear to see her baby hurt. The last thing she wanted was for him to gain more power, but he'd threatened her with the one thing that would truly force her to obey.

"What do you want me to do?" she asked in a small voice, staring at the floor.

Haldreth laughed. "I knew you'd see reason. You will stay close to me," he said. "And you will be silent, watching and waiting. I will perform the ritual that will bring a creature of dark power into being. Do not touch it or let it touch you. Make sure nothing breaks the circle. The ritual will tear open my heart, and you will use the ring to heal me. You must do it quickly, for this dark creature will be under my control alone, and only I will be able to prevent it from killing you. If I do not return alive and well by midnight, my soldiers will kill the child. You cannot let me fail."

Icy dread settled on Allia like a weight. As she came to stand by Haldreth, she could sense his triumph and iron determination. He spoke words she couldn't understand and took out a familiar black cylinder, gripping it in his hand. The gate pin. Haldreth must have discovered how to use it.

His voice droned on and beads of sweat appeared on his forehead, a look of concentration on his face. She heard a strange sound, like someone screaming a long way off. She couldn't tell where it came from, but it terrified her. Afraid to move or speak, she waited, while Haldreth's chanting continued, growing louder as the shrieking grew closer.

The air in the center of the circle shimmered. As Allia looked on, terrified, a spot appeared, growing into a hole in the air just above the center of the circle. The sound came from it.

The voice screamed in fury while Haldreth kept speaking, concentrating on that spot. He trembled.

The fissure grew, and Allia glanced from it to Haldreth, hoping he would fail in this unholy attempt but sure that his failure would kill them both. But then she thought of Cirana. Her infant daughter's life depended on her, and she couldn't let him fail.

Haldreth was bleeding. He had opened a wound in the air that was reflected in his own flesh. Blood soaked through the front of his shirt.

Something moved in the hole, and slowly, a large black shape emerged, shrieking in rage. There were words in its cry, but Allia couldn't understand them. The sound of its voice sent shivers through her.

As the creature emerged, Allia sensed a terrifyingly empty darkness unlike anything she'd ever experienced before. The figure craved to consume every living thing. What else could it be, but a demon? In a moment, it tore itself free and the opening vanished.

Beside her, Haldreth screamed in agony. Blood poured from a gaping rent in his chest, and he collapsed. The black thing was coming for them fast and, fighting to control her panic, Allia reached for Haldreth.

The pain was unimaginable. She screamed, feeling her body torn apart. She could not tell if she felt Haldreth's pain or the long claws of the black creature. Oblivion claimed her.

CHAPTER THIRTY-ONE

YEAR OF WARDING 22, HAKVERE, ARA

ALLIA

ALLIA AWOKE WITH A feeling of revulsion. How long had it been since Haldreth summoned the demon?

Looking around, she saw her room. She didn't have the strength to rise. Was Cirana safe?

Her eyes fell on the cradle near her bed, where her child slept quietly. Cirana was alive. Allia's head fell back in relief. Haldreth had kept his promise. The baby was safe, but at what cost? He had done something unspeakable, and she had helped him do it.

Two more days passed before Allia could take care of Cirana on her own again. She hated hearing the infant cry and not being able to go to her. The grim-faced woman came from time to time to help, but sometimes the baby cried for hours before she arrived, and Allia could do nothing.

Her strength came back slowly. When she left her bed, her bones ached and her muscles felt stiff. She rested and held Cirana every moment she could.

The very evening she was able to get up, Haldreth came, his body healthy, his eyes triumphant. Whatever he was attempting, it must be working. Allia's heart sank.

"I want to show you something," he said. Again, they walked down the stairs to the room where Haldreth practiced his magic. "Stay close to me," he ordered.

Against the far wall of the room, she saw two men in chains. One sat with his back resting against the wall, the other lay on the floor. They wore the dark-green tunics of Sarine's army. Allia's insides seemed to shrink with horror. Did she know them? One of the soldiers looked their way, and she was sure she had seen him before, back in the White City. She followed Haldreth as he crossed the room toward the men.

Drawing nearer, Allia saw that the seated man appeared unharmed, while the man on the floor had beads of sweat standing on his forehead. His eyes were closed, but he didn't rest quietly. He muttered and twitched.

"Please! He needs help!" The soldier nodded toward his friend.

Haldreth ignored his plea. "These men dared to violate my borders. They will die."

"No!" she cried, clutching his arm. "Don't do it. Let them go."

"I want you to see how the poison works. Venom has always been an interest of mine. And this one is even more deadly than the worst kind of spider bite." Haldreth's voice was casual, uncaring. He knelt beside the soldier and pulled up the hem of his bloodstained tunic to expose three long gashes wrapping from his side around to his belly. The wounds were badly swollen, the liquid oozing from them a sickly black color.

Allia gasped, horrified. She sensed the man's pain.

"I could have allowed my demon to tear him apart," Haldreth said. "But I wanted you to see this. Even a tiny scratch from its claws is lethal. And there's no cure for it, unless... perhaps, you."

Allia met his cold gaze. "How could you do this?" She meant the injured soldier, but even more, she couldn't believe he had brought an evil like this into the world. She looked down at the suffering man again. "Please, let me heal him. Let them both go. They haven't harmed you."

A flash of hope crossed the unharmed soldier's face.

But Haldreth laughed. "No." He glanced toward the doorway, where a black figure had appeared. It spoke in a voice that made Allia want to run. She couldn't understand the words, but the sound entered her mind, threatening to overthrow her reason.

At a nod from Haldreth, it advanced upon the prisoners. The unharmed man stared at it, frozen, the muscles of his jaw clenching. The black figure raised a clawed hand, and with lightning quickness, slashed him across the face. Blood ran down his cheek.

The demon turned back toward Haldreth, standing still, waiting for orders. He smiled and addressed it. "I need you to do something else for me. Find my brother Callonen and kill him."

"No!" Allia screamed, seizing the front of his shirt. "Please! He's your brother. You can't do this!"

But the black figure had already stalked out the door.

"It's time to continue our work," Haldreth said, pulling her hands free. "It's too late for my brother, and for these soldiers. But you can still save your child. You will help me, or the same thing could happen to her."

Allia sank to the floor, curled into a ball of agony. Callonen. Where was Cal? The demons would destroy him, and she couldn't stop it. It would be better to be dead than to live with having helped Haldreth cause that. She had nothing left. Nothing except Cirana.

Haldreth came over and prodded her with his boot. "Get up. I need you. It's time to continue our work."

"No!" she cried.

"Very well," he said. "It's time to kill the child." He stared down at her, waiting for the response she couldn't help giving. He knew she couldn't bear it.

"No! Please don't!" She had no choice but to help him.

Again, Allia watched, transfixed with horror, as he began his terrifying ritual. And again, she healed him as he was torn apart.

The pain surpassed anything she had ever experienced, and when she woke days later, she felt all but dead.

As soon as she could, she dragged herself to the window and looked out. She wondered where Callonen and his men were. Maybe the demons had killed every one of them. They were creatures of darkness, and their touch was poisonous. Stories from her childhood crept into her mind. Creatures just like this had destroyed the old kingdom. They had a name. Shekkar.

CALLONEN

By late summer, Callonen felt fit again. Only a slight limp remained in his left leg, but he couldn't leave Iron Bridge to return to the White City. What he needed was to find a way into Hakvere. Talon wouldn't be happy about that plan, but Callonen had already decided to go, with or without him. He found Talon sharpening his weapons.

Callonen took a seat across from his friend. "I'm going out again."

Talon put down his sharpening stone and stared back at Callonen.

"You can come with me or not, but I am going." Callonen refused to back down.

"We didn't get shot enough on the last trip?" Talon raised one eyebrow.

Callonen's recovery had been long and painful. "I intend to be more careful. I don't want anyone to be injured this time."

"What if we're dead?" Talon asked bluntly. He slid his sword into its sheath. "What would your father do without you?"

"We will do everything we can to stay safe," Callonen promised, "but I can't give up and leave Allia to suffer. Will you come?"

"How do you even know she's still alive?"

"I know she is. My brother won't have killed her."

Finally, Talon nodded. "I'll come on one condition."

"Which is?"

"That you will listen to me. And if I think a situation is too dangerous, I will tell you to get out, and I expect you to obey."

"What about you?"

"I'll be right behind you."

∽

With his agreement with Talon in place, Callonen left the Warding, riding east, five men with him. The heat of summer had eased, and the skies were clear. He planned to steal uniforms when they crossed the border into Ara. In disguise, he hoped no one would notice them among the other troops.

Two weeks after leaving Iron Bridge, they crossed the North Road under cover of darkness and moved stealthily toward Hakvere. One night, Talon had selected a hidden space behind a thicket of trees for their camp. There was barely room for them and their horses. Two men at a time stood guard. Patrols of Aran soldiers had already passed near them several times.

Callonen rolled into his blanket and settled down to sleep. The late summer night was balmy.

In the deep hours of the night, it was his turn on guard, and Callonen grabbed his weapons and took his post. The woods were silent around him. Looking back over the camp, he saw the others asleep. He should never have allowed any of them to join him on his hopeless quest. Talon should have gone back to his wife instead of agreeing to come. The stars turned, and the night grew old.

The sound came from some distance off the first time he heard it. A faint shriek. Inhuman. What kind of animal made that sound? Callonen gripped his sword hilt. The second cry sounded nearer, and he ran back to the camp to raise the alarm.

"Wake up! Something is coming."

They started out of sleep reaching for their weapons. Talon rolled to his feet and came to stand beside him. "What is it?"

Another shriek echoed through the woods, and they all heard it that time. "We need to get out of here!" Talon ordered.

Too late. The next sound they heard was a scream from the other man on guard.

"Run!" Talon yelled. The men scattered, and Callonen ran with Talon beside him. Something pursued them. They heard it growling and snarling in the undergrowth. It was definitely following their trail.

With his pulse pounding in his ears and his breath coming in gasps, Callonen ran. Brush whipped against him, and the uneven ground attempted to trip him.

"This way," Talon pointed. "Toward the river. There's a place we can hide."

They could hear the water before they could see it. The rushing flow drowned out the sound of the creature behind them. They came out into the open, stumbling through the uneven stones on the bank. Plunging into the river, they crossed to the far side where the water had undercut the bank to create a small, damp cavern. The two of them crawled inside, sitting shoulder to shoulder in the cramped space. Talon kept a knife in his hand, watching back the way they had come.

Callonen drew his own blade and waited.

A black figure slunk to the edge of the water. It walked on two feet like a man, but its shape and movement were distinctly inhuman. Its form was a patch of utter blackness, reflecting nothing, making it difficult to see its exact outline.

In the light of a quarter moon, they watched it pacing the bank. Callonen felt a powerful urge to run again, but it was near now, and if they moved, it would catch them. It snarled in their direction as if it knew they were there, but didn't try to cross. He gripped the hilt of his knife.

Talon put a hand on his arm, reminding him to stay still.

Callonen nodded.

Moments crawled by. He expected to fight for his life at any moment. But the black creature on the bank kept pacing. Not giving up, but never coming any nearer. Callonen waited, silent and tense.

At the end of its path, instead of returning, the black thing abruptly disappeared into the woods.

Callonen took in a deep breath. Neither of them dared move for a long time after it left. The gray light of dawn filtered down through the trees. "I'll go see if it's gone." He moved toward the opening.

"No, stay here," Talon ordered. "I'll go." He left their hiding place, the knife still in his hand, slipped back through the water, up the stony bank, and into the trees. A few moments later, he came back into view, unharmed, beckoning Callonen out of hiding. He crawled out, stretching cramped muscles.

"I can't find any sign of it nearby," Talon said. "I followed its tracks here, but I don't see where it went when it left."

"We need to find the others," Callonen said.

They found one of their men on their way back to the camp. They overtook him as he made his way through the trees.

"Faris?" Callonen asked. "You're hurt?" He could see blood on his neck above the edge of his armor.

"It's not bad," Faris said firmly. "Whatever that thing was, it hit me with its claws, but my armor took most of it. It could have been worse." He tilted his head to the side and Callonen examined the two cuts that ran across Faris's neck.

They found the rest of their friends at the campsite. Several of them gathered around a prostrate form on the ground. Callonen went to them and saw Will. He had been on guard last night, and whatever the thing was, it had found him first. Deep slashes crossed his face and throat.

"Is he alive?" Callonen asked.

"Barely," one of the others replied.

Will was unconscious. When they removed his armor and examined him, they found several deep wounds, which they tended as well as they could.

Callonen looked at Talon. "Have you ever seen anything like that before?"

"Never," Talon admitted. "I don't know what that thing was."

Callonen rubbed his forehead. "Remember when my father used to tell us stories about fighting demons? He said they only came out at night."

Talon's expression was grim. "I think we should get as far from here as we can while the daylight lasts."

No one disagreed with him. They had only been able to find two of their horses after they had bolted. Two men lifted Will onto a horse, with one of them riding behind to keep him in the saddle. Faris rode the other horse.

The day passed all too quickly. Callonen felt a shiver run down his spine as darkness fell. They didn't stop, but kept moving until it was very late.

The men camped against a cliff face in a hidden place under an overhanging boulder. Callonen helped the others pull Will off the horse. The soldier didn't respond at all. His skin felt cold. They laid him on the ground, and Callonen knelt beside him, listening for any sign of breath. He felt the side of his neck for a pulse, and he waited for several anxious moments. Finding no sign of life, he shook his head and pulled a blanket up over Will's face.

While Callonen had been working over Will, the others had kindled a tiny fire in a hidden spot.

Faris sat beside the fire, and Callonen saw beads of sweat on his forehead. "Are you all right, Faris?"

"I don't feel good," Faris admitted.

In the light of the little fire, Callonen inspected the wounds again. The cuts had swollen badly since dawn, and they were an ugly dark color. Callonen helped him clean and wrap them. Faris was shivering by then, even though the night wasn't cold.

Callonen remembered the old stories of demons with poisoned claws. His father called them Shekkar.

The night wore on, and it was past midnight when they heard the creature shriek. Talon kicked dirt into the fire, extinguishing it. "Split up," he ordered. "You two, take one horse and help Faris. We'll take the other and meet you again at dawn."

By morning, it was obvious that the creature pursued Callonen. "It could have followed any of us," he told the others when they had gathered. "With one man on foot, you were moving more slowly, but still it came after me. I don't know if the Warding will stop it, but I hope it will. We need to separate. The rest of you get back to the border as quickly as you can. I will go by another route. It's never attacked us in the daylight. Rest for a few hours now, then go."

"We're not leaving you alone, Your Highness," they protested.

"I'll take one horse and ride for the border."

"The rest of you will be safe once Callonen is gone," Talon said to his men. "Make your way back on foot. I'll take the other horse and stay with Prince Callonen."

"They need the horse so Faris can ride. Talon, you have to go with them," Callonen objected.

Talon folded his muscular arms across his chest and stared back at Callonen stubbornly. "I don't think so."

"I order you!" Callonen said through clenched teeth.

Talon smiled slowly. "Your Highness, normally that would work, but not this time."

"And why not, Captain Talon?"

"You're not yet Emperor of Sarine. My orders came from Emperor Caldoreth. I promised him I would keep you safe. And that means I'm not leaving you."

Callonen didn't have an answer to that. He knew Talon well enough to know he was incredibly stubborn.

It took them three days and nights of riding to get back to the Warding. Callonen heard the Shekkar growling and snarling behind them as they galloped the last mile through the moonlit fields to the border. The dark creature seemed to gain on them until suddenly it stopped as if it had hit a wall. It shrieked in frustration, but came no farther.

Callonen halted, breathing hard. "It's stopped!" He glanced back to see two of the dark creatures. "They can't get through," he exclaimed. Relief flooded through him. Dismounting, Callonen and Talon walked side by side back toward the edge of the Warding. They didn't cross the line again, but stood facing the dark figures. This was the first time they'd seen them so close. The white moonlight shone on two man-like shapes. But there was something about the way they moved that didn't look human. Perhaps their joints moved differently or their proportions were off. Darkness made it impossible to identify exactly what it was. "Can these really be Shekkar?" Callonen asked.

"Demons," Talon said. He drew his sword and moved closer to the border. The demons snarled and snapped at him, and beckoned to him with their claws. Talon had no intention of crossing the line, but he moved closer, near enough to drive his blade into the middle of one of the dark creatures. It screamed and jerked back, but it didn't fall. A few moments later, it was back at the border, trying to get through again.

Talon thrust his blade at it a second time, with no better result. He turned to Callonen, shaking his head. "It should be dead. My sword doesn't hurt it."

"No," Callonen agreed. "There's only one weapon that can destroy them. We need Blackbane."

CHAPTER THIRTY-TWO

YEAR OF WARDING 22, HAKVERE, ARA

ALLIA

N O SOONER HAD ALLIA recovered from healing Haldreth enough to walk again than he was back, and the agonizing cycle repeated itself. She counted the times, scratching marks into the battered wood of her bed frame.

When she had any strength, she took care of her baby, cherishing every moment with her. Every time she woke after a healing, Cirana looked bigger. Her hair grew perceptibly, her face subtly changed. Allia wanted to watch her grow, hating how much time she missed. And she felt considerably weaker after each time she healed. Haldreth wasn't allowing enough time in between for her to fully recover.

He was slowly killing her. It took longer and longer to wake up after each healing and more time for her to be able to move or walk again.

It wouldn't be long before she didn't wake up at all. Then what would happen to Cirana?

Haldreth would have her. Perhaps he would torment her, as he had Allia. Perhaps he would teach her to be like him. With Allia gone, the baby would grow up with no memory of her mother, and if Haldreth were her only influence...

That possibility was the worst of all.

CALLONEN

Heading from the border toward the White City, Callonen and Talon rode for nearly a full day before they met a company of soldiers. They borrowed blankets and food, and two of the soldiers rode with them. Making good time, they reached the city walls as the sun was going down on the fourth day. They rode through the streets to the palace and left the horses with a groom.

To Callonen, the palace halls seemed familiar and strange at the same time. How long had he been gone? The last time he'd been here, Allia had been by his side. How could he have come back without her?

With Talon following him, Callonen entered his father's study and found Caldoreth sitting behind his desk. He appeared older, somehow. Caldoreth jumped to his feet. "Callonen!" He came around the desk to embrace his son. "I'm so relieved you're safe. Talon, thank you for protecting him."

Callonen returned his father's embrace. He'd missed him.

Finally, Caldoreth drew back and looked at him. "Is there good news? Have you brought her home?"

Callonen bowed his head, overwhelmed with guilt and sorrow. "No, Father," he murmured.

Caldoreth embraced him again. "I'm sorry. I'm so sorry, son."

A hot pain twisted through his chest. "I tried. And I can't give up. I won't. But the situation keeps getting worse. Shekkar attacked us outside the border."

The emperor's face fell, his features frozen in shock. "That can't be true. We destroyed them years ago. There's been no word of demons in over twenty years. This must be a mistake."

"It's not a mistake, Emperor," Talon said.

"I saw them, Father. They clawed two of my men and poisoned them. They are Shekkar."

"Who would bring such vile creatures back into the world?" Caldoreth shook his head in sorrow. He took a deep breath. "There's only one thing we can do. Come with me."

Callonen and Talon followed Caldoreth to the treasury. It was heavily guarded, as always, and the emperor took the key from its chain around his neck. He inserted it in the lock and turned it. Slowly, the heavy latch opened and the massive door swung outward. He took a lantern from a bracket in the hall, and they entered the room. In this room the most valuable of Sarine's treasures were stored. Jewelry, gold, weapons and strange items that he couldn't identify.

Caldoreth didn't stop to look around. He moved confidently to the back of the room, stopping before a wooden chest. It was long and narrow, with designs and runes carved into the wood. "This contains the sword, Blackbane," Caldoreth said. "The one I found after the demons killed your mother. With this enchanted blade, I destroyed the Shekkar and won an empire. It saved the lives of countless thousands of people. I had hoped we would never need it again. Now, we do."

Callonen stood at his father's shoulder, eagerly looking on as Caldoreth fit another key into the lock and opened it. The heavy lid creaked slowly open.

The chest was empty.

☙

Unwilling to wait in the city, knowing the Shekkar were roaming the land, Callonen and Talon returned to the border. By the time they got there, the number of demons had grown to four.

A camp had taken root just inside the Warding. Callonen and his friends sheltered in the small cluster of tents. The town of Varda wasn't far away, but it lay outside the shield, and like all the lands beyond, it was now out of reach to Callonen.

Every night, the demons waited outside. Over the next few months, their number grew to a dozen.

Callonen remained there through the autumn, watching the border as the season changed to winter. The place was cold and uncomfortable, and with the enchanted sword gone, they couldn't do anything other than count the number of demons as they increased. They still appeared every single night. Not always the same number, but there were at least three consistently.

Callonen seethed with frustration. If he wanted to live for more than a day, he couldn't leave the border.

A messenger from the city arrived one evening as the soldiers were preparing to settle down for the night. Wordlessly, he held the parchment out to Callonen. As he opened it and scanned the words, his stomach tightened into a knot.

"What is it?" Talon asked, putting a hand on his arm in concern.

"My father. He's very ill."

"This situation is dangerous, Cal. The demons are roaming our borders, trying to get in. If they find a way..." Talon shook his head.

"We can't allow that to happen. They would destroy Sarine. I need to go to him. But..."

"I know." Talon shook his head. "I'm so sorry, Cal. Allia didn't deserve this. And I know how badly it hurts not to rescue her yourself."

"I love her. And that's exactly what I should do," Callonen said.

Talon took a deep breath and met Callonen's eyes. "I know you don't want to consider it, but he might have killed her. We have no way of knowing whether she's alive after all this time."

Callonen closed his eyes. "She's alive. I know she is."

"But everyone in Sarine depends on you to take care of them. How bad is your father's illness?"

"It sounds very serious," Callonen said. "I wondered if something was wrong. The last time we saw him, he seemed worn and tired, but he didn't say anything about it."

Talon took a deep breath. "Go back to your father, Cal. Protect the Warding. I'll try one last time to go after Allia."

"What could you do that we haven't already tried?"

"One of our scouts found a passageway that leads from the canyon wall into the dungeon of Hakvere," Talon said.

"Why didn't you tell me this before?" Callonen demanded.

"He just returned with the news this afternoon. I knew you couldn't leave the Warding safely, and I was trying to decide what to do. If you go back to the city, I'll find a way to get her out. Harrow can come with me. There is less risk of either of us being recognized."

"But it's too dangerous!" Callonen protested.

"We'll be careful," Talon assured him. "I can't stand the thought of Allia being held captive any more than you can. But I won't do anything stupid. I'll find a way in and figure out how to release her."

Callonen couldn't help feeling a surge of hope at the idea. Talon could do it. He could bring Allia back. But the plan was dangerous, and the demons still roamed outside the Warding.

Maybe Callonen shouldn't agree to it, but he longed to. "Can you promise me you'll be safe?"

Talon nodded. "We'll be fine. And we'll find her."

Callonen rode hard to get from the camp at the eastern edge of the Warding back to the city. When he arrived, the afternoon was fading and silence filled the palace. His footsteps echoed in the hallways as he went straight to his father's rooms. The royal healer met him at the door.

"Your Highness." He bowed. "I'm relieved to see you back."

"How is he?" Callonen asked.

The healer shook his head. "Not well. It's grown much more serious since you were last home. We've been doing everything we can think of for months now, but the last two weeks have been worse."

"When do you expect him to recover?" Callonen asked.

The healer put his hand on Callonen's shoulder. "I'm sorry, Your Highness. I'm doing everything I can, but I'm not sure he will recover."

His father had seemed in perfect health before... before his second son had betrayed them.

Callonen entered the room and saw another healer bending over the bed. He went straight to his father's side, and the healer moved to make room for him.

"Father!" Callonen knelt beside the bed and took the emperor's hand.

"Callonen?" Caldoreth's voice sounded weak, nothing like the powerful man who ruled an empire. His face looked deeply lined and old, the skin fragile and translucent.

"How did this happen?" Callonen asked. On his last visit, he'd noticed that his father had aged, but nothing like this. How had he gone from a vigorous man to someone who appeared ancient and frail? "Why didn't you tell me?"

"You were trying to find Allia," Caldoreth murmured. "I know you love her, and I expected you would come home when you rescued her."

He sat with his father late into the night before relinquishing his place to a healer. Back in his own room, Callonen got very little sleep in his soft bed. How could he rest in luxury when Allia was a prisoner? And how could he help her if he was tied to the Warding?

For the next several days, Callonen divided his time between sitting beside his father and handling the business of the empire. He'd assisted with much of it for years, but handling it alone was harder than he'd expected.

Emperor Caldoreth's condition continued to deteriorate.

Callonen questioned the healers about the progression of his father's illness.

"The first time we noticed anything was last winter," a healer said. "Nearly a year ago. But his illness seemed minor at first. He just couldn't seem to recover, though. In the last couple of months, since you were home, everything accelerated. He didn't want us to send for you, but we had to."

Callonen nodded. "I know you've done everything you could."

The man nodded. "I wish I could do more. With your permission, I will depart for now."

Callonen nodded, and the healer left him sitting alone in his father's study. The emperor's health had been failing for nearly a year, and Callonen hadn't known until the message reached him a few days ago. He'd been too focused on Allia and everything else that had happened.

Callonen rubbed his forehead. There was something about this illness. Something he should remember. He got up and paced back and forth, searching for that elusive thought.

Suddenly, the memory surfaced. His mind went back to the spring day nearly two years ago when he had gone looking for Allia in the storage rooms beneath the palace. They had found many unexpected items. He had held a spell book and read the beginning of an incantation that would cause someone to die of old age in a year. Callonen took a lantern and three of the Emperor's Guard. They went to the farthest corner of the palace, to the storage room where he'd seen the books. The room where he and Allia had found the spider.

He paused in the doorway, memories of Allia as painful as a blade in his skin. "We're looking for crates that contain spell books," Callonen instructed the guards. They spread out, searching.

The glass-sided container that had housed the monstrous spider was nowhere to be seen. Callonen and the others examined dozens of crates. Only a few contained books, but none of them had anything to do with magic. They found nothing out of the ordinary. Someone had removed them from the room.

Had it been Haldreth? A shaft of pain penetrated Callonen's heart. Had his brother taken the strange glass case and the crates of artifacts and spell books? Had he studied them? Was Haldreth trying to murder their father? Could he have stolen Blackbane too? There must be some way to help his father, some way to stop the progression of the illness. Where was the healing ring now, when they needed it so badly?

⌇

For days, the emperor's condition worsened and Callonen stayed beside his father, holding his withered hand. Just before the sun set, Caldoreth took a few final shallow breaths, and then nothing. He was gone.

Grief flooded through Callonen. His father's absence left a stinging hole in his heart. Caldoreth had been the only family he had left besides Haldreth.

Suddenly, Callonen's mind was exploding, filled with thousands of thoughts and voices. The sudden crushing weight pressed down on him, causing him to cry out, writing to escape it. The noise was unbearable. He put his hands on either side of his head, as if he could hold his skull together.

Callonen tried to breathe—in and out. The steady rhythm pushed the noise and weight back a little.

He took a deep breath. The pressure receded enough that he could think again. Opening his eyes, he found himself on the floor beside his father's bed, the healer bending over him.

"What happened?" Callonen rubbed his forehead as he tried to concentrate.

When he focused hard on his own thoughts, everything else moved to the background. He could think. All the people of Sarine were there, somewhere in his mind. If he concentrated on someone, he could tell where they were and what they were feeling.

He looked at the healer kneeling beside him. "I know now how much you really cared about my father. You gave up time with your own family to help him."

The man's eyes widened. He bowed in the deepest respect. "Yes, Emperor Callonen."

ALLIA

Winter was passing, and by now, Haldreth had summoned sixteen of the dark creatures. Allia woke with the all-too-familiar weakness of having healed Haldreth again. The night was silent. The faint glow of moonlight lit her room while Cirana slept in her cradle. Allia heard someone open the door stealthily.

Was it Haldreth? He hadn't made any nighttime visits since before Cirana was born. Had he come back?

Allia's stomach knotted. It could be someone else, any of the soldiers. Her eyes followed the dark shape of a man against the moonlight, and she shrank away in fear. She didn't have the strength to even try to fight if he attacked her. If she cried out, it might alert a guard, but would probably not result in help for her. The man crept silently nearer.

"Allia?" a voice whispered.

No one here dared speak to her, aside from Haldreth. Who could it be? What was he going to do to her? She couldn't even raise her arms. Fear flooded through her, and her breathing became rapid and shallow.

A familiar voice spoke to her out of the dark. "Don't be afraid. It's Talon."

For a long moment, her tired brain struggled to process the information. Talon? But he couldn't be here. That wasn't possible.

"Talon?" she murmured.

"Yes, it's me. Please don't be afraid."

She relaxed against the pillow and tears of relief slipped from her eyes. "How?"

"We didn't have enough men to attack the fortress directly, so we had to find another way in. I'm sorry it took so long."

"Talon! I was afraid you were dead. He sent the demons to kill Callonen. Is he dead?"

"He's alive and sent me to help you. We need to get you out of here."

"It's not just me. My baby too."

If the revelation shocked Talon, he didn't show it. He looked down into the cradle at the blanket-covered bundle.

"There has to be a way to stop Haldreth!" she continued. "He is using dark magic to summon demons, and he's forced me to help him. He said he would kill my baby if I didn't! I should have let him kill us both. Now so many other people have died... But I couldn't!" She couldn't stop the tears now. When she explained it all out loud, it sounded even worse.

"Shh..." Talon hissed, putting a gentle hand on her shoulder. "It will be all right."

"How can you say that? We have to stop him!"

"Yes," Talon agreed. "But first we have to get you away from here."

"You would take me home?" It was too good to be true. "I was afraid Callonen wouldn't forgive me... He's not angry with me?"

"Angry?" Talon asked. "No. He knows you were taken against your will, and he loves you. We've just spent a long time finding a way in. If not for the demons, he would still be trying. They can't get into the Warding. Callonen had to get back inside before they killed him."

Allia took in a deep breath. "Then he's all right?"

"He's fine, but he had to return to the city when Emperor Caldoreth became ill. Without the Warding, no one would have any protection from the Shekkar. He couldn't come himself, but I'm here to take you home."

For so long, Allia had thought Callonen was dead because of her. "Thank you, Talon," Allia whispered. "I've been so alone here."

"Let's go now," he urged. "Come with me."

"Haldreth forced me to heal him. I can't get up."

"I'll carry you."

For a moment, a surge of hope welled up in Allia's heart. He would take her and Cirana away. They would be rid of Haldreth forever. But what would happen after they left? Haldreth would send his demons after them. Perhaps there might be a way to stop his plans... Maybe the gate pin Haldreth used in his ritual? She tried to gather the remaining shreds of her courage.

"Wait," she whispered. "There's a powerful magical object... Without it, and the ring, he can't create any more demons."

"How can I steal it?" Talon asked.

Allia shook her head. "It has to be me. He guards it carefully. But I would need a replica to put in its place. Could you find someone skilled at metalwork to make one?"

"I can do it," Talon said. "Before I became a soldier, I was a blacksmith. What's this thing like?"

"It's almost exactly the length of my hand."

Talon measured the size against his own hand, nodding.

"It's a rod as thick as my finger with six equal sides and looks like black iron."

"I'll do the best I can," Talon said. "I'll make a few, and you can pick the best one when I come back."

"A fake won't fool him for long," she said, "but perhaps long enough for us to get away."

"When?" he asked.

Allia had kept count of the healings by scratching marks into the battered wood of the bed frame. She had no way of knowing exactly how long she was unconscious after each healing, but from the time she woke up, Haldreth had been consistent in his schedule of returning to demand she assist him again.

"In four more days, he will force me to heal him again. If I refuse, his guards will kill my baby. But I don't have the strength to continue. It's killing me. There isn't much time left to get Cirana away from him."

"Cirana? Is that your baby's name?"

"Yes."

"We'll get her out," Talon promised.

Allia sighed. "That's more important than what happens to me. We have to do this. Bring me the replica before then. That night, I will exchange them, and he will bring me back here. I will not be conscious for two or three days. Can you still get Cirana and me out?"

"Yes. Harrow is with me."

"Please be careful! No matter what happens, we have to get Cirana away from him. But what about you? Talon, he will send the demons after us."

"I know." Talon took a deep breath. "But if we don't do this, he'll create an army of demons, and no one will ever be able to stop him. We'll just have to get back into the Warding before they catch us."

CHAPTER THIRTY-THREE

ALLIA

AS THE FOUR DAYS passed, Allia regained some strength and started to convince herself that their plan might work. Talon had slipped back in one night and given her a choice of three black, six-sided iron cylinders. He had done well, and they were all excellent reproductions. She selected the one that best matched the original. Hopefully, Haldreth wouldn't look too closely at it for a few days. She hid it in her pocket, waiting for her chance to act. That evening, Haldreth came to her room as usual, and Allia went with him wordlessly. They descended to the chamber with the circle. Night had fallen. He began speaking the strange words, which by now were grotesquely familiar to Allia. She kept her face blank, but nervousness twisted her stomach.

The shrieking came, and the hole opened. Haldreth's chest was torn apart. As the new demon emerged, Haldreth collapsed, bleeding, onto the floor. The demon faced him. While its attention focused on Haldreth, Allia grabbed the pin from his hand, replacing it with Talon's replica. She hid the real artifact inside her dress. The demon dove toward her, as she reached down to heal Haldreth. When she touched him, the pain was so intense that she couldn't tell if the demon's claws had reached her.

❧

When Allia opened her eyes, she saw the night sky. She blinked in confusion. Where was she? She shivered with the cold and felt the chill of stone beneath her. A dark shape loomed, silhouetted against the stars. A startled gasp escaped her.

"Allia?"

Relieved, she recognized Talon's voice. Had they made it out of the fortress? "Talon?"

"I'm here." He took her hand and gave it a reassuring squeeze.

"Are we out?" It seemed too good to be true.

"We're out," he said.

Tears filled her eyes. "I thought I would never escape!" she cried. "Thank you! Where's Cirana?"

"Harrow has her, right here. She's sleeping."

Allia hadn't meant to let her emotions get the best of her, but she had been trapped for so long with no hope or help. Silent sobs shook her, and tears ran down her cheeks.

"It will be all right," Talon said, putting a comforting hand on her shoulder. "Would you like some water?"

He supported her head so she could drink.

"Thank you," she murmured, taking a deep breath and trying to pull herself together. She and Cirana were both *outside* the fortress of Hakvere.

"Can you eat?" Talon offered her a piece of hard bread.

She couldn't use her arms, so he broke off pieces, and she opened her mouth to accept them. He helped her wash it down with another swallow of water.

"We need to keep moving," Talon said.

She nodded, eager to put as much distance as possible between herself and Haldreth, but she couldn't walk or even move. There was no way she could have gotten out on her own.

"With your permission, Lady Allia?" Talon said.

He knew they had no other choice but offered what respect he could, and Allia was grateful. She nodded, and he picked her up in his arms. Harrow appeared as another dark outline beside him. They moved through the rocks, along the edge of the river. Sheer canyon walls rose on either side.

"We left horses and supplies hidden on the other side," Talon said. "Do you have the gate pin?"

She could feel the hard outline of it against her ribs. "Yes."

"There are villages across the river. We'll find a forge and destroy it."

"Thank you." She closed her eyes to rest.

TALON

The four of them traveled through the rest of that night and early morning. Allia had only been awake for a brief period before she passed out again. When the terrain grew more difficult, Talon carried her over his shoulder instead of in his arms. She had not objected or even moved. It felt like he was carrying a lifeless body.

No. She still lived and would regain her strength with time and care.

The sun was growing high when the baby demanded a halt. Harrow had nestled her inside his coat to keep her warm, and she'd slept resting against his chest. Now she woke, wiggled and informed them she was hungry.

They found a protected hollow, out of sight. Haldreth's men were surely searching along the rim of the canyon.

Talon set Allia down on the rocks. She reacted as little as if she were already dead. In the full light of day, her face looked haggard. Her cheeks were hollow, and she had dark circles beneath her eyes with heavy bruises along her cheek and jaw. As he'd carried her, he could feel how thin she was. Her body felt frail, as if anything might break her.

Knowing they would need to care for an infant, Talon had brought milk with them. It would stay good for days yet in the cold weather.

Harrow pulled the baby out of his jacket and wrapped her in a blanket.

Talon soaked bits of the hard bread in the milk and gave them to the baby. She stared up at him with large brown eyes. "Good girl," he said as she accepted the food. "I'm sorry it's not warm. We're doing the best we can."

"You're pretty good at that," Harrow commented.

"Of course," Talon said. "It's been a while since my son was a baby, but I haven't forgotten everything."

"Good." Harrow wrinkled his nose. "Then you can change her."

Talon laughed.

❧

As the sun sank, they halted, hiding in the rocks, looking down toward the river. "We have to get across." Talon eyed the wide, fast-flowing waters.

"How are we going to get them across?" Harrow gestured to Allia and Cirana.

Talon pointed to the baby. "She's tiny. You can swim and keep her out of the water, can't you?"

"Maybe," Harrow replied. "What about Allia?"

Talon shook his head. "There's no way to keep her dry. We'll wait until nightfall so we can stay out of sight."

They rested quietly as the afternoon faded. "Talon?" Allia's voice was weak. "Where's Cirana?"

He turned to see her eyes open. "She's fine. She's napping beside Harrow. He'll keep her warm."

"Thank you both for taking care of her," she whispered.

"Of course," Talon replied. "He didn't have any experience with babies, but he's learning quickly."

She raised her arm to her chest and pulled something wrapped in cloth from the front of her dress. "Please, take it."

He took the parcel and felt a slender piece of metal inside. The gate pin. "There's a village on the other side, and they'll have a forge."

"Heat the iron until it's red hot, then dunk it in a solution of cold vinegar and salt. Then repeat the process until it shatters."

"I will." Talon nodded, looking out over the river. "The crossing will be painful."

"I understand," she murmured. "Can you keep Cirana dry?"

"We'll do our best," Talon promised.

The night was dark, with heavy clouds blocking the stars. A chilly wind rose, but they couldn't put this off. Haldreth would already have the demons searching for Allia. Harrow wrapped the baby tightly so she couldn't wiggle free. They pulled off their boots and shirts and stuffed everything in their packs. Harrow took the precious blanket-wrapped bundle and waded out into the river. Talon confirmed his axe was tightly buckled to the side of his pack, his sword at his belt. With his weapons secure, he shouldered his pack and took Allia in his arms.

The water was icy on his feet, causing a sharp ache. Soon, it reached his waist, then his chest. He clutched the girl and the pack in one arm, and swam hard with the other. The cold was painful, and his limbs dragged through the water. The current pulled them, and he fought against it. Finally, his foot struck the bottom on the far side, and he pushed himself forward, trying to force his frozen muscles to work.

Harrow appeared in the shallows and pulled them onto the bank where Talon lay gasping and shaking. Allia had lost consciousness. Harrow picked her up, and Talon followed him. He'd done a good job keeping the baby dry, and their packs were only partially wet.

Talon pulled out clothes and quickly changed. At least now he was only damp. Harrow did the same.

Talon knelt beside her. "Allia?"

She didn't respond at all. Her skin was icy to the touch. "We're almost back to the horses. When we get there, we have to get her warm."

But when they reached the place, there was nothing left. No horses, no warm clothing or food. They searched the area carefully, but to no avail. "Come on," Talon said. "The village is near." He wrapped a damp blanket from his pack around Allia and picked her up. "Hurry."

Slipping quietly into the village, they found the forge.

"I'll be right back," Talon promised. Harrow waited with Allia and the baby behind the building.

There was no one on the streets. Everyone in town seemed to be in a hurry to be indoors now that darkness had fallen. Choosing the little house beside the forge, he knocked on the door. No response. He took a gold coin from his pouch and slid it under the door.

Abruptly it opened, and Talon faced a man who appeared to be the blacksmith. His arms and chest were heavily muscled. He stared at Talon.

"I have more gold, if you'll let me borrow your tools." Talon held up a coin.

"What if I kill you and take your gold?" the man growled. He took a step forward.

By the time he took the next step, Talon's knife point was against his chest. "Don't do that," Talon said. "My plan is better. I won't be long. Aside from the gold, you'll never even know I was here."

Talon wasn't sure if it was the knife or the promise of money that finally convinced the man. But the blacksmith led him into his shop and pulled out a hammer, a pair of tongs, and a bellows.

"Thank you," Talon said. "Now, if I might borrow vinegar and salt from your kitchen?"

The smith stomped away, but returned with the items. "Anything else?"

Talon shook his head. "No, thank you." He tossed the man a few coins. "I'll leave the rest on the anvil when I'm finished."

The man cleared his throat. "Thank you. The money will help feed my family."

"I wish you well," Talon said. "Hide the money until we're long gone and forget you saw us. Is there anyone in town who might sell a horse?"

The smith shook his head. "The army took the horses."

"All of them?"

"They take anything they want." The man shook his head in disgust. "If you go to the last house at the end, there's a man with a pony. A sickly old animal, but he might part with it for the right price. If you ride it, it'll be dead in a week."

That hadn't been the news Talon wanted. But what else could they do? "Thank you," he said.

The smith nodded and hurried back to the house.

As soon as the man disappeared, Talon ran to the back of the building. He grabbed the packs and the baby. Harrow picked up Allia. They hurried into the warmth of the blacksmith's shop.

Harrow placed Allia near the forge. "She's freezing, Talon. What if she doesn't wake up again?"

Talon knelt beside her and tried to rub some life back into her arms and hands. Her ragged dress was soaked and freezing, clinging to her skin. "We have to find something dry for her to wear." Talon rummaged through his pack, finding only the wet pants he'd worn through the river. He pulled off his jacket and shirt.

"Allia!" He tried to wake her. She didn't respond. "I'm sorry," he apologized. If he couldn't warm her, she'd die. He started to unlace her soaked dress.

Eyes still closed, she gasped and pulled away. "Haldreth! No. Leave me alone."

Talon shook her shoulder. "Allia. Wake up. Haldreth isn't here. I'm only trying to save your life."

She blinked. "What happened?"

"The river," he explained.

"River?" she blinked. "I-Is that why it's so cold?"

"Yes, you need dry clothes."

"You were only helping me," she said.

"Yes!"

"I'm sorry, Talon."

She took a deep breath and undid the lacing herself. Talon helped her, then put his shirt on her and wrapped her in the blanket. "That's so much better," she murmured, still shivering violently. "Where's Cirana?"

Talon tucked the baby into the blanket beside her. "Just rest and get warm."

He turned to Harrow. "The smith said the man in the last house on the other end of town had a pony he might sell. Will you try to get it?" Harrow nodded and left.

As Talon fed the fire, a welcome warmth spread through the room. He found the smith's leather apron and put it on to protect his skin. The bellows increased the temperature, and when it was ready, he picked up the gate pin with the tongs and put it in the hottest part of the flames. While he waited for it to heat, he mixed the vinegar and salt in a bucket.

When the metal glowed red-hot, he took it out of the fire and dunked it into the liquid. The piece of metal screamed when it touched the mixture. Talon jumped and almost dropped the tongs. Horrified, he stared at it. The metal seemed to twist and writhe beneath the surface. Finally, it lay completely cool and still.

He heated it again and repeated the process. It shrieked louder the second time.

And the third.

On his fourth attempt, the shrieking rose into an unearthly wail of agony, and the metal shattered, leaving a ringing silence in the forge. Allia and baby Cirana watched with wide eyes. If anyone in the little house beside the forge heard the sound, they did not respond.

Talon took a deep breath, peering down at the fragments floating in the liquid. He put his jacket on, borrowed a shovel, and took the bucket out behind the building and dug a hole, pouring in the contents of the bucket and covering them with earth.

Harrow returned with the pony, and they quickly gathered their things. "We need to get away from here," Talon said. "Haldreth's soldiers won't be far behind us."

Talon left the gold as he'd promised. The pony was a decrepit beast, but it seemed as though it could carry Allia, at least for a while. Harrow tucked the baby back into his jacket. They hurried away into the night. The faint lights of the village disappeared behind them.

They covered as much ground as they could before dawn came. As it got light, they hid in a thicket in a little patch of woods. Allia's strength was returning, and with Talon's help, she fed and changed the baby, and wrapped her again.

"How old is she now?" Talon asked, tucking the blanket snuggly around her. He couldn't help but ask. The little girl had brown eyes the exact shade of Callonen's.

"I don't know exactly." Allia shrugged. "The only way I could tell was by how many times I healed Haldreth. Seventeen now. It must be about six months. It seems shorter, but I've been unconscious half the time."

This child was too young to have been conceived in Sarine. It had been too long. And Talon knew Callonen well enough to know that he'd treated Allia with honor. He hadn't fathered this child. There was no need to ask Allia what had happened. Instead, he looked down at the baby and said, "I remember when my son was this age. He was less... well-behaved. She's beautiful, Allia."

"Thank you," she whispered.

As soon as they had eaten a quick meal, she curled up with the baby in her arms and dozed off. She muttered and twitched in her sleep.

"Stay here," Talon said to Harrow. "I'm going to have a look behind us."

Harrow nodded.

Talon went back along their trail. It didn't take long to see the tracks following them. He hurried back to the others. "The demons are behind us," he said to Harrow when he returned. "I saw their tracks."

"How close are they?" Allia asked.

They turned to see Allia pushing herself up into a sitting position. Despair filled her eyes.

"Did you learn anything about them that might help us?" Talon asked.

"I know they only move at night, and they obey Haldreth. Their claws are poisonous. If they break the skin, it's deadly. He forced me to watch how it worked."

"Ordinary weapons don't hurt them," Talon said. He had already tested that for himself. "Is there a way we can kill them?"

Allia shook her head. "I don't know how."

"Do you know any way we can stop them?"

She shook her head again. "You told me they can't get past the Warding. When Haldreth ordered them to kill Callonen, they would have obeyed if they could."

"We'll head for the Warding," Talon said. "We could be back there in ten days on horseback. Walking will take longer."

"He sent them to follow me," Allia said, her tone heavy. "You two should take Cirana and leave. Without me, you might escape."

Talon stared back at her, his eyebrows raised in disbelief. How could she ask that? He shook his head. "We are *all* escaping. Since they move at night, we'll go now." He offered his hand to help Allia to her feet.

CHAPTER THIRTY-FOUR

YEAR OF WARDING 23, ARA'S COUNTRYSIDE

TALON

TALON LED THEM, DAY and night, through the hills and farmlands of Ara. They passed several little villages. They barely paused to rest or sleep, and they were all tired, especially Allia, who had been nearly dead as they began their journey. But somehow, they kept going. Talon watched her with growing concern.

At dawn, Talon slipped out to find a place where he could look down on the North Road. They needed to cross it. The most direct road to Sarine lay beyond the outpost of Iron Bridge. The emperor's army had always guarded the bridge the garrison was named for, but now, with the demons hunting, they would have been forced back within the Warding. Assuming that enemy forces controlled the crossing, Talon would have to find a way through the mountains into Sarine once they made it across the road.

When Talon reached the ridge and looked down, his stomach clenched in horror. Army camps stretched for miles in both directions, farther than he could see. They flew the banner of Ara and wore blue uniforms with black armor. How could he get Allia through? He and Harrow would have a good chance in disguise, but how could they hide a girl with a baby?

On the road below him, a supply wagon rolled by, heading toward the camps. One man drove and two others rode as guards. Talon rubbed his chin thoughtfully. Where could he find a bow? He crept away from the edge and turned back the way he'd come. Staying out of sight among the trees, he made his way back. Motion caught his eye. Two Aran scouts came up the hill. One of them carried a bow. Talon reached for his knife.

By the time Talon returned to the others, he carried the bow and two uniforms. "How many Arans did you see?" Harrow asked.

Talon sighed, not wanting to answer. "Quite a few," he finally admitted. "Are you ready to join the Aran army?" He tossed Harrow a uniform and some armor. "We'll be taking a load of supplies to them."

If Harrow didn't like the plan, he kept his objections to himself and began changing his clothes. Talon turned to Allia. "We have to get through the army camps. We'll leave the pony here, and you and the baby can hide in a wagon."

They waited, hidden in the rocks, for another wagon to pass. One came by with two dozen men guarding it. Talon shook his head. They remained hidden, waiting.

The next wagon had only two guards riding behind. Talon shot twice in quick succession, and he and Harrow ran out of hiding to take the guards' places as they toppled out of their saddles. The wagon rolled on, unaware. Talon took aim and shot the driver. Harrow urged his horse into a gallop and jumped onto the wagon seat. Shoving the fallen man off, he took the reins and pulled the team to a stop.

Talon pulled up beside him, taking the reins. "Go get Allia," he instructed.

Harrow remounted his horse and galloped back toward the hiding place. While he was gone, Talon dragged the fallen soldiers into a patch of thick brush, out of sight. He arranged the crates and barrels in the wagon bed to create a space big enough to conceal a person. Harrow returned quickly with Allia and the baby.

Talon took the child while Harrow helped Allia into the wagon. They wrapped all the blankets they had around her and put the baby in her arms. "Just stay quiet," Talon urged. "We'll be all right."

They resumed their course, directly into the Aran army.

Despite the situation, Talon slouched comfortably on the wagon seat and drove at a relaxed pace. They must appear unhurried. Nothing about this wagon must draw attention. None of the sentries questioned them or stopped them until they reached the main road. Talon began to turn the wagon north toward the bridge and Sarine's border.

"No, no!" a group of guards yelled, waving their arms at him. "Not that way! Those supplies go south. Didn't they tell you where to go?" Talon shrugged and tried to keep his expression bored. He turned south. What other choice did he have? More camps lined the road. The wagon rolled along and they were undiscovered for now, but every step took them farther from safety.

The Aran army clustered along the eastern edge of the North Road. If Talon could get Allia through them and away from the road, they could ride into the hills and escape. He watched the sinking sun, waiting for the cover of darkness.

When the wagon came to a gully, out of sight for the moment, Talon turned the horses aside into a dry riverbed. He jumped to the ground and started unhitching the team. Harrow climbed into the wagon and helped Allia out of her hiding place. He took the baby in his arms and returned to his saddle. Talon jumped onto one of the horses, and Allia slid from the wagon onto the other.

Following the gully up into the hills, they rode away into the gathering darkness. If they continued west through the mountains, they would reach Varda. From there, it was only a day's ride to the edge of the Warding.

They kept moving all night, even though their progress was slow through the rough terrain. The wagon horse Talon rode grew slower and slower. They paused, and he slid to the ground to check its hooves.

"He's lame," Talon said, shaking his head. He'd seen more than his share of horseshoes, and he might have been able to help if he had time and tools. They had neither. Talon got on behind Allia, and they rode into the hills.

At dawn, they dismounted to rest. Talon and Harrow took off the blue uniforms and put back on their own clothes. Allia cared for the baby and then curled up to sleep. Exhaustion showed on her face and in the dark circles under her eyes. Talon brought another blanket and wrapped it around her.

They rested for half the day and went on in the afternoon. A cold north wind came up, and clouds gathered. Talon looked at the sky and shook his head. Darkness fell early, and the storm rolled through the mountains, drenching them in an icy soaking rain. He didn't dare stop and look for shelter, but they moved slowly because of the slippery footing and poor visibility.

They were all badly chilled, and Talon felt Allia shivering. Was the baby all right? By the time the rain finally stopped, it was morning. The clouds broke to let in the light of a cold gray dawn. They dismounted to rest themselves and the horses a little.

Allia went straight to Harrow. "I-Is s-she warm?"

Harrow had the tiny girl tucked inside his jacket. She looked up at them with wide brown eyes. "She's all right," he said.

Talon found enough dry wood to start a little fire. Allia huddled desperately close to it, though it wasn't large enough to put out much heat, and the damp fuel smoked.

"If we do well tonight, we should be near Varda by morning."

"Varda?" Allia raised her head in alarm. None of them had forgotten their last visit there.

Harrow rubbed the two round scars on the back of his neck.

"We won't be going anywhere near the forest," Talon assured them. "We'll stay alert anyway. Our path will be straight west toward the Warding. Rest now. I'm going to check our trail."

Talon hadn't gone far along their trail before he found demon footprints. His stomach sank. Their detour with the Aran army and the storm must have slowed them down too much. How were they going to escape?

They would have liked to rest longer, but after a brief halt, they struggled on. The sun shone fitfully through the broken clouds. The day passed all too quickly, and darkness would come early.

As they rode, Talon heard the sudden hiss of an arrow flying past his ear. Ahead of him, Harrow ducked another shaft that nearly hit his head.

"Go!" Talon yelled, urging the wagon horse into a gallop. He followed Harrow, who had turned to the side and raced into the trees. More arrows flew, and a few Aran soldiers tried to block their path. Harrow drew his sword. He held his other arm protectively over his chest. A quick blow severed the shaft of a spear aimed at him and he thrust his sword at a second attacker.

Then he was past them, and Talon drew his own blade. A few quick strokes and they were through. They galloped on, not sure how quickly the pursuit would reach them.

The horse lurched violently beneath Talon and Allia, throwing them as it fell. He released the weapon in his hand and rolled as he struck the ground. His elbow and side throbbed with pain, and he would have bruises, but he wasn't seriously hurt. Allia had landed a few paces away.

She was gasping, trying to catch her breath from the shock. Her forehead was scraped, and she was holding her shoulder.

"How bad is it?" he asked.

She shook her head. "It's not bad."

Talon helped her back to her feet. He stooped to retrieve his sword and returned it to its sheath. Looking for the horse, he saw it lying on the ground, a troop of Aran soldiers not far behind. "Run!" He followed Allia into the trees. They turned aside and hid in the brush.

The sound of their rapid breathing faded into quiet. Around then, the light was already fading. Talon listened carefully, his hand on the hilt of his sword. But he didn't hear any footsteps approaching. They waited until full dark had fallen. Talon slipped from cover to look around. "I think it's safe."

Allia crawled out after him, and they went on.

They'd walked for an hour before they found Harrow again. He expelled a sigh of relief when he saw them. "I was beginning to fear the worst," he admitted.

"They're not far behind us," Talon said. "We need to move."

Harrow nodded. "Will you ride for a while, Allia?"

"Cirana?" she asked.

Harrow curled his arm around her protectively. "I fed her. She's just gone to sleep."

Allia mounted, and they departed. They were all weary, but she seemed almost ready to collapse.

The night grew black and a chill wind came up. The weather was turning bad. Talon listened to the wind. For a moment, he almost thought he'd heard something. But there was no time to investigate. They hurried on.

A short while later, the shriek behind them was plain. "Demons!" Allia cried, pulling the horse to a stop. "They're going to find us!" Panic filled her voice. She looked at Talon as if there might be something he could do.

How he wished there was. If only there was a river nearby.

She had depended on him for protection, and he had failed utterly. They weren't far from the Warding now. But they had no time left.

Tears welled in her eyes. "Please don't let them take Cirana! I would rather die than to know Haldreth has her again." She glanced behind them into the forest. "It's too late. They've caught up."

Allia took in a deep breath and slid down from the horse. "I'll stay here. You and Harrow take the horse and get Cirana away! Please! Two people on a horse might outrun them. And I can't let Haldreth have the ring."

"You take the ring and go. It won't come off your finger," Talon protested.

Allia took a deep breath. "If we do that, we'll all be killed because of me. The demons are following me, and I have to stay behind. But Haldreth can't have the ring." Her desperate gaze fell on him. "I need your help."

Nausea churned in his stomach. Talon couldn't do what she asked. He just couldn't.

She hugged and kissed the child in Harrow's arms. "I love you, Cirana." She looked up at Harrow. "Thank you for taking care of her."

He nodded in response.

Allia moved quickly, though her hands shook visibly. "Give me your pack," she instructed Talon.

He obeyed, and she grabbed it, unstrapped the axe from the side, and rummaged through the interior. She pulled out an old piece of cloth. Putting the pack down, she spread one of its leather straps across a rock. She seized the front of Talon's jacket and pulled him to face her. "You have to do it. Now." She placed the axe in his hand.

"I can't—" he choked out the words, staring at the weapon.

She met his eyes, and they both knew there was no other way to prevent Haldreth from regaining the power of the ring. Could he create more demons with it? Other dark magic? Talon clenched his jaw. He took the axe, and she extended her ring finger across the leather strap and onto the rock, tucking the rest of her fingers beneath its edge.

"Are you sure?"

Allia nodded resolutely.

Talon gripped her hand, holding it in place. It only took one swift stroke. The blade was sharp and his aim was true. He wadded the cloth and held it firmly against the wound, guiding Allia's other hand to hold it in place. The severed finger had fallen to the ground, and he picked up the ring that had landed beside it.

Talon found a length of cord and threaded the ring onto it. He tied the ends securely and handed it to Harrow, who still held the tiny girl.

"Keep the ring away from Haldreth and see that Cirana's safe," Allia said through clenched teeth. "Go! They'll be here any moment!"

A flash of lightning illuminated the forest. Thunder roared and rain fell.

Talon put his hand on Harrow's shoulder. "That horse can't carry both of us. Guard the baby with your life," he instructed. "Ride hard back to the Warding. Take this to Callonen." He gave Harrow a piece of parchment.

"No!" Harrow protested. "You have a family back there waiting for you. I'll stay. You take the horse and the child and run."

Talon shook his head. "I can't do that. Go now, Harrow. There's no time."

Harrow tucked the baby securely into his jacket, jumped on the horse, and disappeared between the trees.

Talon knelt beside Allia. "We need to find someplace we can defend."

"I told you to go!"

"Harrow is gone," he answered.

Allia's eyes welled with tears. "You were supposed to go with him!"

"If I was going to put anyone else on that horse, it would have been you."

"Talon, they'll be here any moment. Run!"

"What about you?"

"It's too late for me."

Talon offered her his hand. "We knew he would hunt us down, and we almost reached the Warding. We've stopped him from creating more demons. Cirana will escape."

She stared up at him, tears on her face. But she took his hand, and he pulled her to her feet.

"Let's go." As they hurried through the forest, a shriek echoed through the trees.

Talon led them toward a rocky outcropping. It wasn't much, but better than nothing. It had a ledge ten or twelve feet off the ground. Above that, a cliff face rose. He climbed up, turning back to help Allia. When they were both on the ledge, he dropped his pack and checked his weapons. Lightning flashed again. In the brief illumination, he saw several black shapes.

Allia leaned against the rock wall, her wounded hand held close to her chest. Talon wished for some way to ease her suffering. A shriek sounded through the rain.

"Talon!"

He turned to face her. Her shoulders slumped in defeat, and despair filled her eyes.

"Thank you for all you've done."

He nodded, pulling the axe from his back. "Stay against the cliff," he instructed, drawing his sword. "I'll keep you safe as long as I can." He wiped the rain from his eyes with the back of his hand. The demons were at the base of the rocks now. They snarled and growled, almost as if they were talking to each other. He gripped his sword in one hand and his axe in the other.

Before the first demon was fully onto the ledge, Talon struck it with his axe. When the blade made contact, the blow felt solid enough. The demon shrieked, but it sounded angry rather than hurt. Talon planted his boot against it and shoved it away with all his strength. It disappeared, falling backward out of sight.

Another demon had climbed onto the ledge while he had been focused on the first. It slashed at him with razor-sharp claws, but he blocked them with his sword. It forced him toward the edge until Talon was only a foot away from the brink.

More demons were climbing up. Talon felt searing pain as their claws dug into his feet and legs. They jerked him off balance, shrieking in triumph as they pulled him off the ledge.

ALLIA

Allia stood with her back against the stone, her breathing ragged with panic. She stared at the demon, waiting for it to attack. It snarled at her, but came no closer. Another demon joined the first, and they conversed with each other in their language, but neither of them attacked. She remained frozen, leaning against the cliff face, the icy rain drenching her.

The light grew silvery, and the rain changed to snow. Allia was so cold she could no longer feel her feet or hands. Even the harsh throbbing of her injury faded. She sank to her knees. The demons watched her, keeping their distance. Why? Did Haldreth want her alive? Maybe he intended to make her wish the demons had torn her apart.

Allia brushed the snowflakes from her eyes. She saw torches coming through the forest. Demons didn't carry torches. And whoever carried the lights was not fleeing from them. Instead, they came nearer.

She didn't want to go back to Ara. Allia scanned the bare cliff face. Nowhere to hide. Her mind too numb to come up with any sort of plan, she stumbled toward the edge, thinking only that she had to climb down and get away.

A black shape loomed on one side of her. Blindly, she lurched away from it, her feet stumbling against the rocks. One foot came down on air, throwing her off balance. She clawed at the rocks with her good hand, trying to hold on, but she found nothing solid.

The rocky ground below struck hard. The falling snowflakes turned into bright points of light. She lay trying to breathe.

Run. She needed to run. Her limbs refused to obey. She couldn't hold on to consciousness any longer.

From a long way off, she heard a man scream in agony. Talon? She had to help him.

Somehow...

CHAPTER THIRTY-FIVE

YEAR OF WARDING 23, WHITE CITY, SARINE

CALLONEN

CALLONEN WOKE TO SEE the light of dawn shining through his bedroom windows. Five weeks had passed since Talon left for Ara, and three weeks since the weight of the Warding settled on Callonen. Despite the early hour, he jumped from his bed and hastily threw on clothes. At least today, the Warding had provided him with vital information.

Harrow had just crossed the border.

Callonen threw open the door to see Tess standing outside it holding a breakfast tray as if she'd been about to knock. He took the tray from her. "Tess. Harrow's come back into the Warding."

Her eyes widened in shock. "Is he all right?"

He put a hand on her shoulder. "He's hurt, but I'm not sure how badly. I'm sorry."

"We have to help him," Tess exclaimed.

"Yes, of course we do. Will you ride with me?" Callonen asked.

Her mouth tightened into a determined line. "Yes. I'll be ready in a few moments."

Callonen hurried to Mirithel's rooms and knocked. She opened the door in a dressing gown, her golden hair unbound. "Emperor? What's happened?"

"Harrow has come back into the Warding."

Her hand flew to her mouth, her eyes widening. "Then Talon should be with him. They were together. Will you please tell me when Talon is safely inside?"

"I will, of course, Lady Mirithel," Callonen said. "But so far, he has not come back. I am riding immediately to find Harrow. You may join me if you choose."

She stared at him. "It will take us a few moments to be ready. Where is Harrow?"

"He wasn't far from Varda when he crossed the border. We will ride that way."

Callonen made swift preparations, and soon he, Tess, Mirithel and Zarek were riding out of the city with a detachment of guards. The winter day was chilly, with a biting wind blowing from the north. They rode all day and spent the night at an outpost. At first light, they were riding again. Tess looked as though she'd barely slept. She directed her horse close to him. "Emperor Callonen, is Harrow still alone? Where are the others?"

Callonen shook his head. "I don't know." He would have sensed if Allia or Talon had been there. He kept hoping they might cross the border. Maybe they still would.

At the end of another long day of riding, they passed through a line of rocky hills and reached an army camp. It had a few permanent buildings clustered against the base of the hill. Rows of tents surrounded it. All the soldiers stood at attention and saluted as the emperor and his guard appeared.

"We're close," Callonen assured Tess. "He's not far away."

"Your orders, Emperor?" the sergeant in command asked.

"We are here to assist an injured soldier," Callonen said. "If you and a few of your men will follow me?"

"Of course, Emperor."

Darkness fell, and several soldiers brought lanterns. Even in the dark, Callonen knew exactly where he was going. Only a short distance outside the camp, the light fell on a solitary figure limping slowly toward them. His shoulders were hunched, his head hanging down. As the horses drew near, he slowly raised his eyes to squint into the light.

Callonen dismounted and ran to him. "Harrow!"

"Prince Callonen?" Harrow stared in disbelief. "How did I get to the city?" His clothes were torn and bloodstained, and he no longer carried any weapons or gear.

Callonen pulled Harrow's arm around his shoulders to support him. Tess did the same on his other side. They helped him to the emperor's horse. Several soldiers came forward to lift him into the saddle. Callonen mounted behind him and held him steady.

In only a few moments, they were back at the camp. Two soldiers lowered Harrow from the horse. Callonen and Tess followed them as they carried the wounded man into the shelter and warmth of the building.

They set him carefully down on a cot. In the lantern light, beads of sweat stood out on his forehead.

Tess knelt beside the bed and took his hand. "Harrow!"

He turned to look at her, just now realizing she was there. "Tess?" She smiled and held his hand in both of hers.

"What are you doing out here?" he asked. "You're in danger. The demons aren't far away."

"It's all right now," Tess said. "You're home safe. We'll take care of you."

"They can't get into the Warding," Callonen said.

Harrow nodded. "Then I did it," he muttered. "I made it home."

Lady Mirithel entered the room and stood beside Callonen at the end of the cot. Her expression was strained as she stared down at the man who had spent so much time with her husband.

Harrow didn't notice her, but looked up at Callonen. "I didn't want to leave them. Allia knew the demons were hunting her. And she begged me to take her baby somewhere safe. But I couldn't stop her from going back to meet them. I told Talon to take the child and run, but he wouldn't. I had to get the girl to safety." Harrow's eyes closed.

The healers gathered around him. "Give us some room, please," one said, ushering Tess away from the side of the cot. She came to stand with Callonen and Lady Mirithel.

As the healers removed Harrow's torn shirt and jacket, they revealed long gashes crossing his body. They shifted him onto his side, revealing more slashes across his back. The wounds were a sickly dark shade and badly swollen.

Callonen heard a sharp intake of breath next to him. He turned and saw the color drain from Tess's face as she got a closer look at Harrow's injuries. Her hands clenched into fists. Callonen put a comforting arm around her shoulders. The small gesture appeared to break her control, and she began to cry. He hugged her, sensing her grief as it added to his own.

Mirithel appeared to be digesting the words the injured man had spoken.

Awareness of what Harrow had just said dawned on Callonen. Allia had gone back to meet them. And Talon had still been with her, trying to protect her to the end. Allia and Talon were dead. Callonen's mind conjured images of her body, torn by demon claws, her blood draining onto the ground, the light leaving her eyes. And Talon, fighting bravely to the end, even if there was no way to win. "She's never coming back." Callonen felt his heart break as he spoke the words.

"You did this!" Mirithel glared at Callonen. Her voice was cold and heavy with accusation. "You sent him to find her and now Talon's dead because of you. How could you?"

"I'm sorry," Callonen choked out the words. He took a step back, away from her. "I'd rather be dead myself."

Unable to face her, he stumbled out of the room. Pain twisted through his body as he ran. He was the worst person in the world. His actions had destroyed the woman he loved and killed his best friend.

With no clear thought other than to get away, Callonen left the building. It was dark and quiet outside. The indistinct form of the hill rose steeply behind the outpost, and he started climbing.

When Callonen scrambled to the top, he found the far side of the hill cut off in a line of sheer cliffs. He stood on the brink of the precipice. Although he couldn't measure the height exactly in the starlight, he saw the shapes of rocks far below. High enough. Callonen stood on the edge, the icy wind driving through his clothes. The chill was barely noticeable above the pain in his heart. His attempt to rescue Allia hadn't saved her. Instead, she, Talon and Harrow had all suffered an agonizing fate. Because of Callonen's choices. Allia had spent over a year in Ara with Haldreth tormenting her.

She would never have chosen to have a child under those circumstances. But he wasn't surprised that she loved the baby, even if the situation had been forced on her. Now she had sacrificed herself to save her daughter.

Callonen deserved to suffer as much pain as she had. A fall from this height would only hurt for a moment. When his body struck the rocks, it would all be over. The pain, the guilt, the responsibility for everyone would be finished.

He took a step closer to the edge.

For a long moment, Callonen stood alone on the hilltop gazing down. Except that as Emperor of Sarine, he was never alone. He felt all of his people with him, especially the ones nearest. Harrow, still in pain. Tess, hopes for the future dashed. Mirithel, tortured by grief, her small son with her. Callonen sensed Zarek. Despite his youth, he was determined to be brave and take care of his mother. He was Talon's son.

If Callonen jumped, the boy would likely be killed. When Callonen died, the Warding would fall, the demons would rush over the border. This is where they would come first, and there would be no protection.

Zarek would die, and Tess and Mirithel, and all the brave men who served Sarine. And that would only be the beginning...

Callonen stepped back. He couldn't do it. No matter how much pain he felt, he couldn't abandon the others. He stumbled away from the precipice and collapsed to the ground. A cry of frustration and pain escaped his lips.

He should never have allowed Allia into his life. If he had only left her alone, she could have been happy, married someone else, and had the joy of a family.

Instead, Haldreth had stolen her future. All that remained was a lost child, the last remnant of Allia left in the world. Callonen had to find her baby. It was the least he could do for the devastation he had brought on the woman he loved.

And Talon. Time and again, he had saved Callonen. Talon had endured injury, cold, hunger and terrible danger in order to help his friend. He had never once complained. And now his family was left to go on without him.

And Tess. Callonen had seen the way she looked at Harrow and noticed how he watched over her and appeared whenever she needed help. They would have been happy together.

Callonen barely noticed when footsteps surrounded him. He hadn't heard them coming. All he'd been aware of was the biting wind and the voices in his head. "Emperor! Are you all right?"

They were asking if he was hurt. Oh, yes… He was injured. But there was nothing anyone could do.

Supporting his frozen limbs, two of his soldiers helped him back down the hill. They'd taken him inside and wrapped him in blankets and tried to force him to have something warm to drink. After a few sips, he set it aside.

It took a long time for him to stop shivering. Callonen remained where they had put him for a while. When the middle of the night had passed, he rose again and paced the building. He found Tess dozing in the chair at Harrow's bedside. His eyes were closed, but he shifted restlessly in his sleep. Beads of sweat stood out on his forehead.

Callonen brought a blanket and covered Tess, yet he couldn't rest himself. If he kept his feet moving, it was easier to endure the pain of what had happened. It had been his decision to allow Talon and Harrow to go after Allia, hoping against hope they could get her out.

A soldier approached Callonen. "Emperor? Lady Mirithel and her son rode out a short while ago. I sent guards with them." The man held out a piece of parchment. "This was in Harrow's pocket."

It was addressed to Callonen. Taking a deep breath, he took the letter and opened it.

Cal, Harrow and I found a way into Hakvere to rescue Allia and her infant daughter, Cirana. Allia's condition was serious when we found her, but she is already improving. The child appears to be in good health and seems to like Harrow. Harrow's service to Sarine has been exemplary. He is capable and courageous, and deserves your highest honor when he returns. We destroyed the artifact Haldreth used to summon demons. The healing ring was also vital to the spell he cast, and we have the ring with us. When you find your father's sword, you'll be able to destroy these creatures, but at least we have stopped Haldreth from creating more. Allia is desperate to keep her child out of Haldreth's hands, and we're heading for the Warding. If we don't make it back, please tell Mirithel and Zarek how much I love them, that I think of them every moment. I did this to protect them and Sarine. Tell Zarek how proud I am of him. Allia loves you. I can see it in her eyes and hear it in her voice when she speaks of you. She was afraid you'd be angry with her because of what happened. I told her you understood that none of this was her choice. I will do all I can to protect her. Thank you for your friendship. –Talon

It was nearly dawn when Callonen sank into a chair near Tess. He hadn't realized he had dozed until Harrow stirred, waking them both.

Harrow blinked and looked around in confusion. His eyes fell on Tess. "You're here," he murmured. "I thought I dreamed it."

"No. I'm here." She put a hand on his shoulder. He covered her hand with his.

"I missed you," he said. "I've been thinking about you."

Tears flowed down her cheeks. "I missed you too. Just hold on," she pleaded. "You'll feel better soon."

"This is the second time you helped me when I was dying." His eyes drifting closed. Tess gripped his hand in both of hers.

Callonen moved forward and knelt beside the cot. "Harrow? Can you tell me where Talon and Allia are? And where is the baby?" At his words, Harrow turned to look at him, but he no longer recognized Callonen.

"Talon, I should have stayed with Allia and sent you home to your family. But you can tell Allia that the demons won't find her baby or the ring. Cirana still has the ring, and I hid her."

"Where?" Callonen asked. Was the baby out there alone?

"I found someone to take care of her while I led the demons away," Harrow said, and Callonen breathed a sigh of relief.

"Where is she?" Callonen asked. But Harrow's eyes closed, and this time he didn't respond.

Callonen and Tess sat beside him all day as his fever rose ever higher. "Isn't there anything else we can do?" Callonen asked the healers.

"We're doing everything we can, my lord."

Tess never left Harrow's side, and Callonen stayed with them.

Harrow didn't speak again.

They watched through the day and on into the dark hours. Harrow died in the middle of the night. A healer shook his head sadly and pulled the blanket up to cover Harrow's face.

Callonen held Tess as she cried. How could he have allowed this to happen? His own emotions overcame him. He'd intended to comfort Tess, but now he clung to her as if she could comfort him. Eventually, he convinced her to find a place to lie down and rest.

He pulled a blanket over her, hoping she could sleep.

He couldn't.

CHAPTER THIRTY-SIX

Year of Warding 23, Sarine's Countryside

MIRITHEL

MIRITHEL TOOK HER SON and began the journey home. What else could she do? She'd known this would happen when Callonen sent Talon on this fool's errand. She couldn't bear to see Emperor Callonen right now.

As she and her son rode side by side, the icy wind stung her face. Her jaw was firmly set as she kept her features composed. Talon was dead.

A voice interrupted her grief.

"Mother? Will you tell me what's happened?" Zarek asked. "All you told me last night was that Father was gone."

What should she tell him? How could she say the words?

He looked at her with earnest gray eyes, the exact shade of his father's. "Tell me."

She sighed. "Demons attacked Harrow, but he escaped and made it back to the Warding. He said your father went back to meet them."

"Do you know anything else?"

Mirithel shook her head.

"Then we don't know what happened, not for sure. Maybe he's still out there somewhere," Zarek said. "I think he'll come back."

Mirithel shook her head. "Not this time. Your father is dead."

"But he's the strongest man in the world. Even demons couldn't kill him. Father will come back. And I'm going to make sure he's proud of me when he does!"

Zarek lapsed into silence, his small face set stubbornly.

The boy had faith in his father. But this time, Zarek was wrong. He didn't understand that this was final. Talon wouldn't be coming home.

The day after they returned to the city, Zarek came back to their rooms wearing a sword too big for him. Mirithel stared at the weapon in shock.

"I spoke to the new captain and asked him to train me," Zarek announced. "He said he would."

"Take that thing off!" she screamed. "Don't ever let me see it again."

He took her hand and met her eyes. "Mother, I will do this." His face was determined, and his voice calm—much calmer than Mirithel felt. When he looked up at her with serious gray eyes, her anger dissolved and she hugged him. "I couldn't stand to lose you too."

"You won't lose me," he promised instantly. "But I need the training."

"No! You mustn't."

Over the months that followed, Mirithel tried everything she could think of to change his mind, but still she caught him practicing constantly. She wanted time to stop, for him to be a little boy forever. But on the day they received word about Talon, Zarek's childhood had ended.

ALLIA

Allia woke slowly to the sight of bare stone walls. The last several days were a jumble of confused images, pain and the motion of traveling. Now that she was entirely awake, she realized she was in the same room she'd been locked in since Haldreth had brought her to Ara. Her head pounded, and a fit of coughing racked her body.

When she could breathe again, her eyes fell on the empty cradle beside her bed. Cirana was gone. She wrapped her arms around herself and felt tears spilling from her eyes. But Harrow had taken her to safety. Her daughter had escaped.

Talon must be dead. She'd seen the demons claw him. If only she could have made him go with Harrow.

When Allia lifted her head, she saw a guard in a blue uniform standing by the door, watching her. Once he saw she was awake, he left the room. She didn't have much longer to live. Haldreth would be coming to question her.

Slowly, Allia sat up and realized that an iron manacle secured her ankle to a heavy chain that ran to an anchor in the wall.

Moving caused her head to spin. She felt sick and faint, and it was difficult to breathe. Even so, she savored the sensation of air coming and going, knowing that her heart still beat. Life filled her body. She concentrated on the love she felt for Callonen and for Cirana, wishing them happiness.

When Haldreth stormed through the door, she knew her time was up. Her stomach clenched, and her hands gripped the edge of her cot when she saw him. His dark eyes burned with fury. His skin was flushed, and a vein throbbed in his temple. She'd watched him kill people, and he'd never been this angry.

At least she could no longer sense what he was feeling. She would never have to share his darkness again. But she didn't need to sense him to know he would kill her. Allia tensed, trying to prepare for the pain. Hopefully, it would be over quickly.

He crossed the room, seized her arm, and pulled her up. He struck her face and her head snapped back, pain radiating from her cheekbone.

"Where are the ring and gate pin?" he demanded, grabbing her wounded hand. He tightened his grip, and she groaned in pain.

"Gone," she gasped. "They're gone."

"Don't lie to me," he warned. "I'll make you tell me everything." He struck her again. Her vision burst into white light.

She tried to catch her breath. "There's nothing left to tell. It's all gone. I destroyed the gate pin and the ring." She felt liberated, knowing that he couldn't force her to help him anymore. There would be no more demons.

"Tell me where you hid them! Tell me everything or I'll make you beg for me to kill you," he hissed.

Her body shook with terror. He excelled at causing pain. She desperately needed to escape.

He seemed to read her mind. "There's no way out."

His words echoed in her head. No way out.

"I melted them!"

The blow struck her jaw, knocking her backward over the cot, her head slamming into the rough stone wall.

The world receded.

What a relief. Now she heard only a faint echo of Haldreth's angry voice. Some pain remained. Her head ached, and her heart was broken.

Her mind had shattered into pieces. Fleeing from despair and suffering, Allia's consciousness escaped into memories bright with Callonen's presence. Nothing else remained for her.

CHAPTER THIRTY-SEVEN

YEAR OF WARDING 37, WHITE CITY, SARINE

CALLONEN

MISSING ALLIA EVERY DAY had not kept time from passing, and Callonen had carried the Warding for over fourteen years. He knew she wouldn't be back. Though his heart was broken and he hadn't been able to save her, he dedicated his life to protecting the rest of his nation. From the moment he had learned of the existence of Allia's child, he had been determined to help her if he could. He had sent several groups of men out of the Warding in an attempt to find her, but so far, none had succeeded.

One morning, Callonen woke feeling that something was wrong. Exhaustion weighed him down, and waking up felt difficult. His bones ached. When he washed, he stared in shock at his face in the mirror. He had aged noticeably, and he couldn't help but remember how his father's health had failed so quickly. No one had been able to do anything to help Caldoreth. Was Callonen doomed to die the same way?

The healers tried every cure they knew on him, but over the next several days, Callonen only grew worse. He called a meeting of his closest councilors. Before entering the room, he paused outside the door and took a deep breath.

A few of his councilors gasped as they saw him, but he ignored them and took his place at the head of the table. The room fell silent. It would be best to be direct.

"I am not well. And we need to make some plans in case my health does not improve. I fear that if we can't find a cure, the same thing will happen to me that happened to my father, and my life will end within a year."

He looked around the table as everyone began talking at once. A few of his noblemen, advisers and the best of his military were represented, General Gray, Captain Toren, Captain Dane and...

As Callonen's eyes rested on Zarek, he felt his throat tighten. Zarek had been abroad to complete his studies, and Callonen hadn't seen him for years. He'd heard the boy had returned after completing the last of his training. All the reports praised his abilities, saying he had far surpassed the other soldiers. Now here he sat at the council table looking just like Talon.

Taking another deep breath, Callonen said, "If I die, the Warding will fall. Should that happen, the demons will destroy our nation. There won't be anything that can be done at that point. We tried every remedy we knew of to help my father, and nothing worked."

"If we could find the ring," Zarek said, "it could heal you and protect the Warding."

Callonen's memory went back to a much smaller Zarek lying on the ground, near death after a poisoned spider bite. The boy had experienced the power of the ring firsthand. It would have been the perfect solution. If only it were possible.

"True," Callonen replied. "But none of our people have found any trace of it, not in all these years."

A councilor spoke up. "You might consider... marriage, Emperor."

A sudden unreasonable wave of fury rose in Callonen. They wanted him to forget Allia and take some other woman into his arms in the hope they could produce a child? The thought sharpened the bitter ache in his chest. The room had gone completely silent. He took a slow breath. "I realize that having an heir would protect the Warding. And..." He forced his voice to sound calm. "Maybe I should have done that years ago. It's too late now. Even if I married today and fathered a child at once, it might not even be born before I died. Even if it was, I cannot pass the weight of the Warding to an innocent baby."

"Then our only chance is to find the ring."

"When Harrow came back here, he said that he'd given the ring to Allia's baby and hidden her. The child would be fifteen years old by now."

"So, we have to find a girl around that age who has a ring with a green stone," Zarek said.

"But Ara's forces have been looking for her too," Callonen said, "and the demons."

"I'll go. We can do it," Dane said. "Zarek and I will find her and bring her back to heal you. We'll keep searching until we do."

Late that afternoon, Callonen sat behind his desk, working through a stack of correspondence. At a knock, he glanced up to see Zarek in the doorway. "You sent for me, Emperor?"

"Zarek, come in. Please sit."

The young man took a chair opposite him, looking at him expectantly.

"Dane told me you received high praise from all your instructors, that your abilities are extraordinary."

"Thank you, Emperor." Zarek flushed slightly. "I look forward to beginning my duties."

Callonen met his gaze. "Have you spoken to your mother about your plans?"

Zarek's expression tightened. "I did. It was the same as always. She wants to keep me locked up, and she's angry that I won't agree to it. I understand that she only wants me to be safe, but I have to live my life, and I'm committed to serve the empire."

Callonen sighed. "She blames me for your father's death, and the fact that you wish to serve only makes her angrier with me."

Zarek shook his head. "She always knew that the work he did was dangerous. I think because he was so good at it... Maybe she thought... Maybe we all thought he was invincible, that nothing could ever defeat him."

His throat tightened. It was true. Maybe that's why he'd allowed Talon to go to Ara. Callonen should never have agreed to it. "I let him go." He rubbed his forehead. "I'm very sorry, Zarek. He was your father. I should have thought more about what his loss might mean to you."

"He was a good father," Zarek said. "Not everyone has such a blessing in their lives. The best way to honor his memory is by carrying on his work. Dane and I are ready to leave tomorrow."

"I wouldn't let you go at all if the Warding were not in such danger. If it falls, you'll be safer far away. But I have something to protect you on your journey." He opened a drawer and took out a sheathed dagger. He pulled the blade a little way out, and it glowed softly. "This weapon was made by the wizard Zarekathus. There's enchantment in the blade that can defend against dark magic."

Zarek took the dagger. "Thank you, Emperor. And don't worry, we'll find the ring in time."

PART THREE

HOMECOMING

Chapter Thirty-Eight

Year of Warding 42, Sarine-Ara Border

ANA

Ana opened her eyes and saw darkness. She felt the motion of a horse. The weakness following healing paralyzed her. Heavy fabric covered her face, making it difficult to breathe. In the dark, she had no way to orient herself. Before long, she slipped back into unconsciousness.

When she woke again, Ana saw the night sky above her. The last thing she remembered was Gavin and Toren beside her as she'd healed Rosie after her accident. Something must have happened. But Toren wouldn't let anything harm her. He had to be somewhere nearby.

"Toren? Can you help me?"

Ana needed to know if Rosie was all right, but she didn't have the strength to look around, and no one responded to her.

The next time she opened her eyes, Ana saw the light of dawn. She shifted her head slightly to look around, glimpsing a bare rocky hill. Before she had time to see anything further, the light vanished as someone threw a cloak over her head. Still weak from the healing, she struggled unsuccessfully to throw it off.

Someone thrust a cloth soaked with a pungent liquid against her face. It had a strong, sweet smell that stung her nose. Her eyelids became as heavy as lead. Everything faded.

❧

When Ana woke fully at last, she saw nothing but darkness. It was so black that she lay there trying to figure out if she had been struck blind or if her eyes were really open. Unyielding rock pressed against her back. She heard nothing except for a few small rodents scurrying and the drip of water. Slowly, she sat up. With her hands, she explored a little around her.

Ana felt a stone floor, not very smooth, but not rough enough to be a natural cave. She felt weak, nauseated, and desperately thirsty. Her mouth felt dry and gritty. How long had it been since she'd healed Rosie?

Eventually, Ana saw dim gray light. Morning? It illuminated a rough stone room with a heavy door bound with iron. Near the door sat a small wooden bucket with a little liquid at the bottom. Leaning close to smell it, she found it was water and drank greedily. It refreshed her somewhat, and she looked around.

She explored every corner of the room. Trying the door, she found it locked. The light came through a grate in the high ceiling. A steady drip of water fell in one corner, so she placed the bucket to catch it. Ana found a slender crack at the bottom of one wall, far too small to be a means of escape. The door was sturdy, and the stone surrounding it, impenetrable.

There was no way out.

A great weariness and despair came over her as she finished her search. She sank to the floor and rested her back against the wall, pulling her knees up to her chest.

Why would anyone lock her in here? Did someone hate her? Did she have enemies she didn't know about? She could think of no one who would want to imprison her. Unless maybe they wanted to make Callonen suffer. Or maybe it was because he had named her his heir.

Or perhaps because of the ring. Did someone need its power? But if that was the case, why didn't they just come to her? Her questions spun around in her mind as she sat alone in the dark. Eventually, she drifted into sleep.

The sound of the heavy door shutting woke her. She struggled to her feet and stumbled to the door. "Wait!" she cried. "Who are you? Where am I?"

There was no reply. Someone had provided a fresh bucket of water and left a dish of food. She called and pounded on the door until her hands hurt, but no one answered. Ana slumped to the floor in despair.

She drank the water. Her stomach still churned, but she did not know how long it had been since she'd eaten, so she tried a bite of the food. It wasn't good, but she got a few more bites down before giving up.

Tedious hours passed. When the light faded, she huddled against one wall, staring out into the dark.

Days and nights passed, and she quickly lost count of them. They were all exactly the same. Once a day, the door opened a crack, and her captor gave her water and food. A few times, she glimpsed the person, but he was hooded and dressed in featureless black.

She sensed he felt sorry for her. At first, when he came, she would ask for help or beg for him to let her out. When he never answered her, eventually she gave up. He might feel sorry, but she could sense that his fear of consequences was so great that he would never help her.

As time went on, she lost hope of ever seeing the sun again. Unless someone helped her, there was no way she could escape. She'd been over every inch of the room a hundred times. There was nothing new to find.

How had she gotten here? Somehow, she was outside the Warding. Something terrible had happened while she was unconscious. But what?

The last thing she remembered was finding Rosie. She'd never found out if her injured friend was safe. And where were Gavin and Toren? Had they tried to protect her?

Of course, Callonen would find her if he could. She had only intended to be gone for a week, and she missed him terribly. Being away made her realize how completely the White City had become her home and Callonen her family. He'd been there every day to talk to. Even when he was busy, he made time for her. She felt special when he asked important people to wait while he focused on her. Was he even now trying to rescue her? That thought encouraged her, but when nothing happened as the days slipped by, her small hope faded.

There had been hard times before. When she had fled for her life from the Shekkar, it had been Zarek who had encouraged her, protected her, calmed her fears, and promised her they would make it. And when things were at their worst, he would try to lie about it. She smiled at the memory. She could always tell when he was lying. But despite the danger, they had survived. Zarek had saved her.

If only he were here to help her now. He had been so steady, so strong. She would have given anything to have him back. Nearly four years had passed since she'd last seen him, and she had heard nothing from him since then. Maybe their enemies had caught him. Maybe he was dead. And even if he was still alive, there was no way he would find her here.

Alone in the dark, Ana cried.

❧

As the days and weeks passed, Ana heard whispers. The longer she listened, the more she thought she heard a voice. At times, she could almost understand the words, but at other times, it sounded like gibberish. Maybe her mind was going, and she would rot here in the dark, insane and terribly alone.

Her mind drifted. Thoughts of Zarek helped keep her from utter despair. He was always so resourceful when things went wrong. She wished he was here now. Was he even still alive? Was he safe?

She remembered the way his wavy hair looked untidy when he ran his hands through it, and the spark of mischief in his gray eyes when he smiled. Those same eyes had hardened as he promised to protect her with his life. He had, too.

It was so easy to feel safe around him, despite any danger, and he had comforted her when she was frightened. He had been her best friend.

One day, as she sat against the wall, a memory came of a song Zarek had sung to her when she was afraid, an old familiar tune. Fire and water, hammer and tongs... It was about a blacksmith, that much he had explained to her. She sang softly to herself, but then she stopped, unable to remember all the words. Her small voice faded away into the darkness.

Then she heard the song again, like an echo—only it wasn't her voice. She felt along the wall until she found the crack. The sound came from there.

As she crawled closer to the opening, despair washed over her in a wave. No hope remained. Broken remnants of memories were all that was left. Black loneliness drowned her.

Ana gasped, scrambling away from the wall. She sat in the middle of the room, breathing hard. Once away from the crack, the despair disappeared. Her own worries and fears burdened her, but the broken, hopeless feeling was gone. Ana turned to stare at the opening. Slowly, she walked closer. When she reached the wall, she felt the despair again and heard a hoarse voice faintly following the old melody.

She sensed this. The feelings belonged to a person. She knelt on the floor, searching until she found the crack.

"Hello?" she called.

The singing stopped. "I'm dreaming again," a faint voice moaned. "I thought I heard an old song."

"You're not dreaming. I'm here," Ana said. "Who's there?"

"Hello?"

The voice belonged to a real person. For a moment, she felt nothing but relief that she had not lost her mind. It was a man's voice, deep but hoarse from disuse.

"Hello?" He repeated, more urgently now. His voice grew fainter and louder, and she heard scuffling as he moved slowly back and forth, searching for her. It stopped on the other side of the crack. "There's someone there." He sounded incredulous. "Are you real?"

"I am real," Ana responded.

"I've been so long in the dark and never spoken to another person. What year is it?"

"Year of Warding forty-two."

"Forty-two…" the voice muttered for a moment, counting. "It's been twenty years, I think. I don't really remember."

"Who are you?"

"I don't know," he sighed. "I was someone once. The song you sang reminded me of something… I can't… I can't recall. Perhaps if I could escape from here and see the sky, I would remember who I am."

"I hope there's a way out for both of us."

His voice was grim. "It's too late. There's no way out except death."

Her chest tightened. She'd been hoping to find a way. But if he'd been here so long… "I'm not ready to die," she said. "But I don't know any way to escape."

"All these years I have never found one." He sighed heavily. "There's no hope. Not anymore. If I could see my wife and son again, I'd be happy to die. I can't remember their faces. But I have to remember. I should remember…"

"I wish there was a way you could see them again."

He laughed bitterly. "I can see the way out. He left it within reach just to torment me. There is a shaft in the ceiling with a passageway that leads out into the canyon. I could climb it, if only…"

"If only what?" Ana asked.

"They cut off my legs. He knew I could see the way out, but never climb it."

"Who?"

"The king. He told me I have to call him the king now, even though that wasn't always his name. Nothing else. Just the king, the king." He chanted it, and she felt the potency of his despair.

She drew in a sharp breath, her stomach tightening in horror. What had happened to this man?

ↄ

Ana slept next to the crack in the wall and dreamed of looking up to see the vast, clear sky above her with the stars glittering like diamonds. She woke with a start, shivering from the cold, and the white stars vanished, leaving only blackness. "I'm afraid," she said. "It's so dark."

He must have been just on the other side of the wall, because he answered, "It will be all right."

His voice sounded soothing, as if he wanted to comfort her, and she sensed he truly wished to make her feel better. Why should he care if he couldn't even remember his own life? He was a compassionate person.

Suddenly, it struck her. He had been a good person, and someone had locked him in here, determined to crush his spirit. His torment here in the dark had been so great that he had lost his mind. Yet he still tried to comfort her.

The person who had done this must be truly merciless. If this man had been here all these years and no one had helped him, what hope did she have of escaping?

"Thank you for comforting me," she said to the crack in the wall.

He was glad to hear her voice and giving assistance, even in such a small way, brought him a scrap of satisfaction.

"I'm not a child anymore," she said. "I shouldn't be afraid of the dark. It's just that... terrible things have come after me in the dark."

"I know," he replied, drawing in a ragged breath.

"Do you remember?" she asked. "Did the Shekkar come after you too?"

"I... I can't. I don't remember. They're all around..." His voice grew frantic. She could hear a sound like fingernails scraping against the rock.

"Stop, please!" she pleaded. "I'm sorry I asked you. They aren't here now. We're alone. It's all right."

She heard him breathing hard and sensed his panic. "Please," she called through the crack. "It's all right."

"All right?" he whispered hoarsely.

She sang him the song about the blacksmith, and it calmed him.

After a while, he sighed. "Better now," he murmured.

"I can hear you more clearly." She pushed at the stone on the edge of the hole. It crumbled a little.

"Yes," he replied. "I've pulled away as much of the loose stone as I can, and the opening is larger. I can reach into the crack."

"Can you reach my hand?" she asked. "I can help you."

"It's too late for me," he said with a sad sigh. "But it would be good to feel someone's touch. I've been alone for so long."

"I can help you," she repeated. "Will they notice if you climb out and run away?"

"Run away?" He laughed madly. "The king knows a man with no legs can't run away. But if I could, they wouldn't notice. They put a dish of food and a bucket of water through a hole in the door. That's all. They never check. When I die, they won't know it. I'll lie here and rot in the dark. Alone."

"No you won't. I'll do what I can," Ana said. "Try to reach my hand." The wall was very thick, and the opening small. But she worked her hand into the crack as far as she could. The man put his hand through from the other side. They were close, but still she couldn't reach. Ana pushed harder until the rough rock cut into her skin but she managed to touch his fingertip.

Her mind exploded. Nothing remained but darkness and fear. Her memories were gone. Hope was gone. She was isolated from all human contact. Blank darkness surrounded her, and a lingering terror that she could not name. Ana felt all the bitter pain of twenty years alone in the dark, crawling like a snake on the filthy floor. She couldn't stand. Her legs were gone, but she could still feel the pain. There was someone she had sworn to protect, and she'd failed. Crushing despair.

Ana knew no more.

When Ana opened her eyes, it was utterly silent. She no longer sensed anyone on the other side of the wall. Had the man escaped? She hoped so. Her arm remained painfully wedged into the hole. She barely had the strength to pull it free before she passed out again.

Ana opened her eyes and squinted against the light of a torch, which seemed dazzlingly bright after the long darkness. The light came nearer, and a hand touched her. Someone whispered her name.

"Cirana."

She realized she knew the voice. Gavin. He had found her and come to take her home. It had been so long since she'd seen another person that she wanted to reach out to him, to ask him for help, but she didn't have the strength. A barely audible whisper escaped her lips. "Please, help."

He heard her. "I'm here," he murmured, touching her face. "It's all right now. Please forgive me. I found you as quickly as I could." Gratitude washed over her. She wasn't alone anymore. He would take her out of the darkness. She felt his arms lifting her and the motion of being carried, then nothing more.

CHAPTER THIRTY-NINE

YEAR OF WARDING 42, HAKVERE, ARA

ANA

ANA DID NOT KNOW where she was when she woke again. She lay in a large, soft, canopied bed. It felt delicious to her after the dirty stone floor of the cell. Looking down, she noticed she was clean again and wore a white nightdress made of a smooth, rich cloth.

An ornately furnished room surrounded her, with soft rugs and elaborate tapestries. A fireplace stood opposite a tall window covered with thick velvet drapes. Nothing looked familiar to her, and the luxury of her surroundings was a shock after the cell she had been trapped in for so long.

A servant came in with a tray of food and set it on Ana's lap. "Where am I?" Ana asked, but the woman behaved as if she had not heard. She kept her eyes on her hands, not looking up, then left without a word.

The food smelled delicious. The tray contained freshly baked bread, roast beef and apples. She had dreamed of a meal like this while she had been so hungry and weary of the dismal prison fare. But she remained so weak that it took great effort to move her hand from the tray to her mouth. After eating a few bites, she slid the tray aside and tried to stand, but she didn't have the strength. Desperate to know where she was, she slid out of bed and crawled across the floor to the window. Pulling herself up to the sill and pushing aside the heavy drapes, she looked out to see flickering torchlight on stone walls, and far above, clear white stars. For a moment, she thought she must be dreaming again.

Ana didn't know how long it had been since she'd seen the sky. She gazed at the beautiful stars until exhaustion overwhelmed her, and she crawled back into bed.

She lay still, staring at the surrounding room. None of this made any sense. Had she lost her mind, after all? Finding herself in this luxurious room was even stranger than hearing voices in the dark. Maybe she would wake up in the White City and discover it had all been a dream. Or maybe she'd wake up back in the dungeon, alone in the dark.

She closed her eyes, but when she opened them again, the room was still there. Examining her arm, she found scrapes from the edges of the crack in the rocks. It hadn't been a dream.

What had happened to the man in the other cell? She hoped he had escaped, that he was all right and could go home now.

If Ana had more energy, she would have tried the door. For now, she had no choice but to rest. She didn't want to sleep in this strange place without even knowing if she was safe. But weariness forced her eyelids closed.

When she awoke, Ana saw actual golden sunlight coming in the window. It was the most beautiful thing she had ever seen. She wanted to run to the window and look out, but she still felt so exhausted she couldn't even get out of bed. Her eyes closed, and she dozed again.

Ana felt a hand gently brush her cheek. "Cirana?"

She woke up to Gavin looking down at her with warm brown eyes. "How are you feeling?"

"So tired," she whispered. "But I'm grateful to be out of the dark."

"I'm sorry it took so long to rescue you," he apologized, taking her hand.

"What happened? Where was I?"

"A group of outlaws who hide in caves in the hills captured you. They had you locked in their stronghold, and it took some time to figure out how to get you out. I think they intended to hold you for ransom. I'm sure Emperor Callonen would pay a mountain of gold to get you back."

"A mountain of gold?" That idea shocked her. But if it were true, then her captivity had been an attempt to attack Callonen after all.

"He'd trade whatever he had," Gavin said. "I'm sorry I couldn't get there sooner. When I finally found a way to get you out, I came here for help. The king of this land is a very kind man. He offered us his hospitality until you are well again."

"How did I get outside the Warding?" she asked.

Gavin shook his head, his brows furrowed in concern. "Your bodyguard... I saw him take money from a man who came to the city. Maybe they paid him to betray you. After you healed Rosie, he attacked us. He tried to kill me, but I escaped. I was wounded in the fight and couldn't catch up with him. He took you out of the Warding. I followed as soon as I could."

"My guard? Toren?" She knew him well. They had spent a lot of time together, and she'd sensed nothing from him but loyalty. She tried to imagine him betraying them, but she couldn't. "Toren can't have done it," she whispered in disbelief.

"I know it's hard to believe."

It was. Gavin seemed and sounded so sincere. Ana couldn't sense any deceit from him. But she couldn't believe Toren betrayed her. Was Gavin lying? "There must be some other explanation."

"Perhaps," Gavin said, rubbing his forehead.

"When can we go home?" Ana asked. "I want to go home. Please, Gavin? Please help me get home. Don't you miss the White City?"

Abruptly, she realized why he looked so different. In Sarine, he'd nearly always worn the white-and-gold uniform that marked him as a member of Callonen's guard. Now, he wore a dark red tunic in a rich fabric.

"Of course I do," he said, holding her hand reassuringly. "But we must get you well first."

"Why aren't you wearing your uniform?"

He smiled slightly. "It's been many weeks, dearest, and I had to travel in disguise. Outside Sarine, it's not very safe to wear that uniform."

"But we'll be able to go home soon?"

"Of course. We're only waiting until you're strong enough to travel. Don't worry, you're safe here in the meantime." He bent to kiss her forehead, then left her alone.

Ana didn't see Gavin again until the next morning. His kiss woke her. Though they had kissed many times before, she felt something was different. He still enjoyed it, but there was more he wanted from her now.

She broke away and looked up at him.

"What's the matter?" he asked.

"Nothing, I was just thinking..." Anything to distract him. "I was thinking how grateful the emperor will be to you for helping me."

"Yes," he said. "But you don't have to worry about traveling until you feel better. We are safe, and it's nice here. I brought you something." He took out an ornately carved wooden box and opened it.

Ana sat up to look inside and gasped at the sight of a gold necklace, heavy with emeralds. She knew what they looked like because Emperor Callonen had a large one on his crown, which he only wore for formal affairs. He hated wearing it and always removed it at the earliest possible moment. But she remembered the dark-green stone. The necklace Gavin had brought was set with several similar gems, and it must have been worth a huge sum.

"Where did you get this?" she asked breathlessly. It was beautiful, but she didn't want to keep something so valuable. She'd grown up in a tiny village where no one wore jewelry and had kept her ring hidden throughout her childhood.

"It is a gift from the king. And from me," he said, smiling warmly at her. "Do you like it?"

"It's overwhelming," she said honestly. He fastened the jewelry around her neck, and it felt heavy and cold against her skin. "Why would you give me this?" she asked.

"Because I love you," Gavin said. "And it's the most beautiful thing I could find to give you."

"Thank you." There was nothing else she could say. That day when she'd healed Rosie, she'd been about to tell him she didn't want to see him anymore. She really wanted to tell him now, but how could she push away the only familiar person in this strange place?

"Are you strong enough to get up? Our host is occupied today, but would you like to see the castle?" he asked.

She wanted to know where she was. "Yes, please. I think I can walk for a while."

"Will you join me for breakfast before we go?" he asked smoothly. "I'll wait in the hall to give you time to dress."

"Thank you," Ana said.

"I'll see you soon," he smiled at her and went out the door.

As soon as he left, a woman came in with a dark-green gown draped over one arm. The dress was rich velvet and finer even than anything Ana had worn in the emperor's palace. The woman helped her put it on and arranged her hair elaborately.

"Thank you," Ana said kindly when she was done. The woman bowed and left without a word.

Gavin was at her door so soon after the woman left that Ana thought he must have been waiting. He offered his arm, and she took it. They walked through rooms, corridors and staircases, and finally into an elegant dining room. Gavin helped her into a chair and sat opposite her. Ana felt nervous, overwhelmed by the unfamiliar surroundings.

Servants brought them an amazing variety of food, all expertly prepared. Ana watched Gavin as they ate, and his manners were perfect. He appeared very comfortable issuing orders to the people waiting on them. In the back of her mind, she wondered if that was usual for a young man who was the newest member of the Emperor's Guard. More than just his clothing seemed different here.

When they had finished, he offered his arm again and asked, "Would you like me to show you around?"

"Yes, thank you," she said.

They strolled until Ana was lost. After a while, they came to a set of stairs. Exhaustion forced her to climb them slowly. They reached the top, coming out onto a high wall. The sun shone between broken clouds, and a chill wind blew. She shivered, but at last she could see where she was.

All around her, thick stone walls and towers seemed to go on for miles in every direction. This place was larger than she had imagined. On one side, a bridge spanned a deep canyon like a crack in the earth. She couldn't see the bottom from where they stood. On all the walls and towers, she saw guards dressed in blue uniforms and black armor. There was something familiar about them.

"Your friend has a lot of guards," Ana observed.

"Your safety is very important. The guards are there to protect you."

"Of course," she said. She felt trapped by the walls and battlements. They seemed so strong, so impenetrable, and she did not recognize any of the surrounding land. The fortress seemed to be within a wide valley fenced in by rolling hills. There was no way to tell in which direction the White City lay, even if she could escape.

Escape.

But how? She could barely walk. Even the small exertion of climbing up the stairs had been difficult. Her legs trembled, and she clung to the wall for support.

"You're tired." Gavin offered his arm. "Let's go back now. You should rest."

She took the proffered arm, not wanting to be so close to him, but needing his help. Ana would have much preferred to walk on her own.

There was something different about Gavin. He acted... possessive, and she didn't like it. She couldn't sense anything wrong from him, but her intuition warned her not to trust him. Everything that had happened to her was confusing, and his explanations didn't make sense. She was sure there was more going on than she knew. But Gavin had found her and rescued her from the dungeon. She was very grateful for that, even if none of the rest of it made sense. And he seemed so at home here.

Ana knew it was a bad idea to ask too many questions. For the time being, it would be better to go along, at least until she knew more about her situation.

❦

The next morning, just as Ana had been dressed in another elaborate gown, Gavin met her at the door to her room. "Would you like to meet our host?"

"Yes, of course." Ana's voice sounded much more confident than she felt, but she hoped it would be helpful to learn more about the master of this place. She might discover something that could aid in her escape. Hiding these thoughts behind a smile, she took Gavin's arm.

He led her to an enormous hall in the center of the castle. Slender high windows provided dim light to the room. Rich tapestries and heavy draperies covered much of the stone walls, and two thrones stood on a dais at one end. A man sat in one of them.

Gavin didn't hesitate, and Ana walked forward with him. She couldn't really see the man on the throne until he glanced up and light fell across a face so very familiar to her. Her heart leapt and relief flooded through her. Emperor Callonen.

She would have run to him, but suddenly she knew something was wrong and stood there frozen. She could feel that he was someone else.

The man smiled in greeting and rose. He wore a black tunic made of rich fabric and wore a cape trimmed with dark fur, and he looked exactly like Callonen.

"Cirana, can it really be you? I'm so glad to see you, my dear." He extended his hand and, numbly, she took it, staring up at him.

His face was hard, despite the smile he wore. With a horrible sinking feeling in her middle, Ana realized he wasn't Callonen, though his features were identical.

"You've grown up! It's been so long since I've seen you." He bent to kiss her cheek.

"I..." She faltered. Her throat felt tight, and her lungs constricted. She had been so relieved when she thought he was Callonen, but it wasn't... it couldn't be him.

Gavin appeared at her elbow, steadying her. "Please sit down," their host said.

Ana looked for a place to sit. There were no other chairs, only the two thrones.

"Sit here," he commanded, pointing to the seat beside him.

"But... I..." she stammered.

"Sit down." His tone implied he was used to being obeyed.

Her knees felt alarmingly weak, and she said no more as Gavin helped her to her seat.

He smiled encouragingly at her and held out his hand toward the man. "May I present the king of this land? Everything you see is his to command."

Ana bowed her head to the king and wondered if he usually allowed people to sit in his presence in his own throne room. King. King of what land? Where were they?

She remembered years before, when Emperor Callonen had told her about his brother, who wanted to destroy him and the White City. Callonen's brother... Haldreth... The king of Ara was Callonen's brother. Of course, it had to be. Had anyone ever told her they wore the same face? This had to be Ara. She remembered tales about a dark fortress here. Hakvere. That must be where she was. Of course. That was why the guards seemed familiar. They wore the same uniform as the men who had killed Dane and attacked her years ago. The soldiers would have taken her if Zarek hadn't stopped them.

"How are you feeling?" the king asked her.

"I am growing stronger every day," Ana replied, trying to keep her face a calm mask.

"I'm so glad you are improving. It was fortunate that young Gavin brought you here. I have already sent men out to hunt the bandits who held you captive. If I had only known where you were, I would have sent every man I had to your aid. I have been so worried all this time and have been searching for you for years. I can't thank Gavin enough for finding you and bringing you home." He sounded deeply concerned.

"Searching for me?" she asked.

"Yes, of course. After all, I am your father."

Ana felt as if the ceiling were coming down on her, crushing her. She couldn't breathe. The room spun in circles and voices faded into a distant buzzing sound. Then everything went dark.

CHAPTER FORTY

YEAR OF WARDING 42, HAKVERE, ARA

ANA

THE SOFTNESS AND WARMTH of her bed surrounded Ana. Opening her eyes, she saw that someone had brought her back to her room and wrapped the blanket around her. "I must have fainted," she murmured. Abruptly, the reason for her shock came back to her. The king of Ara. He was the master of the demons, the one who had sent them after her. He had caused the desperate journey years ago that had nearly killed Zarek and killed Dane.

Ana recalled the cold and the toil, the pain of it. But worst of all, she remembered Zarek lying on the ground, covered with blood. Haldreth had been behind all that. He couldn't be her father. It just was not possible.

She lay back on the pillow, trying to control her emotions. In her mind, she reviewed everything Callonen had told her. His brother Haldreth had left the White City and gone to Ara. He had taken her mother away with him all those years ago. Maybe he had brought her here?

Ana burst into tears. Was Haldreth being dishonest? She could sense his deceit, yet she didn't think he was lying about this.

Could he really be her father? And if it were true, what had he done to her mother? She wept until the pain in her heart dulled as she drifted into an uneasy sleep.

A knock at the door woke her. She hastily rubbed her tear-stained face with her sleeve. The door opened, and it was him.

"Are you feeling better, my dear?" Haldreth asked, pulling up a chair and sitting beside her bed.

She looked at him. Though the same color as his brother's, his eyes were cold and hard. She had always loved Callonen's warm brown eyes, and that hers were the same. She had never dared tell anyone, but in her heart, she had wished Callonen was her father and that was why they shared the same eye color.

Ana struggled to find words. "I'm all right," she said. "I'm sorry about before. I..."

"You didn't know who your parents were?" he asked.

"No."

"Then perhaps it was a shock," he said soothingly.

"Yes," she agreed. "I'm sorry."

He smiled. "I'm just happy to have you here. I have missed you all these years." He bent and kissed her forehead gently. She wanted to pull away. Being so near him was uncomfortable, but she forced herself to remain still.

"Will you tell me what happened?" she asked.

He straightened up and met her eyes. "You were born here, in this castle. This is your home. I intended you should grow up here, at my side—a princess."

She felt that he spoke honestly about this.

"The entire kingdom loved you. But, one terrible day, an assassin slipped through our defenses. He murdered your mother and stole you away. I caught him, of course, and gave him the fate he had justly earned. But it was too late—he had hidden you or given you to another, and I couldn't find you. Please forgive me?"

Forgive him? The story seemed believable enough. But did she believe it? She knew there were lies mixed in. And he asked for her forgiveness. How could she offer him that? But it would be safer to go along. He must not find out how desperately she wanted to escape from this place.

Finally, she spoke. "It's all right, Father." The word felt strange on her lips. She'd never called anyone that in her life, but it seemed to please him.

"Rest now," he murmured. "I will see you again soon." He rose and went out the door, leaving her alone. She lay turning everything over in her mind until she fell asleep.

In her dreams, Ana saw his face, and sometimes as she drew near, he would smile, his brown eyes gentle. She hugged him and called him Callonen. And sometimes, his eyes were hard. He looked down and laughed at her cruelly, and she fled from him in terror.

The king sat in the dining room the next morning, Gavin beside him. Ana shared breakfast with them. The marvelous food tasted like ashes in her mouth, and she felt as if she choked on every bite. But she knew she mustn't show it. She kept her expression calm to hide the panic that threatened to erupt at any moment. She sensed malice and deceit from the king. From Gavin, she felt only a mild warmth.

After breakfast, a servant brought a small chest of dark wood and knelt, offering it to Haldreth. As he took the box and set it on the table, the servant scurried away.

"Cirana," Haldreth said, "this is something special. Come and see."

She got to her feet and stood near him, looking down at the polished wood of the box.

"The memory of your mother is painful for me. But I wanted you to have this." He opened the lid, and there, nestled in a bed of velvet, lay a crown of diamonds.

"This was hers?" Ana asked.

"Yes, and now it's yours." He took the crown and gave it to her.

His words sounded sincere, but Ana could tell he was lying about her mother.

It felt heavy in her hands, the hard edges of the gems sharp against her fingers. She stared at it in disbelief.

"I will make sure you have an occasion to wear it soon," he promised, taking it back from her and returning it to its box. "Would you like to see more of our kingdom?" Her father stood, offering his arm. She could tell that he kept his feelings tightly controlled.

They walked through halls filled with treasures and rooms full of paintings and sculptures. He showed her stables with fine horses. "Do you like to ride?" he asked.

"Yes," she answered eagerly, "it was one of my favorite things to do." Back at the White City. But she dared not mention the city out loud. "Do you think we might go riding?" she asked. Would he permit her to go outside the walls?

"Later, perhaps, when you are stronger and the weather is not so cold," he assured her. "You've been ill, and you must be careful."

Haldreth would not let her out. She had feared he wouldn't. If he gave her a horse and let her pass through the gates, she would ride away just as far and as fast as she could.

"You're right," she said. "It would be too tiring now."

Haldreth came to see Ana often, bringing her beautiful presents and treating her with meticulous kindness. But Ana wore the ring, and she could sense that his caring was superficial. When the time came, he would reveal his true motives. He wanted something from her.

Gavin came to visit her every day as well. Often, the three of them spent time together, and as Ana watched them, she realized that Haldreth and Gavin knew each other well. This wasn't a new friendship begun when he had brought her here, asking for help. He must have been working for Haldreth the whole time. Why hadn't she sensed it?

All these years, Ana had thought she could sense anyone's feelings. She'd never encountered someone who could hide their true emotions from her. But somehow, Gavin could.

Of course, she hadn't seen what happened after she had healed Rosie. But it couldn't have been the faithful Toren who had betrayed her. She felt a fool. How had she ever trusted Gavin? How had Callonen? He said he hadn't sensed the man was hiding anything. So, she wasn't the only one Gavin had fooled.

But now she was in the middle of a well-guarded fortress, and couldn't get away. It would be unwise to defy the king openly, and she said nothing to Gavin of her realizations. She remained pleasant and courteous to them both, and in this way, she hoped to buy herself time to come up with a plan.

Days and weeks passed, and the weather turned colder. Sometimes snow covered the valley. The silence of winter lay heavy over the castle. Time wore on, yet she still didn't have a plan.

Whenever Gavin and Ana went anywhere in the castle, she carefully observed her surroundings. The halls and corridors grew familiar, and she came to know her way around at least. But the king's guards were everywhere.

Gavin often took her walking, and one day they came out onto a balcony that overlooked the outer wall.

"What a beautiful view," Ana exclaimed. She couldn't see any landmark in the surrounding valley that would tell her which direction the White City lay. It must be west, though. Zarek had told her that Ara lay east of Sarine. The deep canyon blocked her path in that direction. She would need a way over or around it, other than the well-guarded bridge.

"No scenery could compare with your beauty," Gavin said with a charming smile. He bent and kissed her.

Ana found him repulsive now and pulled away after a moment. "I'm sorry," she murmured. "I'm not feeling very well today."

"Shall we go back?"

"Yes, please," she said.

He was kind and solicitous as he helped her back to her room. But she knew better now. It was all an act.

Finally alone, she sighed in relief. This situation grew worse all the time, and Gavin's attention more insistent. How long could she pretend to cooperate? She had to find a way out.

Bare, rocky hills lay to the north and south of Hakvere. A little village huddled into its shadow to the east, and to the west, the fortress faced the deep chasm, the bridge spanning the precipice apparently providing the main entrance. But Ana would be caught if she tried to cross the bridge. The balcony where she had strolled with Gavin was only an arm's length from the outer wall. If she could find a way to climb down it, she might be able to slip away.

If she had a rope, perhaps she could lower herself to the ground. It was a long way, and she considered whether she had the strength to make the descent.

"I don't have to get back in," she said. "I only want to get away." Rope. She fingered the fabric of her skirt.

Before she slept that night, she braided yards of rope made from a stack of blankets she found in her wardrobe into a thickness that she hoped would bear her weight. She hid it and slept, content to have at least the beginnings of a plan.

The rope grew longer as she worked on it every moment she was alone in her room. She learned to listen carefully for the sound of footsteps approaching her door and to hide her work quickly and quietly when she heard someone coming.

How long did the rope need to be? Zarek had laughed at her once for not being able to estimate distances by sight. This was certainly not the time to make a mistake.

One day, when Ana's rope had grown quite long, Gavin came to her door. "Would you like to take a walk?"

"I would. Let's go to that balcony again. The one with the beautiful view," she said.

They walked there, and Ana smiled and looked out at the lands around.

"It is nice here," Gavin said, standing beside her at the wall.

"You can see so far up here. How high are we?" Ana asked, widening her eyes.

Gavin smiled. "About twenty of you, end to end."

She peeked over the wall and gasped, putting her hand over her heart. "It makes me dizzy."

"Maybe I can help," he said, putting his arm around her. "Better?"

"Yes, thank you," Ana replied.

❦

The next morning, a servant woke her, saying, "Your father has asked you to join him for breakfast."

As Ana came to the door of the dining room, she saw the king. His jaw was clenched, and the scowl on his face frightened her. She could feel his anger. But when he glanced up and saw her, he put on a pleasant expression and she sensed his hostility dissipating.

"Cirana, come in. Sit down." He held a chair for her. She sat.

"I wanted to tell you I'm hosting a special banquet for you in ten days."

"For me?"

"Of course. I promised you a chance to wear your crown, and I want you to meet everyone. We've received so much help and support as we have rebuilt this nation. I'd like to introduce you to the people who help me lead Ara. They are eager to meet you."

"I would be honored. Thank you." A quiver of unease settled in her belly.

Before she made any attempt to escape, Ana needed all the information she could gather. That night, when the halls became silent as the household went to bed, she slipped out of her room. The passages were empty. She had learned where the guards were stationed, and she avoided them.

Voices echoed through the hall ahead of her, and she slipped into a dark room, out of sight. Her father was talking to Gavin.

"I'm ready," Haldreth said.

"And you really think Callonen will cooperate?"

Haldreth's voice was icy. "He will. Or I will kill Allia right in front of him, and then I'll take it anyway."

Ana's chest constricted. Her mother was alive. She was here.

Haldreth asked, "How is she?"

"The same. She just sits in her room, doesn't speak, doesn't do anything."

"That might be the best part." Cruel humor tinged the king's voice. "I'll let Callonen exchange his empire for the woman he loves. He'll be desperate for her to run to him with open arms, and she won't even recognize him. Let him enjoy seeing that I destroyed her mind."

Ana stood, her heart pounding and her limbs frozen in horror. What had Haldreth done to her mother? What had Allia suffered, friendless in this place for all these years?

"Do you still have the shroudstone?" Haldreth asked.

"I've kept it close. We don't need Cirana sensing anything from me that she shouldn't. We're almost ready to complete our plans. She still thinks I care about her. I'm going to ask her to marry me."

"Very well," Haldreth replied. "Finish overseeing the preparations. I'm going to have a word with Allia."

"Yes, my king." Gavin's footsteps retreated.

Ana heard her father pass her hiding place. It was foolish and dangerous, but she couldn't stop herself from following him. She'd already suspected they'd found a way to deceive her abilities. If not, she'd have known Gavin's true nature a long time ago. Now she knew for sure.

Her soft steps were soundless as she slipped through the dark. The sound of his footfalls stopped. Peeking around a corner, she saw him lift a bar and heard a heavy door creak open. Inside the room, she heard his voice, gloating. "Gavin has Ana totally fooled. She can't sense what we're doing any better than you could. I find that very amusing, don't you?" Silence answered his question.

A few moments later, he left the room, replacing the bar on the door, and passing the dark hallway where she hid. When everything was quiet, she crept to the door.

Ana lifted the heavy plank and set it silently on the floor. She slipped into the small room, bare except for a low cot in one corner and a single chair. The barred window let in a chill breeze with a sliver of moonlight. At first glance, the room seemed empty. But as her eyes adjusted, Ana noticed a person huddled against the wall.

She crept nearer. Wide eyes stared at her from a pale, haggard face. A heavy chain secured the woman's ankle to the wall.

"Hello?" Ana whispered. There was no response. Those eyes stared back at her blankly, with no sign that she'd even heard. Ana saw the woman's hand where her arms wrapped around her knees. Her left ring finger was missing.

Ana reached out, taking the crippled hand in her own, willing the injury to heal. The green stone glowed and agony ripped through her. This pain wasn't new. The weight of it felt as ancient as a mountain.

Moving suddenly, the woman reached out her hand to grip Ana's tightly, covering the ring, holding on.

Now another person bore the weight of the pain with her. They suffered the pain together, the ring binding them to each other. Their hearts were broken, their minds shattered. Heavy chains bound them. They had lost everything and everyone they held dear. Nothing remained but darkness and pain.

Ana collapsed to the floor, the darkness overwhelming her.

CHAPTER FORTY-ONE

YEAR OF WARDING 42, HAKVERE, ARA

ANA

SURROUNDED BY DARKNESS, ANA gasped, trying to breathe against the tightness in her chest. Gradually, she recognized the cold stone floor beneath her. The warmth of another person pressed against her arm. She wasn't alone.

"What happened?" a voice beside her asked.

Allia. It was the first time Ana remembered hearing her mother's voice. Beside her, Allia moved, struggling to get up from the floor. Dragging in another breath, Ana tried to do the same. How long had they lain there unconscious? It had been long enough for the chill from the floor to seep into her body.

With great effort, Allia pushed herself up to sit leaning against the wall. She stared down at Ana. "Please wake up! I don't know how you got in here, but the guards will be back, and they can't find you here! Who are you?"

Ana swallowed, trying to find her voice. "Cirana."

Allia's eyes widened. "That's impossible. You were a baby." She looked around the dim room. "I... I know this room. This is

Hakvere. And... the ring?" Allia grabbed Ana's hand and held it up to the moonlight. "How is this possible? How can you be Cirana?"

"But it is me!"

Ana fought to make her limbs obey her, managing to sit up, braced against the wall.

"Is it really you?" Allia asked.

"Yes, Mother."

She pulled Ana into her arms, and they cried together. "Oh, I've missed you. Every day. Every moment," Allia sobbed.

"Me too," Ana said. "I thought you were dead." It seemed unreal to be looking at her mother's face. Allia's hair looked pale in the growing light of dawn, fairer than Ana's, and she saw the strong resemblance between them.

Allia put her hands on either side of Ana's face and stared at her. "You are so beautiful! But you're grown up. How long have I been here?"

"I'm twenty," Ana said.

"So long? I did everything I could to get you out of Ara when you were a baby. Please tell me you haven't been here the whole time? That Haldreth hasn't controlled your life?"

"No." Ana shook her head. "Harrow gave me to a kind woman who was my grandmother until she died. I lived at an inn until Zarek found me when I was sixteen and brought me to the White City. When I got there, Callonen took care of me." Her heart ached. She missed him so much.

Allia burst into tears. "He's alive?"

"Yes, he's alive," Ana said.

"Is he happy? Did he have a good life, a family?"

"He... He waited for you," Ana said. "He missed you every day. There was never anyone else. We have been each other's family."

Allia met her eyes. "I healed Haldreth seventeen times, once for each demon he created. I sacrificed everything to stop him and get you to safety. How did you come to be here now?"

"I'm sorry," Ana whispered. "They tricked me... But... I have a plan to escape. Come with me."

"I can't," Allia said, extending her foot with the chain. "Nothing can be done for me now. You must go without me."

"But I can't leave you here," Ana protested.

Allia's expression became stern. "You have to. Be strong. Please, my dearest. I know you don't know me, but please obey me this one time. There is no way out for me. If you've found one, you must take it. Tell Callonen I never stopped loving him. We've been lying here for hours. It will be morning soon, and you must go quickly now, before the guards come. Can you walk?"

"I'm not sure." Ana felt weak. Healing the old injuries had taken its toll, even though she had regained consciousness sooner than usual after a healing. With her mother holding the ring beside her, she felt something she'd never felt before, the will and strength of another person bent on supporting her as the magic worked.

"You can't let him catch you here."

That was true. Ana did not know what her father would do to her if he discovered what she had done. Or what he might do to Allia. She had to get away from here.

With Allia's help, Ana got to her feet, leaning against the wall. "I'll come back for you," Ana promised.

"Don't worry about me, just get yourself to safety." Allia helped her toward the door. Before they reached it, the chain pulled taut, forcing Allia to stop. She pulled Ana into an embrace and kissed her cheek. "I love you. I've always loved you, more than anything."

Ana held onto her, wondering if she obeyed her mother and left without her, would they ever be together again? "I love you too." She stumbled to the door and shut it behind her. The bar felt a dozen times heavier now. By the time Ana wrestled it into place, she sank to the floor, breathing hard. Somehow, she had to make it back to her room before they caught her.

Gathering her determination, she pushed herself up against the wall. Leaning heavily against it, she inched her way down the hall. She was still a long way from her room, and she saw the faint light of dawn through the windows.

Ana got as far away as she could from Allia's room before she collapsed.

What could she do now? The fortress would be waking up, and someone would find her. She couldn't let Haldreth find out that she'd seen Allia.

Looking around a corner, Ana saw a flight of stairs. As quickly as she could, she crawled to the bottom of them. She used the last of her strength to get there, collapsing to the floor.

Only a moment later, a guard came down the corridor and hurried toward her. As he bent over her, he realized who she was. "Princess? What are you doing here?"

"I'm so grateful you found me," Ana said in a weak voice. "My room felt stuffy, and I only wanted a breath of air. I decided to walk to the balcony. At first, everything was fine, but then I started to feel faint. I turned back, but... the stairs... I think I fainted, and I fell."

The guard had brown hair and a serious expression as he knelt beside her. "You fell? You must be hurt. Shall I bring a healer?"

Ana shook her head. "I don't think it's that serious. I still feel faint, but mostly, it's my ankle. I can't walk on it."

The guard rubbed his chin, looking worried. "I must inform the king at once."

"Could you please help me back to my room first?" she asked weakly.

"Of course, Princess."

The guard lifted her into his arms and set off down the hall, carrying her. No one stopped them or questioned them on the way. He took her back to her own room and set her gently on the bed. His eyes seemed concerned.

"Thank you," she said. "You're very kind to help me."

"Of course, Princess." He moved quickly back toward the door. "I wish you a speedy recovery."

Ana had only been in bed for a short while when a knock came at the door, and her father entered, hurrying to her side.

"Cirana! What happened?"

Ana shook her head, her expression contrite. "I'm so sorry, Father. I couldn't sleep, and all I wanted was a breath of fresh air. I was in the hall when I started to feel light-headed. I turned back, but I think I fainted, and I fell."

"How badly are you hurt?" he asked.

"Nothing serious," she assured him. "My ankle was sore, but it's already improving. I think if I can just rest a little, I'll be fine."

"I've already called the healer to take a look at you."

Ana's stomach tightened. Hopefully, the healer wouldn't tell her father that there was nothing wrong with her ankle. She maintained a grateful expression. "Thank you, Father."

He stayed until the healer arrived, an older woman with gray hair. After a brief examination, the healer agreed that rest was the best treatment. "I don't see any swelling in your ankle."

Ana sighed in relief. "That's good news. It should be fine in a few days."

"Good," Haldreth said, dismissing the healer with a nod. His expression was concerned as he looked at Ana. "Just rest for now. I'm sure you'll be fine."

"I will be. Thank you, Father."

Kissing her forehead gently, he left her alone. A moment later, Ana fell into an exhausted slumber.

Later in the morning, Ana's maid woke her with a breakfast tray. Ana blinked and covered her eyes against the bright sunlight streaming in through the window. Exhaustion weighed her down, and she ached all over. It took all her strength to sit up in bed.

The maid placed the tray on her lap. Eating would help her regain her strength, but she was too tired to swallow more than a few bites. Gavin appeared as she finished her meal. "Cirana?" He took the chair beside the bed. "Your father told me what happened. I'm so sorry."

"I'm all right, just still exhausted."

He leaned closer and took her hand. "Don't worry. We'll take care of you until you feel better."

Ana shook her head, covering her face with an expression of embarrassment. "The whole thing is so silly. It seemed so much worse last night. I'm already beginning to feel better."

"You still look tired. Don't worry about anything now," he bent forward to kiss her forehead. He took the tray from her lap and set it aside as she lay down again, then pulled the covers back up around her.

"Thank you," she smiled weakly at him.

Gavin rose. "Rest. I'll have the maid come in a little while to check on you and see if you need anything."

Ana spent the day in bed. Would she be able to get up if she tried? Usually, after healing someone, it was at least four days before she could function again. But she'd never had someone lending her their strength before. Hopefully, her recovery would be quicker this time. Would her father realize what she had done? If he went to visit Allia, he would know Ana had been there. She needed to regain her strength and get out of here.

Three days saw Ana past the worst of the weakness. As soon as she was able, she left her bed and gradually resumed her activities, taking care to limp slightly for a few more days.

"My dear," Haldreth exclaimed, as she entered the dining room on the first morning she left her room. He hurried to assist her to a seat. "I'm so pleased that you are feeling better."

"Thank you, Father," she said. "I am much better than I was."

"Good, good. I feared we would have to postpone the banquet. But since you're on the mend, I believe we can keep our plans. You still have five days to prepare."

Ana had been trying to forget about the event.

The next several days passed all too quickly. On the day of the banquet, Gavin came to Ana's room, a servant following him. "I'm sure you want to look your best tonight," he said, smiling. "The king will introduce you as the princess of Ara." He gestured to the woman behind him, whose arms were full of shimmering silk. "This dress is something special. Your father paid a fortune for it, and you will make him so happy if you wear it."

Make him happy? What Gavin really meant was that Haldreth would be angry if she didn't, and no one liked it when he was angry. When Gavin had gone, the woman helped her put on the dress.

She realized then why he had come himself to bring it to her. It was not something she would ever wear by choice. Its neckline was far too revealing and would attract unwelcome attention. Her mind went back to all the parties she had gone to in the White City. She remembered putting on beautiful gowns and meeting with kings and queens and ambassadors. Callonen would never have let her leave her room dressed like this.

Her hands clenched into fists. She looked in the mirror, her cheeks coloring a little with anger.

This dress had probably been Gavin's idea. They wanted to control her and for her to feel like a possession. What would they do if she refused to wear it?

Especially today, when the king had planned a party and her plans for escape were nearly complete—today, of all days, she had to go along with his request.

When Ana arrived in the great hall, it glittered with thousands of lights. She took a deep breath and tried to slow her pounding heart. Everyone in the room bowed low as she entered.

Haldreth came to her side. "My daughter, Princess Cirana." The people cheered and applauded.

Ana glanced back at them. The diamond crown felt heavy on her head, and the priceless jewelry weighed her down. Her bare shoulders and low neckline made her horribly uncomfortable. They had intended for her to feel as if she were on display. She stood up straight and tried to ignore the sensation.

The king offered his arm and led her across the hall.

There was music and dancing, and everywhere the people bowed to her. She looked into their faces.

They're afraid of me. There's fear in their eyes.

Not me, she realized. Him. I am with Haldreth. The king.

She could sense the darkness in him. He was powerful and would destroy anyone who tried to oppose him.

Eight soldiers in blue uniforms stood along one side of the room. "These are the best of my captains," Haldreth said. None of them looked pleasant. Some were clean and well groomed, but their eyes were cold. Others appeared surly and unkempt.

The king introduced her. "My daughter, Princess Cirana." Each one bowed to her in turn.

"This is Captain Kaemar."

A big man with dark hair took her hand. "A pleasure to meet you, Princess." His eyes lingered too long as he looked her over, and she tried not to let her face show her discomfort.

They moved on down the line to the man at the end. He was easily the most untidy of them all. His hair hadn't been cut in years, and scars marked the part of his face not hidden behind his beard. He wore a collection of small knives across his chest, with a couple more at his belt. A sword hung at his side, and an ax was slung across his back.

"Captain Tack, this is my daughter, Princess Cirana."

The man nodded but didn't speak and kissed her hand as briefly as possible. Their eyes met for only a second before he glanced away. He seemed angry about something. And she could sense it wasn't just his outward appearance. He was genuinely furious about something. She certainly didn't know why he felt that way, but it frightened her.

She was grateful when they moved on.

The king bent to speak in her ear, nodding toward Tack. "He doesn't like to talk, but he keeps the men in line. They're all terrified of him. There was a fight once. I didn't see it myself, but the others told me that eight men attacked him and he beat them all. He never goes anywhere without his weapons. Not even to a party." Ana wondered if Haldreth was trying to frighten her more that she already was. Maybe. All of his captains were intimidating men.

She shivered.

The king introduced Ana to many more people, and they sat at the table in the front of the room to eat a magnificent dinner. The fine food did not make Ana feel more comfortable. She longed to escape. The soldiers' eyes followed her, staring at her in the ridiculous gown. It made her want to crawl away and hide.

Once, she met Tack's gaze from the other end of the table. He wasn't leering at her like the others. Quite the opposite; he still seemed angry. She resolved to stay well away from him.

At length, the meal ended and gradually the guests left the tables to form small groups, chatting. Ana found herself surrounded by people, noblemen and women who seemed eager to get to know her better and soldiers who had been staring at her all evening.

Of course, her outfit probably gave them an unrealistic idea of how she might behave. She could sense what they wanted from her. She felt her cheeks heat and took a deep breath.

Breaking into a circle of conversation, Gavin offered Ana his arm. "If you'll all excuse us for a moment. I need to have a word with the princess." He led her outside to an empty balcony. In the dark, the cold moonlight shone on the towers. "Do you like the party?" he asked. "Everyone adores you."

Adored her? That was not what she had felt from any of them. "Yes, they've been very kind," she said, her voice only a little stiff. She hated being on display. And some of the guests had been afraid of her. No one had ever feared her before, and she did not like it at all.

"You look wonderful," Gavin said, stepping nearer.

"Thank you." She shivered as the chill night breeze brushed her bare skin.

"Tonight is only the beginning," he said, putting his arms around her. "You can have anything you want here. You can live in luxury and command all the resources of this land. Your father will give you anything you ask. There's no reason to go back to Sarine. He wants you to stay here. And he's offered me a permanent place here too. I want us to be together. We could be happy here, couldn't we?"

The question startled her. Happy? How could he think she'd ever be happy here? But she couldn't let him know she suspected his deceit. "Perhaps we could, but I still miss home," she admitted.

"Is there anything you want? Anything at all that your father hasn't given you?"

"No," she said.

"The king wants you here. It's your place to rule after him as queen of Ara, and I would have you stay at my side. You're so beautiful," he whispered. "I have always thought so, since the first moment I saw you. I need you. I love you. Don't put me off any longer. Your father will give his blessing, if you would consent to be my wife."

He brushed his fingertips along the side of her neck. She still could not sense any concealed feelings from him. But now, she knew Gavin hid his true intentions from her. An icy shiver of alarm went through her as his fingers trailed along her jaw to her chin, lifting her face to his. He kissed her hungrily. When his hands touched the skin of her neck and shoulders, she shivered. She didn't know what to say to him, but she couldn't endure him kissing her like this. There was only one way to get him to stop without revealing her true feelings.

"I'm sorry, Gavin," she apologized. She allowed her knees to buckle and her head to fall to one side. "I don't know what's wrong with me. I don't feel well... I..." She collapsed and felt him catch her. Ana forced herself to remain unmoving, feigning unconsciousness, even though she saw bright lights through her eyelids and heard a sudden buzz of whispering voices. Gavin was carrying her across the ballroom. She relaxed when the noise died down and all she could hear were his steps as he walked.

She let her eyelids flutter. "What happened?" she murmured.

"You fainted," Gavin said.

"I'm so sorry," she said weakly. "I didn't mean to. I heard everything you said."

"Good," he said gently. "Get some rest now, and you can think about it."

"Thank you, Gavin. That's just what I need, a little time to think."

He laid her on the bed in her room and covered her with a blanket. "Rest," he said. "I'll see you in the morning."

She waited for a while after he left to make sure he wasn't coming back or sending someone else. Her time was up. She had to get away. Ana rose and took off the ball gown, then put the finishing touches on her rope and measured it against her own height. The rope had reached the length she needed plus a little more. She wound it around her waist and hips and put on a plain riding dress and the boots that went with it.

It grew later, and the castle quieted. Ana waited until midnight had passed, then slipped from her room. There were guards in the halls, but she remembered how to avoid them. With her stomach quivering, she tiptoed through the corridors toward the balcony. She heard voices in the hall ahead. One of them belonged to her father. Terrified, Ana ducked into a room and hid behind the door.

"My brother cannot defeat my demons," the king said contemptuously. "Callonen still has no way to stop them. And after all this time, I'm ready to cast the spell that will undo the Warding. All I need is to get close enough to touch it. We'll be marching soon. Sarine will be mine."

Chapter Forty-Two

Year of Warding 42, Hakvere, Ara

Ana

Ana's chest constricted until she couldn't breathe. Haldreth had found a way to break the Warding. Without its protective power, so many people would die. She had to warn Callonen. Ana realized she was shaking and took a deep, silent breath, trying to calm herself.

"Do we have enough men to beat him?" Gavin asked.

"We have more men than he has, even without the demons," Haldreth said. "But I won't need them. I have something he wants more than anything else. Callonen will give me the city."

"You really think he will?"

Her father laughed, and Ana quailed at the sound. "Of course he will. You saw him. Don't you know how it's tortured him all these years, knowing I took Allia? There was only one other thing that would hurt him like that. And you made that happen."

Gavin laughed. "It took a great deal of work to get close enough to abduct her."

Ana held her breath in shock. They were talking about her. Her guess had been right. They had taken her.

"You should have seen Callonen's face when he came after her and got to the edge of the Warding. He went crazy! The demons were there, and he didn't even care. If his men hadn't stopped him, it would have already been over. Callonen was still screaming when I left."

Their voices and footsteps faded and then disappeared, leaving Ana alone in the hallway.

Tears ran down her cheeks. Callonen had tried to come after her. He would have died attempting to save her. Ana went out into the hall. All was quiet, and no one challenged her as she made her way toward the walls. It seemed to take hours, but at last she made it to the balcony.

During her previous visits, she had watched the positions and movements of the guards, and she knew this corner would be unobserved for a short while. When she saw the soldiers moving away, she unwound her makeshift rope, fixed it around the railing, and dropped both ends over the wall.

It was dark. Clouds covered the moon, and she couldn't see if the rope was long enough to reach the ground. But the guards would be back soon, and this was no time to hesitate. Grasping it with both hands, she swung onto the rope. It held her weight, at least for the moment, and she wrapped the rope beneath her, bracing it against her thigh to control her descent and resting her boots against the wall, just as she had once watched Zarek do. The darkness disoriented her, and after a few moments, she lost all sense of time. She clung to the rope desperately, and the muscles of her arms and hands burned with the effort. Down she went, several times slipping when her grip weakened.

Finally, she reached the ground, banging her knee against a rock. Gritting her teeth, she rubbed it. She had made the climb safely. Pulling one end of the rope, she gathered it up, hiding it between two large stones.

Trying to be absolutely silent, she slipped off through the rocks and patches of snow. After a while, the clouds parted, and she saw the moon, three-quarters full. It provided enough light to let her see her way and to make sure she didn't get too close to the sheer edge of the canyon. She chose a path that ran southward, parallel to the cliff.

Ana walked briskly for the rest of the night. It was cold, but the exercise kept her warm. When dawn came, she went on in the new light. She needed to get farther away from Hakvere. But she was tired. Gathering her will, she continued on.

At midday, she came to a tiny stream, the first water she had seen except for the river running far below through the canyon. She knew that as soon as night came, her father would send the Shekkar to hunt her. Perhaps she had been foolish to escape. But she had to warn Callonen. She followed the stream uphill, crossing and re-crossing it, using the water to hide her trail.

Despite her exhaustion, she walked all day, with only a few brief halts. But all too quickly, the sun sank into the cloudy west, and night covered the barren landscape.

Bone weary, Ana pushed on, stumbling through the dark. She was reminded of her journey before with Zarek and Dane. They had often felt like this, but somehow, they had kept going. And when she couldn't go on anymore, Zarek had carried her. Now she was alone, with no one to help.

By midnight, she heard the sound she dreaded hearing. Demons. She stopped for a moment, listening. The sound of their voices came from up the hill ahead of her. Were they behind her too? She wasn't sure.

Her heart pounding in her throat, she turned and hurried back the way she had come, stumbling along in the dark. Panic gnawed in her belly. If the Shekkar caught her, would they kill her? Or would they take her back to her father?

The Shekkar grew closer, driving her downhill toward the sheer edge of the cliff. By their voices, there were at least six of them. She had nowhere to go. And she wasn't fast enough to escape them. Her attempt to get away had failed. Wouldn't it be better to lie down and accept her fate? But the stubborn part of her kept her feet moving.

When Ana reached the edge of the canyon, it was too late. As the demons surrounded her, she turned to face them. They stood in a half circle, a wall of darkness, blacker than the night around them. They waited, not moving.

"Zarek," she whispered. If he still lived, he was far away, but saying his name gave her strength. She would try to be brave, like he was. She took a step backward, away from the demons, then another and another. They followed her silently, drawing no nearer. The tiny stream ran nearby. Ana heard falling water and knew that she had come to the brink of the cliff. The depths were utterly dark, and far, far below, she heard the river.

She stopped on the edge of the precipice, her heart pounding in her throat. She heard horses pull up behind the demons. Men gathered behind the dark creatures, Gavin among them.

"There's nowhere to go," he called. "Please come back."

"No!" she protested.

"What are you going to do then?"

"I won't go back to him!" she cried.

"You'd rather die?" he asked.

"I..." Her voice faltered. Despair and terror rushed over her. There was nowhere else to go. No help. It was over.

She jumped.

Something seized the skirt of her dress. Her momentum carried her into the rocks, and when her head hit them, everything faded.

Maybe she was dead. Ana didn't know. Strong arms carried her gently. It felt so familiar and safe. She'd been held like this before, a long time ago. She whispered his name. "Zarek."

Other voices sorted themselves out in her head. Someone shouted angrily. She heard the demons snarling and begged, "Don't let them take me."

Ana felt pain as something soft pressed against her head, and she groaned. Little by little, the world reassembled itself. She was in trouble. She'd tried to jump into the canyon and had failed. Opening her eyes, she found it wasn't Zarek who held her but one of the king's men, the one with all the knives who she had met at the banquet. The demons had drawn back a little, and Gavin was there.

He glowered at her. "What were you thinking?"

"I—" she faltered.

"Get my horse," he ordered over his shoulder, and when he had mounted, he turned back to the man holding Ana. "Give her to me."

"I can take her back," the soldier said.

Gavin's voice was harsh. "Give her to me now, Tack, or you won't live to see the dawn."

She felt herself handed to Gavin, and she quailed before the fury on his face. Even if she hadn't seen it, this close to him, she could sense his feelings. He was terrified that Ana had almost lost the ring and the king would blame him for her escape. He was determined to make her bend to them.

Whatever method he had been using to deceive her abilities, the shield was gone now.

Gavin despised her. He'd only been using her.

Ana's stomach clenched at the force of his emotions.

"You lied to me! We offered you everything!" Gavin held her so tightly his fingers were bruising her arm.

"Please stop," she pleaded. "You're hurting me. You said you loved me."

"I do! And I would have made you a queen, if only you hadn't betrayed your father. I would have done anything for you. What am I supposed to do now? You told me you needed time. Then you tried to sneak away! You must have finished your... thinking." His voice was hard and angry. She could sense his deceit and his craving for power.

He urged his horse back toward the castle.

The ride back didn't last long enough. All too soon, they could see the fortress, black against the starlight. They rode up to the walls and through a back gate that Ana hadn't seen before. Gavin dismounted, still holding her. Then he abruptly released her. She still felt woozy from hitting her head. Her knees buckled, and she sank to the ground.

"Get up!" Gavin yelled. "No more pretending to faint." He grasped Ana's wrist in an iron grip and pulled her up. She was still trying to get her feet under her when Tack appeared to support her from the other side. His hands were gentle, in stark contrast to Gavin's. Tack wanted to help her. She could feel it. But he couldn't stop Haldreth, even though it was clear to her he wanted to. No one could.

Gavin dragged Ana through the torchlit halls. Her head still throbbed with pain. The Shekkar followed them like an honor guard. Ana had never had them nearby for so long, and their voices made her want to scream. She could sense the empty darkness in them and dared not look directly at them.

They came to the room where Haldreth sat on his throne, his face flushed with rage.

Marching her across the room, Gavin threw her down at the foot of the throne. Ana fell, bruising her knees and one elbow against the stone floor. She stared at Haldreth's boots, not daring to look up at him.

"What happened?" the king demanded.

"We caught up with her on the cliff edge, a few hours ride from here. She tried to jump, but Tack caught her," Gavin explained.

Tack was still there and wanted to help her, but he was terrified. It didn't show on the outside, though. His face remained stony and impassive. The king's cold voice said, "Both of you, find out who is responsible for this. Any guard who let her get past him will die."

He would kill his own men? Just like that? She heard Gavin and Tack retreating. There was nothing Tack could do. The demons were right there, and there was no way to stop her father.

When Haldreth spoke again, his voice was soft and tightly controlled. "Why?" he asked. "Why would you run away?"

Reluctantly, her gaze traveled slowly higher until she saw the fury burning in his eyes. Facing him made dying out there on the cliff seem much more attractive. She felt his hatred and malice.

The demons hissed behind her.

Ana shuddered at the sound, but she couldn't look away from the king.

"Why would you betray me?" He shook his head.

Ana stared at him in disbelief, her head still pounding. Why? Into her mind flashed the horrifying memory of Zarek, bloody and motionless on the ground. She thought of her mother, a prisoner of Haldreth's hatred for all these years. And he had sent Gavin to trick her and steal Ana from her home.

But what could she say now?

He continued, in injured tones, "I have given you luxury, gold and treasure, and the honor of sharing my throne. Would you really refuse all this?"

Silently, Ana nodded.

The king sighed, as if sad and weary. "I tried to make this easy for you."

"If you care about me at all, let me go home!" Ana cried, finding her voice. "Why do you take everything from everyone? You think the world belongs to you! I will never join you."

"No more games!" he snarled. "This is your last chance. If you won't help me, you're no longer valuable to me."

Haldreth intended to destroy Callonen and the city, everyone in Sarine she cared about, and so many other innocent people. And she had no way to stop him. Tears welled up in her eyes, and her hands shook.

"Well?" he demanded.

She tried to gather her courage. Zarek had always been brave, and she wished she knew how he did it.

"Choose!" the king demanded, pounding his fist on the table beside the throne. At the jolt, something small and silver slid off the tabletop to land on the floor at his feet.

Ana picked it up. It was a silver charm on a chain, the familiar figure of a hammer and sword crossed upon it. Zarek's charm.

"Where did you get this?" she cried, holding it up.

"That? It belonged to someone who betrayed me. I have kept it all these years because it reminds me of what happens to people who try to humiliate me. Even though he tried to escape, I caught him and made him suffer."

"No!" she cried, sensing Haldreth wasn't lying about this. So Zarek was gone. The news settled like a stone in her gut. Zarek.

He had been the most alive person she had known, always in motion. And Ana would try to be as brave as he had been. She could never join Haldreth. She couldn't help him. Never. No matter what.

"Forget him. Forget the charm," the king demanded. "Will you join me?"

"No," she said, trying not to choke on the word.

As the Shekkar drew nearer, she shrank away from them, against the foot of the throne. One of them reached out its claw until it almost touched her cheek. Ana froze.

"You know their touch is deadly." Her father bent to whisper in her ear. "A single scratch will kill you."

Tears rolled down her cheeks. Ana expected him to give the command that would cause the demons to rush forward, shrieking, to tear her apart. She waited for oblivion. But she couldn't join him. It seemed he wasn't ready to kill her quite yet. All at once, the demons departed, and the guards caught hold of her. One raised a sword. Ana struggled and fought against them, but they jammed her knuckles against the edge of the table top, extending the third finger onto the surface.

"Father, no! Please!" It was her last desperate plea for mercy, but he remained unmoved. He nodded, and the blade fell. She screamed.

"Take her back to the dungeon." Haldreth laughed as he picked up the ring.

CHAPTER FORTY-THREE

YEAR OF WARDING 42, HAKVERE, ARA

ANA

THE DOOR CLANGED SHUT, leaving Ana alone in the dark. Shaking from shock, she sank down with her back against the wall. She still had Zarek's silver charm clutched in her right hand, and she hung its chain around her neck.

Ana tore a piece of fabric from the hem of her skirt and held it firmly against her wounded hand. In the dark, she couldn't see it, but she felt blood soaking the cloth.

When her eyes adjusted, she recognized the same cell she had been locked in before. There had been plenty of time earlier to memorize every detail of the room, and it was horribly familiar. Only now, she knew this was Ara's dungeon.

The king had expected Gavin's charm to win her. She had been in Haldreth's power all along. Her pretended rescue had been nothing more than an attempt to manipulate. They wanted her to feel undying gratitude to them for saving her.

How could she ever have liked Gavin? It had all been a trick. Her father had been behind all of it, and now he had the ring.

She tore off a fresh piece of her hem and pressed it against the wound. Ana raised her hand above her head, trying to slow the bleeding, but that did nothing to ease the throbbing, and she was too tired to hold her arm up for long. Her skull felt like it was splitting where she'd struck it against the rock.

Slumped against the hard floor, the chill stone stole the warmth from her body, and she shivered. Silence surrounded her. She tried calling through the crack into the next cell, but whoever had been there before was gone now, and she was left with only pain for company.

Today had been her last chance with Haldreth. Ana lowered her pounding head to rest against her knees. No one could help her now. Zarek was dead or a prisoner. She had no way of communicating with her mother, and neither of them could help the other. Shivering, she fell into a restless slumber.

HALDRETH

Haldreth, the king of Ara, stared thoughtfully into the green depths of the stone. He shook his head. Why did the girl have to be so stubborn? It would accomplish nothing. He controlled the whole situation, and she couldn't change that. If only he'd been able to raise her by his side here in Ara... He could have taken care of her, made sure she never lacked any luxury. If those thieves hadn't kidnapped her as a baby, he'd have had the chance to be a real father to her. Maybe then she would have understood his work better and the wisdom of helping him.

Seeing her after all these years had brought up so many emotions. She reminded him of Allia, which was unfortunate, but her brown eyes were the exact shade of his. And her face had lit up when she saw him, as if she loved him and wanted to be with him. He'd felt a sharp twist of pain when he realized that wasn't actually the case.

Callonen had gotten to her first. She hadn't been happy to see him. She'd mistaken him for his brother. And it stung, even after all this time. His self-righteous, self-absorbed brother had such a way of luring people to his side. They fell for it every time. They would do whatever he asked of them. It was disgusting.

But Haldreth had found a better way to get people to do what he wanted. Fear. They did everything for him because he would end their worthless lives if they didn't. Maybe his unfortunate daughter didn't fully realize that. Well, she had made her choice, and he would go forward with his plans without her.

Footsteps approached. He looked up to see Gavin. The young man might be loyal and resourceful, but Haldreth wasn't certain he had the backbone to be a leader. Yet his talent for deception rivaled Haldreth's own. Gavin had made himself valuable. He'd worked his way into Callonen's guard, far closer to his brother than any of his other spies had ever come.

"We have work to do," Haldreth announced, gripping the ring in his hand.

"The Warding?" Gavin asked. "Is it time?"

The king smiled. "It's time. All we need is to get there. The spell will be dangerous, and I will keep the ring close by as a precaution. If you prove yourself worthy, I may permit you to wear it. Once the Warding is broken, the demons can destroy Callonen and his friends. We'll be leaving in a week. Go and check on the preparations. Be sure our armies are ready to march. There's just one thing left. We'll take Allia with us in case Callonen escapes the Shekkar and we still need him to cooperate." Gavin bowed and departed.

Haldreth went to Allia's door and lifted the bar. In the light of the lantern he carried, he saw her sitting motionless against the wall, staring into the darkness. She did not respond to the sound of the door or to the light.

He moved closer, bending to one knee to search her features. Her face held no expression, not even the utter blankness he'd seen there for years. Did he detect a new awareness in her eyes? She sat still, as if she were carved from stone, a graceful statue, ageless. It reminded him of how she'd looked when he first brought her here. "Are you well, my lady?" he asked. "You do look well. Better than you have for many years. Has something changed?" Allia still did not respond.

He put the lantern on the table and seized her left hand, holding it up to the light. Her hand was whole. The missing finger had been restored.

Haldreth smiled. "So, Cirana was here. Our darling child." Then he laughed. "Did you think she got away?" He dropped Allia's hand and held up the ring so she could see it. "My men caught her."

Moving for the first time, Allia's eyes followed the ring as he brought it to his lips. "You can still taste her blood on it."

For a long moment, they stared at each other, horror blossoming in Allia's eyes. "What have you done to her?" she demanded.

"She tried to run away with the ring. What could I do? There was no reason for her to do it. I treated her well, offered her a chance to rule at my side. But instead, she chose to betray me. She's been gone for nearly twenty years!" Haldreth seized the front of Allia's dress and jerked her to her feet. "You saw her once in all that time. Explain to me why she's just. Like. You." He struck her to punctuate the words, the last blow knocking her back against the wall, where she slid to the floor.

Allia had repeatedly attempted to thwart his work. Why should he be surprised when her child behaved the same way?

She slowly climbed back to her feet, the heavy chain clanking as she moved. "What have you done to her?"

"What do you expect? I gave her every opportunity to help me willingly. Instead, she betrayed me." There was only so much he could do, and it was sad. "Now I'll have to kill her."

"No, Haldreth. Please!" Allia straightened and faced him. "You can't do this. There must be something else you want! I'll do anything!"

It was good to see a little cooperation from her finally, even if it was belated, but his plans were already underway. He shook his head. "You're too late."

Allia screamed at him and leapt forward. Before he had time to react, she had seized the knife at his belt. She drove it at his chest, but his hidden armor deflected the blade, and he seized her hand. "You tried that before, years ago. I know you don't really want to kill me."

She twisted away from him and turned the dagger on herself. Haldreth seized her wrists, forcing the knife from her hand. She fell to her knees.

"You can't die yet," Haldreth kept his grip on her wrists and bent forward to speak in her ear. "We're going back to Sarine. I've waited far too long. Now it's time for me to claim my father's throne. Callonen will give it to me in exchange for you."

Allia struggled, trying to free herself. "I'd rather die than help you!"

Haldreth tightened his grip. "I thought it would be touching to take you back to him as you were, blank and broken. Watching him suffer would have been gratifying. But now, here you are, well and whole, and you remember him. You still want him. I think it will be even better for him to see you now and know that you've lost so many years already and I still won't let him have you."

Haldreth gripped her wrists tighter until she moaned in pain.

He released her and picked up his dagger from the floor. "I will get everything I want." He got to his feet and stood over her. "You've tried to stop me every step of the way, but it won't work. I will rule. You will never see your daughter again, and you will never be with Callonen. I'll see to that."

ANA

Ana had lost all track of time. It must have been days since they dragged her back here, maybe three or four. Her head felt like it was going to crack open where it had hit the rock. As time passed, the pain eased, and the throbbing in her hand lessened a little, unless she moved it too quickly or bumped it against something.

No one had given her food or drink. She collected a small amount of water from the drip in the corner, enough to keep her alive. Yet she felt weaker every day, and so cold.

The sound of the heavy door opening broke the silence. Someone came in with a torch and then locked the door behind them. She had to shield her eyes with her hand. When her vision adjusted, she saw Gavin and scrambled to her feet.

He placed his torch in a hole in the wall and bowed mockingly. "How are you, my lady?"

"Please, just leave me alone," Ana said, turning away from him.

"I'll go if you ask," he said. "I only came to bring you food and water. You are hungry, aren't you?"

Warily, she nodded.

He held out a basket and a bottle of water, and she took them. Her lips were cracked, her mouth dry. The water felt wonderful, and for a moment, she thought of nothing else and drank deeply.

"Please, sit. Be comfortable." He gestured to the stone floor.

She sat down, resting her back against the wall, and ate the food in the basket.

"There's no need to thank me," he said sarcastically as she ate in silence. He took a seat beside her.

"Thank you for the food and water," she said, turning to meet his gaze as she finished eating.

It felt strange not to have any sense of what he was feeling. He still looked the same—dark curly hair, handsome features. But now she couldn't sense anything from him. She had not expected how lost she would feel without that ability. Looking into his eyes, she tried to read his intent there.

"You made a big mistake," he said conversationally. "I'm sure you realize that by now." He shook his head. "He would have treated you well if only you'd obeyed him. You forced him to mistreat you. He never wanted to. But you have to do your part. I've done everything I can to help you."

Now she heard the undercurrent of anger in his voice.

"You owe me your gratitude." He grabbed her wrist.

She turned to stare at him. For a long moment, he held her gaze, and the look in his eyes terrified her.

"Let me go." She twisted out of his grip and regained her feet.

He stood, following her. "I don't want to let you go." He caressed her neck.

She pushed his hand away.

"You should appreciate me," he whispered, his dark eyes holding hers. "The king said there was no reason to feed you if we're just going to kill you. He was ready to do it today, but I asked him to wait. I saved your life." His fingers wandered across her collarbone and down the front of her dress.

"Stop." She jerked away and ran to the far corner of the room.

"I stood up for you. And this is the thanks I get? Do you want me to let him kill you?" He shook his head in disgust. "I offered you the honor of being my wife. I would have committed to spend the rest of my life with you. And you refused me. For some reason, I'm not *good* enough for you. I'm sorry you feel that way. But I don't have to ask you for anything. I can take whatever I want." Slowly, he came closer.

"Please, leave me alone," she said.

"Is that really what you want? I can't stop thinking about you." He seized her arms, pulled her against him, and pressed his mouth against hers. "You enjoy kissing me. I know you do."

She struggled and tried to escape his grasp. His grip loosened, and she pushed him away. "You'll change your mind," he said in a low voice. "I know you will. I've saved your life, and I'm the only thing keeping you alive. Don't deny it anymore. You've always wanted me."

His handsome face was still the same, but Ana could not even remember a time when she had thought him attractive. "I do not want you!"

A blinding pain erupted across her face, knocking her to the floor.

"You have no choice! You will want me if you stay in here long enough!" he yelled. "The only way out of this room alive is in my arms. They won't bring you food. Only I will. And you can ask for me anytime. They will tell me. Otherwise, you can starve in here."

Shrinking away from him against the wall, she struggled back to her feet.

She ducked, but not fast enough to avoid his second blow. It drove her back to the rocky floor, the room spinning around her. She felt a crushing kick to her side. Another impact followed the first, forcing the air from her lungs, and she couldn't seem to get it back. The door slammed as he left, leaving the room in darkness.

Ana couldn't catch her breath for a long time, and pain stabbed through her ribs with every lungful of air. The dark was now a relief, and to be alone, a blessing. Gingerly, she felt her bruised face with her good hand. It hurt, but nothing compared to the pain in her side.

With a groan, she wrapped her arms around her injured ribs and curled up on the stone floor. Couldn't they just kill her quickly? There was no other way this could end. She'd rather die before Gavin carried out his plans for her. Was he waiting for her to change her mind? To submit? To at least pretend to want him?

༄

Two days and nights passed with no food or water besides the drip in the corner—and thankfully, no Gavin. She was alone and in pain, with nothing to do but think about her options. She had no good ones.

It was easy to decide that she'd rather die than submit to Gavin, but she had no way of carrying out that choice. She could do nothing, but wait for death to take her or for Gavin to come back. When he did, she could either fight or give up.

The time passed in silence, and Ana started at even the slightest noise. She feared and waited for the sound of the door opening. Each day, she grew weaker. If Gavin waited long enough, there would be no choice left to make.

CHAPTER FORTY-FOUR

YEAR OF WARDING 42, HAKVERE, ARA

ANA

ONE NIGHT, ANA HEARD the sound she had been dreading. The creak of her cell door opening startled her out of sleep, and she huddled against the wall, her knees pulled up to her chest. She no longer had the strength to fight Gavin. He stood over her as if assessing exactly how defeated she'd become.

She wanted to resist him. She had to. But she lacked the strength. As Gavin came slowly closer, his dark eyes mocked her. Ana knew he could see her fear and despair—that he enjoyed it. He stopped a short way from her, placing the torch into a hole in the wall, and held out a parcel.

"Are you hungry?" He knew she was starving. The guards had obeyed his command and brought her nothing since his last visit.

Ana did not answer. He had made his intentions clear the last time he was here, and she knew he hadn't come to give her food. This was the end. Tonight, he would kill her if she tried to fight. Maybe he would kill her either way.

His eyes never left her face. When she said nothing, he continued softly, "I'm sorry about before. I shouldn't have hurt you. I was angry, and I didn't mean it."

Ana didn't believe him. She didn't need the ring to guess what he was going to do next. She kept her silence, and slowly he came nearer.

Her breath came in an involuntary gasp when he knelt beside her and put his hand on her shoulder.

"Cirana," he whispered. "Why are you so stubborn? It would be so much better if you joined us. You can have your room back with a comfortable bed and have anything you'd like to eat or drink. I can take you there right now."

"Please, Gavin. I just want to go home." She looked up to meet his eyes. "Please let me go."

"Let you go?" He caressed her cheek. "But you are home. I can't let you go," he said. He shoved her knees away from her body, laid down beside her putting an arm around her waist, and pulled her close.

"No." She tried to push him away with her good hand.

"You still want to fight me?" he asked in disbelief. "It won't accomplish anything but cause you more pain."

Ana couldn't help but struggle. He only held her tighter, crushing her body against his, and she clenched her jaw to keep from crying out.

"Please stop!" She couldn't catch her breath.

"Then stop fighting. It's over." Releasing her, he drew a knife and held the tip against her throat. "I can kill you. Now. Later. Whenever I choose. Stop trying to fight me!"

"You really don't care if you hurt me?" she asked. "If you had ever felt another person's pain, you wouldn't do this." She couldn't imagine intentionally harming someone herself.

For a moment, he simply stared at her wordlessly, with no expression on his face. Had he really listened?

He lowered the knife a little, but it didn't last. The cruel sneer came back to his features. "Don't try to make this about me! I offered you my heart, and you lied to me! You betrayed the king after all he's done for you. I gave you everything, and you threw it back in my face. You deserve this," he snapped. "All of it."

Ana's momentary hope vanished.

"You are mine, Cirana." He returned the blade to her throat. "Body and soul."

"No!" she cried. The word came out almost involuntarily.

The knife bit into her skin, and warm blood ran down the side of her neck. He slid the blade inside the neckline of her dress, along the top of her shoulder. With a quick jerk, he sliced the fabric, purposely cutting her as he did so.

Hot pain tore along Ana's shoulder, and she clenched her teeth to hold back a cry. Gavin pinned her against the wall with his body and kissed her. His weight sent pain stabbing from her injured side. Even the agony couldn't stop her from shuddering as his fingers caressed the bare skin of her neck.

"You liked me once," he whispered, his lips by her ear. "I think you still like it when I hold you." His hands were gentle for a moment, caressing her.

"I don't!" she cried, trying to twist away from him.

He pulled her closer, crushing her injured ribs as his lips pressed against her throat. She could not hold back a cry of pain.

"Gavin!" Another man's voice broke into their struggle.

Gavin glared over his shoulder, enraged at the interruption. "Get out of here, Tack!"

Captain Tack stood in the doorway, armored and covered with weapons, his expression furious. "No," he growled. "The king sent me. He told me to bring her."

Ana stared at Tack. The only possible way this could get worse was for her to be taken back to the king. He would not have ordered her brought to him unless he planned to do something even more horrible to her.

"No!" Gavin hissed, his arms tightening around her possessively, bringing a gasp of pain from her. "She's mine. He promised."

"He said to bring her," Tack repeated sullenly.

"You tell him—"

Tacks heavy brows drew together. "I'm not your messenger," he growled. "Tell him yourself."

"You're not taking her," Gavin said flatly. He released Ana and got to his feet, standing between her and Tack, the knife still in his hand. Ana pushed herself up from the floor and sat, her back against the wall, trying to catch her breath and holding the wound to slow the bleeding.

Tack glanced at Ana, then back at Gavin and his blade. "Why did you cut her?"

"That's not your business!"

Tack stared back at Gavin, then rolled his eyes. "I understand. No woman will go to bed with you unless you force her."

Gavin yelled in rage, raised the blade, and lunged for Tack. But before Gavin could reach him, Tack already had a knife in his hand.

"You'll go to the demons for this!" Gavin yelled.

He thrust his knife at Tack, who deftly blocked the blow and smashed his fist into Gavin's nose, causing blood to pour down over his mouth and chin. He howled in pain.

Gavin's next attack came a little slower. Tack seized his wrist, holding his weapon immobile, and left a long cut on Gavin's shoulder. He screamed in rage and twisted out of Tack's grip, staggering a few steps back.

Tack stood casually, waiting. Gavin rushed forward, but his injuries and his rage slowed him. Tack was obviously far more skilled, and he dodged. Each time Gavin attacked, Tack easily blocked, dealing Gavin another injury. He was bleeding now from several wounds, the worst a deep gash in his thigh.

Finally, Tack wrenched Gavin's arm behind him hard enough that he shrieked as his shoulder popped out of joint. The knife fell from his hand. Raising his own weapon, Tack slammed the pommel into Gavin's head. Tack released him and watched him slowly crumple to the floor.

Tack undid Gavin's belt and pulled it off. A hard shove from his boot rolled the unconscious man onto his stomach. Tack bound the man's hands behind him and tore a strip of cloth from the hem of his tunic, using it to gag him.

Ana watched in horrified fascination. Tack turned from Gavin to look at her. He had beaten Gavin so easily. She could see why all the others were afraid of him.

Despite how intimidating he was, he'd wanted to help her on the night she'd been captured.

But instead of helping, he'd given her to the king. He would do the same thing again.

Tack held out his hand.

She shrank away. "Please don't take me to the king!" She could no longer sense whether he had any desire to help her. She didn't know what he would do. Maybe he only intended to finish what Gavin had started. Tack was bigger and a better fighter than Gavin. He was the one who'd beaten eight men at once. What chance did she have? Beneath his beard, his jaw clenched, and his eyes burned with fury. He still had his weapon in his hand, with Gavin's blood staining the blade. He took a step toward her.

"Please don't..." Ana pleaded, her eyes on the knife.

Meeting her gaze, Tack lowered the weapon slowly. Wiping the blade on his pants, he put it away. When he knelt beside her, Ana shrank away, but he pulled her to her feet and toward the door.

"I don't want to go to the king!" she protested.

Picking up the parcel of food Gavin had brought, Tack guided Ana out of the room, took the torch, and locked the door behind them. She twisted out of his grip and ran down the hall away from him.

Coming to a dead end in front of another door, she looked around for another means of escape.

Tack paused to pick up a blanket-wrapped bundle and a thick coil of rope before he followed her down the hall.

Her panic increased as he approached. "I can't go back to him! It would be kinder to kill me. Help me, please!" She met his gaze, feeling desperate tears welling in her eyes. "You wanted to help me before, but you didn't."

"I still want to help," he said. "The last time, I couldn't. The demons were right there. But now I will. I'm not taking you to the king. We're leaving."

"Leaving?"

"We're going home, Ana."

"What?" She stared at him in confusion. In the torchlight, she saw his eyes were gray. Just like... The world spun around her. After a few deep breaths, everything settled back into place. She grabbed the edge of his breastplate and pulled him closer to examine his face.

When she pushed the hair back off his forehead, she saw the familiar scars. "It can't be," she gasped.

"Before, I thought you recognized me." He sounded confused. "That night by the cliff, you said my name when I picked you up."

Underneath the long hair and beard, was Zarek.

"Zarek? But it can't be you..." With shaking hands, she pulled out his charm on its chain still around her neck. "He had this, and he told me he had tortured you." She leaned against the wall, feeling weak as her fear subsided.

Zarek's features froze. For a moment, he held his head in his hands and took a few deep breaths. Then he reached under his collar and took out an identical charm. "Remember? Two of them were made. My mother gave me hers when my father didn't return, before I left to look for you. That one belonged to my father."

"Oh, Zarek! Haldreth kept this on the table next to his throne. Is your father still here? Could he be a prisoner?" She pointed to the door. "There was a man in the room next to mine several weeks ago, but he's gone now."

"Do you think it could have been him?"

Ana remembered the man who had spoken to her through the crack in the wall. He had suffered beyond imagining. "Well, he recognized your song about the blacksmith, but he couldn't tell me who he was. I healed him, and I hope he got away."

"So he was here... I searched for years and never found him. I thought he was dead," Zarek said. "Maybe I'll get another chance to look for him after I get you home. But we need to get out of here now, before they come looking for Gavin."

"Whoever it was in the next room told me there was a passageway that led outside."

Zarek opened the door to that room. They looked inside, finding it empty. He explored it quickly and gazed up at the shaft in the ceiling. Faint moonlight shone down from an opening. "There is a passageway."

It seemed like a long climb to Ana.

"This is better than the plan I had," Zarek said, wedging the torch into a crack in the wall and studying the shaft. "If we can get out this way, no one will see you. Wait here while I check. Sit down and have something to eat." He handed her the parcel of food he'd picked up from Gavin and removed the bundle, setting it beside her. He slung a coil of rope over his shoulders and headed for the shaft.

Without intending to, Ana took a few steps after him, grasping his arm. "Please don't leave me."

He turned back and covered her hand with his. "It will only be for a few moments. You'll be safe. If I can find a good path ahead, I'll lower the rope to pull you up. Can you bring this up with you?" He nudged the bundle with his toe.

She took a deep breath, trying to calm herself. It was quiet. There was no sign of other danger. She met Zarek's eyes and nodded.

"It won't take long." He began to climb.

Ana sat down and opened the parcel of food. Despite her unease, it felt so good to eat. She turned her head, listening hard. Some small sound had disturbed the stillness. Had Gavin woken in the next room? Several times, the flickering light of the torch caused her to think she saw movement from the corner of her eye. When she turned to look, she saw nothing.

"Ana?"

She heard Zarek's voice clearly in the silence and walked over to the bottom of the shaft. In the dimness, she couldn't see him.

"Are you all right?" he asked.

"Yes," she replied.

"Good. Let's get out of here."

She picked up the bundle he had left on the floor. It gave a metallic clank as she slung it across her back.

A moment later, he tossed the line down, with a large loop at the end. "Put out the torch, so they won't know we were here. Are you ready?"

Ana was not. But she had to be. She snuffed the torch out against the floor, then tossed it into a dark corner. As her eyes adjusted, she noticed a faint light coming down the shaft. She grasped the rope. The rock looked sheer above her. How could she go forward? She wasn't strong enough to climb a rope.

"Slide the rope around you," Zarek instructed. Ana obeyed, placing the loop so she could sit in it.

"Are you in?"

"Yes."

"Just hold on, and I'll pull you up. Are you ready?"

Ana gripped it tightly and clenched her jaw. "Ready."

Zarek pulled slowly and steadily. When the rope grew taut, Ana held on even tighter. She clung to it as her feet left the rock and she swung out into space. All her muscles tightened as she held herself steady, and the effort sent a stabbing pain through her wounded ribs.

Ana set her jaw and closed her eyes, holding on.

CHAPTER FORTY-FIVE

YEAR OF WARDING 42, HAKVERE, ARA

ANA

ANA CLUNG TO THE rope as Zarek lifted her an arm-length at a time. She never felt herself slipping back. Even so, she kept her eyes firmly closed until she heard his voice nearby.

"Almost there."

He pulled her onto the rocks with him. Relieved beyond words to find solid stone beneath her, she clung to him. The pain in her ribs eased a little, and she tried to catch her breath.

"Are you all right? We need to keep moving." Zarek's voice echoed in the cavern surrounding them.

"Yes," she said, trying to slow her breathing. Of course, they had to go on.

Zarek took the bundle from her and slung it across his back. After coiling the remaining rope, he did the same with it. He offered his hand. "Stay close. I found a way down into the canyon."

It took only a few steps to bring them out into the starlight. A cold breeze rushed past them, and Ana shivered. She glanced up in gratitude to see the open sky above her, but turned hastily back to watch her feet as she stumbled through the rocks, following Zarek. The mouth of another cavern opened in front of them.

"We have to go through," Zarek said. "The passage is damp, and a little tight in one place, but we can do it."

Hoping he was right, Ana followed him into the dark.

Zarek crouched ahead of her as the uneven rock ceiling grew lower. Soon, they were forced to crawl. Ahead, the passage became still tighter. "This will be easier feet first." Zarek lay full length against the floor and slid through.

On the other side, the space must have been wider, because he turned back to help her. She could just see his outstretched arms as a little light came in through the other end of the passage.

Ana clenched her teeth and laid against the rock with her boots pointing into the hole. That position sent pain shooting from her injured side. Using her toes and elbow, she inched her way forward, scraping her skin against the rough rock.

"You're almost through," Zarek promised. "Wait there while I anchor the rope."

A moment later, she felt his hand on her ankle.

"Now slide forward carefully. There's a ledge about two feet below the opening." He guided her until she stood on solid rock.

Ana's stomach clenched when she saw the sheer canyon wall falling away below them. They stood on a narrow outcropping on the brink of the cliff.

She sucked in a terrified breath, gripping his arm. "H-How are we going to get down?"

"Do you see that ledge?" He pointed. She couldn't.

"The rope is long enough to get us there. From there, I see a wider ledge farther down and another beyond that. I think we can climb from that point."

"Zarek," she protested. "I can't climb with one hand."

"We've done this before," he reminded her. "Have you forgotten?"

Ana's mind flew back to years ago when she'd fallen and broken her arm. She'd been stuck on a ledge, unable to climb up or down. At the time, she'd been sure she was going to die. But she hadn't. Zarek had gotten them both down safely.

"I remember," she said. "I trust you."

"Good."

Ana closed her eyes against the sight of the deep canyon.

He swung the blanket-wrapped bundle to the front of his body. "I'm ready." His voice sounded steady.

Ana took a deep breath. He probably wasn't even afraid.

"I'm holding onto the rope. You need to climb on to my back. Can you do it?" He turned his back to her.

He wouldn't be able to let go of the rope and help her without them both falling to their deaths. Her hands shook. She set her jaw. No one was going to fall. Slowly, she grabbed his armored shoulder with her good hand. "Are you ready?" she asked him.

"Ready," he confirmed. He reached down with his free hand to offer her a foothold.

She stepped into his palm and hoisted herself up, pressing against the hardened leather covering his back, and wrapped her arms around his neck. Her good hand gripped her other wrist. She circled his waist with her legs, supporting some of her weight.

"Stay still," he warned.

He committed their weight to the rope and began lowering them down. Ana stared at the rock in front of her, not looking up, and definitely not looking down. Zarek lowered them steadily, using his boots to push them back from the cliff face. After a few moments, they reached the next ledge. Ana wasn't sure she'd been breathing.

The narrow, rocky shelf had barely space for them both to stand. Ana lowered her feet to the rock and released Zarek. She huddled as close as she could to the canyon wall and sank down to rest. Her ribs throbbed where she had pressed against him.

Zarek pulled the rope free and repositioned it for the next leg of their climb. They repeated the process twice more until they scrambled between the last boulders to reach the bottom of the canyon.

When they finally arrived at the edge of the river, Ana sank onto the damp stone, holding her injured side. She heard nothing but the sound of the water crashing over the rocks. They'd survived the climb, and they were outside of Hakvere. It was a miracle. Her cuts, her ribs, and most of all, her hand throbbed, and she felt weak. But they couldn't stay on this ledge beside the river.

"Can you walk?" Zarek asked above the roar of the water. "We need to get out of here."

He was right. They couldn't rest here. They had to get away. Ana couldn't bear it if she slowed him down too much and they caught him because of her. She got to her feet, still holding her side. It hurt to breathe, but they had to go on.

He pointed upstream. "We have to get out of sight before it gets light." He slung the bundle across his back. "Ready?"

She took a deep breath and nodded.

Ana followed him as they climbed through the rocks at the edge of the water. They kept near the canyon wall, choosing the driest path. Even though faint moonlight touched the tops of the boulders, Ana stumbled often. She had forgotten how hard it was to keep up with Zarek. The night felt endless, nothing but cold, slippery stones and water frozen into ice at the edges of the river. They followed it steadily upstream. Thankfully, the water was low, leaving them room to walk between the canyon wall and the water's edge.

Only a few thin rays of moonlight reached the bottom of the canyon. She saw his outline ahead of her in the dim light. How could he be Zarek? She had been introduced to Captain Tack at the banquet. His black armor and weapons had been memorable. The king knew him well and had trusted him with command of a portion of his army. Had Zarek been in Ara all this time?

The last time she'd seen him, he'd looked very different. How many times had he worn the crisp white-and-gold uniform of the Emperor's Guard? He'd been a fine young man, someone kind and helpful, who she could always trust to take care of her.

When she'd met Tack, she had felt no hint of recognition. He'd appeared unwashed, unkempt and unpleasant. His eyes hard and angry. And it had been years since she'd seen him. They were both older, and he had filled out. The thought that he could be Zarek had never even entered her mind. That night on the cliff edge, she hadn't known. In the aftermath of hitting her head, she imagined it had been him because the way he held her reminded her of Zarek. She'd wished he was there, but she had not recognized him.

The winter night was long and cold. Ana moved as fast as she could, but her long ordeal had seriously drained her. She felt light-headed, her side throbbed with pain at every breath, and her injured hand made it difficult to climb. Ana tried to hurry. She couldn't slow Zarek down and allow her father catch him. Someone would come looking for Gavin, and they would find her gone. Haldreth would send the demons after them.

Ana pushed on, using every bit of energy she could find and more. The night grew darker. How could that be? They'd been traveling for so long, it had to be nearly dawn. It had to. But the stars faded, the canyon blurred, and suddenly the rocks leapt up to meet her.

She had to get up.

"Ana!"

When she heard Zarek's voice, she tried to answer. She felt him lift her, and that was all she was aware of for a while.

Hours later, Ana woke as Zarek set her down on the rocks. With an effort, she forced her eyelids open. She blinked and focused. The first thing she saw was a knife in his hand. Instantly awake, she lunged away from him in terror. They were in a small space between two boulders sheltered by overhanging stone. She reached the rock face at the back of it and found nowhere else to go. Zarek had put the knife away, holding out his open hands. He looked at her with a calm expression.

"Ana, I would never hurt you," he promised, his steady gray eyes meeting hers.

She nodded, trying to slow her racing heart.

He came slowly closer. "I'm sorry I frightened you. I was going to borrow some cloth from your hem."

This was Zarek. He wasn't like her father or Gavin. He would not hurt her. She knew it, but after everything that had happened, she'd reacted without thinking at all. She gave a little nod. He took out the knife and cut strips of cloth from the hem of her dress. When he finished, he put the blade away. His hands were gentle and careful as he wrapped her wounded hand.

"Are you hurt anywhere else?"

"It hurts to breathe," she admitted, pointing to the injured place on her side. "Here."

"Will you allow me to look at it?"

She hadn't wanted to see the injury herself and felt reluctant to reveal it. But this was Zarek. He would never do anything to harm her. She began to undo the buttons of the riding dress.

Zarek turned his back, but not before she saw his face color slightly.

Ana pulled her arms out of the sleeves and lifted the bottom of her chemise to reveal her ribs. "All right," she said.

He turned back to her. Zarek no longer appeared embarrassed. Instead, fury burned hot in his eyes and his hands closed into fists.

Her stomach clenched, and she shrank away from him.

He blinked and stared at her. She could see when he realized his anger had frightened her. He took a deep breath, and his expression softened visibly. "Please forgive me, Ana." He pointed to her ribs. "Did Gavin do that?"

She nodded.

He reached out and, softly, his fingers brushed her cheek. "Striking you and using his knife on you wasn't enough?"

Ana didn't know how to respond to that question. She looked down at her side and saw ugly black bruising across her ribs. It had been better not to see it. Zarek was still watching her.

"Are your ribs broken?" he asked.

She didn't know. Probably. She gave a small shrug. Zarek reached out his hand. "May I?"

She nodded.

He explored the area with his fingers.

Ana clenched her teeth when he reached the most painful spots. "I think two or three ribs are cracked. Ana, why didn't you tell me last night? Everything we did must have been very painful. It was, wasn't it?" He stared at her.

"Yes," she admitted.

"Will you allow me to wrap it? It will help with the pain."

"Yes, thank you."

He cut a piece from the edge of the blanket and folded it into a soft pad. Using strips of cloth from her hem, he bound it snuggly over the injured ribs.

"It helps," she said, inhaling. "It doesn't hurt as much to breathe. Thank you."

He moved to her shoulder and neck, cleaning and bandaging the cuts. When he finished, she pulled the sleeves of the dress back over her arms and redid the buttons.

"You should rest now," he said.

She nodded, leaning against the rocks and closing her eyes. It was freezing, and she shivered as the chill of the stone leached the warmth from her body. Zarek sat beside her, and she finally warmed up enough to fall into a deep sleep.

When Ana woke, the sun hung low in the sky. She found herself wrapped in a blanket, huddled close to Zarek, her body pressed against him. His arm was around her. Even through the hardened leather of his armor, she felt his warmth and was grateful. She remembered their journey four years earlier. He'd kept her warm many times back then. It felt different now. His arm felt so right around her, and the feel of his strong body against hers made her want to be closer still.

She peeked up at his face and found him watching her. "You saved my life last night," she said. "Thank you."

"Ana, I..." He took a deep breath, his eyes sad. "Can you forgive me?"

She was confused. "What for? You rescued me."

"That night when you escaped and we caught you on the cliff edge, I wanted to help you, but I did nothing. I'm so sorry. I've never been so afraid in my life." The muscles of his jaw clenched. "I didn't know if he would kill you, and I couldn't stop him."

Ana remembered. "I knew you wanted to help. And I knew you couldn't."

"It was one of the worst things I have ever done." He shook his head "You were hurt, and I left you behind as if I didn't care. I'm so sorry."

"But what could you do?" she asked. "The demons were right there. If you had done anything, they would have killed you. I knew why you didn't try."

"Ana," he whispered, pulling her closer.

"I forgive you," she said. "I know you did the best you could."

"It's more than I deserve," he replied. "I promise I will never let anyone hurt you again."

Tears welled in her eyes, and she remembered a younger Zarek promising he would get her to the White City.

They got up and he picked up his things. Soon, they were walking again, making their way slowly up the canyon, climbing along the edge of the rocky riverbed. They headed north, away from Hakvere.

In the middle of the night, Ana paused, looking back over her shoulder and listening intently. The water crashing over the rocks masked other sounds. For a moment, she thought she'd heard something behind them.

Zarek had gotten a little ahead, and she hurried to catch up. He paused on top of a ledge and reached down to help her. Just as she grasped his hand, the sound behind was unmistakable. Demons.

CHAPTER FORTY-SIX

YEAR OF WARDING 42, ARA'S COUNTRYSIDE

ANA

T HE SHEKKAR WERE COMING. Ana drew in a ragged gasp, her heart suddenly pounding in her chest. She never really expected to escape her father's clutches, but now, if she acted quickly, Zarek could. There was no safe place nearby to enter the water. If they did, the river would sweep them away and crush them against the rocks.

Ana's eyes met Zarek's. "Go upstream! Find a place to get out of reach. I'm going back to draw them away. Run!"

"No! Ana, stop!"

But she tore her hand free of his and headed back the way they had come. The only chance of keeping him safe was for the demons to think she was alone. A memory flashed into her mind of Zarek's ruined body on the ground. That would happen again if the demons found him. Her stomach clenched.

A hand seized her arm, halting her flight. Zarek hadn't obeyed her instructions. Now his arms closed around her. Ana struggled, twisting and kicking. "No! If they find you, they'll kill you. Let me go!"

"Ana, please listen!"

"They're coming. Leave me and run!"

"Ana!"

His arms felt like iron bars around her, unyielding as she fought against them. She pushed against his armored chest.

"You're running back to them because you think it will save me?" he demanded.

"It's the only way!"

"Ana! You're the bravest, craziest person I know. Don't kill yourself before you listen!"

He pulled her closer until he held her immobile against his body. One arm across her shoulders and the other around her waist, deliberately avoiding her injured ribs. "Please, Ana? I left Ara because I have a weapon to fight the demons."

His words penetrated her panic. "You... what?" Ana drew in a breath and stopped struggling.

"I found the emperor's sword, Blackbane. I hope it will stop them, and I intend to try. It's a risk. But running back to them will mean certain death."

"You found a weapon that can defeat them?" A ray of hope penetrated her fear.

"Yes, Ana! Promise me you won't give up before I try? Please!"

She was shaking all over. She'd expected pain and death, and still wasn't sure she believed Zarek. Was what he said possible? Above the crashing water, a demon shrieked, and the foremost of the Shekkar came into view, rushing toward them through the narrow passage between the rocks.

Zarek released her, positioning himself between her and the deadly attack. He slid the bundle from his back and pulled the ropes loose to take out a long sword, tossing the rest to Ana. "Stay behind me in the rocks. Tell me if you see more of them."

When he drew the sword, the blade glowed faintly green.

The demon leapt at Zarek, claws outstretched. Ana clenched her jaws to hold back a scream. He slashed at the creature with the blade, and she heard it hiss in pain. Could it be true? Was it possible this weapon could harm them?

The injured demon rushed directly at Zarek as if it did not expect to be resisted. He blocked the poisonous claws with his blade. Ana didn't dare breathe. It tried to distract him with a feint to one side, followed by a sudden attack to the other, but Zarek was too quick. When he slashed at it again, the demon fell to the ground. He drove the weapon through it. With a final fading shriek, it lay still.

Zarek whirled to face Ana, the sword still in his hand. "Did it cut you?" She asked desperately.

"No. I'm fine. The sword worked. You… You would have died trying to save me." He stared at her, his eyes wide with disbelief. Then he lowered the sword, crossed the distance between them in two quick strides, using his free arm to pull her against him into a hug. "Ana!" She could feel him breathing hard. His arms were around her, her cheek pressed against his armor and the row of small knives across his chest.

"I didn't know," she said. "Why didn't you tell me about the sword?"

"I was going to! I thought if you were afraid, you would run toward me, not away. And never toward the demons. I thought I could tell you anytime." Zarek pulled her close again. "You are not going to die. Not today. Not tomorrow. Not anytime soon. Promise me you won't do anything like that again."

Wrapping her arms around him, she held him. He was here, and they were both alive. "I'm sorry, Zarek. But I couldn't stand to watch you die. What if all of them came at you at once?"

A shriek interrupted her question. Zarek pushed Ana back against the rock, standing in front of her, his blade ready as another demon charged at them, snarling.

Ana's chest constricted as she watched him battle. It seemed impossible that any person could stand against the Shekkar. Any slight mistake could be deadly.

The demon moved quickly, dodging to one side and then the other, attempting to find a way around the sword. It shrieked in frustration and rushed straight at him. Zarek drove the blade deep into its body, and after that, its efforts grew weaker. Soon, it lay on the ground beside its fellow. One more blow cut off its voice with a gurgle, and it lay still.

There was no time to celebrate. A third demon attacked, but after Zarek had dispatched it, the night grew quiet; the only sound, the flow of the water over the rocks. For a long moment, they waited, listening.

Ana felt a surge of joy. She ran to him and threw her arms around him. Zarek had fought the demons and won. "You did it!"

He was safe. They were alive, and they had a chance.

Zarek pulled her close, letting out a long breath of relief. "It's going to be all right now," he murmured. "I'll keep you safe. There's no need to put yourself in harm's way. We can do this. Do you believe me?"

She looked up at him. "I'm trying."

"You had no hope." His eyes were solemn. "That's why you were so ready to die. That's the second time I've caught you as you jumped." Zarek pointed to the ruined remains of the Shekkar. "Look at them. They aren't coming back. It's possible. I killed one demon in Bright Springs on the first night I met you and two more in the mountains when we ran for the Warding. Now, three more have died tonight."

"So only eleven left." She nodded. Maybe there was hope.

"Ana!" He stared at her, his eyes wide in disbelief. "You found out how many there are? How? I've been in Ara for years, trying to uncover that exact piece of information. Did the king tell you?"

"Not him." She shook her head and felt tears welling in her eyes. "My mother is alive. She's back there, and she told me. I wanted to help her, but I couldn't. She sent me away."

Zarek put his hands on her shoulders. "Allia's alive?"

She nodded, her chest aching with guilt and sadness. "I left her back there."

"We'll help her, Ana. When we finish killing the demons and get you home safely, I can return and look for her."

Ana felt tears coming faster now. "But you just escaped. You can't go back to Ara."

He put his arms around her. "That means I know my way around Hakvere. I'm sorry for everything that happened to both of you. But there is still hope. I promise."

A sob escaped her. "I'm sorry. I'm so tired and scared. I didn't think we had a chance."

He wiped the tears from her eyes with his thumb. "Can you make it a little farther? We'll get away from this place, and then we can rest."

How different it felt to be near Zarek now. Ana longed to stay in his arms. She wished she still had the ring, so she could tell if he felt the same. Even though he appeared forbidding, inside he was still Zarek. And holding him close was still the best thing in the world.

But the moment passed, and Zarek released her and gathered his weapons. He cleaned Blackbane's blade and put it back in its sheath. "Are you ready?" he asked. "I have supplies waiting—food, blankets, warm clothes. We just have to get to them."

Ana picked up the remains of the bundle that had held the sword. "What else do you have in here?"

He returned the sword to the blanket and rolled it again. "There are two more daggers like the one Emperor Callonen gave me when I left Sarine to look for you."

HALDRETH

Haldreth's lantern illuminated the long room full of artifacts. He set it down and rummaged through the collection of objects. Some were treasures, others were merely interesting. No one else was allowed in this room unless he brought them here, and he had only afforded the honor to a few. Several items appeared to have been subtly disturbed. Fury rose through Haldreth's body. When he found out who was responsible, he'd make them regret it.

Haldreth searched for the long slender box made of plain dark wood. When he found it on a shelf, he opened it. Instead of his father's enchanted sword, he saw an empty case.

Empty. His jaw clenched.

Just as Haldreth turned to storm from the room, it happened. Tonight, he had sent three of his demons to destroy Cirana after he had discovered she escaped from her cell. He was finished waiting for her to change her mind, to be less stubborn.

Since the Shekkar were bound to his will, his thoughts followed them. They fulfilled Haldreth's wishes, pursuing Cirana, and the first of them had nearly reached her when it stopped, unable to complete its quest. Something stood in its way. The demon struggled, trying to find a way around. It fought on until a shaft of deadly green light impaled it, and it exploded into nothingness.

Two more Shekkar followed the first. Haldreth had taken a few steps toward the door, when the first of the pair attacked. He expected it to sweep away any opposition. In a few moments, Cirana would feel its claws in her flesh. Haldreth would grant his daughter the small comfort of dying quickly. She wouldn't suffer for long. The demon charged forward, only to encounter the same mysterious opposition. It fought hard, trying to get past the enemy to reach its prey. Cirana was very near. She had no defense against them. Her soft skin would provide no resistance to their razor-sharp claws. She had no way to drive them back. Soon, those brown eyes, the same color as Haldreth's, would close forever. His will remained focused on her.

But instead of completing its mission, another demon died.

Haldreth yelled in rage. This couldn't be happening.

Drawn by the noise, Gavin appeared in the doorway, a lantern in his hand. "What's wrong?"

A moment later, the third demon met with oblivion, and Haldreth shouted again and threw the box. It crashed into the doorframe and splintered into pieces.

Gavin took a step back. "My king? What happened?"

"Someone is killing my demons!" Haldreth seized a glass jar from a shelf, throwing it toward the stone wall where it smashed into a carpet of broken pieces.

"I thought they couldn't be killed?"

"Someone has stolen Blackbane!" Haldreth punctuated his sentence by smashing a few more items. He stood, his breath ragged, trying to regain control. He had put too much time, effort and pain into his plans to see them ruined now.

"Are you all right?" Gavin asked.

Haldreth dragged in a long breath before he answered. "I'll make them pay," he said through clenched jaws. Picking up his lantern, he strode to the door, the shards of glass crunching under his boot soles.

Gavin backed out of the doorway, and Haldreth slammed the door shut behind him, locking it.

"Inform our army that we march at dawn," Haldreth ordered. "It's time to break the Warding."

CHAPTER FORTY-SEVEN

YEAR OF WARDING 42, ARA'S COUNTRYSIDE

ANA

THAT DAY, ANA AND Zarek climbed the treacherous path to the western rim of the canyon. They traversed narrow ledges above sheer cliffs where Ana feared she would fall and die. Beside them, a waterfall with columns of ice mingling with flowing water, crashed down into the rocky depths. In the end, they made it safely to the top and came out into a cheerless landscape of brown winter hills with patches of snow. Hakvere loomed behind them. "I hoped we were farther away," Ana said.

"Soon," he promised. "If we follow this river, it will take us back to Sarine." He pointed to the water that flowed from the west down into the canyon. "We have to move. There are soldiers nearby, and I need to keep you out of sight."

Zarek found a cluster of rocks where she could hide. They stood no more than waist high, but had spaces between them. When Ana sat down and pulled her knees to her chest, she was hidden.

"Good," he said. "Don't move. I'll be back soon."

With Zarek gone, she heard nothing except for the sound of the cold wind in the dead grass. The chill air went right through the thin fabric of her dress, and now that she sat still, she began to shiver. Her empty stomach pinched. The quick meal as they'd left the dungeon was long past, and she'd gone hungry for weeks before that.

At the sound of horses, Ana forgot her discomfort as her stomach clenched in fear. She froze, not even daring to breathe. A large troop of Aran soldiers in blue tunics rode by. She felt terribly visible. But Zarek had told her not to move, so she remained hidden in the rocks.

Finally, when they passed out of sight, she drew in a deep breath.

Where was Zarek?

Another group of soldiers rode past, even closer to her hiding place than the others. She tensed again. This time, she heard their voices as they stopped in front of the rocks. One of them was giving orders to the rest. His voice was cold, and he sounded angry. "The king sent us out two days ago, and we haven't found anything yet. But she can't have gotten too far. Six men go north, and the rest of you split up and check the edge of the canyon. We completed our search below. Keep your eyes open. And give me one of those extra horses. Sergeant Aman is still down in the canyon. He'll need a mount when he rejoins us."

"Yes, Captain."

Ana shivered. They were looking for her. Had Zarek already been caught? What could she do? The horsemen rode off in different directions until only the captain remained. He rode toward her hiding place, leading a spare horse. Ana's heart pounded wildly. Did he know she had hidden here? She tensed to run.

The man stopped. When he took off his helmet, she recognized Zarek. He had been the one giving orders. She took a deep breath and shook her head. He played his part extremely well.

He jumped to the ground. "Ana?" He pulled a blue tunic and dark trousers out of his saddlebag. Taking a deep breath to slow her racing heart, she looked in all directions. She saw no one else.

"Put these on, quickly." Zarek handed her the clothes. "They won't fit. Here's a belt."

Ana pulled the pants on under her skirt, got to her feet, and then belted them in place. She undid the buttons of her dress. Sliding her arms out of the sleeves, she dropped it and pulled the blue tunic over her head.

By the size, it was his and much too big for her. She rolled up the sleeves until she uncovered her hands.

"Here." Zarek lifted a set of armor over her head. A pair of black leather plates shielded her chest and back, and metal pauldrons covered her shoulders. The protective gear felt heavy and cumbersome, and didn't even come close to fitting. He buckled the plates together on each side and added a helmet that partially covered her face, then belted a sword to her waist. Standing back to examine her critically, he said, "Tuck your hair inside your collar."

Ana did as he asked.

Zarek nodded. "You'll be fine, as long as no one looks too closely. If we pass other soldiers, don't draw attention to yourself." He picked up her dress, stuffed it into his saddlebag, and tossed her a biscuit. "Eat while we ride."

As Zarek and Ana rode northwest along the river, they passed a few isolated settlements and farms, but the only people they saw were Aran soldiers. Ana felt her muscles tense when any of them got too close, but Zarek saluted and spoke to them. When she saw his face, it looked fierce, and his voice sounded angry. The people he spoke to were afraid of him.

She had to remind herself that it was an act. This was Zarek. She didn't need to fear him, and he had to play his part.

They rode a long way that day, passing swiftly through the hills. After a while, they saw no more soldiers. When the terrain allowed, they rode side by side.

"Where are we going?" Ana asked. "I've never been north of the Warding."

Zarek nodded toward the water flowing beside them. "If we follow this river to its source, we'll come to the northeastern boundary of the Warding."

"Will there be more soldiers there?"

"A few," Zarek said. "The king has sent most of his troops toward Iron Bridge. It's the most direct route toward the White City. But if we went that way, we'd have to get through the entire army without them discovering you. And there are many miles with no water nearby, which would make it even riskier for us."

"Will we reach the Warding in time?"

Zarek nodded. "This way is only a little longer. If anything happens to me, just follow the river."

By afternoon, Ana caught herself nodding in the saddle. They stopped in the shelter of a grove of trees. When Zarek offered his hand to help her down, she took it gratefully. She was so stiff and tired from riding that she leaned on him until she sat down, removing her sword and resting her back against a tree trunk. Her injuries ached, and she was exhausted.

Zarek unsaddled the horses, rubbed them down, and tethered them where they could reach grass and water. He brought his saddlebags, took off his helmet, and sat beside her, handing her a couple of biscuits.

"Good, aren't they?" he asked sarcastically as he chewed.

"I'm grateful to have them," she said honestly.

He took a long look at her, then nodded slowly. "I guess you would be after being locked up. It's nothing compared to the king's table, though. He has many faults, but he serves excellent food."

"That's true," she admitted. She remembered dining with her father, sitting so carefully, weighing each word before she said it, wearing some ridiculously ornate gown and a crown on her head. It was such a relief to get away. She never wanted to see him again. "I'd rather eat hard bread with you," she said truthfully, looking up at Zarek.

His expression softened visibly. When he smiled, it changed his entire face, and he looked more like the Zarek she remembered.

"I missed you so much," she said. "When we didn't hear anything, I worried you were dead. It's been so long. Were you all right?"

His smile faded. "It has been a long time. And I've been alone. There was no one to talk to and no safe way to send messages. Every moment, I pretended to be someone else, and I couldn't let them catch me. I got used to lying all the time and tried to stay focused on my job."

She had only been in Hakvere for a few months. He'd been there for years. How had he done it, alone and friendless? "It must have been awful," she said, leaning against him. "All this time."

He put his arm around her. "It was hard," he admitted. "But I'm fine."

"You did this to protect us."

"I promised long ago that I would keep you safe." He took a deep breath. "Ana..." He rubbed his hand over his face. "I'm sorry Haldreth took you. I would never have left you in Sarine unless I believed you were safe. Callonen swore to guard you. I never thought they'd be able to take you from the Warding."

"And I promised you I'd never leave it. Gavin tricked me," she admitted. "I was a fool..."

"He was your... friend?" he asked. "I'm sure he acted differently. A sincere, generous man."

"Yes. But it was all an act. Even Callonen didn't suspect. Gavin was a member of the Emperor's Guard."

"What?" Zarek exclaimed. "How did he manage that? Callonen knows everything about everybody. How did Gavin fool him? And you? You can tell what other people are feeling."

"Not anymore," she said, sadly. "Not without the ring. But even then, I didn't feel anything bad from him. I've never failed to sense someone's feelings before, and I guess I didn't realize it was possible. In Hakvere, I overheard Gavin talking to the king about a stone that would shield his true intentions from me. I assume it did the same for the Warding. The whole time, I never realized. But I knew I didn't want to see him anymore, and I was about to tell him so. Toren was with me in Hale Bridge, guarding me. Our old friend Rosie was injured. Without help, she would have been gone in a few moments. So I healed her. I don't know what happened after that, but I think Gavin must have killed him. Otherwise, Toren would have stopped him from taking me."

Zarek pulled her close. "I'm sorry. I didn't know Toren well, but Emperor Callonen always spoke highly of him."

"He didn't deserve to die because of me." Ana wiped her eyes.

"It wasn't your fault. Haldreth caused this. The whole plan must have taken years of preparation. He knows exactly how the magic works. This is the first time I've heard of anything that could shield someone from the Warding." Zarek shook his head. "I shouldn't be surprised they had the same idea I did. But I never thought they could get to you."

She heard the caring in his words. "You rescued me from Hakvere." Tears welled in her eyes. "I thought I was going to die in there."

❧

Ana and Zarek continued to follow the river upstream as it ran smoothly through the hills. The weather was cold enough to freeze the shallows, but the sky remained clear. That night, they walked together, leading their horses. Ana reached out and laced her fingers through his. He didn't object or try to pull away. His hand felt big and rough and warm in hers.

Suddenly, Zarek froze, listening. She heard them too. Demons. "Get up." Zarek boosted her into the saddle. "Take this." He handed her one of the wizard's daggers. "Ride out into the water."

Ana fastened the weapon to her belt and nudged the horse into the stream. The water was calm, but still fast flowing, deep in the middle, and icy cold. She felt grateful to the horse for standing in the water, so she didn't have to.

Zarek drew Blackbane and stood on the bank, waiting for the Shekkar. The black shapes ran along the riverbank, shrieking in anticipation. His horse bolted in panic, and Ana felt her own mount shift fearfully. She patted the animal's neck, trying to calm it. Were there too many demons for Zarek? She saw the sword flash, but it was too dark to see anything else clearly. He stood with his back to the river, and as they pressed their attack, he retreated a step into the water.

Some of the demons rushed toward Ana. They stopped at the bank, but the horse shied away from them. Despite her efforts to calm the animal, it plunged into the deeper part of the river. Freezing water soaked her legs, taking her breath away.

"Stop! Go back!" She tried to turn the horse, but the Shekkar were still behind her, and despite her direction, the animal plunged even deeper. Her mount was swimming now, but found its feet on the opposite side and climbed up the bank.

A demon shrieked right in front of them. The horse reared in panic, throwing Ana back into the water. She went under, and the current pushed her hard. She tried to swim, but the armor was too heavy. Ana felt the bottom and managed to find her footing enough to push herself into shallower water. As she struggled toward the bank, a black shape, dark against the starry sky, loomed above her. Ana staggered back, stopping waist deep in the water. The demon paced back and forth. It hissed, trying to reach her, but it couldn't. Instead, they stood there, facing each other. Ana took a few steps upstream, but she couldn't fight against the strong current for long. The horse had disappeared, and so had Zarek. She heard nothing but the rush of water and the insane voice of the demon.

The force of the current pushed her downstream. She stumbled and lost her footing on the slippery rocks.

The river took her, tossing her in all directions. She struck rocks, sending pain shooting from her injured ribs. As she washed up against a clump of debris that had built up midstream, she clung to the branches. Her body felt numb. She dragged herself farther out of the water.

On the bank, the demon kept pace with her. It stood just a short way off, hissing and trying to reach her.

Her head rested against the wet branches. Time seemed to stop. The demon waited on the shore, while Ana hung on to the mass of limbs. The river flowed by, while she grew colder every moment. Everything seemed to happen from a great distance. She fought to keep her eyes open, but she was so sleepy that her eyelids felt like lead.

CHAPTER FORTY-EIGHT

YEAR OF WARDING 42, SARINE-ARA BORDER

ANA

Zarek's footsteps splashed through the water toward her. "Ana!" She heard him calling her and blinked, seeing dawn light the sky.

The demon on the bank had disappeared, and Zarek forced his way through the water to reach her. She felt him pull her toward the bank and out of the water. Her limbs were frozen. She couldn't move. When he released her, she collapsed. The sound of the river seemed faint and far away. Her eyes closed.

Strong arms lifted her. Everything seemed confused and distant. She smelled wood smoke, then opened her eyes to see a fire burning. Shaking, she reached out gratefully for the warmth.

They were in a little sheltered hollow beside a large boulder. Zarek finished adding more wood to the blaze and knelt beside her to unbuckle her helmet and armor. Pulling off her sodden boots, he tried to rub some life into her frozen feet.

He must have found her horse, for it stood nearby, without its saddle. She didn't see the second animal anywhere. Zarek went to the saddlebags, pulled everything out, and spread it to dry on the rocks. He found a shirt that was damp, but not soaked, and held it near the flames. "This is the driest," he said, his breath showing in the chill air. "You need to get those wet clothes off."

She wasn't sure she could force her arms and legs to work, but her water-logged clothes were painfully cold. He tossed her the shirt and politely turned his back. She managed to pull off the wet tunic and pants and put it on. "Th-Thanks," she said through her shivers.

Zarek spread her wet clothes out with everything else. The warmth of the fire felt delicious, and she huddled close to it, warming her hands and feet.

Sitting here, shivering by the fire, reminded Ana of their earlier journey. The routine felt familiar. Fleeing from demons seemed to guarantee being constantly wet.

Zarek set his weapons aside, unbuckled his armor, removed it, then peeled off his wet shirt. It had been so long since Ana had traveled with him, and she hadn't seen his bare skin since before that terrible night in the mountains years ago, when the demons had attacked them.

He'd filled out considerably since then. She hadn't meant to watch him, but after a glimpse of his muscled torso, she couldn't make herself look away.

Zarek hung the wet shirt on the brush. When he turned around, her eyes fell on the scars on his shoulder and arm, and the long one across his chest. Her throat tightened, and her stomach clenched.

She drew in a shocked breath, and for a moment, she was back on the mountain, staring down in horror at his slashed and bloody form. The memory of the pain they had shared as she healed him was still sharp, even after all this time.

He heard the gasp and knelt beside her. "What is it?"

"Sorry." She shook her head to clear away the memory.

He sat down next to her and put his arm around her. "What's wrong?"

"I'm sorry," she repeated, huddling close to him. "I've never seen the scar before. When I did..."—she touched his chest with her fingertips—"I was back there, looking down at your body.

There was no way you could survive it, no way you could live. I thought I was watching you die, and I won't ever forget that."

"Me neither," he said, holding her close. "You saved my life. I'm not sure anyone else understands what that night was like. You're the only one who knows."

She nestled closer to him. "I'm so glad you're safe. We believed you were dead. I'd given up hope... We have missed you so much!"

"I missed you too," he whispered. "Is everyone all right back in Sarine? My mother, Callonen, all our friends?"

"Yes," she replied. "But Mirithel might still be mad at you."

He laughed. "She's been mad at me every day since I was seven."

Ana felt the warmth of his breath by her ear, and her cheek lay against his chest. She grew suddenly very conscious of his arm around her, the sensation of his skin against hers. It had never felt anything like this when they'd been together before, even though they had become very close through all the danger and trouble they'd shared. They'd spent every moment together during their journey. She'd come to know all his moods. He had protected her and helped her. They had laughed and cried together.

Ana still knew him well. But being with him felt so different now. She'd never felt such a magnetic attraction to anyone before. She wanted to reach out and touch him, to feel his smooth skin and hard muscles under her fingers, and in return, to feel the touch of his hands on her body. Being with Gavin had never felt like this.

"It will be all right, Ana. Soon, we'll be home safe again, and everything will be all right."

His fingertips brushed her cheek. "Rest if you can," he whispered. "We had a long night. Sleep for a little while."

Ana didn't want to sleep. She wanted to enjoy the way it felt when he held her. But exhaustion took over, and her eyes closed.

ZAREK

Zarek felt her relax against him as she dozed off. She still shivered, but she grew slowly warmer. Last night, he'd been frantic when the horse had thrown her into the river. Ana had caught herself on a pile of debris, so at least she wouldn't drown. But the night was freezing, the water, icy. Another demon had died last night. As soon as dawn broke and the rest of them had vanished, Zarek had gone to her rescue.

Now she was here, safe for the moment. He brushed a few silken strands of honey-colored hair away from her face. Moving carefully so he didn't disturb her, he tossed a few more pieces of wood on the fire.

In many ways, Ana was exactly the same as he remembered, delicate features, beautiful brown eyes framed by heavy lashes. She'd always been brave and pigheaded, and her bright smile was the same, showing a dimple on one side.

How had he never noticed before how lovely she was? Or the softness of her skin under his fingers? Had her lips always been that enchanting shade of pink? The desire to pull her closer and kiss her was new. He longed to discover if her mouth was as sweet as he imagined.

That night at the banquet back in Ara, Zarek hadn't recognized her on Haldreth's arm. He'd seen only a stunning young woman in a daring gown. Every man in the room had been staring at her. And every rational thought had left Zarek's head. He'd never seen anyone so beautiful. Then they'd announced the arrival of Princess Cirana of Ara and he'd realized who she was. He'd been furious that they had taken her outside the Warding when he thought she was safe.

Now he held her in his arms, her skin against his. It had been so long since Zarek had been close to anyone. During all his time in Ara, he'd been on his guard constantly. Even moments of friendship had been very rare.

Having her so close made him long for something that went far beyond friendship. Years ago, they had promised to be friends forever. There was no reason now to believe she felt any different toward him. But he couldn't help feeling differently toward her. Her touch awakened new feelings in him. When she gazed up at him, he wanted desperately to wrap her in his arms, to hold her close, and never let her go.

But that was crazy. This was Ana. She'd been his best friend. She looked up to him, trusted him. He could not take advantage of her like that. Especially not after what she'd just been through with Gavin.

Zarek brushed his fingertips along her neck. Her skin felt as smooth as silk.

He forced himself to keep his hands still. She sighed in her sleep and nestled closer to him, one hand resting on his chest.

She was driving him crazy.

The sound of hooves pounded loud and near, and Zarek cursed himself for allowing Ana to distract him so badly. "Captain Tack," a lazy voice drawled.

Zarek looked up to see a big, black-armored man on a horse. Three other soldiers flanked him. The man dismounted and came over to them, sitting on a rock by the fire.

"Captain Kaemar," Zarek said, nodding.

Ana woke with a little gasp as she heard him speak.

Kaemar grinned. "This is a pretty picture. Such a touching scene. Instead of leading your men into battle, I find you here, giving aid to a lady in distress." Kaemar's eyes followed the lines of Ana's bare legs. "She is lovely." He stared at Zarek and smiled coldly. "I've never seen you out of uniform before. And for a woman? For the princess? The king will skin you alive if he finds you with his daughter! He has plans for her, and none of them include you."

"I have done nothing to dishonor the princess. The king ordered me to find her. It's not my fault I succeeded before anyone else," Zarek said. He felt Ana's arms tighten around him. She was afraid.

Captain Kaemar looked her over again. "Give her to me. I'll take her back and split the reward with you."

Zarek pretended to deliberate. "A fair offer, unless you forget I found her first and take all the credit yourself."

"Would I do that, Tack?" Kaemar smiled. His voice had an edge to it now. "You'd better give her to me. I have three men with me, and you are alone."

"I'll take my chances."

"Don't be a fool, Tack." Kaemar gripped his weapon.

Zarek seized his own sword, stood up, and drew it. He pulled Ana to her feet beside him. They had their backs to the boulder. "Ride on, Kaemar," he said coldly. "I will guard the princess myself."

Kaemar drew his own blade. "I don't have a problem with killing you before I take her."

Zarek grinned and held his sword ready.

The other soldiers hung back, watching. He had seen Kaemar fight many times, and the man was average at best. Zarek would never allow him to take Ana.

Kaemar attacked with a yell. Their blades crashed together. Zarek ducked under Kaemar's blow and threw his shoulder into the other man, knocking him off balance so he stumbled awkwardly. Furious, Kaemar straightened up and attacked again.

Zarek stood his ground. He could read the other man's movements before he made them. He was ready for every thrust, anticipated every blow. This would not last long.

In a moment, he had knocked the weapon from Kaemar's hand. Zarek's sword swung in a graceful arc, slashing his opponent's arm below the edge of his armor. Kaemar yelled in rage and clutched the wound, blood flowing from between his fingers. Zarek delivered a hard kick to the man's knee, knocking him over. Cursing, Kaemar tried to rise, but his leg wouldn't bear his weight.

Zarek faced him, waiting.

"You're a dead man, Tack!" Kaemar snarled, pulling out a knife.

Zarek shook his head. How badly did the man want to die? A quick kick to his hand sent Kaemar's weapon flying.

"Kill him!" Kaemar commanded his companions.

Zarek slammed the pommel of his sword against Kaemar's head, causing the man to crumple. Seizing the reins of the fallen captain's horse, Zarek leaped into the saddle and turned to confront the other three.

Not as eager to engage after Kaemar's defeat, the three soldiers exchanged glances with each other and urged their horses forward. "Do you really want to fight?" Zarek glared at them, his sword ready. "The king ordered me to find her, and I won't enjoy explaining to him that things didn't go as planned."

They continued to advance, but by the time Zarek had crossed blades with the nearest and knocked him from his horse, the other two turned their mounts and fled.

Zarek dismounted and held the point of his sword against the man's chest.

The soldier on the ground held up his empty hands. "Please, Captain, don't kill me!"

Zarek paused for a long moment, turning to glance at Ana and then back to the man on the ground. "I'll leave you alive, but only because it's bad manners to kill you in front of the princess. Don't follow me. If I see you again, you're dead."

The man's eyes were wide with terror, and he nodded in agreement. Zarek swiftly gathered their things and saddled their horse. He kicked dirt onto the fire and buckled his sword around his waist. After helping Ana onto Kaemar's horse, he got on the other soldier's mount and took up the reins of their own to lead it, leaving Kaemar and his comrade on foot.

Zarek looked at Ana. "Are you all right?" he asked. She nodded.

"Follow me," he said.

They rode north toward the border, not stopping until Kaemar and his friends were far behind them. Out in the open, they fought against a steady chill wind. Knowing Ana needed to rest, Zarek searched for a sheltered spot where he could see anyone trying to approach. He stopped under a rocky outcropping that would guard their backs.

Zarek got off the horse and helped Ana down, trying not to let his eyes linger on the smooth skin of her legs. She looked frozen again; her bare feet, blue.

"Sorry," he said. "That was my fault. I shouldn't have let him find us."

"He p-p-probably saw the fire," she said through her shivers.

"Maybe," he said. "I should have been more careful."

"W-Were you worried? There were four of them."

Zarek shook his head. "Not for a second."

She desperately needed warmth and rest after last night. Zarek could see how tired and cold she was. He pulled out the damp blankets. "This one is almost dry." He gave it to her, and she wrapped it around herself gratefully.

"Thank you for protecting me," she said, stepping nearer and putting her hand on his arm.

"Didn't I promise I would?" he asked.

Her lips looked so soft. He shook himself mentally. No matter how much he wanted her, he had to stay in control. He forced himself to look away into the trees. "Try to get some sleep," he said.

Ana nodded and pulled the blanket tighter. She curled up with her back against the rock. Fear lingered in her eyes as she glanced around, watching for danger.

"It's all right to sleep," he said, sitting beside her. "Don't be afraid. I will keep watch."

It only took her a moment to doze off. He gazed at her as she slept. A sudden memory came back to him from four years ago. He and Dane had teased her about being a princess, traveling in disguise. They had all laughed about it then, none of them realizing that it was actually true.

Chapter Forty-nine

Year of Warding 42, Sarine-Ara Border

ZAREK

ANA AND ZAREK RESTED. Nothing disturbed her slumber while he kept watch. By midafternoon, it was time to move on. Dark clouds gathered, obscuring the sky.

It was possible that Kaemar would find other troops in the area and send them after him.

Zarek increased their pace. He needed to get through the Aran patrols outside the Warding before they were on alert, looking for the missing princess.

Ana and Zarek hurried on through the evening and into the night. The clouds thickened, and an icy rain fell. They kept ahead of the demons, but they had to cross the river again. Dawn found them soaking wet and dangerously chilled. It was unwise to build a fire this close to the Aran army.

They stopped in a clearing surrounded by thick brush. The rain had finally stopped. A few things in the pack had managed not to get wet. He tossed her a shirt. "Dry off and put this on." His breath hung in the cold air as he spoke.

Zarek was sick of being wet. He sat down, took off his sodden boots, and rubbed his feet. The soaked fabric chilled his skin, and he pulled off his armor, jacket and shirt. A glimpse of Ana changing caused him to close his eyes tightly. Creamy skin, soft curves. Given the choice, he would have looked at her forever.

He shook his head, furious with himself. No. He had to stay in control. He had to get Ana back into the Warding and then kill the rest of the Shekkar. He couldn't let anything, or anyone, keep him from getting it done. And Ana... What kind of man would he be if he took advantage of her? He could not—

When he opened his eyes, she stood right in front of him, wearing his spare shirt. "Zarek? What's wrong?"

"Nothing." His tone sounded harsher than he intended.

She took a step back from him, hurt plain in her brown eyes.

And it was his fault.

"Will you tell me?" she asked.

"No," he said, trying not to grind his teeth.

She took another step back, then turned away.

No. He couldn't stand to see her hurt. And if he told her the truth, she would pull away. She'd be frightened of him. She'd look at him like she'd looked at Gavin. But her brown eyes filled with pain, and he couldn't stand that either.

He went to her, bent to one knee, and kissed her hand. "Ana, please forgive me?"

"Zarek, what's wrong? With the ring, I could always tell what you were feeling. But not now. Now I can't tell what's bothering you. Have I done something to upset you?"

"You think this is your fault?" he asked.

"I can't imagine what else it could be. We could always talk to each other so easily, but now you're pulling away."

She was about as far as she could get from the truth right now.

Her eyes met his. "Tell me why."

He got back to his feet. "Ana, I know you. Until the last few days, it's always been easy to talk to you."

"What's different?"

She sounded angry now.

He took a deep breath. "Ana, I..."

She gazed at him with those beautiful dark eyes, and it almost made him forget what he'd been about to say. He began again. "I was gone for a very long time. I hadn't seen you for years. That night at Haldreth's banquet, he walked in with you beside him, and you looked... Well, I didn't recognize you. I never expected you to be in Ara."

"That does not explain why it would be difficult to talk with me."

"Ana, I'm not angry with you. I was angry with myself. Sometimes I feel out of control, and I can't risk that, not now. I need to get you home and finish my work. No one is safe until the demons are dead. Please forgive me for being angry. It's not your fault. It's not—"

Very gently, he put his hands on her shoulders and looked down at her. "It's not that I don't like your company. It's the opposite. I enjoy it too much. How do you think it feels when I've been alone all these years? When you look at me, and smile at me, and touch me, I feel..."

She gazed up at him with tears welling in her beautiful eyes. "It must have been hard to be so alone, but I promised to always be your friend."

"But I can't just be friends like when we were younger," he protested, lowering his hands back to his sides. "I've tried. When I look at you... You're so beautiful. I want to..." Zarek shook his head. His explanation was getting worse.

He clamped his jaw shut. She would be angry and want nothing more to do with him.

Instead, she smiled, leaving him baffled by her response. "You think I'm beautiful?"

"The most beautiful girl I've ever seen," he said honestly.

She stood on her tiptoes, resting her hands on his shoulders, and kissed him. Her lips were even softer and sweeter than he'd imagined. Perfect. It was perfect, and it threatened to make him forget everything else.

"Ana..." He took a step back, breathing fast. "You can't do that. I can't stand it. If you do that, I'll—"

"What?" Her eyes widened.

"I'll kiss you back," he warned. "I only have a certain amount of willpower, and I've wanted to kiss you ever since I saw you at Haldreth's banquet." Maybe she didn't realize how badly he'd wanted to.

"Why didn't you?"

"Lots of reasons," he exclaimed. "We were friends, and you trust me. I didn't think you felt the same. I wanted you to have choices, to decide what you want. I couldn't stand to be like Gavin."

"Those are the reasons you've kept your distance? Not because you didn't want me?"

"Yes," he said. "I hope you understand that—"

When she kissed him again, he stopped trying to object. He drew her close, his fingers tangled in her hair. Her arms slid around his neck, holding him tightly. He'd never felt anything like her sweet mouth on his. No one else could compare.

He pulled back for a moment. "Are you sure this is what you want?"

"I'm sure," she said firmly, kissing him again.

She felt exactly right in his arms, and he pulled her closer still. He wanted that moment to last forever, her lips moving against his, the feel of her soft curves against him. He put his mouth to the satin skin of her neck, and she gasped. The sound tugged at his heart and threatened to snap the remaining threads of his control. "We have to go..." he murmured, his lips still against her skin. He couldn't remember where exactly... but...

Regretfully, he pulled back.

He never wanted to stop, but he still had to get her past the Warding and the Aran troops. And they had to hurry.

"We have to go," he said sternly. But he grinned at her, and she returned the smile. He'd been wrong about how she felt, and he'd never been so happy to be wrong.

ANA

Ana and Zarek gathered their gear. She dressed in the uniform of an Aran soldier and tucked her long hair into her collar. Her mouth remained warm with the memory of Zarek's kiss. He'd been gone for so long, but she'd thought of him often during those years. He was still the same person, and she knew him well. His appearance might have changed, but inside he was the same young man who had put himself in harm's way to keep her safe. The memory of him had remained with her, and maybe she had unconsciously measured every other man she met against him. Now she was actually with him again, and it had been all too easy to fall for him. Or she simply realized how much she had cared about him all along.

Zarek held up the leather armor for her. She made a face.

He grinned and settled the armor into place. "You might not like it," he said, "but it will keep you safe." He slid his hands from her shoulders and stepped closer to her as he tightened the buckles.

She felt her breathing quicken. "I don't have much experience," she said, looking up at him. "Is this how you help all the soldiers put on their armor?"

"Raise your arms," he growled.

She lifted her arms and wrapped them around him, nuzzling his neck. "Is that better?" she whispered.

He stopped tugging on the buckles and kissed her. She would have stayed there in his arms, but they needed to go.

"I'm sorry," she murmured. "I didn't mean to distract you."

"Yes, you did," Zarek protested. "I'm very sure it was intentional."

She laughed and pulled back to do up the buckles. When they were done, she put her helmet on.

He hung a sword and a knife around her waist and an axe across her back.

"It's too heavy." She shrugged her shoulders under the extra weight. "I can't move."

"Then don't move," he said. "You just have to ride, and they need to think you are just another soldier. Don't speak and don't look anyone in the eye. Here, this will help." He removed the axe and hung it from the saddle.

Ana took a deep breath. Maybe Zarek wasn't afraid, but she was. If the Aran soldiers knew he had betrayed the king, they'd take both of them back to him. And her father would kill them.

She had to be honest with herself. Being killed was by far the best option if her father caught them. She felt butterflies in her stomach as they gathered the rest of their things and mounted. It was time. Zarek led the extra horse.

Her worries spun around in her head as they rode. But she tried to keep her back straight and follow Zarek. He seemed relaxed in the saddle and so much more comfortable wearing the armor and weapons than she felt.

Ahead, Ana saw a military camp ahead filled with Aran troops. There were so many. If she and Zarek were discovered, they wouldn't have a chance against that many soldiers. What if Captain Kaemar had arrived ahead of them?

Zarek rode up to the checkpoint and saluted the guards. As instructed, Ana made the same gesture.

"Good morning, Captain," the guard said politely.

"Good morning," Zarek growled. He sounded irritated.

Taking in his weapons and his hostile expression, the guard swallowed. "Where are you going, sir?"

"The king ordered us to gather information along the border, some special project he's planning for. I hope you have been doing your job here. Which one of your soldiers is missing his horse?" He stared hard at the guard, who swallowed again. Zarek handed him the reins.

"I will find out, Captain. Is there any assistance we can provide? Do you know where the border is?"

"Yes," Zarek said. "This is our third assignment in this area. Just keep a sharp lookout."

"Of course," the man said. "Good luck, Captain. And watch out. There are enemy soldiers just on the other side of those hills."

"They won't even see us," Zarek promised. Passing the guards, they rode into camp, through a cluster of tents, stacks of weapons, and groups of soldiers, maintaining an unhurried pace. No one questioned them.

At the far edge of the camp, Zarek saluted the guards as they left. The soldiers returned the gesture and watched as Ana and Zarek rode away.

When the troops were out of sight behind them, Ana's stomach calmed. They rode for the rest of the afternoon until the shadows were long. It would be dark soon.

They came to the base of a line of rocky hills, partially covered in snow, and had to lead the horses through them. The sunset had faded from the sky, but from the tops of the hills, they could see distant lights. They were almost home.

How many times had Ana thought she would never get back there? Now her long ordeal was nearly over. She could return to her life. She could see Callonen again...

Ana shook her head. It wasn't nearly that simple. They still had to save Allia. And they had to stop her father and his army or there would be no peaceful city to go home to. His army was marching toward the White City, ready to attack.

They led the horses over the uneven ground in the dark hills. Ana's knees and shins were bruised, and it was so hard to walk carrying all the extra weight, but she didn't dare lay aside the armor. At least the effort warmed her. On they went until finally they left the hills and the ground leveled out so they could travel more easily.

Zarek turned his head, listening.

"They're coming," he said. They mounted their horses and rode. She could hear the demons too, coming down through the rocks behind them. They urged their horses to greater speed. Where was the boundary? They had to be almost there.

Ana's horse stumbled in the dark, throwing her through the air before she hit the ground hard. She lay there for a moment, dazed.

But she couldn't stay here. The Shekkar were coming. She scanned the area for her horse, but didn't see it anywhere. There was no time to search, so she dragged herself to her feet and ran. Her muscles burned and her breath came in gasps, but she couldn't stop. She could hear the demons close behind her.

In a blind panic, she ran on. How long till she stumbled or couldn't run anymore? Then they would have her, and it would be like their journey years before when the demons had caught up with them in the pass.

She saw white spots in her vision.

But the demons' shrieks faded behind her.

Was it possible? Looking back over her shoulder, she saw them clawing at the invisible wall of the Warding. They couldn't come any closer. She sank to her knees, gasping. Where was Zarek?

He appeared a moment later, pulling his terrified horse behind him. "Ana! Are you hurt? They didn't touch you?"

"I'm all right," she said, still gasping for breath. She got back to her feet.

"Can you hold the horse?" he asked. She took the reins from him and tried to soothe the terrified animal.

Zarek drew Blackbane and turned back. "Stay away from the border," he said as he approached the demons.

She counted six or seven black shapes at least. But they couldn't cross the line. They stood shrieking and hissing, waiting for Zarek.

One of them, he killed quickly, almost easily, as it stood against the barrier. The others moved back after that.

When Zarek stepped outside the border, they attacked instantly, trying to surround him. He kept the Warding at his back, and when too many got close, he ducked back within the protected area. They followed as far as they could, and he drove the sword into another of them. It screamed and struggled, but Zarek cut it down. Another demon dead.

He kept fighting, but dawn was coming. A moment later, the Shekkar disappeared. He kicked the ground in frustration and walked back toward Ana. "I could have killed all of them like that. It's the perfect place to fight them."

"You killed two more," she said. "Only eight left. And we're home. We made it back to Sarine."

CHAPTER FIFTY

YEAR OF WARDING 42, SARINE'S COUNTRYSIDE

ANA

A CHILL DAWN SURROUNDED Ana and Zarek. For the moment, they were safe. Gripping the horse's reins, Ana's rapid breath steamed in the icy air. Zarek stood with Blackbane in his hand, staring back toward the Warding. The morning grew brighter around them.

A sudden pounding of hooves announced the arrival of four riders in the dark-green uniforms of Sarine. At the sight of Zarek with his sword drawn, two of them drew their own blades. The other two confronted Ana.

She looked from the sword point aimed at her throat up into a very familiar face, his eyes wide with shock. "Toren!" she cried. "You're all right! I feared you were dead!"

He put his weapon away immediately and yelled at his companions. "Stop! It's Lady Cirana."

At his words, his men backed up, keeping their weapons ready, staring at Zarek warily.

Ana pulled off her helmet. "Please, Toren, order them not to harm Zarek!" She went to stand between the men.

Toren's men lowered their weapons.

Dismounting, Toren came to face Ana. "You brought an Aran captain back with you, my lady?" He eyed Zarek uncertainly.

"He's not Aran," Ana protested. "We had to dress this way to escape. This is Zarek."

Toren stared intently at him. "Zarek? Weren't you the one who brought Lady Cirana to the White City four years ago?"

"That's right," Zarek said.

Looking unconvinced, Toren glanced at Ana. "Are you sure that's the same man?"

"Absolutely," she said firmly.

Toren stared at her for a long moment. His eyes came to rest on her bandaged hand, and his expression tightened in pain. "Whatever they did to you... it's my fault. Your safety was my responsibility, and I failed you."

"No, you didn't. He... deceived all of us. I was so afraid he'd killed you."

He took a sudden step forward and hugged her. "And you... you're alive. You're all right. I thought we'd never see you again. Emperor Callonen has been insane with worry. I've never seen him like that before."

Ana returned the hug, feeling her eyes fill with tears. "I'm home now. We'll find Callonen soon and let him know. What about you? What happened that day?"

Toren released her and looked down. "Gavin nearly killed me. For several days, I thought I was going to die. It took months to recover. I've only been back on duty for two weeks." Ana's mouth fell open in shock, and her eyes filled with tears. "No! You wouldn't have been hurt if not for me... I'm so sorry that happened to you. But you're recovered now?"

"Yes," Toren said, "except for the shame of being tricked by that spineless traitor. If I ever see him again, I'll..." He gripped the hilt of his sword.

"If I find him first, there won't be enough of him left for you to bother with," Zarek growled.

"What about Rosie?" Ana asked. "Is she all right?"

"She is anxiously waiting for news of you, but she's fine," Toren said. "She'll be so happy you're safe."

"Zarek helped me escape." Ana turned to meet his eyes and smiled. "He saved my life."

Toren held out his hand to Zarek. "The Empire of Sarine will be forever in your debt."

Putting his sword away, Zarek took the offered hand, allowing a smile onto his face.

"You'll go straight to the city and let the emperor know you're safe?" Toren asked, turning back to Ana. "We must finish our patrol and check in with the others or they will assume something is wrong. I can send two men with you."

Zarek met Ana's eyes and then glanced back to Toren. "I will stay here and fight the demons at the border. Ana should go back to the city." Zarek took Ana's hand. "I will only be a few days behind you."

Ana took a deep breath, considering her options. "We have an urgent message for the emperor. Haldreth is planning to break the Warding and send the Shekkar after him. His army is marching toward the White City now. They may already be inside Sarine." Toren exchanged glances with his companions. "We need to alert the rest of our troops patrolling the border. Do you know when?"

"It could be any time," Ana said. "Zarek found Blackbane, and he's been killing the demons one by one. Once they are gone, we will have a chance of defending Sarine."

Toren's eyes widened as he noticed the legendary blade at Zarek's side.

"We need to let Emperor Callonen know there is hope," Zarek said. He turned to Ana. "Go with them and take the message to him. I'll meet you at the city. You'll be safe there."

She saw his determined expression. But she would not leave him. "What will you do when the Warding falls?"

"I'll take out as many of them as I can before that," he said. "I'll keep fighting. All the more reason for you not to be with me when it happens."

Ana squared her shoulders and straightened to her full height. "We will send these soldiers to take Callonen the message. I'm staying with you."

His eyebrows drew together. "That would put you in more danger."

"Will it? The demons are following me. As soon as the Warding falls, they will hunt me. They won't wait here for you to kill them. Please?" She put her hand on his arm. "Don't try to make me leave. I need you. The sword is the best protection I have."

Zarek didn't look happy, but she had forced him to consider her viewpoint. Beneath his beard, his jaw was clenched.

She turned back to Toren. "Which of you will take our message to Callonen?"

Toren nodded toward two of his men.

Ana turned to them. "Let the emperor know everything we learned. Zarek has already killed nine of the Shekkar, and we will try to destroy the remaining eight. But everyone needs to be ready to fight."

The two men nodded.

"Ride to the city as fast as you can," Toren instructed them. They turned their mounts south and rode off at a gallop. He put his hand on Ana's shoulder. "I have to meet the others, but when that is done, I'll gather some men and come back to find you. Take care of yourself in the meantime."

"You too," Ana answered. "There's a large group of Arans not far away. Watch for them."

Toren nodded. "We will." He looked at Zarek. "Everything depends on you. Please keep her safe."

"I swear on my life," Zarek said, his hand on his sword hilt. Toren and his remaining companion mounted and rode away, following the border.

Ana and Zarek took shelter in a thicket of trees not far from the Warding, where the dense growth would hide them. A little stream moved past, slowing into a wide pool crusted with ice, before flowing on its way. He unsaddled the horse, then watered and rubbed it down.

Ana sat down nearby with her back against a tree, watching for any sign of danger. "Get some sleep. I'll watch for a while."

Zarek nodded in agreement and spread a blanket on a patch of dry grass and laid down. He drifted off immediately.

The day was quiet, and her eyes strayed to Zarek as he slept. As her gaze traced his features, realization flooded through her. Even through the years they had spent apart, he was the same man. She loved him. The feeling filled her entire body, and she knew it wouldn't change. Being with him again had only reminded her how much she had already loved him for years. He was the one she wanted to spend the rest of her life with. There had never been anyone else, not really. No other man could measure up.

Zarek's face was peaceful. Anger had vanished from his expression, as had the guarded look she'd so often seen him wear. He had been through so much, alone among his enemies, and was truly a remarkable person who had given many years of his life to help his people. His abilities, which could have been used to gain power or fame for himself, instead, had been used to protect others. He had been willing to stand against the man who wanted to destroy Sarine.

The king of Ara. Her father... who intended to slaughter everyone she cared about.

The afternoon passed slowly. Ana saw no sign of soldiers, and everything was quiet. As the sun dipped behind the distant mountains, shadows fell over them. She shivered as the temperature dropped. Before she had a chance to wake him, Zarek sat up and stretched. When his eyes met hers, he smiled.

She returned his smile, despite the knots forming in her belly.

It would be dark soon.

They shared a quick meal, and Ana rolled up their blankets while Zarek saddled the horse and tethered it in the trees. He checked his weapons. Blackbane hung ready at his side, beside one of the enchanted daggers.

She put her hand on the matching knife at her belt.

"Keep your weapon close, just in case..." His voice trailed into silence. "Wait for me here." He nodded at the pool. "If something goes wrong, stay in the water, out of their reach."

The light was fading quickly, and he turned toward the Warding. Ana took his arm and pulled him back. "Zarek, wait!" She couldn't let him go without telling him what she'd been thinking.

She threw her arms around his neck and kissed him. "I love you, Zarek. I had to tell you—"

"Ana." He pulled her close.

She never wanted that moment to end. His strong arms held her, and her lips pressed against his. Even without the ring, she felt the love, desire and desperate fear of loss in his kiss. But their time was up. Darkness had fallen, and the demons were coming.

They both heard a shriek in the distance, and Zarek drew back. He made a final check of his weapons and headed toward the Warding.

CALLONEN

Callonen, son of Caldoreth, Emperor of Sarine, stood on the tower and looked out over the White City, while the last light of sunset faded. The city was hushed, despite being packed with people who had come from the outlying lands for protection.

The latest news from the border reported that the Aran army was massing outside the Warding, preparing to invade. Callonen's forces were ready to meet them. The Warding kept the Shekkar out, but it did not prevent human invaders from entering his lands. His army could defend against men; the demons, they had no defense for. Maybe the walls would stop them, but not all of Sarine's people could fit into the city.

Callonen had just turned to head inside when a sudden shock of power struck him. He saw nothing; he only felt it. And it was directed at the Warding. His chest constricted as the surge rushed through his body. His knees buckled, and he fell, each of his muscles clenching.

It passed after a moment, and he lay stunned, trying to breathe.

His guards ran to his side and bent over him. "Emperor! What is it?"

He couldn't speak, couldn't do anything for several moments. Finally, he was able to get some air into his lungs. With their help, he slowly staggered to his feet. His body felt weak, and he wondered if he would fall again. He heard no one else's thoughts, felt no one's emotions, and sensed nothing beyond his own physical senses. For the first time since his father had died, Callonen was completely alone.

"What is it? What can we do?" the guards asked.

"I can't—" Callonen struggled to speak. "It's gone. The Warding is gone."

❧

As the afternoon lengthened, a widening column of refugees streamed through the city gates. Another wave of his people seeking protection.

Callonen watched from the top of the wall. It had been two days since the Warding failed. How quickly could the demons travel? They would probably arrive tonight.

By nightfall, everyone was inside. The space within the wall overflowed with people, and the gates were shut and barred. Darkness covered the city.

Two large braziers had been lit just inside the gates. General Gray posted several guards there, while many more patrolled the battlements.

Callonen stood among his men, Gray's solid presence at his side. "We've set up the defense, Emperor," the general reported. "This afternoon, they finished filling a pool of water in front of the gates. We hope it will offer some protection."

"Thank you, Gray," Callonen said.

"You should move someplace more secure," Gray advised.

"No," Callonen said. "The demons will look for me. If they find a way in, I'm going to meet them. Otherwise, they will slaughter anyone they encounter."

"You don't know that."

Callonen tightened his jaw. "After all this time? After everything that's happened? I know."

As the night deepened, he kept watch from the walls. The demons could arrive at any time.

CHAPTER FIFTY-ONE

YEAR OF WARDING 42, SARINE'S COUNTRYSIDE

ANA

ANA WATCHED ZAREK DISAPPEAR into the darkness. She wasn't far from the Warding, and she could hear the horrible voices of the demons calling to each other. Several of them shrieked, probably announcing Zarek's arrival. From this distance, she could see only a faint glow of green from his sword blade.

So far, the protection of the barrier held. Zarek would be safe fighting them. He had to be. Ana felt a strong temptation to leave the safety of the water's edge and creep nearer to find out what was happening.

She took a few steps away from the pool. With great effort, she stopped herself. Zarek was all right. He would protect himself. Gripping the hilt of the wizard's dagger, she paced. For several long moments, she listened to the distant sounds of battle.

Another demon shrieked. Abruptly, she realized the glowing green blade was moving fast, coming back in her direction. She knew at once what had happened.

The Warding had broken.

Zarek sprinted toward Ana and the safety of the water. She could barely make out the black shapes of the Shekkar as they pursued him. How many were still alive?

The glowing sword blade gave a sudden jerk, as if he had fallen. Ana's stomach clenched in terror. Had they caught him? A demon shrieked in mortal agony, and she saw his sword moving toward her again. But now the Shekkar were between them, running straight for her.

Ana retreated into the pool, gasping as the icy water soaked her boots. She drew her dagger.

In the dim light, she saw four demons on the bank snarling as they reached out for her.

Zarek struck one down as he charged into the water, breathing hard. "Ana? Are you all right?"

"Yes!" she assured him.

He turned back to the three remaining demons. Standing just out of their reach in the shallow water, he held the sword ready. With his left hand, he drew his dagger. The demons slashed at him with their claws. Zarek blocked them with his blade.

The Shekkar spread out along the bank. One of them shoved him so he stumbled to one side where another of them reached out to slash at him.

Ana lunged forward to block its blow with her dagger before it could reach him.

The creature's claws grated against the blade, and it swung at her with its other hand, forcing her to jump back out of reach.

"Ana, get back! Please!"

Why would he say that when she'd just prevented the demon from slicing his arm?

Zarek drove his blade into a demon's throat, and it crumpled with a gurgling cry. Only two remained.

"Don't risk yourself," he ordered.

There were only two demons left. Zarek killed another, but moving forward to deal the fatal blow allowed the remaining one to slash at his arm.

It had hit him.

"No!" Ana screamed. "I could have stopped it!"

From the sound of his voice, his jaw was clenched. "Just keep yourself safe. It's already too late for me."

Her stomach dropped. No. She felt numb and dead inside as the realization flooded through her like icy water. They had already poisoned him.

Zarek kept fighting, though his movements grew slower. Only one demon left. They couldn't let the last one escape.

Moving swiftly, Zarek charged forward and drove his blade through the demon's chest. It slashed at him, and Ana heard him gasp in pain. The last demon fell to its knees. Zarek drove his blade twice more through its body until it stopped moving.

He left the water, slowly, methodically retracing his steps, making sure each demon was dead.

The night was now silent. Ana didn't hear a sound around them. With the dagger still in her hand, she stepped out of the pool and followed him.

Zarek walked back to the line where the Warding had been. He was counting their fallen enemies. "Eight," he said when they reached the last one. "That's all."

Ana ran to him and threw her arms around him. "You did it! You killed them! Sarine has a chance now."

"Yes."

"But you—" She burst into tears. "Zarek, no!"

His arms tightened around her. "I'm sorry, Ana. There were too many. When the Warding fell, I ran, but they were too close."

Her mind flew back to the moment when she saw the sword fall in the darkness. Was that when it had happened?

She wiped her eyes and took a deep breath. Maybe they would still fail, but she couldn't give up yet. "My father has the ring, and he's heading for the White City. If we can find him, we have a chance. Let's ride."

Zarek had left the horse saddled and ready to go. He mounted and pulled her up behind him, and they rode away in the faint moonlight.

CALLONEN

Callonen spent most of the dark hours on the walls keeping watch. The night remained silent with no sign of the Shekkar. When dawn was only a couple of hours away, Callonen yielded to General Gray and agreed to get some rest.

After a few brief hours of sleep, Callonen donned his armor and went back to the city walls with the general. Sarine's troops were in position to defend the walls and gates. An army approached. These weren't demons, but men in the blue uniforms of Ara. Why hadn't the Arans attacked during the night, when the Shekkar could have fought beside them?

The troops marched closer, stopping just out of bow range, while a small group rode forward. They carried the blue banner of Ara. A tall man on a dark horse led them. He wore black armor and a helm that hid part of his face. A dark beard covered his chin, but Callonen recognized him. And there was no mistaking that voice.

"I want to speak with Callonen, Emperor of Sarine."

Haldreth. His long-lost brother had come home. Callonen seized a bow from a soldier, nocked an arrow and drew, taking aim at Haldreth's throat. "Tell me why I shouldn't shoot you right here!" His arms trembled with the need to fire. Here was the man who had taken Allia, likely tortured and killed her. He'd sent Gavin to steal Cirana.

Haldreth laughed. "Is that any way to greet your brother after all this time?" He stopped laughing and stared at Callonen. "Don't shoot. I brought someone with me to ensure your good behavior. If you harm me or any of my people, she will die immediately."

Callonen lowered the bow, his heart hammering in his chest. They had Cirana. What was he going to do? What would Haldreth ask for? Callonen's insides twisted like snakes.

"Don't worry, brother. I want to talk first."

"You brought an army here just to talk?"

Haldreth laughed again. "Oh, no. They're ready to attack the city on my command. But first..." He gestured to one of his men, who rode forward.

When Gavin took off his helmet, Callonen's hands raised the bow again before he could stop them. As much as he wanted revenge, he couldn't risk them harming Cirana. His jaw clenched and with tremendous effort, he lowered the weapon.

"I trusted you," Callonen spat. "You claimed to love Cirana and then betrayed her."

Gavin didn't reply.

It was Haldreth who responded. "Cirana belonged in Ara. She was born there, after all. And now the power of the ring will remain in my control."

Gavin raised his hand to reveal the healing ring.

Haldreth turned back to face Callonen. "You should be grateful the Warding is gone, otherwise you would know everything about Cirana's experiences during her time as our guest."

Feeling his muscles slacken, Callonen sank to one knee. His deepest desire was to protect his loved ones, and he had entirely failed at that. Tears stung his eyes. He loved Ana as if she were his own daughter. But in the end, he had failed her, and everyone else he loved. He reached inside his collar and took out a battered silver band hung on a chain. Allia had intended to put her father's ring on his hand when they married. He closed his fist around it.

"Callonen?" Haldreth called. "Don't go yet. I came to present you with an offer."

Forcing himself back to his feet, Callonen looked down at his brother.

"I'll make this an easy decision for you," Haldreth said. "I will order my army to retreat. We won't attack the city or harm anyone. All you have to do is walk out here alone and give yourself up. It's time you and I resolved our differences." Summoning another horse forward, Haldreth commanded, "Bring her!"

One of his guards rode up with a black-shrouded figure in front of him. Haldreth pulled the cloak away, and Callonen saw a golden-haired woman in a white dress.

It couldn't be.

For a moment, Callonen's heart stopped. Their hostage wasn't Ana. Did this mean that Haldreth had killed her?

Haldreth did not allow time for his brother to cope with the shock. "Come out now or I will kill Allia."

She struggled against the man who held her, very much alive. "Don't listen to him, Cal!"

Haldreth struck her with the back of his armored fist. Her head snapped back at the impact and blood welled on her cheek. The guard behind her held her arms, and Haldreth drew his knife, pointing it at her heart.

Callonen saw her stiffen as his brother pushed the point into her skin. A stain of red blossomed on the white fabric.

"Stop!" Callonen yelled. "I'll come!"

"No!" Allia screamed. The guard behind her put his hand over her mouth, silencing her.

Haldreth smiled, lowering his knife.

Callonen turned to General Gray. "Keep the city safe. Guard the gates at night so the demons can't get in." He pulled the chain over his head and held Allia's ring out to Gray. "Please keep this safe for me. Don't let anything happen to it. Hold on to it until I ask for it again."

Gray nodded and took it.

Callonen looked around at his men. They all stared at him in disbelief. These were his friends, men who had been at his side for many years. "I thank you all for your excellent service," he said, unbuckling his sword belt and setting the weapon aside. He turned toward the stairs down to the gate.

"Emperor, you can't do this!" Gray put a hand on his arm.

"My whole life I've put Sarine first! You cannot ask me to watch Allia die." Callonen threw off the hand.

"But he's going to kill you!" Gray protested.

Callonen stopped and turned to look him in the eye.

"He will torture you," Gray said.

"I know." Callonen turned to leave.

Gray didn't try to stop him as he walked down toward the gates. It would be over soon. The Warding was broken, and the demons would kill him when night fell. With Callonen gone, hopefully Haldreth wouldn't harm anyone else. Without the Warding, Sarine had no more protection against the demons and Haldreth would control everything.

"Open the gates," Callonen ordered. His stomach knotted.

The guards stared at him with wide eyes, but no one dared disobey him. The heavy gates opened, and Callonen passed through them alone. As they shut behind him, he approached Haldreth's men. He could see Allia. A guard still held her, but she was alive. And she had been all this time. Her eyes were dark with despair and there was blood on her cheek where Haldreth had struck her, but she was just as beautiful as he remembered. If anything, he'd forgotten exactly how lovely she was. Or maybe it was just that he'd never been happier to see anyone in his life. But not like this. Gray was right. They were going to die. At least he had seen her one last time.

Haldreth called up to the men on the walls. "Don't worry. We won't harm him," he promised. "We will have a friendly chat, work things out between us, and you'll have your emperor back soon." From horseback, Haldreth glared down in triumph at Callonen, who met his brother's eyes, but didn't speak. What was left to say? The Arans brought a horse and Callonen mounted. A guard held the reins. As if Callonen would try to bolt after all of this.

They rode away, and Callonen didn't look back at the city. He glimpsed Allia a few horses ahead. She turned and met his gaze for a moment, and he recognized the heartache in her eyes.

Seeing her beloved face made him feel more alive than he'd felt for many years. She looked thin, worn and older now. The pain Haldreth had caused would have changed her. Everything that had happened during these years apart had changed him too. Did she think he hadn't tried to rescue her? Or that he'd forgotten her? He knew he still loved her, no matter what.

The thought gave him no hope. They were both in Haldreth's power, and they were going to die. At least it would finally be over. Without the Warding, there was no longer anything forcing him to keep going. He could finally be at peace. All he wanted was a chance first to tell her how sorry he was.

They rode over a hill into a little dell where a few patches of snow lingered. He saw a peaceful farm with a patch of trees behind it. The place was empty now, and a camp of Aran soldiers surrounded it. They took Callonen past the tilled fields to the edge of the woods. "Now," Haldreth said, "we can deliver a proper greeting to my brother."

The soldiers laughed and dragged Callonen from his horse. He saw others tying Allia against a tree. As he glanced toward her, one of the men slammed his fist into Callonen's face.

"Wait, wait," Haldreth ordered. "Just a moment." He stepped in front of Callonen. "We can't let any blood get on his clothes." He fingered the edge of Callonen's white tunic.

When he nodded to the others, they jeered and surrounded Callonen, pulling off his armor, clothes and boots, even the signet ring his father had given him just before he died. They gathered everything and took it into a nearby tent, leaving Callonen standing there in his underclothes. He felt so alone. No guards, no friends, no Warding.

"That's better!" Haldreth took off his helmet and rubbed his bearded chin, staring at Callonen appraisingly. "You look good, brother, you really do." He touched the scar on Callonen's chest, a reminder of the day he had stabbed his brother in the heart, a day Callonen would never forget.

Haldreth turned to his men. "Where is Cob?"

A short, nervous-looking man hurried over to them. He held a razor and a pair of scissors. Another servant followed him with a small table and chair. Haldreth beckoned them forward. "Take your time. Get a good look." The man stared at Callonen intently, then he nodded to Haldreth.

"You! Bring that chair over here," Haldreth ordered. He sat down, and the barber copied Callonen's haircut.

When Cob had finished, he handed Haldreth a mirror. "The left side is uneven, idiot!"

Cob rushed to correct it.

Haldreth consulted the mirror again. "That's better."

The barber proceeded to give Haldreth a shave.

When Cob finished, Haldreth nodded to his men, and they shoved Callonen against a tree a few paces away from where Allia was bound and tied him to it.

Callonen tried to prepare himself for the pain. He was going to die. In the end, his brother had won.

CHAPTER FIFTY-TWO

YEAR OF WARDING 42, SARINE'S COUNTRYSIDE

CALLONEN

BLOWS CAME AT CALLONEN from all directions. He clenched his
jaw and tightened his muscles. Something smashed into his
left knee, and pain radiated up his leg. He would have fallen if
it weren't for the ropes holding him. A hammer-like blow struck
his right arm below the shoulder. He had stayed silent until then,
but he screamed as the bone broke. Everything seemed distant
after that, except the pain. It started in his arm, but it spread
everywhere. He couldn't think, couldn't do anything.

The blows stopped for a moment, and Callonen inhaled, trying
to clear his head.

Gavin stood in front of him. The others backed away a
little. The traitor raised his knife and leaned close to Callonen,
whispering, "I used this blade on Cirana."

"No!" Callonen cried. It was too late. There was nothing he
could do now to help her.

"I made sure she suffered."

Callonen shut his eyes, trying to block out the image of Cirana
captive in Ara.

White-hot pain exploded from the side of Callonen's head. Blood poured down his neck onto his shoulder, and Gavin dropped a severed ear to the ground.

Callonen sagged against the ropes, gasping. Gavin stepped away, and the other soldiers pulled back. For a moment, Callonen just breathed, and the absence of any fresh injury seemed a relief. He tried to get control of himself. The shouts and mocking laughter stopped abruptly.

He raised his eyes a little.

The group of soldiers parted to make room, and Callonen saw himself walking nearer—white tunic, silver armor, his favorite boots, and his signet ring.

I'm dead. I've died, and I'm looking at myself.

Blinking hard, he looked down at his battered body, his bare feet. Still here.

It was Haldreth.

He walked forward to face Callonen. Now that he'd put on Callonen's clothes, the effect was uncanny. "Enjoy your time out there, dear brother." Haldreth paced back and forth in front of him. "I regret I can't stay, but I'll be back. You must remain alive long enough to provide every bit of information I need. Then your time will be over."

"It won't work," Callonen mumbled through swollen lips. "You haven't been here in over twenty years. So much has changed."

"That's true," Haldreth admitted. "But Gavin recently spent a great deal of time near you, observing every part of your life. After your reaction to him this morning, I'll have to keep him out of sight, but he'll still be close at hand."

Callonen's brief hope collapsed. It was true. Gavin could fill in many of the missing details, maybe enough to convince everyone.

"If you try to stop me, it'll only be worse for her," Haldreth said, drawing the dagger. He turned toward Allia, where she remained tied against a tree. With a careless slash of his blade, he left a long cut across her arm. She gasped in pain, and red blood flowed down her sleeve, standing out sharply against the white of her dress.

"Stop!" Callonen cried. "Don't hurt her. You've already caused enough pain."

"There's no such thing. I'll see you soon, brother," he said, mounting a horse. In a moment, he was gone.

Callonen stared at Allia, unable to look away. After missing her for so many years, he could never get enough of her. He longed to touch her, to remove the ropes that bound her and bandage her injuries and comfort her. But he couldn't move. She gazed back at him, her golden hair hanging loose and one side of her face bruised and cut where Haldreth had hit her. Dried blood stained her dress.

"Callonen." She said his name softly, so no one else would hear.

He could see the mist of her breath in the chill air.

"I'm sorry I ruined your life. I failed you. I failed everyone."

Tears welled in her eyes. "None of it was your fault."

"But I should have seen. I should have known what he was going to do. You warned me about him!"

"No one knew what he was going to do."

"I can't ask you to forgive me," Callonen said. "But I had to tell you how sorry I am. I would give my life to make you happy."

"Callonen...?"

He couldn't see her anymore. Everything spun and blurred around him.

Pain and cold dragged Callonen back to consciousness. The coarse ropes bit into his chest and arms as the rough bark of the tree scraped against his back. He shivered uncontrollably. The night air stole the warmth from his body.

Where were the Shekkar? He'd expected them as soon as darkness fell. Were they in the city killing his people?

And Allia?

He raised his head to look at her. In the dark, he couldn't see her face. Several guards stood at their posts, not far away. It was too late for him. He couldn't save himself, but he had to do something to help her.

His brother's threats echoed in his mind. There must be some way to free her. Pulling against the ropes sent waves of agony from his arm, and he passed out again.

When Callonen opened his eyes next, the sun was up. It wasn't much warmer, but enough to keep him alive. He didn't even have the energy to move. Pain burned through his body. Maybe it wouldn't be such a bad thing if his brother finished him. But what about Allia? Callonen could sense her. She was only a short distance away, hurt, cold and afraid. He could feel it.

It was the Warding that provided him insight into her feelings. But wasn't it gone forever?

He sensed she had done things she was ashamed of in order to survive. Fear and desperation had driven her to violence. She felt a terrible weight of guilt for helping Haldreth summon the Shekkar, and was convinced she shared responsibility for the deaths of everyone the demons had killed.

Callonen raised his head a little to look at her. She hadn't moved or responded, but he knew how she felt.

He'd been in so much pain, he hadn't realized the Warding was returning. Not until now. But it gradually expanded around him. At first, he was only aware of Allia. She was nearest to him. He felt the goodness in her, the strength, love and virtue, mixed with the dark things she had done out of desperation. She felt the horror of driving a knife into Haldreth's flesh. Determined to stop his plans, she wanted to kill him.

Callonen couldn't blame her for any of it. He didn't need to know exactly what had happened to know that Haldreth had forced her. She'd endured so much.

As time dragged on and his reach extended, Callonen realized he could sense the other men in the camp. Some were terrified. They obeyed out of fear of Haldreth and his demons. Others were violent, greedy or angry. When they looked at Allia, they felt lust. Sensing it made him sick.

The Warding was definitely coming back. Not that it would matter much at this point. Callonen wouldn't last long like this. Even if his brother didn't come back to kill him, he didn't think he'd survive another night out in the cold.

A long, painful day passed. But Callonen was with Allia. It was agony to see her alive and right in front of him when he'd thought her dead for so long, only to realize that Haldreth was going to kill her. Callonen's eyes traced the line of red across her arm where his brother had cut her. Blood had soaked down her sleeve. More suffering would follow. Haldreth would make sure they didn't die too quickly. But Callonen would endure anything if he could prevent that from happening to Allia. When their eyes met, he saw love and despair.

Darkness fell, and the cold chilled him to the bone. Callonen had no way to warm himself, and he knew Allia suffered the same. How long would it take them to freeze to death?

Sometime in the middle of the night, their watch changed. One of the new guards appeared to be ill. The other slapped his friend's back. "Nothing's happening here, and nothing is going to happen. I'll watch. You can sleep for a while. I'll wake you before the guard changes, so no one will know."

The sick guard nodded. "Thanks," he said, sitting at the base of a tree, wrapping a blanket around himself, and dozing off.

Last night, Callonen had seen several guards. Now he saw only one that was awake.

Nothing else moved, and the camp was silent. Instead of slumping comfortably where he could watch them, the guard disappeared. He returned with two saddled horses and looped their reins over a branch. Then he approached Allia.

Callonen sensed she was frightened as the man drew near. Callonen pulled at the ropes. If the man wanted to harm Allia, what could he do about it? The guard was a big man, powerfully built. A beard and long hair hid his face. His blue uniform was old and stained.

If not for the extra perception granted by the Warding, Callonen might have yielded to the urge to yell at him to leave Allia alone. Instead, Callonen didn't make a sound. He knew the man wanted to help her. Why?

As the man spoke softly to Allia, Callonen sensed her fear turn to surprise and then relief. She knew him.

He cut the ropes binding her and caught Allia as she collapsed. He supported her back to her feet and over to the horses, then helped her into the saddle.

Approaching Callonen, he began sawing at the ropes. His presence felt so familiar. In the dim light, Callonen couldn't see him well, but he knew him.

"Talon?" he whispered. "Is it really you?"

"I didn't think you'd recognize me, Cal," his long-lost friend said. "When I escaped from Ara, I joined the army and followed Allia here, waiting for the chance to help."

"I didn't recognize you. I wouldn't have known except for the Warding. It's coming back."

"Good," Talon replied. "It will keep the demons back and give us a chance."

Talon finally cut through the last strands holding Callonen up, and his injured leg buckled under him. Pulling Callonen's good arm around his shoulders, Talon helped him to the horse. He couldn't put any weight on his injured knee without pain jolting through him. Supported by Talon's shoulder, he set the bare foot of his good leg in the stirrup and, with help from his friend, pulled himself onto the horse. Talon mounted behind him. They slipped out of the camp, heading back toward the city.

The motion of the horse sent searing pain from Callonen's injuries at every stride. Although he tried to focus on the woods and farmland they rode through, the landscape blurred together. He didn't even know he had passed out until he woke up again. Talon had kept him on the horse. Now they had stopped beside a rocky outcropping in the woods.

"We'll stop here and rest. I remember this place," Talon said as he dismounted.

Leaning on Talon, Callonen swung his leg over the horse and slid to the ground. Talon supported him again, and they passed through the narrow entrance of a cave. He saw a large space with a sandy floor before everything blurred again.

When Callonen woke, he saw daylight filtering in through the cave mouth. The room had a lofty ceiling, big enough that Talon had even coaxed the horses inside. Someone had wrapped Callonen in a blanket, and he was grateful for the warmth. He didn't try to move. His arm hurt less than it had, but still throbbed.

He felt a warm weight on his shoulder and the silken texture of hair brushing his bare skin. Looking down, he saw Allia's head resting against him and her hand on his chest. He felt the warmth of her body all along his side.

Tears welled in his eyes. Allia was here, alive. They had escaped from Haldreth and his men. They would not hurt her anymore. She lay still, her breathing slow and gentle in slumber.

No one had ever slept beside him like this, not in his whole life. He'd rarely allowed himself to dream of her next to him. Even after years had passed, the wound left by her absence had refused to heal. But how could she ever forgive him? His uninjured arm cradled her closer. She sighed in her sleep, and he felt her warm breath against his skin.

It was the most amazing sensation. He had wanted this more than anything else and had thought he would never feel it. The silken softness of her hair, the touch of her fingers against his chest. Callonen remained there for hours, still and silent, doing nothing more than enjoying that she was here.

Callonen sensed Talon returning. He came through the mouth of the cave and saw Callonen awake. "Can you swallow some water?" Talon asked.

Allia stirred at his words and sat up. She had cleaned the blood from her face, but two red lines remained atop a darkening bruise. The cut on her arm was neatly bandaged. His own injuries had been tended to as well.

Now she helped Callonen raise his head enough to drink. Moving sent stabbing pains through his body, and he gasped.

But the water eased his dry mouth. "Thank you," he murmured.

"Can you eat?" Talon asked.

Callonen shook his head. "Not hungry. Can't move my jaw much."

"Try a little."

Allia fed him, and he accepted a few bites. Finally, he lifted his good hand to stop her.

He looked up at Allia. "Is there any news of Cirana?"

Allia nodded. "I saw her in Ara. After all these years wondering if she was safe, she found me a few weeks ago. She told me you'd taken care of her all this time. She was so brave and beautiful. But Haldreth said he killed her." Her voice trailed off into a whisper. Pain filled her expression.

Callonen shut his eyes and breathed deeply, trying to calm himself. "My fault again," he said in an agonized whisper. "I never believed he could reach her. I thought I could keep her safe." He felt as if his heart had turned to stone in his chest. "I can't fight anymore. Ana is dead. Haldreth has the throne. Both my army and the Aran army answer to him. He controls the Shekkar. And with them at his side, we have no way of fighting him. It's over."

His defeat was total. Ana, lost. Sarine, finished. His empire had crumbled. There was nothing else he could do but fade into oblivion. It was the only chance of keeping Allia safe.

Talon seemed as if he wanted to object, but he said nothing. Maybe Allia wanted to protest too, but instead, she brought another blanket from the saddlebag and wrapped it around him. He felt her fingers gently brush his cheek.

"How can you tolerate me?" he murmured. "I'm nothing but a curse to everyone I love." He allowed sleep to take him, the pain pursuing him there.

It began as a dream. Callonen was back in the city, in his private dining room. Morning sun streamed in the windows, and he sat across the table from Ana. She laughed with him, her face carefree, her smile warming his heart.

Suddenly, fear crossed her face. She was in danger. In the dream, she looked up at him. "I'm searching for Zarek. Please help?"

Callonen woke with a start that disturbed his injuries and sent pain flaring through his body.

"What is it?" came Allia's urgent whisper beside him. "Ana!" Callonen opened his eyes and saw only darkness.

"A dream?"

Callonen took in a deep breath and searched his feelings. "I was dreaming of her. But now... I think I sense her."

"Could she be alive?" Allia's voice contained a desperate hope.

Callonen searched his mind. The Warding continued to expand gradually, not yet back to its original strength. Ana. Warmth grew in his chest.

"I can feel her," he said. "Ana's alive. She's alive! And inside the Warding, not far away." He wanted to get up and shout.

Callonen concentrated on her again. "She's afraid. We have to help her!"

Talon struck a spark and lit a bit of wood. In its light, he stared at Callonen. "You said you were done fighting."

"I don't care what I said." Callonen struggled to push himself into a sitting position. "We have to help her. There's someone with her..." A familiar presence, but one he hadn't sensed for years. "Zarek is with her."

Talon grinned. "Good. Then get dressed. We'll find them." He went to the saddlebag and pulled out a blue uniform, tossing it to Allia. "I stole these before we left." He took a second one to Callonen and helped him into it.

CHAPTER FIFTY-THREE

YEAR OF WARDING 42, SARINE'S COUNTRYSIDE

ANA

A S THE STARS TURNED above them, Ana and Zarek rode at a steady pace, heading south toward the city. The chill night was quiet around them, and they saw no sign of danger. Ana clung to Zarek. For the moment, he was here with her, alive.

"I love you," she murmured, tightening her hold. He placed one of his hands over hers.

"Ana, I love you too," he said. "I always have."

"You need to hold on until we get to the city. No matter what."

"I'll do my best."

As dawn came, the sun warmed the frosty air. They passed fields, farms and villages. The land appeared deserted. People were hiding, or they had fled to the city for protection. With only a few short breaks, they rode on into the afternoon. By then, Ana felt Zarek swaying in the saddle.

"We should rest," she suggested, expecting him to argue. He didn't. They stopped in the shelter of a boulder.

Moving slowly, Zarek dismounted, leaning heavily against the saddle. Ana slid down after him.

"I can... take care of the horse," he mumbled.

"Don't worry about that now," Ana said. "Just rest."

Instead of protesting, he sank to the ground with his back against the rock.

Ana wasn't sure she could resaddle the horse by herself when they were ready to go on, so she left it in place, hauling the saddlebags over to where Zarek sat.

"Are you all right?" he murmured, looking up at her, his gaze unfocused. "I should... keep watch."

But already he slumped to one side, and she took out a blanket and wrapped it around him. "Rest." She kissed his cheek.

She cleaned the wounds on his arm and back and found a piece of cloth and used it to wrap the gashes. Zarek's eyes were closed and beads of sweat stood out on his forehead despite the rapidly cooling evening.

The night was chill and the ground cold. She took off her helmet and curled up beside Zarek.

She'd intended to stay awake and alert, but when Ana opened her eyes, it was dawn.

Zarek hadn't moved, and when she tried to rouse him, it took a long time for him to respond. Finally, he blinked and opened his eyes. "Ana? Where are we?"

She bent over him, brushing her fingers across his hot forehead. "Still trying to get to the city. We're not far away. If you can get back on the horse, we should be there later today."

"I can't." He shook his head. "I love you... You should leave... Get yourself to safety. Haldreth's army is coming."

Her eyes widened. "No. I won't abandon you! You wouldn't leave me behind when the demons were coming."

A slight smile crossed his face. "I guess that's true."

"Besides that, we are going to find the ring, and I need you close by when I do."

He nodded slightly, but didn't speak again.

Ana brought him food and water, but he wouldn't eat and took only a few swallows. His skin was burning hot.

When she heard the sound of an approaching horse, Ana grabbed her helmet and put it on, tucking her hair into her collar. She picked up her sword.

The rider came into view, a lone Aran soldier. He looked at her, and at Zarek where he lay on the ground. "Can I help?"

Ana shook her head.

He didn't leave. Dismounting, he came nearer.

Ana stood her ground, raising the sword in her hand. "Go back," she ordered. She had no training with a blade, and she'd never hurt anyone before in her life. But this man wouldn't be alone, his companions must be nearby, and she would rather die here trying to fight than go back to the king. And she couldn't let him harm Zarek.

The soldier was a big man, his hair uncut, his face bearded, wearing a sword at his side. But he hadn't drawn it. Something about him seemed familiar, though she felt sure she'd never seen him before.

Her own blade felt heavy, but she gripped it with both hands despite her wound.

He scrutinized her for several moments, then raised his empty hands. "Cirana?"

Everyone in Ara knew her name, and many would recognize her. "Who are you?" She didn't lower the weapon.

He took a step nearer.

"Stay back!" she warned.

"I'm Talon. Callonen sent me to help you."

Her eyes widened in disbelief. That was why he seemed familiar. He strongly resembled Zarek, even down to the blue uniform. In her hands, the sword wavered slightly. "You're Zarek's father?"

He nodded. "Yes. And Callonen is with me." He nodded toward the hills. "He's just over there."

"Why isn't he in the city?"

"Haldreth captured him and took his place."

Ana's stomach twisted into a knot. Haldreth was there now, pretending to be Callonen. She couldn't allow that. And if Zarek was to have any chance of surviving, they had to get back to the city. Ana needed help, and this man's resemblance to Zarek was undeniable. Could she trust him? Without the ring, she had no sense of his emotions.

He remained still, making no threatening move. "I know you don't know me," he said. "But I know you. You were only a baby the last time I saw you, but I've actually been waiting for a chance to thank you."

Her brows raised in surprise. "Me? Why?" What had she ever done to help him?

Meeting her eyes, he sang a few lines of an old song about a blacksmith.

For a moment, his familiar voice took her back to a dark cell beneath Hakvere. Black memories surrounded her. She drew in a deep breath, lowering the sword. "It *was* you. I hoped you escaped, but I didn't know."

Talon's voice grew thick with emotion. "By the time you found me, I had nothing left. My body was ruined, my mind broken. Yours was the only voice I had heard in twenty years. When you spoke to me, I remembered I had been a person once. And you were locked in that dark hole just as I was. Why did you help me?"

He came nearer, but Ana no longer felt afraid.

"I had to!" Ana said, pulling the helmet from her head. "When I learned what the king had done to you, I knew he hated you. And even after all you'd been through, you tried to help me, and I knew you were a good person."

Talon's steady gray eyes, so like his son's, met hers. "You don't know what it means to me to be standing here, walking, breathing fresh air, looking up at the sky. It wasn't just my legs. The ring healed my mind and my spirit. I had hope again and the will to live. After the healing, I called out to you, but you didn't answer. So I climbed out. I stole weapons and tools to open the lock and I came back. But the room you were in was empty. I'm so sorry I couldn't get you out too."

Ana reached out, and he took her hand and gripped it. "It's all right. Zarek helped me escape. We never have to go back there again." She knelt beside Zarek and touched his forehead.

Talon bent beside her. "What happened?"

Ana's eyes welled with tears. "Demons."

"We have to get back to the others," Talon said. "Can you help me get him on the horse?"

Talon knelt beside the unconscious Zarek, pulling him first into a sitting position, and then to his feet, leaning against the horse. From the other side, Ana gripped Zarek's hands and pulled while Talon pushed from behind until he lay across the saddle.

Ana climbed onto her own mount, while Talon led the horse with Zarek on its back. She followed him through the rocky hills.

A short while later, Ana saw a hidden hollow containing two horses and two people. One of them called out to her. "Ana!"

She knew Callonen's voice, though she would never have recognized him. Bruises and dried blood covered his face; his head was wrapped in bandages. "Callonen! What have they done to you?" She rushed to him and carefully put her arms around his neck.

Heavy splints covered one of his arms, but with the other, he pulled her close. "I thought you were dead. I'm so sorry."

"It wasn't your fault." Her eyes filled with tears as she noticed Allia and reached out to include her in the hug. "Mother. You're here."

The three of them held each other and cried.

The overwhelming events of the day had almost made Ana forget why she needed to speak to Callonen so urgently. She turned back to him. "Callonen! You have to know, Zarek stole your father's sword back from Hakvere, and when Haldreth sent the demons after us, Zarek killed them."

Callonen gasped. "Can it be true? All? Did he kill all of them?"

Her heart swelled. No one but Zarek could have done it. He was so brave. And now, unless she helped him, he wouldn't survive. "Yes, but they poisoned him!" Her voice broke. "Please tell me you know where the ring is. We can't let him die!"

"No, we can't," Callonen said. "We have to get back to the city. Gavin is there with your ring. And Haldreth is pretending to be me. Ana, the news you bring is vital. With the demons gone, we have hope."

"I know you look alike, but can't people tell the difference?" Ana exclaimed. "If they spent any time with you, couldn't they tell?"

"I hope so. But I don't look like myself anymore," Callonen pointed out. "And everyone knew the Warding fell, but they don't know it's back. I still wield its power. Not him."

"And I will tell them who you are," Ana said.

"What if they don't believe you?" Allia protested.

Ana squared her shoulders. "I am heir to the empire of Sarine, and I will make them believe."

"It's a dangerous plan," Talon said. "We'll be totally in his hands if we fail. There will probably be fighting, and Callonen and Zarek are in no condition to defend themselves."

"But we have many friends there," Ana protested. "They'll help us. If the ring is there, it's our only chance to get it back in time to save Zarek. Come on!"

Talon helped Allia and Ana get Callonen upright. With assistance, Callonen made it to his horse, and Talon helped him on. Ana mounted behind Zarek, still slung over the saddle. She would make sure he didn't fall off.

Around them the land was quiet. The only other people moving were Aran patrols. The day was cold, and Ana warmed her frozen fingers against Zarek's feverish skin.

They increased their pace. The way grew easier as they approached the city. Soon, they traveled on smooth roads. Almost there.

"Our men are going to shoot us from the walls," Talon said, shaking his head and looking up at the city. "I would."

In the bright afternoon sunshine, they paused a little distance from the gate.

"Stay here, all of you, out of bowshot," Ana ordered. She took her helmet off and shook out her hair. She gave Talon her weapon and rode forward.

When she reached the city gate, a voice demanded, "Who are you? Speak quickly. We're ready to shoot."

She knew the voice. In her years there, she'd gotten to know nearly everyone in the palace. "Is that any way to welcome me home, Renard?" she called back. "I know you couldn't hit a barn at this distance, but I don't want to risk it. So please don't shoot."

Inside, she heard an oath and then a laugh, followed by several voices arguing. "They ordered no one gets in," one protested.

"But it's Lady Cirana," Renard countered. "I don't want to be the man who tells the emperor we refused to let *her* in."

Ana heard murmurs of agreement from the others. The gate opened, and she rode in. They surrounded her with welcomes and questions. Renard's tall frame and bright blue eyes foremost among them. Ana glanced back outside. "Three more friends are waiting out there. I need you to trust me and let them in as well. We've been hiding from Aran soldiers. We had to disguise ourselves in their uniforms."

The guards shifted uncomfortably, but they didn't object as Ana waved the others in. She dismounted and gathered the soldiers close around her. "Something terrible has happened. You all saw Callonen leave the city?"

"Yes," Renard replied, "But he came back the next day and seemed fine. The king of Ara didn't hurt him. I think they made some kind of deal."

"No," Ana explained. "Callonen didn't come back. It was his twin brother Haldreth."

They made exclamations of shock.

"He looked just like Emperor Callonen," Renard protested. "How can you be sure he wasn't?"

"Because I am the emperor." Callonen pulled his hood back.

For a long moment, they stared in shock at his injured face.

Renard gasped, his blue eyes wide. "Emperor! What did they do to you?"

"That's not important now," Callonen said. "You can stop staring. It's me. I saw you the day before they attacked, Renard. I asked you if your mother was feeling better yet. And Wes, you hurt your shoulder when we were sparring last week. I hope it hasn't given you too much trouble."

Renard leaned close and stared hard at him. "It is you," he said, straightening up and saluting. The others followed his example. "What is your command, Emperor?"

Callonen put his hand on the unconscious Zarek's shoulder. "This is Zarek. He might look like an Aran now, but he saved Sarine. Wes, please take him someplace he can rest and guard him."

Ana put her hand on Wes's arm. "Please, make sure he's safe."

"I will, my lady," Wes replied. "We'll take him to the healers at the palace. They'll do everything they can to help him." He and another of the guards brought a stretcher from the guardhouse. They slid Zarek off the horse and onto it, throwing a blanket over him to hide his blue uniform. Then they lifted him and carried him to a nearby wagon.

Ana wanted to go with him, but they had to finish this first.

"Now," Callonen said, "Will you find out where my brother is?" Another guard saluted and hurried off.

"Renard, we can't walk through my city looking like the enemy. But we can't be recognized either. Please bring us something to wear," Callonen requested.

Talon dismounted and began helping Callonen down.

"Don't try to walk, Emperor," Renard protested, waving two of his companions forward with another stretcher.

"Don't be ridiculous! Of course, I can walk," Callonen objected. As he hobbled a single step, his face tightened in pain.

"Now is not the time to be stubborn," Talon said. "Lie down."

Relenting, Callonen got onto the stretcher and allowed them to carry him into the guardhouse. His friends followed along. Before long, they had dressed to blend in with the Emperor's Guard.

The soldier who had gone to look for Haldreth returned. "Your brother is on his way to the throne room. Many members of the court are already there."

"It's time to finish this," Callonen said grimly. "Help me up."

Ana felt her stomach tighten. It was time to face her father. But this was her home, and she didn't need to stand alone.

They helped Callonen into a borrowed carriage. Allia and Ana got in with him. Talon, Renard and his friends followed on horseback. It didn't take long to pass through the city and up the hill, stopping at the palace gates.

Ana followed Renard to the barracks housing the Emperor's Guard, while the others waited in the carriage. She spoke to the sentry at the door. "We need your help. It's very important."

He bowed with one hand on his heart. "Anything, Lady Cirana. What can I do?"

"Haldreth is pretending to be Emperor Callonen. I need to stop him. Will you help me?"

"But how—?"

"Wake everyone up. We need to go now," Ana said. "I'll explain when the men are gathered."

"Yes, Lady Cirana. Wait here." He opened the door to the barracks and yelled, "Everyone up! It's time to serve our empire."

Only a few moments later, the entire company of guards came out. Some looked half awake, but they were dressed and armed.

Ana gave them a quick explanation. "Emperor Callonen's twin brother is impersonating him. We need to protect the emperor as he confronts Haldreth. Callonen is badly hurt and needs our help." Their faces registered shock and disbelief, but prepared to serve, they all followed her back to where she had left the emperor. They waited in silence as Talon and Renard helped Callonen out of the carriage. He stood there, leaning heavily on them, looking around at the guards. "I can't tell you how much I appreciate your loyalty right now," he said.

"We're with you, Emperor," one of them said. The others nodded.

Callonen looked at Ana. She took a deep breath. It was time. She led the way to the throne room.

CHAPTER FIFTY-FOUR

YEAR OF WARDING 42, WHITE CITY, SARINE

ANA

DESPITE ANA'S TIME AWAY from Sarine, the palace halls were familiar. It felt strange to be leading so many people, but she felt supported by their presence. They gathered more with them as they went—guards, courtiers and friends.

Ana paused at the door to the throne room, her heart pounding. The king was in there. Haldreth. Her father. Her missing finger throbbed. She would rather have run the other way and never stopped running than confront him. But it was time to be brave.

She glanced at the others. Renard and his friends helped Callonen. Allia and Talon stood beside him, and the rest of the guards surrounded them.

"Ready?" Ana asked. Everyone nodded.

"Stay out of sight until it's time," she directed them. "Renard, will you walk with me?"

He smiled. "Gladly, my lady. Wherever you lead." Another man took his place supporting Callonen.

"Thanks," she said. She inhaled deeply and entered the room.

Though her heart raced, Ana kept her expression calm and happy as she met the eyes of the man on the throne. She walked forward eagerly. His eyes widened slightly, and his lips tightened for a moment.

He stood up and opened his arms. "Lady Cirana! Home safely! It's a miracle, and we are so grateful." He embraced her. "I've been so worried! I was afraid he had killed you. Cirana, I am so relieved to have you back."

Even without the ring, his kind tone never would have fooled Ana. He turned back to the people. "Let everyone rejoice with us! The heir to our empire, my beautiful Cirana, has returned safely." The crowd cheered and applauded.

Ana took a deep breath. "And I…" The room quieted to hear her. She felt like she was going to throw up. But she couldn't fail now. She could not let him win. And she refused to live in fear of him anymore. She took another breath. "I'm so grateful to be home, but imagine my surprise to find you here, my father, Haldreth, king of Ara."

The room exploded with noise, everyone speaking at once. The man in the crown held up his hand for silence.

"My dear, you must be exhausted after your long journey and distraught after whatever they did to you in Ara. You're safe. You're back in Sarine. Don't you recognize me? Please tell me how I can help you."

"I recognize you perfectly," Ana's voice rang in the silent room. "You forced Callonen from the city, took his clothes, and ordered your men to beat him. Then you came back here, dressed as the emperor, to replace him. I'm sure you only did it because, without the Shekkar, it will be too hard to defeat us. The demons are dead!" She yelled it to the entire room, and they cheered. "The emperor's sword, Blackbane, killed them all. Now there's no one left to fight against Sarine but ordinary men!"

For a moment, Haldreth seemed paralyzed by shock, but he quickly recovered. "Guards!" he cried. "Send for the healers, and take Lady Cirana someplace secure, where she can rest until her delusions have passed." Four of his own guards surrounded Ana and Renard. As they tried to seize Ana, he jumped forward with a yell, knocking the foremost of them down. The others drew their swords, and Renard's friends rushed to join the fight.

"Stop!"

Everyone paused, looking around to see who had spoken. The voice commanded everyone's attention.

Leaning heavily on a guard, the emperor hobbled to the front of the room. "I am Callonen, son of Caldoreth, Emperor of Sarine."

Everyone stared at him in shock. His damaged face bore little resemblance to the emperor they knew.

"He is Emperor Callonen!" Ana yelled, still struggling against the guards, who refused to release her. One clamped a hand over her mouth, silencing her.

Slowly, Callonen stepped forward to face his brother, Talon at his side. "It's over, Haldreth. I am the emperor. The Warding belongs to me."

"The Warding is broken!" Haldreth protested. "It's gone."

"It disappeared for a while," Callonen agreed. "But it has returned. I know how much you hate me and that you tortured Allia and Cirana. She's your own child. How could you?"

"You're very bold to confront me in my throne room and claim I am not myself," Haldreth said. "Guards. Seize the impostor."

As Haldreth's soldiers hurried forward, Callonen called out to his own men. He knew every one of them by name, and when he called, they gathered to him.

"Well, Haldreth? Do you know their names?"

While all the soldiers wore the white-and-gold uniform of the Emperor's Guard, they had divided themselves into two groups. The crowd in the hall pushed closer to Callonen as if to express support.

"Release Lady Cirana," Callonen ordered.

Ana struggled against the men holding her, but they were loyal to Haldreth and didn't obey the emperor's command.

The impostor moved a step nearer, his eyes locked with his brother's. "This is my empire." His tone was icy.

As his hand moved suddenly toward Callonen, Ana couldn't see a weapon, but the emperor stiffened, his battered features tightening in pain. She fought against the guards holding her. Her father had attacked his brother somehow.

Ana barely saw Talon move, but his knife appeared, buried in Haldreth's throat.

Disbelief on his face, Haldreth jerked the blade out as he crumpled, and the weapon fell from his hand. His soldiers attacked Talon and the rest of the Emperor's Guard. In the confusion, Ana saw a man slip between the combatants.

Horrified, she recognized Gavin.

She tried to shout a warning, but the guard still had his hand over her mouth. She drove her boot-heel into his foot and her elbow into his belly. He grunted in pain and his grip loosened, allowing her to twist free.

But it was too late. Gavin was already reaching for Haldreth with her ring on his finger. Talon dove toward him, but the young man reached Haldreth first and touched him.

With a flash of green light, Gavin screamed in agony and collapsed to the floor just before Talon's blade struck him.

Haldreth leapt back to his feet, heedless of the bright blood staining his neck. He retreated a few steps, and his guards blocked Callonen's men. Now the king of Ara stood in the center of a black circle drawn on the marble floor.

Ana fought her way through the crowd, trying to reach Callonen.

"So that's how it is!" Haldreth stared at his brother in fury. "You feel justified in attempting to assassinate me? After all this time, you still think you're better than me. You think the people love you and want you to take care of them? That ends today. This empire is mine!"

Haldreth chanted in an unfamiliar language, and a sharp tearing noise filled the room. A piercing, unearthly shriek followed, causing everyone to cover their ears. It sounded like a demon, only much louder.

Ana stopped and clasped her hands over her ears.

Talon and the emperor's guards attacked Haldreth's men, attempting to get through to stop him. The sound of blades clashing filled the room.

Haldreth's spell had torn a hole in reality. It looked as if the air had split along an invisible seam, revealing an opening to... somewhere else. It was utterly dark inside. Haldreth continued the incantation—his powerful voice carrying above the noise.

Something huge pushed its way out of the hole. Screams and cries of fear echoed throughout the room.

Whatever it was, it would be worse than the demons. The thing shrieked again, and Ana felt like the sound penetrated her mind.

Where was Callonen? The crowd had closed in, blocking him from view.

At another roar from the creature, her eyes riveted on it as more became visible. It had sleek, dark, scaly skin and sharp claws. It opened its enormous jaws to display long, deadly teeth.

Talon knocked the last of his opponents to the ground and ran toward the circle. Its boundary stopped him as if he'd hit a solid wall. One of his men shot an arrow, but it rebounded off the invisible barrier.

Haldreth continued reciting. Even more of the creature slid out, proving it was even bigger than it had first appeared. It snapped its jaws, fixing its gaze on the people outside the circle. With more shouts and screams, people backed away from the line, the crowd packing together against the walls. Many ran from the room in panic.

Ana caught sight of her mother, nearly invisible in the confusion of the room, kneeling on the floor at the edge of the circle. She was far too close to Haldreth and his spell. Silent and nearly motionless, she worked on something on the floor, concentrating, despite all the chaos happening around her.

When Haldreth turned his head and spotted Allia, a look of horror appeared on his face. But he couldn't stop chanting. Even his slight pause had caused the monster to turn its attention to him. Now its eyes followed his every move.

Sweat beaded on Haldreth's face. He kept speaking, increasing his pace. But Allia didn't stop, even though the creature roared again and everyone in the room shrank from the sound. The monster began pushing a leg through the opening, when a flash of brilliant crimson lit the room.

Haldreth yelled, "Allia, stop!"

But it was too late.

The circle was broken, the binding words interrupted. Now the black creature turned to snap at Haldreth. It lunged toward him, clamping his arm in its teeth. He screamed. "Allia! Please! Repair the circle. I'll give you anything you want... Please!"

Allia stood, the blade still in her hand. "No!" Her voice carried through the hall, clear and powerful.

With the spell incomplete, the scaly creature was being pulled back into the opening. Haldreth struggled desperately as it dragged him with it, his boot heels scraping against the polished floor. "Allia, please! Help me!"

The creature disappeared, taking Haldreth with it. The sound of his screaming abruptly cut off as the tear in reality sealed itself.

Silence fell.

The quiet only lasted for one shocked moment. Then the crowd burst into cheering, yelling and crying in relief.

Allia raised the knife over her head and shouted in triumph. "He's gone!" she exclaimed. "I'm finally free." She held up her knife and shouted the words. "I'm free!"

Talon and the rest of Callonen's guard swarmed over Haldreth's remaining men, disarming them.

Ana ran to her mother. Leaning heavily on a guard, Callonen hobbled toward them. "Allia! Are you all right?"

Allia held up her knife. "I scraped away the markings. He can only control the magic as long as the circle stays intact."

"You did it!" Callonen put his good arm around her, pulling her close. He turned to Ana. "Find the ring and save Zarek. Hurry!"

His voice sounded strained, and underneath the bruises, his skin looked pale.

"Are you all right?" she asked him, worry tightening her stomach.

"It's nothing. I'm fine," he insisted. "Help Zarek."

Ana ran to Gavin. He lay on his side where he'd fallen after healing Haldreth. His body was crumpled, one hand across his chest, a pool of blood spreading from a mortal wound. She'd been so terrified of him, but now he looked like nothing more than an ordinary young man. The cruelty was gone from his face.

She knelt beside him as he took one last breath. Then, nothing. The ring slipped from his finger to the floor. She picked it up and put it on. Talon joined her as she ran from the room, heading for the infirmary where they had taken Zarek.

CHAPTER FIFTY-FIVE

YEAR OF WARDING 42, WHITE CITY, SARINE

ZAREK

WHEN ZAREK OPENED HIS eyes, he realized he was dead. It was quiet. He saw a man's familiar features above him, resembling the face that stared back at him every time he looked in a mirror. Fine lines at the corners of the man's eyes made him look older. He was someone Zarek hadn't seen since he was a child.

"Father, it didn't hurt as much as I thought it would," he said.

"What didn't?" Talon asked.

"Dying. It doesn't hurt at all. I feel fine." He stared at his father. "The next world must be hard. You look awful, and you're still wearing all your weapons."

Talon laughed. "Get up, son. You're not dead."

Zarek raised his eyebrows. "Then why can I see you?"

"I'm alive, Zarek," Talon said. "I came home as soon as I could."

"Is it really you?" Zarek asked in wonder.

"It's me." Talon grinned, then his expression grew sad. "I'm sorry I was gone for so long. You're all grown up."

"That happened a long time ago," Zarek reminded him. "How did you get here? You're dressed in an Aran army uniform, so I'm guessing you came with them?"

"Yes. But there will be time later to tell you all the details," Talon promised.

"Where's Ana?" Zarek sat up suddenly, only to realize she lay cradled in Talon's arms, unconscious.

"Don't worry. She's fine," Talon said soothingly. "She healed you." He must have caught her as she collapsed.

"How'd she get the ring back?" Zarek asked in confusion. "We have to stop Haldreth."

"It's over, Zarek. He's dead."

Zarek got to his feet, and Talon placed the unconscious girl gently onto the cot where his son had lain.

Out in the hall, they heard the sudden sound of running feet, and Mirithel appeared in the doorway. It had been years, and she looked older, though he knew her at once. She stared back at him without recognition. "The guards told me my son was here. Where is Zarek? They said he was injured."

"I'm here," he said.

She blinked at him in disbelief and stepped closer. "I'm looking for Zarek."

"Mother, it's me."

Finally, her eyes widened in recognition, and she burst into tears as she put a hand to her heart. "It is you!" She hugged him, and he held her close.

After a moment, Zarek cleared his throat and nodded toward his father. Mirithel turned to see Talon. She recognized him at once, which wasn't fair. He was just as unwashed, untrimmed and unshaven as Zarek. She gasped and ran to him, crying, "You're alive! How?"

Talon took her in his arms, his embrace lifting her from the floor. "I've missed you!" They laughed and cried together. He set her back down and kissed her. "I've missed both of you," he said, putting one arm around Zarek's shoulders.

"We've missed you too," Zarek said.

His family was reunited. It had seemed impossible. But they were here, holding each other with tears of joy in their eyes. Zarek felt moisture in his own too and realized how long it had been since he'd cried. He'd been completely focused on becoming another person—Captain Tack—cold, dangerous and alone. Zarek wasn't alone anymore. He'd come home, and his family was beside him and Ana was here, safe and alive.

And she loved him. That was a miracle in itself. He looked down at her and saw her face, peaceful as she slept. She wore a borrowed white-and-gold tunic, her honey-colored hair hanging loose. The pain and fear were gone from her expression. She'd been so brave.

When Talon kissed Mirithel again, Zarek released his parents and took a step back. "I'll give the two of you some time alone," he said.

Mirithel turned from her husband to brush her hand along Zarek's face and kiss his cheek. "Welcome home, Zarek. We'll see you again soon." His mother smiled at him, and no bitterness or judgment remained in her eyes. She took Talon's hand and led him out the door.

Someone had left Zarek's weapons on a chair beside the cot where he had lain. He picked up the precious enchanted sword. A trip to the armory could replace other lost weapons, but not this one. Zarek buckled the belt around his waist.

He lifted Ana in his arms and carried her back toward her room. A woman with red hair ran up to him in the hall. "Ana!" she cried in alarm, bending over the girl in his arms.

"She's all right," Zarek assured her. "The ring..."

"Where are you taking her?" the woman demanded, looking at him suspiciously.

Tess. Her name was Tess. He remembered her.

"I was taking her to her room if it's still the same one?" Zarek had thought he remembered every room and hallway of the palace, but everything seemed strange to him after all this time.

"We can take care of her," Tess said, beckoning a pair of guards over. They didn't recognize him or trust him. He should have expected that. But he wasn't going to give Ana to the guards. "Tess," he said. "I'm Zarek."

"You're who?" She stared at him, completely without recognition.

"I'm Zarek," he repeated.

She stared at him, and slowly, he saw the realization dawn on her face. "Zarek?" She looked him up and down. "I... I... can't believe it. I didn't recognize you."

"It is me, Tess," he said. "We need to take care of Ana."

"Of course," she agreed. Tess turned to the two guards, who stood waiting for her instructions. "It's all right," she told them.

They nodded to her and resumed their posts.

If Zarek wanted to be welcomed home, he would need to get cleaned up and changed.

When they reached Ana's room, Zarek set her down gently on the bed. She remained unconscious, but her breathing was steady and she looked peaceful.

"We need to get the healers," Tess exclaimed, looking down at her.

"Yes," Zarek said. He felt his stomach clench in guilt as he took in an assortment of cuts and bruises. Ana's horse had thrown her, and they'd fought the demons. After that, some of the details became a little fuzzy.

"Please ask them to care for her hand." He pointed to the bandages he'd put there. "She has some cuts on her shoulder and neck. And her ribs—I wrapped them, but two or three are cracked."

Tess looked increasingly alarmed as he spoke.

"I did what I could for her," he said awkwardly.

"I will send for a healer at once," Tess said. "We'll take care of her."

"Thank you," Zarek said. "I need to see Callonen. Do you know where he is?"

"He was in the throne room," Tess replied.

Zarek went to look for the emperor. When he got to the throne room, he heard a confusion of many voices. A member of the guard stood at the door.

"Where Emperor Callonen?" Zarek asked.

"What are you doing here?" the guard asked.

"I need to see Emperor Callonen."

"He's injured. He's not seeing anyone."

"Please, just tell me where he is!"

The guard put a hand on Zarek's arm. Throwing off the hand, Zarek took a step back.

Just then, a group of guards came around the corner. They stared at the two men facing off and dropped their hands to their weapons. Zarek recognized Renard among them.

"Stop! He's one of ours," Renard commanded the rest of the guards. He grinned at Zarek. "You look better than when we brought you in." He turned to the others. "This is Zarek, don't you recognize him?"

"No. It's who?" They shook their heads, still staring at him.

"You don't remember Zarek, son of Talon? He's the best soldier Sarine ever had," Renard told the guards. "He returned with Lady Cirana."

Renard escorted Zarek to the emperor's rooms, and though the guards at the door stared suspiciously at Zarek, they allowed him to enter.

Inside, four healers worked busily. A woman with golden hair knelt beside the bed, holding Callonen's hand. The healers stepped around her to reach the bed. Zarek went to stand next to her. His belly twisted in shock when he stared down at Callonen. The emperor's face was bruised and swollen. His nose was broken, and bandages swathed one side of his head. Black bruises covered his chest and stomach. One leg was heavily wrapped, and the opposite arm was splinted. The healers now worked on a knife wound in his side.

Callonen opened his eyes and looked up at him.

"The demons are dead," Zarek said.

"And you're alive." Callonen sounded relieved.

"Ana healed me," Zarek said.

"As she should. I promised her I would do everything I could to help."

"You didn't tell her how badly you were hurt," Zarek said, looking at the knife wound.

Callonen's eyes closed. His breathing remained shallow, slowing a little as unconsciousness brought relief from the pain.

Zarek looked at the woman holding Callonen's hand and with a shock, recognized Allia. Her face was cut and bruised, but she was very much alive. Obviously, many things had happened while he was unconscious.

"Lady Allia," he greeted her with a bow.

She gave him a quick smile and put her hand on his arm. "You remember me?" She sounded surprised. "It's been a long time since you were a little boy."

"Yes, it has," he agreed.

She turned back to Callonen. "He didn't let any of us know how bad it was. Haldreth had a blade hidden in his sleeve. None of us realized what had happened. Callonen sent Ana to heal you. As soon as she left, he collapsed."

"How soon might she heal again?" Zarek asked.

"The ring takes power from the wearer," Allia said. "She must regain enough strength before she heals again, otherwise she will not survive. And she will sleep for days. There's nothing more we can do but wait."

Zarek turned to the healers. "How bad is it?"

"The knife wound is very serious," one of them said. "Not to mention the stress of all his other injuries." He gestured to the bruises. "We don't know how much damage they did to him internally."

"Will he survive?" Zarek asked.

"I'm sorry. It's too soon to tell," the healer said. "We are doing all we can, of course. There's nothing more you can do here. We will tell you if there is any change."

Zarek allowed himself to be led to the door. "I'll come back to check on him soon," he said.

"As you wish. Now leave us to our work."

Renard waited outside the door. "I'll walk with you," he offered.

Zarek clapped him on the shoulder. "Thanks. I don't want to fight anyone before I change my uniform. Where do you think they put my things?"

"After all these years?" Renard shrugged. "I don't know. But Tess will. She knows everything."

When Zarek had dreamed of going home after his years in Ara, he'd pictured himself being welcomed with open arms instead of being treated with hostility and suspicion. But he shouldn't be surprised. He'd worked hard to play his part, to look like a cold and dangerous man. Now it was time to look like himself again.

They returned to the room where Zarek had left Ana and saw Tess just coming out.

"How is she?" Zarek asked.

"She's asleep. The healer is still tending to her injuries. There's nothing more we can do for her at the moment. We have prepared a room, now that you're back. I had someone set out clean clothes for you. The rest of your belongings were packed up and given to your mother. Shall I show you to your room now?"

"Thank you," Zarek said. "And thank you, Renard."

Renard grinned. "I'm glad you're home." He slapped Zarek's shoulder. "I'll see you soon."

He disappeared down the hall, and Zarek followed Tess to a comfortable room with a big bed and a seating area. Two of the household staff were just adding the last bucket of hot water to a bath. Another set a tray of food and drink on the table.

"Thank you," Zarek said gratefully. It was so good to be home. "The barber will be here in a little while," Tess said, eyeing his uncut hair and beard.

Zarek smiled. She really had thought of everything.

"Welcome back," she wished him on her way out the door.

For a long moment, Zarek stood still, looking around, feeling completely out of place. He pulled off his boots and ate the food they'd left for him. He set his weapons aside, handling the ancient sword reverently, then unbuckled his armor.

Black filth crusted Zarek's clothes from the wounds the demon had inflicted. Pulling his shirt off, he saw the new white scars that were all that remained of his injuries. With soap and hot water, he scrubbed away the last remnants of the demon's touch.

CHAPTER FIFTY-SIX

YEAR OF WARDING 42, WHITE CITY, SARINE

ANA

WHEN ANA FINALLY WOKE, it was dawn. The memory of pain remained sharp, but when she opened her eyes, it did not return. She saw her own beautiful room in Callonen's palace. For a moment, she stared around in wonder. Was it real? Would she wake up and discover she'd only been dreaming of home? Her gaze fell on Zarek, asleep in the chair beside her bed.

His appearance had changed dramatically. Now freshly shaved, and his hair trimmed, he looked much more like the old Zarek.

The familiar scars from the demon claws stood out more clearly. He wore a loose white shirt, and she couldn't see a single weapon on him. His expression was peaceful, relaxed in sleep. He looked healthy—well and whole.

He had fallen asleep leaning on the arm of the chair, and she realized he must have been there all night. For several moments, she watched him sleep, his breathing, deep and even. It felt completely right to have him near. She never wanted to be apart from him again.

Now she wore the ring on her right hand. Having it back felt like a part of her that had been missing was restored. But not every part could be returned. She glanced at the bandages on her left hand.

Ana knew she had made no sound to disturb him, but Zarek opened his gray eyes and smiled at her. Her eyes widened in amazement. She could sense what he was feeling again.

He loved her and would do anything for her. He was attracted to her. Even now, he felt a powerful urge to pull her into his arms. He wanted her.

Her cheeks colored. "What is it?" he asked.

She could feel the blush, and he obviously saw it.

"I..." Just a few days ago, she had thought he didn't like her. Now, it was obvious the opposite was true. The two of them would never have had their misunderstanding if she'd had the ring all along. Without it, it had been hard to believe him when he told her how he felt.

"You look embarrassed," he observed.

She smiled. "It's just that I can tell you'd like to..."

He bent over her and kissed her softly. "Do this?" he asked.

She answered his kiss and smiled up at him. "I love you, Zarek."

"I love you too," he replied. "But you already know that. You can feel it, so you know I'm not lying."

"I know," she said.

He smiled again. "It's time for breakfast." He pointed to a tray on the table. "Are you hungry?"

"Yes." She tried in vain to sit up.

"Let me help you." He lifted her shoulders and put a thick pillow behind her.

His arm around her made her forget about breakfast, and she kissed his cheek. "Thank you. I'm so glad you're safe."

"You healed me," he whispered, kissing her again. "My life is yours."

"You don't mean that," she said, drawing back to look at him. "I know you. Another adventure will come along and off you'll go."

"Not this time." Zarek lowered his mouth to hers. "I promise."

He straightened up after a moment, breaking their connection, and if Ana hadn't felt so weak, she would have pulled him back. Instead, he reached for the tray of food. "You need to eat."

One bite at a time, he fed her.

When she'd finished chewing, she asked, "Where is my mother? And Callonen. Are they safe? And are your parents back together at last? Why aren't you with them now?"

Zarek smiled at the flurry of questions. "I saw my parents last night, but they had a lot of catching up to do after all these years. When they are ready to see me, they know where to find me."

Ana giggled, for despite his sun-browned skin, she saw him flush a little. "Where is my mother?" she asked again.

"With Callonen. And they told me Haldreth was dead."

"Yes," Ana said. Perhaps she should feel sad at his passing, but he had caused so much suffering. She felt only relief that he was gone. "He was my father, but he never cared about me, or my mother."

"You're not sad then?"

"No! He was never a father to me," she said fiercely, then paused and took a deep breath. "I've always wished Callonen could be my father. Is he all right? He was hurt."

"He's all right," Zarek said.

Instantly, Ana knew he was lying. "What happened? What's wrong with him? And tell me the truth."

Caught in his attempt at deception, Zarek sighed heavily. "I didn't want to tell you when you're supposed to be resting, but he's hurt pretty badly."

Ana felt tears welling in her eyes. "I thought Haldreth... struck him, but I didn't see what happened. When I asked him, Callonen said it was nothing."

Zarek took her hand. "I know."

"We have to see him!" Ana insisted, tears welling in her eyes. "Will you please help me?"

He lifted her gently, wrapped her in a blanket, and carried her through the halls to the emperor's rooms. The guards outside let them in without question.

Callonen lay in a large bed, wrapped in bandages. Allia sat beside him with his hand clutched in hers. Zarek took a seat next to her with Ana still in his arms.

"How is he?" she asked Allia.

Her mother's worried face answered the question. Callonen didn't respond to their voices. His face was pale, his breathing shallow.

"He said he was all right," Ana said, tears running down her cheeks. "Will he die?"

"I hope not," Allia said quietly.

As they sat watching him, the healers came and went, doing what they could for him.

Ana drew in a deep breath. She couldn't allow Callonen to die. "I can heal him."

"No," Allia protested, abruptly raising her head to look at Ana. "My dearest, it's too soon. If you aren't strong enough, the healing will kill you. Please believe me."

Ana shook her head. "I won't try to heal again after this until I'm stronger, but Callonen can't wait! Carry me closer, Zarek."

He didn't move.

"Callonen needs help now. I'll be all right. If you won't help, I'll crawl to him!" She struggled in Zarek's arms.

"You're only hoping you'll survive it. It's too great a risk!" he protested. "Callonen wouldn't let you do it. You know he wouldn't." She tried to get up again, but couldn't. He refused to let her go.

All the way back to her room, Ana begged him to change his mind. "Don't leave!" she cried as he returned her to her bed and turned to go. "We have to help Callonen!"

"Please rest," Zarek said. "Get your strength back, and when you're stronger, you can help him."

"How can I rest when he is dying?"

"Regain your strength. In a few days…" But they both knew that Callonen didn't have a few days. Zarek couldn't meet her eyes as he said it. He went to the door.

"Wait!" Ana cried desperately. "Take the ring. Give it to someone else, and they can heal him."

"It won't come off without injuring you."

"I know that! It's worth losing another finger to save his life. But I need you to help me do it."

"I'll see you later." Zarek closed the door behind him.

For the first time, Ana was furious with Zarek. The rest of the day, she remained in bed, unable to get up without help. Darkness fell, and the palace became quiet as everyone went to sleep. Ana waited for Zarek to come back, but he didn't.

When everything was silent, Ana slid her feet out of bed. She tried to stand, but crumpled to the floor and crawled slowly to the door. All was quiet in the hall, and she saw no one. With many pauses to rest, she crept toward the emperor's room.

Before she turned the last corner, she dragged herself to her feet. Leaning against the wall, she managed to stay upright. When she came to Callonen's door, a guard opened it for her. Thankfully, he didn't ask questions, even though it was very late. She made it inside, and the door closed behind her before she sank back to her knees.

Allia dozed in the chair beside the bed, still holding Callonen's hand; her back to the door. A healer sat nearby, sound asleep in his chair at the foot of the bed.

Ana crawled across the floor to the side of Callonen's bed and reached up to touch his arm.

CHAPTER FIFTY-SEVEN

YEAR OF WARDING 42, WHITE CITY, SARINE

ALLIA

IN HER CHAIR BESIDE the bed, some instinct startled Allia out of her doze. She realized instantly what was happening. Cirana reached up from the floor, determined to heal Callonen even if it killed her. Already, her hand gripped his arm. She didn't have the strength she would need to complete the healing, and Allia needed to act or her daughter would die.

Allia put her hand over Cirana's, the stone of the ring digging sharply into her palm. A burst of green light flashed from the ring, and in that moment, Allia sensed them both.

Part of her became Callonen, lying on the bed, his body battered, blood seeping from his wounds, pain spreading from his injuries. Allia's muscles clenched against the agony.

Another part of her became Cirana. She loved Callonen and desperately wanted him to be healed, to live. All her will was bent on him, the remaining vitality in her body draining into him.

If Cirana completed the healing, she would die. Despite the pain, Allia focused her will on helping Cirana. They would both heal Callonen. Allia directed her own energy to lend strength to her daughter. Pain surged through her body, and she welcomed it as a sign that the healing was working. She refused to let go until the pain ceased and darkness covered her.

⟡

As she felt the thick rug against her cheek, Allia realized she lay on the floor beside her daughter. She couldn't move or speak. The door banged open, and she heard Zarek's voice and his heavy footsteps.

"Ana!" His tone rang with desperate worry.

Allia blinked and saw him bending over Cirana's motionless form, putting an ear to her chest.

When Allia heard Callonen's voice, her heart leapt. He was alive, his voice strong. "What happened? Is she...?"

Zarek let out a long breath in relief. "She's breathing, and I can hear her heart beating."

The same wave of relief washed over Allia. Her daughter was alive.

"Allia!" Callonen knelt on the floor beside her, still wrapped in bandages. "What happened? Are you all right?"

She couldn't even turn her head, but she focused her eyes on him. When she tried to answer, she was too weak to form the words.

Callonen bent over her. "The ring?"

Allia managed the slightest of nods.

He gathered her in his arms and lifted her, setting her gently on the bed and covering her. "Is there anything I can do?" His concerned brown eyes looked down at her.

She couldn't answer, but her eyes devoured him. He was healed. Safe.

He pulled the bandages from his head, and joy spread through her heart to see him completely whole again. The healing had worked. His arm was no longer broken, the wound in his side, gone. All his injuries had vanished, even his ear had been restored.

Tears of relief welled in Allia's eyes.

From where she lay, she watched Zarek pick Cirana up from the floor to hold her cradled in his arms. "What happened?" he asked. "If Ana healed you, what happened to Allia?"

Callonen turned back to Allia. "You must have helped her... somehow."

Allia nodded again.

"How is that possible?" Zarek asked.

"I've never seen it before," Callonen admitted. "But I have no other explanation."

"Me neither," Zarek said. "Allia warned Ana that she could die if she tried to heal in her weakened condition. Did Allia prevent that from happening?"

Sitting on the edge of the bed, Callonen took her hand and examined her palm. "I can see the imprint of the ring on your hand. Is that what you did?"

She nodded.

Zarek's arms tightened around Cirana. He turned to Allia, and she saw the love this young man felt for her daughter. It was in his eyes, his voice, and obvious in the tender, protective way he held her.

His voice was thick with emotion. "When I found her gone, I knew where she would go, and I ran here, but she had already..." Zarek looked at Callonen. "We're glad you're safe, but you wouldn't approve of Ana sacrificing herself to save you."

Callonen shook his head. "Never."

"Allia, you saved her life." Deep gratitude filled Zarek's voice and moisture welled in his eyes. "I love her. You don't know what it means to me that she's alive."

The only response she could give was a slight nod, but she hoped he understood.

"I'll be right back," Callonen said to Allia.

She could not take her eyes off him. As he stood and turned away, she saw a scar shaped like a sunburst on his back, below his ribs. She wanted to ask him about it and everything else that had happened.

Callonen faced Zarek. "Speaking of actions I don't approve of..."

Guilt grew plain on the young man's face. "I accept any punishment you choose for disobeying your orders. I humbly beg your forgiveness, Emperor."

Putting his arm around Zarek's shoulders, Callonen shook his head. "I won't deny, I was furious when you left. But I've had a few years to cool off. And how could I not welcome you home when you saved Sarine? But we will speak of this more later."

"Thank you, Emperor." Zarek's features relaxed in relief. "I'll take Ana back to her room now."

He departed.

One of the healers was still at his post in a corner, watching everything with wide eyes. "Your orders, Emperor?"

Callonen turned to him. "I am very grateful that I no longer require your services. Would you kindly see to Lady Allia?"

"Of course." The healer came to her side and checked her pulse, listened to her breathing, and examined the bandage on her arm.

"Did you reopen the wound? Are you in any pain?" She shook her head.

He turned back to Callonen. "As far as I can tell, she just needs rest. I can have her moved to one of the guest rooms. And someone should watch her tonight."

"I will see to her myself," Callonen said firmly. "You may go."

"As you command, Emperor," the healer said, bowing. "I am close at hand should you need me."

Callonen walked with the man to the door and opened it. Just outside, two guards were on duty. "Wes," he addressed one of them. "Do you know where General Gray is? He is keeping something for me, and I need it back."

"Of course, Emperor. He's just down the hall."

A moment passed before Allia heard another brief conversation, and then Callonen returned.

When the door clicked shut Allia realized they were alone. How many times had she dreamed of being with him? Only a few moments ago, Callonen had lain in bed, mortally injured. Now unexpectedly, their roles had reversed, and he felt well while she was unable to do anything.

He sat in the chair beside her and took her hand. "Are you sure you're all right? Did you hurt your arm when you fell? Is there anything I can bring you? Anything you need to be more comfortable?"

"You," she tried to say. No sound came out.

He knelt beside the bed and leaned close. "What is it you want?"

"You," she managed a faint whisper.

He must have heard her, because he smiled and gave her the gentlest of kisses. "You can have more later," he murmured. "When you're ready."

She wished she could tell him she wanted more now.

Callonen unwrapped the bandages on his arm and pulled off the splint. He stretched and flexed. "So much better," he exclaimed. He pulled off the wrappings on his side and his leg.

Allia felt her cheeks color. With all the bandages gone, he wore only his shorts. The memory of watching Haldreth's men torture him swept through her. Haldreth had humiliated him and intended to destroy him. Through it all, Callonen never complained. He must have known what would happen that day if he gave himself up to his brother. At the time, he didn't know where the ring was or if he would ever have access to its power again. But Callonen hadn't hesitated. He'd done it to save her life.

Allia couldn't help allowing her eyes to roam his body. She couldn't believe what she saw after watching his enemies attack him so brutally. He appeared strong and fit, his skin unmarred, except for a new white line on his side and the old scar on his chest where his brother had stabbed him. Both of their lives had been thrown violently off course that day.

Her eyes fell on an old silver band hanging from a chain around his neck. It couldn't be... Was it possible he still had her father's ring after all this time?

Callonen met her gaze and smiled. He had not missed her looking at him. "I never dared to hope I would find the woman I adore in my bed."

Allia tried to smile back. One corner of her mouth twitched upward. He knelt beside her, gazing into her eyes. "I know you aren't feeling very strong right now, and you gave your own health to help Ana and me. When we were back in that cave, you came and rested beside me. Waking up to find you so close was the best moment of my life. Will you give me your permission to do the same?"

"Yes," she whispered.

"Are you sure? It must be your choice. If you prefer, I can move you to another room where you can have all the privacy you want while you recover. Do you wish to stay?"

If Allia had felt stronger, she would have answered with more enthusiasm. "Yes," she breathed.

Callonen lay down beside her and put his arms around her, throwing the covers over them both.

She rested her head against his chest.

"Are you comfortable?"

Allia wanted to be close to him more than anything. She felt his warm breath on her hair.

"I never expected to have you back," he murmured. "You're home now. Safe. And Ana is safe. Rest now. I'm here."

Tears of joy welled in her eyes. All was quiet, still and peaceful, and Callonen was beside her, healed of the injuries Haldreth and his men had inflicted. His arms were around her. Nothing would ever keep them apart again.

CHAPTER FIFTY-EIGHT

YEAR OF WARDING 42, WHITE CITY, SARINE

ANA

WHEN ANA WOKE, THE light of morning came through the windows, and she saw Zarek's concerned face above her. The last thing she remembered was the pain of Callonen's injuries. Her mother had been beside her. Somehow, Allia's strength had supported Ana. "Is Callonen healed?"

"He is," Zarek said.

She breathed out a sigh.

"I'm so relieved to see you awake," he said, rubbing his forehead and sitting back in his chair.

"You're angry." Ana realized, sensing it.

Zarek didn't try to deny it. "Do you know what almost happened?" His voice sounded strained. "If not for Allia, you'd be dead. You are too willing to sacrifice yourself if you think it will help someone else."

Ana looked back stubbornly. "What about Sarine? What about the Warding? It would disappear without Callonen. Our people depend on us for safety. I know you disagreed with me, but I couldn't let Callonen die."

"Disagreed?" His eyes widened. "I hope you don't think I would ever agree to you sacrificing your life? Even for Sarine. You almost killed yourself trying to save him! I care about Callonen too, but did you think about how he would feel right now if you'd died? You know him. He would torture himself forever over it. And your mother?"

Ana felt her cheeks heat at his words. He was right, of course. She knew how upset Callonen would have been if he woke up healthy, only to discover she was dead. He wasn't the kind of man who could forget something like that and go on with his life.

Zarek's gray eyes were as dark as a thunderstorm.

"I'm sorry, Zarek," she murmured. Still barely able to move, she tried to reach out to him.

He knelt on the floor beside her bed and brought her hand to his lips, kissing it. "Ana!" He whispered. "I'll do anything for you. But please, please don't ask me to watch you die. After everything we've been through, I don't think I could do it. Promise me you won't do anything like this again?"

"But I watched you fight the demons," she protested. "If I give my word, you have to make the same promise, that you'll never put yourself in danger again."

There was a hint of a smile in his expression now. "You drive a hard bargain. But I admit your terms are fair."

"Well?"

"As you command, my lady." Zarek met her eyes. "I promise to love you forever, to give you my heart, and that I won't put myself in danger unless it's to protect you." He smiled. "Was that good enough?" His words sent heat through her whole body. When their eyes met, she could see the warmth in them, and she could sense that he meant exactly what he said.

"Are you sure?" she asked. "You won't find some other impossible quest and leave me?"

He leaned closer and brought his mouth to hers. For a long moment, Ana thought of nothing besides kissing him. If she had been well, she would have thrown her arms around him and pulled him closer. When the kiss ended, she was gasping for breath. He trailed more kisses down her jaw to her throat. She never wanted him to stop.

But after several delicious moments, he drew back and looked down at her. "For the last three years I was alone, constantly on my guard, hiding my identity, trusting no one. I was feared, tolerated, maybe occasionally admired, but never loved. I took the memory of our friendship with me and kept it in my heart. When I felt alone, I thought of you. Now that I have you back, I won't leave you. I've done enough impossible things for one lifetime. But are you sure you want me to stay? You're safe now. You have your mother and Callonen beside you. There is no more danger to protect you from, nothing to hurt you, nothing to guard against. You don't need me anymore. Do you still want me?"

"Yes," she said, pulling him closer. "As you protected me, you never realized how badly I wanted to be with you. I want you to stay. Now, and for the rest of my life."

"Good then," he murmured, kissing her again. "It's time for your promise."

She looked into his gray eyes. "I promise I won't put myself at risk unless someone I care about is in grave danger." Weakly she reached out and he placed his hand in hers. "I love you, Zarek." She sensed the overwhelming joy he felt at her words.

He smiled and slid his arms around her to pull her close. "Your promise was worthless," he murmured in her ear. "All you have to do is claim that someone was in danger, and you could do exactly as you please."

"I don't think it's fair that..." she protested. His lips met hers and whatever she was about to say became unimportant.

ALLIA

Allia floated in the best dream of her life. The cold hard stone and heavy iron chain were gone, and she rested in a luxurious room. The aching loneliness that had trapped her disappeared, replaced by contentment. She felt a soft mattress beneath her, and a thick blanket kept her warm. Best of all, she wasn't alone. Callonen slept beside her. Her head rested on his chest, and his arms held her close. His love surrounded her. He respected her, cherished her, and would never hurt her.

As she stirred, she knew her body remained weak after the healing. Dark memories rushed in. She couldn't move after using the ring and woke to find Haldreth in her bed. He had used her and intended to destroy her.

Her jaw clenched. No. Haldreth was dead, and she was free.

She took in a long breath, casting out the painful memories in favor of the bliss of the moment.

Reluctantly, Allia opened her eyes, unwilling to leave the beautiful dream.

The light of morning shone in through an opening in the drapes.

It was real. This was Callonen's room. And he was beside her.

Within a few moments, her memory pieced itself together. Last night, Ana had healed Callonen, and Allia had lent her strength to help.

Callonen's breathing remained even. He was asleep.

Allia took in a deep breath, grateful to find her strength had begun to return. Her arms and hands obeyed her will. She touched the silver band on its chain around his neck and ran her fingers over Callonen's arm where it had been injured. Nothing remained but a faint scar. He was really here, alive and healthy. She slid her arms around him, savoring the feel of his skin against hers.

He drew in a quick breath, awake now and aware of her touch. After the night of rest, she had regained the energy to speak.

"Callonen," she whispered.

His arms tightened around her, pulling her closer; her head tucked under his chin. "I'm here."

"How do you feel this morning?" she asked. He'd been very near death when Ana had come.

"I feel perfect. I have never wanted anything more than to wake up with you in my arms. I want to wake up with you every morning for the rest of my life."

"Callonen, we have to talk before you say that. I'm not the same person I was when we parted."

"No," he agreed. "Me neither."

"Haldreth said you would hate me for the things I've done, and you'd never want me back." Allia felt tears welling in her eyes at the memory.

Callonen held her, and she felt his lips against her brow. "That's not true. He lied. I don't hate you. I would never feel that way." His embrace was warm and accepting. Being close to Haldreth had never felt anything like this.

She drew back and looked up at Callonen. "But do you know what I did? Everything? I took a knife and stabbed him. Me. With my own hand. And I... I helped him create the demons. How many good people have died because of that? They nearly killed Talon and Zarek. Because of me, they killed Harrow. I know there are many others." Tears ran down her cheeks.

With care to miss the cuts on her face, Callonen gently brushed the tears away and met her gaze. "I know. The Warding is back, and I know everything. You feared for your life when you attacked Haldreth. And you felt helpless to do anything else when he forced you to help him with his magic. None of this was your fault."

"If I had only been stronger that night! He would have died. Even though he would have killed me first, he would have been dead. There would have been no demons..."

"You can't take that burden on yourself," Callonen said gently. He took her hand in his and brought it to his lips and kissed it. "I know what you did, and why, but Haldreth caused this. Not you. I'm so glad you're here, alive..." He pulled her close again. "It didn't seem possible. I really thought you were dead. Now you're here, and how can you forgive me for not bringing you home sooner? I tried to save you, but Haldreth had you too well guarded. They nearly caught us."

"You were injured, weren't you?" she asked, thinking of the scar she had seen last night.

He nodded. "I failed. I should have protected you!"

"I wish you could have," she said. "But... I have to tell you... Cirana is Haldreth's child. The first time it happened was just after I healed him. And I couldn't even fight back. He knew I wouldn't be able to. He said you'd reject me for that too, even though I had no choice."

"Never!" Callonen gazed down at her, tears welling in his dark eyes. His voice grew choked with emotion. "He knew nothing about me. I love you, Allia. And nothing that he did to either of us can change that!"

She put her arms around him and held him tight. They cried together, sharing the pain, loneliness and despair they had each suffered.

Haldreth couldn't have ever really known his brother. A man who would sacrifice for those he loved would never refuse to forgive them if they asked. And Allia felt lighter now that she'd told Callonen everything. Some part of her had been afraid that Haldreth's lies were true.

Allia wiped her eyes and looked at him. "He didn't try to... force me again after Cirana was born. It's been many years. I think he was more concerned with the demons and building his kingdom. It was a long time ago. What about you? Haldreth told me you'd married someone else. Did that beautiful princess from Paraman come back?"

Callonen shook his head. "I never saw her again. It took years before anyone in Paraman would speak to me. If not for Cirana's astounding diplomatic skills, they would probably still hate me." He pulled her closer. "There was never anyone but you, Allia. I've been alone all this time. I was hoping, if you will accept me, you might change that. Of course, I would understand, after everything that happened with my brother, if you don't feel you can be with me. I look just like him. When you look at me will you think of him?" Allia drew in a deep breath. If she woke in the middle of the night and saw him beside her, would she enjoy the dream of being with Callonen or recall the nightmare of being with Haldreth?

Callonen pulled the chain from around his neck and removed the ring. "You gave this to me all those years ago, and I am still waiting for you to put it on me. I kept it, thinking of you, and I never gave my heart to anyone else."

Allia took the ring and slid it onto his finger.

Callonen examined his hand with the band in place. He held it out for her to see. "I will leave it there for the rest of my life," he vowed. "You gave this to me, a symbol of your love. When you see it, you'll know that it's me, and I am nothing like my brother. It will remind you of my promise that my hands will never hurt you."

Allia felt tears welling in her eyes. "He might have looked like you, but he was never anything like you." Her fingers traced a new white line just below his ear. She was silent for a long moment, the events of the last years passing through her mind. "There are scars from this." She touched the mark on his chest from where his brother had stabbed him. "For both of us. But if you are willing, we can heal them together."

"I am willing," he murmured.

Allia took in a deep breath, allowing her fears and worries to fade away. She gazed up at him and smiled. For a moment she felt like the eighteen-year-old girl who had fallen so hard for the handsome, unattainable prince. There was nothing she wanted more than to stay with him.

She pulled his head down and kissed him. The touch of his lips on hers felt like coming home.

About the Author

aj@ajparkwriting.com
www.ajparkwriting.com
Stay In Touch – Join my email list and download a FREE Story
https://BookHip.com/XKTAJDB

AJ Park is the author of several fantasy adventure books and has won multiple writing awards. She grew up reading everything she could get her hands on, and continues to cultivate her life-long love of stories.

When she's not working on the next book, she loves climbing mountains, being outdoors, and spending time with her family. She loves meeting new friends, being part of the local community, and works for a digital marketing firm that helps businesses grow.

Acknowledgements

Thank you for reading this book! Thank you family, friends and fans for supporting me during the creation process.

I cherish the opportunity to bring to life stories born in my imagination and share them. I hope you enjoy reading them and that we have many future adventures together.

FORGOTTEN REBELLION

CHAPTER ONE

B RIGHT TONGUES OF FLAME from burning buildings lit the evening with an orange glow. From his position outside the village, Andevaar waited. Dark shapes of people ran between the houses and shops, screaming in terror. Andevaar remained, watching. The raid was going exactly as planned. Other horsemen gathered around him, gripping their swords, their eyes locked on the clustered buildings.

"Go?" the stocky man at his shoulder asked.

Andevaar shook his head. "Not yet." They had to be patient. He needed to allow the people enough time to become desperate for help. Soon.

The man wiped a bead of sweat from his brow with the back of his hand.

For several more moments, Andevaar observed, anticipation growing inside him with each flame that burned. Then he gripped his sword and met his companion's eyes. "Ready?" He looked back at the group behind him. They nodded. "You know what to do," he told them.

With a shout, he urged his horse forward, his sword held high. The others followed, yelling and raising their weapons. Picking up speed as they approached, they charged into the village. Farmers and tradespeople, confused and poorly armed, jumped out of their way.

As Andevaar and his men entered the fray, the robbers, faces masked in black, abandoned their looting to do battle with them. Many smaller fights raged, but the thieves, most of them on foot, retreated before the onslaught of the band of mounted men. The riders swept through the area, driving the outlaws before them until only a single man on a black horse remained.

He faced Andevaar in the open space of the village square, his sword raised in defiance. The image of a silver hawk emblazoned on his tunic was the only color he wore. His face was masked in black cloth.

Andevaar charged toward him, his own blade ready to crash against his opponent's. The staged battle was effortless. They had sparred together for years, and they knew each other's every move. They fought, striking and parrying, their skills evenly matched. With equal strength and speed, every blow flowed perfectly into the next, and the crowd watched in fascination.

Andevaar's men returned to the square from their sweep through the village. They joined the crowd at the edges of the open space and watched the fight. The remaining outlaws were gone, already out of sight.

The man on the black horse fought hard. He wouldn't give an inch, until eventually, he pulled back, looking around to assess the crowd of enemies. With a shout of defiance, he wheeled his horse and charged toward the street leading out of the square. He aimed a blow at the horseman blocking his path, and the man parried but retreated, allowing the black horse to gallop away.

A moment of stunned silence fell, then suddenly, the people cheered and gathered around Andevaar. Every eye was on him. Every voice shouted his praise. Their adoration washed over him, and he sat a little taller in the saddle, drawing in a long, satisfied breath. Success. He raised his blade in the air and yelled in triumph. The crowd cheered again.

"Thank you!" a man cried, approaching Andevaar as the noise subsided. He wore a fine tunic, cloak, and a gold magistrate's medallion. "You saved us from the attack."

"My friends and I are happy to have been of service." His men raised their blades, and the people cheered and applauded them eagerly. They had done enough here for one night. None of these villagers would ever forget what had happened. It was time to leave. Andevaar turned to the town leader. "We must go, Magistrate. The criminals who attacked you are escaping, and we will pursue."

"Yes, yes, of course!" the magistrate agreed. "You have saved lives and property tonight. Might we have the name of our hero?"

Bowing his head in acknowledgement, he said, "I am Andevaar."

By the time all the horses were stabled and the men were resting, it was nearly midnight. Andevaar rode out alone through the darkness. The land was silent and sleeping around him, the stars sparkling in the dark sky above. He turned off on a slender side road and drew up in front of a tiny cottage. No lights showed as he dismounted, looped the reins over a fencepost, and went to the door, opening it without knocking. Inside, a small flame burst into life in the fireplace. The black figure of a man crouched, using a long wood shaving to light a candle.

The flickering glow illuminated the silver hawk on the front of his tunic. Andevaar smiled as Drake stood to face him. "It went just as well as the others." Drake laughed, and Andevaar slapped his friend on the shoulder. "Even now, they have no idea!" Drake folded his arms across his chest, a sarcastic smirk on his face.

"Were any of your men hurt?" Andevaar asked.

Drake shook his head. "Nothing more serious than scrapes and bruises."

"And the villagers?"

"Some of them put up a fight. We took several prisoners, but none of them were seriously injured. My men are keeping them secure until we can take them back to Sathar."

Andevaar nodded. "Make sure they're treated well. Some of the men you hired are savages. Don't let them attack your captives."

Drake's mouth set in a firm line. "I can handle them."

Andevaar knew this. Drake had lived in a world of violence all his life. He knew how to maintain order by force over men who understood nothing else. "Good. We have the schedule and the locations for the next raids. After these last two smaller communities, we will hit Edrithil. When we take the city, we'll have all of Edri on our side, and I'll be ready to meet the arrogant Princess Tahlea."

Drake lifted one corner of his mouth. "I'm sure you will impress her."

"If the gratitude of those villagers is any sign, she'll *have* to be impressed." Andevaar raised his chin. "By the time we're finished, the people will beg me to take the throne, so they won't have to endure the royal family's tyranny anymore."

Grinning, Drake put his hand over his heart. "And I will remain your most loyal friend and business partner throughout it all. When we're done, we'll rule this land, and everyone will be treated fairly."

Andevaar nodded. He rubbed his chin, contemplating their plans. "When we're finished in Edri, go to the palace in Namradan. The Stone Ceremony is in a week. They'll let anyone inside for the event. See if there is someone there, a young lady, maybe, who is close to the royal family, that you might become friends with." He stared at Drake appraisingly. "I'm sure you can find some charm as well as brute force. Use it."

Drake bowed with a flourish. "As you command, Lord Andevaar."

(Continue the story in the full version...)